PENNSYLVANIA

THE COMPLETE NOVEL

MICHAEL
BUNKER

PENNSYLVANIA
THE COMPLETE NOVEL

ISBN: 978-1497502758

First Edition

Cover Design by Jason Gurley
http://www.jasongurley.com

Editing by David Gatewood
http://lonetrout.com

Interior Illustrations by Ben Adams
http://www.benjadams.com

Formatting by Stewart Stonger
http://design.nourishingdays.com/

For information on Michael Bunker or to read his blog, visit: http://www.michaelbunker.com

To contact Michael Bunker, please write to:

M. Bunker
1251 CR 132
Santa Anna, Texas 76878

To everyone who dares to start anew.

KNOT 1:
PENNSYLVANIA

Old Pennsylvania

"**E**xplain it to me again, brother. How do you get from here to there?"

Jed pushed his forehead into Zoe's flank to make certain that she didn't kick. She didn't do it often, but she'd nailed him before and he wasn't anxious for a repeat of that performance. He exhaled in mock annoyance at his little brother's questions, but the truth was that he loved talking about the journey. He just pretended to hate it. Talking about it made it seem more real, but somehow less imminent in a way that he wasn't sure he understood completely. He'd explained the whole pilgrimage and the colonization process to Amos a hundred times, at least, but Amos wasn't going to stop talking about it until his older brother was gone.

"An airbus picks me up there," he pointed up the long, winding drive, "and we fly to the Columbia checkpoint. From there, I board an English airbus that takes me to the Speedwell Galactic Transport station out in the desert in far West Texas. From there, all the pilgrims will board a ship bound for New Pennsylvania."

"You're really going, Jed?"

"I don't see any reason why I shouldn't. I've already paid for my ticket, all except the monitoring. Nothing has happened that would change my mind, so I'm going."

Jed finished stripping out the final teat, and the last squirts of milk buzzed into the bucket, which was now almost overflowing. "Our people have been pioneering for a thousand years or more. When our ancestors came here to Pennsylvania, they came on fearsome and incredible ships, traveling in ways that were strange to them at the time."

"I felt sure you'd change your mind; just sure of it," Amos said.

Amos was fourteen, fully four years younger, spry and witty, and he was not old enough yet to go through the initiation and orientation process that was administered to anyone interested in pioneering in New Pennsylvania.

Jed finished wiping down Zoe's udder with warm water mixed with a light and mild soap, and then he stood, hanging the milking stool on the post with practiced dexterity.

"Once we get on our way..." He paused. This was the hard part to explain. "You see, Amos, New Pennsylvania is very, very far away—outside of our galaxy—in a place with another sun altogether. Anyway, once we board the ship, the passengers go to sleep in these things called 'pods,' and, according to the paperwork, we'll sleep for nine full years. But—and this is the tricky thing—when we wake up, we won't have aged any at all."

Amos had heard this explanation from his older brother many times before, but he still whistled at the thought.

"And it will be that nine years will have passed according to the ship's time. But all in all, to the passenger, it will feel like a journey of just a few hours!"

"I don't understand it, Jed," Amos said, screwing up his mouth and shaking his head. "I don't know why the elders have approved of it."

"What else can we do, little brother? Where can we go? We're running out of land here, and no one can afford to buy any more. The government is pushing us out. It's always been this way. The elders approved of this migration for the same reasons that many centuries ago they approved of our migration from Europe to here. Without it, we'll be erased as a people. It's already happening, Amos. Almost everyone we know works in town in the factories. Our population is exploding, and our way of life is dying out. But this isn't the first time this has happened."

"No?"

"No. It's happened many times way far back in history, but it happened during Grandfather's time too, when the wars came, and the population of the English dwindled, and after that, we had room to spread out more."

Amos shrugged and his shoulders dropped. "Right. And this time, there is nowhere to go. But why must you go all the way to another *planet*? And why must Mother and Father never hear from you ever again?"

"When our people left Germany, Holland, and France to come to Pennsylvania, do you think they kept in touch with the old places after that? They didn't rush home for weddings or funerals, Amos. It was too far away, and the travel was too expensive and too dangerous. There were no phones, and letters were expensive. Our people were never much for those forms of communication anyway."

Jed looked at his brother and slapped him on the back. "Once I leave for New Pennsylvania, I'll be in a place where it's *impossible* to communicate back to here. The ships that take us there, they never come back. It's a one-way voyage because those machines travel millions and millions of miles while we just sleep away there in the pods." Jed looked at his brother and smiled. "Don't be sad, little brother. It will only be a few years before you can come too. In fact, if the Lord wills it, when you start on your own journey, you'll already be on your way by rocket ship before I even get there! Hopefully I'll have a place set up for us by the time you arrive, and we'll work the farm together."

Amos shuffled his feet, his eyes down and his voice lowered, almost in a mumble. "Why can't Mother and Father join us? Why don't we all—everyone in the community—travel together at the same time?"

While they talked, Jed poured the milk into a stainless-steel vat, closed the lid, then unhooked Zoe from the tether that kept her in the milking stall. He backed her out and then walked with her out of the barn and into the southwest paddock. Amos followed with his hands thrust deeply into the pockets of his black broadfall pants.

"You know the answers to those questions, Amos. They want young people. Eighteen to twenty-five only. They need people to work the land, and the pioneers who go will need every advantage they can get. It's going to be tough starting out. The new colony cannot yet afford to take care of the elderly and the infirm. Besides, Mother and Father don't want to go. This has always been their home, and though they support us going when it's our time, they agree with the elders: only those who are needed should go."

Jed unhooked the lead from Zoe's halter and she walked only a few steps away before she started grazing on the lush grass. He folded up her lead and stuck it in his front pocket, and as he continued trying to soothe and placate his troubled brother, the two walked across the paddock.

"Eighteen to twenty-five is the perfect age, anyway. The younger children can work the farms here, and those who emigrate are the ones who would be just starting to look for their own land and new farms. Well, there aren't many farms to find any more, so pioneering is the new thing. But it's not new. Like I said before, our people have been doing it since the beginning. There's nothing really new in this at all."

Amos looked up as he followed his brother to the pump near the paddock fence. Jed pumped the handle, and when the cool, clear water came bursting forth, Amos scrubbed the milk pail under it until it was spotless. The grass grew thick and lush around their feet, and the water that splashed over it formed into glassy droplets on the blades and made the grass glisten.

"What if something bad happens to the ship along the way? What if it crashes or you die?"

"What if we were both struck by lightning right here in this field? Everyone dies, Amos. Zoe might've kicked either one of us in the head just now, and it would be over—just like that." He snapped his fingers.

"Well, I think taking a spaceship to another galaxy is a little more dangerous than milking Zoe, brother."

"Maybe, but we wouldn't be here milking Zoe if our ancestors hadn't braved the voyage to a new world. They came to escape religious bigotry and persecution, and to find new lands to farm. That's the same reason I'm going to New Pennsylvania."

"Are you all ready to go?"

"I am. They don't let you take much, so I don't have to pack. Basically you get there with what you're wearing and not much more. They expect me to buy everything new when I arrive. That's why I've been saving money."

"And you won't change your mind?"

"I will not."

"Okay, brother. Then I'll come after you. Four more years and I'll be old enough. Besides, I'd like to see Matthias again. It's been a year since he emigrated. It's funny to think that he's been gone a year and he's not even there yet. It'll be nice to see him again."

Jed smiled and popped his brother's hat up, then pushed it back down on his head. "Well, we'd better go eat. The airbus will be here in an hour."

* * * *

It was hard to say goodbye to his mother and father. They both masked their emotions as much as they could and smiled a lot, but he knew his mother wanted to cry because her eyes were damp and sparkled when the light hit them just right. Abraham Troyer, his father, shook his hand firmly, and then they all prayed together before Jed walked up the long drive to where the airbus would pick him up.

As he walked up, he thought about the journey, and what might lie before him. Jed couldn't help but think about the Plain People who had first come to America to farm and tame the wilds of this Pennsylvania. When he reached the last bend in the drive, he turned slowly to look back at the farm, and his boots crunched the gravel as he rotated. A soft spring gust blew up through the paddock and past the split-rail fence, and it jostled the felt brim of his hat. The breeze carried the fragrance of foxglove and touch-me-not growing wild just outside the fence of the paddock, and the mingled scents—of the wildflowers, of soil, of horse manure and moist grass—framed for his memory the smell of home.

He froze for a moment when he saw the barn. That beautiful old barn. It had been the center of his life for most of his eighteen years. It was made of heavy stone two-thirds of the way up its height and then solid beams the rest of the way. The barn was more than two centuries old, and Jed knew that unless something bad happened to it, it would be standing there two hundred years hence. This Amish barn was constructed back when people built things with the future in mind. Back when people—even the English—thought about the generations to come, and built with the intention of blessing them. There was permanence to the Troyers' old barn. In Jed's mind it stood like a covenant between the ancestors and their progeny. In its Old World style it declared to the temporary society and impermanent culture around it that there had once been another way to live. Strangers in buses liked to tour these country roads just to see the old farms and barns and the Plain People going about their work in the fields. This old barn was definitely a favorite for the tourists due to its classical Amish design, but the structure did have one blemish.

He saw it up there near the top, on the window in the gabled end. The bottom-right pane of glass that wasn't there. Jed had broken it accidentally with his slingshot four years ago. He'd been about Amos's age when it happened, and his father had ordered him to "fix it." So he'd fixed it, all right. What did a fourteen-year-old child know about fixing a window?

He'd found a coffee can—red with white printing, the old-timey kind—and had cut the can until he could stomp it flat. Measuring it out perfectly, he'd carefully snipped the can with metal shears until it fit where the glass pane had been; and now, there it was still, four years later. He'd expected his father to complain about it and to order a new pane of glass for the window, but for some reason the old patriarch thought that the whole thing was terribly funny. He laughed every time he looked up and saw it. He'd slap Jed on the shoulder and say, "Well, boy, your coffee can is staring down on us!"

He turned to finish his walk to the airbus stop. Maybe that coffee-can windowpane is part of the covenant too, he thought. Maybe in a hundred years, that coffee can will still be staring down from the height of the barn as a way of telling the world that it can change all it wants to, but, down deep, the people who live in this place will never change.

DEPARTURE

The airbus picked him up right on time. Leaving his family was tough, but he'd been raised to be practical, and was not as sentimental as other people he'd heard about... *as the English*. He loved his parents very much, and he couldn't yet imagine or fully grasp that he would never see them again, but they all believed in heaven, and Jed's father had told him that the same God who ran the earth also ran every other planet too, so he did have hope that they'd all meet again someday.

Amos would be following on behind him... he hoped. Jed worried that perhaps his little brother had been spoiled a little too much; that he might be overly emotional and unable to see the greater good in emigration and colonization. The younger boy wasn't as learned in the nuances and eccentricities of Amish history as his older brother. Amos couldn't imagine a sailing ship, but then, neither could any of the Plain People who'd fled Europe for the New World. Their hesitancy to embrace technology did not mean that they would avoid it to their own detriment. The forefathers boarded great ships that, to them, were every bit as odd and scary as this airbus, and they had crossed the seas to start anew in a wild and untamed land. There was nothing new under the sun.

The airbus flew smoothly and silently, and even the buffeting of the wind against the cabin was silenced by a system that emitted a type of white noise that altogether contradicted and eliminated the sounds of air travel. That was one thing that Jed appreciated about the airbus: the quiet of it. He'd only flown a few times before, and the silence of flight made it somewhat magical and surreal to him—a lot different than riding into New Holland being pulled in the buckboard by Reba and Jesse.

There was that one time he'd gone with his father to Cruville to bid on some land. They'd lost the bid, but that was the first time he'd flown on an airbus. Another time was when he and his father flew to Richmond for the hearings on whether the Plain People were going to be forced to get TRIDs. That was a trip that ended with a positive outcome. As a result of the Richmond Ruling, there were now two distinct airbus systems: one that operated within the AZ and served the Plain People; and another for the English.

This was a Plain People airbus, and in it, the Plain People could travel anywhere in the AZ without papers. There were four AZs in the North American Union, and Plain airbuses traveled between them non-stop. These buses didn't require TRIDs, either. The Plain People weren't marked with biometric TRIDs like the English were; the Richmond Ruling had seen to that.

Of course, if any passenger was heading out of the AZ, by law they had to stop at the Columbia checkpoint and get papers. And on any bus that stopped or took on passengers outside the Amish Zone, the Plain People had to have their papers with them at all times. If not, things would get bad for them.

●●●●

Columbia was just like Jed remembered it. The hustle and bustle was disconcerting, and the city buzzed with a strange mixture of Plain People and the English. It was a place where two cultures met, and it was the last checkpoint for anyone traveling into or out of the Amish Zone.

The Transport station at Columbia ran smoothly and efficiently. Travel had been streamlined a lot since the wars. In general, people were more docile. Most of them were on the drug *Quadrille* and stayed online anytime they weren't actually standing in front of a government official; and those who weren't on the new drug, and who weren't online, had learned that resistance and misbehavior didn't pay. No one wanted to get sent to Oklahoma, and that was exactly what would happen to you if you got out of line anytime during transport.

The Amish travel advisor had warned Jed numerous times not to "mess up" during transport. Private transport had been almost uniformly outlawed since the end of the wars, and transport law was now rigid, inflexible, and merciless. The Transport Police were feared like no one else in the society.

Jed got in line for his papers, and there were only a dozen or so other Plain People in front of him. The English all had implanted TRIDs, and they just flowed through ticketing and security without having to stop at all.

When he reached the front of the line, Jed presented his emigration papers without saying a word. The customs worker, a pretty young woman, glanced through them with disinterest before stamping each of them with a transport code. Next, the woman smiled at him as she reached over and yanked out a few strands of his hair—without warning him—and placed them into a small glass tube, which she then filled with a bluish liquid. She asked him to roll up his sleeve, and she took a skin sample by scraping the dry skin on his elbow with a sharp tool. She caught the flakes of skin in a second tube which was also filled with a blue liquid. He was asked to look into some kind of eye machine, and there was a flash. Whatever the eye thing was (she didn't explain), Jed knew that Transport was permitted to take material *from* the Plain People, but they couldn't implant anything. No invasive procedures were allowed. The Richmond Ruling was ironclad and court-tested, and the Plain People had won their right, on the basis of their sincerely held religious beliefs, not to be implanted with any identifying devices or markers. Jed figured that the eye scan was some way of identifying him biometrically, much like the hair and skin samples. No one messed with fingerprints anymore. Those had become too easy to fake.

Other than politely barked instructions, the pretty

customs lady made no idle chit-chat. A couple of times she looked up with just her eyes, as if she was sizing him up, but other than that she was going through her checklist almost robotically. She slid the two blue tubes and something in the form of a small plastic chip into a hard rubberized band and slid the band over Jed's left hand, securing it on his wrist. Then she forced his hand into another machine, and he felt the band tighten on his wrist in a way that made it seem like it had been permanently attached, even while he could still feel that it didn't hinder the flow of blood to his hand. *Strange.*

"Unilets?" the woman said with a smile. Not really a question, more of a statement. She stepped out from behind the computer desk for a moment, and as she did he saw her name tag. *Dawn.*

It took Jed a moment to understand what Dawn was asking. *Money.* The English now paid one another in *unis,* and his money had been converted for him when he'd picked up his approval papers. Unilets were originally designed to be a fair representation of time worked. Back when they were first introduced, after the wars, there was some computer algorithm that supposedly determined the value of unis day by day. Eventually, the original idea of unilets as a form of straight trade or barter of human work hours had been dropped, as everyone knew they would be co-opted by governments and banks.

Jed knew a lot about unis because the Plain People had considered accepting the currency early on, back when the new money system was just called *LETS.* The LETS were initially designed to be a local trade and barter system, and that was something Jed's community could really appreciate. But the "wait and see" attitude of the Plain People had paid off once again. It didn't take long before LETS were changed to unilets, and the Plain People chose not to participate in the system. Unilets were not accepted as money anywhere in the AZs.

Jed pulled the plastic card from the front pocket of his vest and handed it to the customs woman. She thanked him and waved the card in front of the monitor on her computer, and then she looked back and forth between his face and whatever now appeared on the screen. She sat staring at the computer for several minutes as if she were frozen in place. She didn't press any keys, and her eyes didn't scan back and forth like she was reading. She just stared blankly for a very long time.

Jed wondered if Dawn was on the Internet in her head. He didn't know what else to call it. He wasn't even really sure what an "Internet" was, except that it was how the English did everything on computers. Now they had some way to get this Internet in their head, and he'd seen the far-off, blank gaze in the faces of tourists before.

After what seemed to be an interminable wait, the customs woman stuck his plastic card into a slot and did some procedure on the computer, typing furiously for a few seconds. Satisfied at last that everything was good and ready to go, she again grabbed his wrist—the one with the black band on it—and flipped it over so it was facing her. She took the card out of the computer and touched it against the armband. A light blinked on the band, which apparently convinced the woman that his unilets were now resident on his band. She then let his wrist down onto the desktop and stared at the computer for a few more seconds.

"Yep," she said. "You're good to go now. Do you know how to use the band to buy things?

"Not really, ma'am."

She smiled, and for the first time it was like a light went on in her mind that indicated to her that she was dealing with a real human. He smiled back, and he noticed that she even blushed a little. Maybe he did, too.

"Okay, well, the band has your unis in it," she said. "Place the wrist portion against or near a charging station and the amount indicated on the charging window will be deducted from your total... got it?"

"I think so."

"Any other questions?"

"Well... yes. Couldn't somebody steal this plastic band and make off with all of my money... or, er... um... my unilets?"

"Nothing to worry about, sir. We've solved those problems long ago. The band can only be used when it's touching your body, and only while you're alive." She nodded like this last part should make him feel more comfortable about carrying all of his money on his wrist. "The unique identifiers are digitized now, and the charging stations will scan your eyes and other biometric identifiers automatically to make sure it's you that's making the purchase and that you're not under duress. So it's totally safe. You have nothing to be concerned about, okay?"

"Okay." It was all Jed could think of to say.

"Anything else?"

"Just... well... thank you, Dawn. Thank you very

much, and... where do I catch the airbus for the next leg of the trip to New Pennsylvania?"

Dawn smiled again. This time there was another look in her eye. It was a far-off look that he couldn't rightly quantify. Perhaps it was sadness, or maybe she felt sorry for him. He really wasn't good at trying to figure out the motivations of the English, but she paused for just a moment, as if a thought, previously unconsidered, passed through her mind. Her smile tightened and she blinked before answering, and all of her mannerisms taken together gave him a weird feeling in his stomach.

"Make a right directly at the end of this counter. Down at the end of the concourse, turn to your left. Then to the end of that walkway and you'll be at Gate 13. Okay?"

"Okay. And thanks."

"No problem. Have a safe and prosperous trip, Jed."

"Yes, ma'am."

Jed looked into her eyes one more time before he turned to leave, and again he saw a hint of sadness there, as if she were saying, "After you are all gone, what will become of us?" But maybe he was projecting his own thoughts into a woman who might not even really care.

● ● ● ●

There was a vending machine at Gate 13 that purportedly served food, but Jed had learned in his few journeys among the English that the term "food" could only be loosely applied to whatever came out of a machine. He was hungry though, and the brochure plainly instructed pilgrims to eat before boarding the airbus to the SGT station out in West Texas. There would be no food for nine years once he boarded this airbus! He thought about that for a moment and shook his head. To think, this machine food was going to be his last meal. *Ech!*

He selected a sandwich and a bowl of chicken soup, and noted that the two items would cost him a total of two thousand unis. *Two thousand unis! For soup and a sandwich!* It was difficult for him to do the conversion in his head, but he was pretty sure he could buy a new pair of work shoes for the equivalent of two thousand unis. He couldn't find anything that was remarkably cheaper, so he tapped his wrist against the charging station on the right side of the glass, and the machine whirred into motion. As he leaned over to pull his meal tray from the slot in the machine, he noticed the computer screen above the slot.

Your charge: 2,000 Unilets

Your balance: 598,000 Unilets

598,000 Unilets! Wait a minute. That's way too much. Something is wrong.

He tried to recall how the money system worked. After converting his AZ money into unis when he'd first picked up his transport orders, he'd had two hundred thousand unis for his trip. That was all. Two hundred thousand unis. No more. That was how much he'd brought with him. Now, for some reason, his uni account had just tripled! *Maybe something is wrong with the machine.* He looked up at the screen again, then glanced all around. His face flushed with embarrassment. He felt guilty for some reason, like maybe he'd stolen the extra unis. Balancing the tray with his right hand, he looked at his wristband to see if there was any readout that might tell him how many unis he really had. There was none... at least there wasn't one that he knew about. He looked around again, and now he felt panic rise up in him; his heart began to beat faster. He felt sweat building up on his brow, and just as he turned around again, he saw Dawn walking quickly toward him.

She wasn't smiling.

3

EN ROUTE

Most Plain People are used to feeling guilty when they've done nothing wrong. It's part of the physiology and culture of being different. Usually this feeling only creeps up on them when they're out among the English. There was something in the way the English looked at them that conveyed a sense of accusation. Even when tourists were smiling and pointing and saying "How cute!" and asking for pictures, or snapping them anyway while pretending not to, there was always a subtle covetousness in the way the English looked at the Plain People. Maybe it was something around the eyes, but the gist of it was that somehow life had been unfair, or maybe the Plain People had done some great wrong to have to live an unadorned life of simplicity. The whole thing was an insoluble enigma. Even though the English man or woman may not want to be plain—wouldn't change places even if they could—there was still the communication of some want, or need... or blame that made the Plain People cringe inside. An elder had once called it "a criminal charge that comes through without words."

Seated in the airbus, Jed was attuned to this feeling of guilt. The situation with Dawn and the extra unis was troubling enough, but now he was on an English airbus by himself for the first time, and the looks and stares from many of the English brought back that oppressive feeling of guilt that Jed could not explain, even to himself. The passengers who were on Quadrille or lost on the Internet in their minds didn't pay him much heed. Others, not on the drug and not busy online, stared openly or secretly, usually one or the other, and always there was the wordless accusation... or maybe it was just a question... *why?*

One man with slicked-back hair—a young man Jed did not know and had never met—openly showed his disdain for Jed. Slicked-back had a sneer on his face, and whenever he caught Jed's eye (which Jed studiously tried to avoid) he'd emphasize the sneer and demonstrably look Jed up and down with disgust. There was hatred in Slicked-back's eyes, and this was not the first time that Jed had seen this attitude among the English. It made matters worse that seats on an airbus were arranged like those on an old subway, with passengers facing one another across an aisle. Slicked-back was across the aisle from him, but one seat over and to his right. Jed decided not to look at him, and he thought back to the incident with Dawn.

Back at the vending machine, when he'd been trying to grasp what was happening with the extra unis, the customs clerk named Dawn had approached him in a way that caused him to experience very real fear. Had he done something wrong?

When she was about five yards away, she'd reached into a pocket of her navy blue vest. Her eyes met his, and then she was extending her hand toward him. In her hand he could see his used electronic unilets card. He'd left it back at the desk. He didn't think he needed it anymore. They were disposable, after all.

"You left this at the desk," Dawn said, and now there was a forced smile on her face.

"I'm sorry... um... listen, I just..." Jed indicated with his head toward the vending machine, but Dawn cut him off before he could say anything about the extra unilets.

"Yes," she said, interrupting him again and nodding her head, "that's all right. Everything is as it should be now. Just take your card and make sure you don't miss your bus."

"But, I..."

"Yes, sir." She raised her hands this time. "Everything is as it should be." Her eyes grew wider, as if she were trying to tell him to shut up and just accept things the way they are. "Just take your card and go get on your bus, sir."

"So..."

"Listen, sir. Everything is fine now. You needn't worry about a thing. I've got to get back to the desk, but... *everything is as it should be*, so have a great trip." She forced the card into his hand, and when she did, he noticed that she was handing him more than just the card. There was also a small, folded piece of paper, and something else. Something heavy. It felt like a large coin.

He didn't look at it.

Not knowing why he did it, but intimidated by the discussion and not sure what else to do, Jed put the card, paper, and coin into his pocket quickly and without argument. He looked up at Dawn and tried to smile, and he noticed that she smiled back. And then she turned and was striding back toward the check-in desk...

In the men's restroom, he examined what Dawn had given him.

There was a note.

Don't say anything about the extra unis to anyone. I can't explain everything right now, but trust me. If you're in trouble in the City, ask at Merrill's Grocery Supply for Pook. Just ask for Pook. Put the gold coin in your shoe, and only pull it out in an emergency. There are no metal detectors anymore since bombs and guns won't work on transport anyway. Unless you get searched, they won't find it. Flush this note when you're done memorizing it. Dawn.

Now he was on the airbus to West Texas, and he could feel the heaviness of the gold coin in his shoe, and somehow the extra unis in his wristband seemed to have an extra weight all their own as well. *I feel guilty,* Jed thought, *and I don't know what I've done wrong. Maybe I should tell someone about the unis and the gold? No. Getting caught with extra unis that don't belong to you would mean automatic deportation.* If he did something stupid, he'd never make it to New Pennsylvania. How was he to know what was stupid in this world? For all he knew, everything he did was stupid. He began to imagine the Transport Police storming into the airbus to haul him off and send him to exile in Oklahoma.

Despite Jed's best attempts to put them out of his mind, crazy ideas started to flood over him. *Maybe I can spend them all at the SGT station when I get there... maybe I can give all the extra unis away... maybe a Quadrille dealer will sell me some drugs and then I can flush them all down the toilet like I did with Dawn's note...* None of his ideas were workable, and most of them would get him deported. It wasn't a far trip from West Texas to Oklahoma. Not far at all.

* * * *

The airbus floated silently through the air, and Jed tried to occupy his mind by looking out the window at the ground way below. The polarized windows and the altitude combined to make the view seem not... quite... right. But he'd never been this high before, so he wasn't sure how things were supposed to look.

Every now and then, looking down, he could see scars on the earth—remnants from the wars—and at one point they passed over what used to be a great city, but from thousands of feet in the air it looked like it was now a massive pile of burned rubble and debris. He wondered why people hadn't fixed up the cities again in the dozens of years that had passed since the wars. Maybe they left everything destroyed like that just to remind everyone how bad the wars had been, and so that the people would be thankful to the Transport Authority and the government for keeping everyone safe and secure.

"Hey, little Amish boy, you ever been up this high

before?"

It was Slicked-back, and he spewed the words, giving the impression that he really didn't care what the answer might be.

"No, sir," Jed replied.

"Yeah, I think it's funny that you Amish get to travel and fly and do everything the rest of us get to do... only you don't have to live by the same rules as everyone else." As he said this, he pointed at Jed's wristband and snorted. He looked around as if everyone else agreed with him, but most of the other passengers seemed to be on the Internet in their heads.

Jed didn't know what playing by the rules had to do with them being up this high, but he figured that Slicked-back was only looking for trouble and a reason to spew. Jed just ignored him and looked out the window.

"That's not very polite, Amish boy. I'm talkin' to you. How come you people don't have to get implanted TRIDs like everyone else? What makes you so special?" He was raising his voice now, and a few of the other passengers looked over, interrupting their music or videos or chats to see what was going on right there on their own bus.

Jed hadn't noticed it, but when Slicked-back began his little rant, a large Hispanic man sitting toward the back of the bus had gotten up, and during the one-sided conversation had been walking forward up the aisle. Now Jed noticed him, and he wondered if this giant of a man was going to give him grief too.

Just as Slicked-back finished his last little broadside, the big Hispanic man leaned over to Slicked-back and spoke to him clearly and concisely.

"Do you want to get sent to Oklahoma?"

"What're you, a Transport cop?" Slicked-back said with a snarl.

"No, friend, but we're about to be over Oklahoma, and if you'd like me to throw you out of one of these windows, then you keep bothering my friend."

Slicked-back didn't reply; he just kicked his feet across the aisle and pushed himself back in his seat. The big man smiled and nodded his head.

"That's right, little man. Now I'm going to talk to my friend. You should take some Q and chill out so that you don't make any permanent mistakes." He stepped over to take the seat next to Jed, but before he did he leaned back over Slicked-back's face and whispered to him. Slicked-back didn't respond, but he slowly drew his legs back so that they weren't blocking the aisle.

● ● ● ●

"I'm sorry that some people feel the need to attack things they don't understand," the big man said. "I'm Jerry Rios." Jerry stuck out his hand and Jed instinctively clasped it with his own.

"Jed. Jedediah Troyer. But you can just call me Jed."

"Okay, Jed. Glad to know you," Jerry said with a smile and a nod. He sat down next to Jed and crossed his long legs.

"What did you whisper to that guy as you walked by?" Jed asked.

"I told him that if his legs were still across the aisle when I walk back to my seat, that I'd remove them and feed them to him."

"Apparently he believed you," Jed said as he looked over at Slicked-back.

"It's good that he did," Jerry replied somberly. "I don't make idle threats."

Jed looked at Jerry to see how serious the young man was. He was serious.

"Anyway," Jed said, "there's no eating on the bus."

Jerry broke down laughing and eventually Jed joined him. Slicked-back just looked up at them and grunted his displeasure.

AMONG THE ENGLISH

Jerry was a little older than Jed, maybe in his mid-twenties, and he looked like someone who was not to be messed with. Talking to Jed though, he was personable and friendly, and the younger man was happy that Jerry had been there on the bus when Slicked-back decided to get aggressive.

"Where're you headed?" Jerry asked.

"I'm a pilgrim. I'm traveling to our colony in New Pennsylvania to live."

"Well then!" Jerry replied, smiling broadly. "We'll almost be neighbors. I'm heading to New PA too, but I'm heading to the City. I'm not a country boy."

Jed stared at Jerry for a minute and blinked several times before he could answer.

"Um... Oh. Uh, I didn't know... that the English... I mean—"

Jerry laughed heartily. "Hey man, don't worry about it. I know that your people call all of us outsiders the

English. It's just strange for me to hear, because I'm as far from English as a man can get!"

"I'm sorry, Jerry. What I meant was that I didn't know that any... *non Plain People...* were also colonizing New Pennsylvania."

"Oh, sure! You didn't think they were going to let you people have the whole planet, did you? Besides, someone has to eat all of that food your people produce!" Jerry laughed again in a friendly way, and Jed was compelled by Jerry's gregarious manner to laugh along with him.

"I guess I just never thought about it," Jed said. "In my world, we only talk about the colony that our people are starting there, so I just never considered that there would be others."

"Well, if you look around, Jed, you'll see that you're the only Amish guy on this bus, and I'd guess that most of us are going to West Texas SGT so that we can catch our transport to New PA. That should tell you that there are probably going to be a lot more of us there than there will be of you."

"I guess it's always that way."

"Well, from what I hear, it won't be bad," Jerry said, shrugging his shoulders. "I've read a lot about the colonization process, and it seems that there's plenty of land and countryside to go around. They say that New PA is almost the same size as Earth, with similar gravity, weather, and all that stuff as this planet, so I figure with such a tiny population, there'll be plenty of room to stretch your legs... without having to block the aisle." Jerry winked again and glanced over at Slicked-back. The man was obviously on the Internet in his head now, because he just stared blankly into the distance and hardly moved at all.

Jed looked sheepishly over at Jerry before speaking. He wasn't sure how exactly to ask what he wanted to ask, but now that he had an honest-to-goodness English fellow here to talk to, he felt like he should take advantage of the education.

"So... how do I say this... you don't look like you're on Quadrille or on the Internet in your head." Jed smiled a little. He thought that he'd made it sound like the Plain People believed that all English were on Quadrille and the Internet all the time. He wanted his interrogation to be taken as benevolent, and he wasn't sure whether he'd said it right. Jerry didn't seem to be offended.

"Oh, Jed... I don't mess with that stuff. But I'm unique in this world. When I need to, I get on the Internet the old-fashioned way. I'd walk down to the IntSta—the Internet Station—near our house a couple of times a week to check email. Frankly, I don't know why they even have the IntStas any more. No one uses them, except a few weirdos like me. Even the ultra-poor have the BICE... do you know what that is?"

Jed shook his head.

"The BICE is the Beta Internet Chip Enhancement. That's what you call 'the Internet in the head.'" Jed noticed Jerry looking at him, and his new friend saw the confusion on Jed's face, but Jed nodded anyway as he tried to keep up.

"Listen, Jed. I'm sorry to be using all of this stupid technology jargon with you. I know your people don't use too much of it. Let's talk about something else."

"No, please. I'm fascinated, and I mean to learn all that I can. I just have to slow down a bit and try to understand it all. I think I'm getting it. There are so many terms to learn. I just got the hang of a whole new vocabulary just for this trip, so you can correct me if I'm wrong on any of this stuff. I studied a lot before I left home. I know that *TRIDs* are Transfer IDs. I know that *unilets* are your kind of invisible money." He was now counting off the terms with his fingers. "Hey, and I even know that the term *unilets* comes from what was once called the *LETS*, which meant Local Exchange Trading System. Then, when the UN took over the money system after the wars, it became UNILETS for United Nations International Local Exchange Trading System. Now, thanks to you, I know that the Internet in the head thing is called BICE, and the Internet that is not in your head is at a place called an IntSta."

"You're doing okay, Jed!" Jerry said, slapping him playfully on the back. "Now I hope you'll get to your colony at New PA and forget all about this nonsense out here in this world. Especially the TRIDs and the BICE and the unilets. Those are just people-control systems. After the wars, everyone was willing to give up whatever freedom they had left just to stop the violence. So now we have TRIDs and unilets... and they have this stupid BICE system that ties it all together so that the power apparatus can control everything down to the minutest detail. It won't be long and the BICE will be mandatory, just like the TRIDs and unilets. I hate the unilets system."

"Why do you hate it?" Jed asked.

"Unis are now just an international currency, governed and regulated by corporations and the international banks. The great wars, which were caused by the collapse of national banks, drove everyone—everyone but you Plain People, that is—to conclude that the only way to prevent massive swings in the values of currency and markets was to have a centrally regulated form of money. The unilet became that currency. In the end, the mechanism designed by so-called "patriots" to free people from the grip of the banking cartels became the tool used to codify and deify the single currency as the de facto monetary unit of the whole world."

Jerry looked around, leaned into Jed, and whispered conspiratorially. "That's why I'm going to New PA, buddy. When I get there, I'm getting my TRID removed. Heck, I might even try to get into the AZ to visit you there. Maybe I'll even convert and become one of you!"

Jed laughed. He really didn't think that Jerry was serious, and as the big man turned to glance out the window, the smile kind of faded slowly until his face communicated more of a wistful look than anything else. The look reminded Jed of Dawn.

● ● ● ●

"In Europe, a long time ago, our people were persecuted horribly. But after a war, or when some king somewhere discovered that his people were nearing starvation, he would open wide the doors of his lands for our people to come in. We've always been prized for our industry and hard work and productivity. For a time, we'd be given tolerance and protection... and things would remain that way until our numbers would multiply, and the people, no longer starving, would grow angry at our successes, and then the kings would banish us, or allow us to be persecuted again to the point where we would have to flee. Then we'd be off to homestead in some other land. There was always another king somewhere with land who wanted us to come and work the ground in his kingdom."

Jerry sat and listened intently. They'd arrived at the SGT Transport Facility in the desert of Loving County, Texas, and now they were sitting in the gate area waiting for their turn in Medical. Medical was their last checkpoint before they could board their ship for New Pennsylvania.

"And now the newest new world is a whole other planet!" Jerry said. He whistled softly and shook his head. "I guess some things never really change, do they?"

"Jerry Rios!" The name crackled out of the speakers and frightened everyone in the waiting room. Most of the people had the BICE, so there was no need to actually call those people's names over the loudspeakers. With the Internet chip in their heads, an alert would indicate to them that a medical station was opened and waiting for them. For the Plain People, and those few like Jerry who didn't have a BICE implant, the old-fashioned building-wide announcement was used.

"Jerry Rios to Medical, please. Jerry Rios."

Jerry stood and reached over to shake Jed's hand. "I guess this is where we part ways, Jed. We probably won't see one another again until we disembark at New PA.

They take us straight from Medical to our pod, so... I guess this is it. Have a great trip, buddy, and I'll see you on the other side."

"Okay, Jerry. Thanks for the nice conversation." Jed squeezed his hand and smiled. "I hope you have a great trip too, and Lord willing, we'll talk when we get to New Pennsylvania."

Jed sat back down as Jerry hurried off toward the main desk. Most of the people had already gone through their checkup and preparation at Medical, and only a few travelers were left in the waiting area. Slicked-back had been one of the first ones called, over an hour ago, and Jed was glad about that.

Jed hadn't had the opportunity to see everyone who was going to be on the trip. The SGT station was a confusing and cavernous facility, and people were seated all over the place. Without access to the Internet queue, to Jed it looked like people would just randomly stand up and head off to Medical, and while he'd been talking to Jerry, maybe two-thirds of the passengers had loaded onto the ship without him even noticing. Now, there were only a few travelers left in the waiting room.

"Jedediah Troyer! Jedediah Troyer to Medical, please. Jedediah Troyer."

∗ ∗ ∗ ∗

Jed was poked and prodded and tested, but, all in all, the process proceeded quite rapidly. The only painful part was when a catheter was inserted into his bladder. He wasn't sure if that process violated the Richmond

Ruling, but the doctors explained to him that it was necessary in order to be able to drain his liquid waste during the trip. He didn't understand every word they said, but it seemed pretty straightforward. After the catheter was installed, he was given a large glass of an orange liquid, and he was told to drink it all down. This was supposed to "clean him out" for the trip, they explained.

Next, a woman came in and went through everything that was going to happen on the trip, explaining basically the same information that had been on the brochures Jed had read, only this briefing was a little more in-depth.

She explained that he was going to be placed in "suspended animation." The trip was going to take nine years in Earth time. He would only age a week or so during the duration of the voyage, but it would seem like he'd slept for only a few hours. There should be no long-term health effects. The one thing she emphasized several times was that he could not return. She made certain that he understood that fact.

When the woman was finished briefing him, she asked if he had any questions. He could feel the orange drink working on him, and he had the urge to go to the bathroom, but he felt like he needed to wait to see what would come next. He said he didn't have any questions, so she smiled and stood to leave. Just as she reached the door, she turned to him and said, "I'm sure you need to use the restroom, so go ahead. It's right through that door. Someone else will meet you when you come out."

Jed nodded his head but didn't spend long saying goodbye. He really needed to go. He rushed into the bathroom, and there he determined that when the Transport authorities told you some drink was going to empty you out for a long voyage, they weren't kidding around.

●●●●

After Jed was done doing his business, he washed his hands and paused to look in the mirror. This was something he'd rarely done in his life. His people didn't generally believe in having mirrors around the house. Mirrors tended to vanity, he was told. But now he really looked at himself, and maybe it was for the very first time.

At eighteen years old, he was a sturdy young man. Handsome enough. He noticed that he looked like a very young version of his father. His hair was dirty blond where it stuck out beneath his black hat, and he was shaved because he wasn't married yet. He was lean and strong from all the hard work on the farm, and he knew that there would be even harder work ahead of him if he was going to be successful in building his own place in New Pennsylvania. Looking at himself in the mirror, he nodded his approval. He knew he'd make it work, no matter what happened next.

Stepping out of the bathroom, Jed was met by two stern-looking men who appeared to be very official. One of the men, the taller one, wore the uniform of the Transport Police. The shorter one was the one who spoke to him.

"Mr. Troyer, my name is Hugh Conrad, and I'm with the Transport Authority. This is Officer Rheems of the TP. You're under arrest for insurrectionist discussions and terroristic intent based on conversations you had with Mr. Jerry Rios aboard the airbus that brought you here. We have the whole conversation recorded. We're going to need you to come with us."

SLEEP

J ed felt the gold coin pressing into the ball of his foot, and the feeling that he'd been doing something terribly wrong made it hard for him to focus on what the TP officer was saying to him.

Every five minutes or so, a small box up near the ceiling in the room would spray a fine mist into the air. The air smelled of artificial flowers and sweet chemicals, and Jed wondered if perhaps this was some aerosolized version of Quadrille, used to make arrested persons more compliant. He didn't know, and not knowing made him feel even worse. Everything in the office was plastic and metal and temporary, and Jed contrasted it with the essence of permanence he'd experienced back at his family's farm.

Officer Rheems of the Transport Police commanded

Jed to "remove his shoes and any articles of jewelry" and place them in the rubber bin under his chair. He slipped off his shoes and made sure to tip them forward so that the gold coin in the right one would slide unnoticed toward the toe. He placed the shoes into the bin and then folded his hands on his lap. He wore no jewelry or other personal adornment of any kind. He didn't like not knowing what was going to happen to him. He was nervous. He was frightened. For the first time that he could remember in all of his life, he felt fully powerless and exposed.

Rheems ordered him to stand up and put his hands on the opposite wall, and a thorough pat-down search commenced, adding to Jed's sense that he was some kind of criminal and that he was, therefore, doomed.

"Sit back down in the chair," Rheems said. The Transport cop looked over to the other man, Conrad, and nodded his head to indicate that the search had been completed.

Conrad glared at him coldly. Jed could detect no human feeling or care or empathy coming from the man. This was a man who did everything by the book, and it was obvious that he didn't let anything—emotions, mercy, kindness—affect his decisions.

"Jed Troyer, son, you are charged with a felony count of insurrectionist discussions with terroristic intent. You are not only charged, but you are already convicted, by the way." Conrad walked around the desk and stood in front of Jed. "Once you left the AZ and boarded official Transport, you were no longer protected under the Richmond Ruling, and you've waived all rights as a Plain

Person in order to travel out of the AZ. Every individual who boards and engages official Transport agrees to waive any right they have to an attorney, to a trial by jury, et cetera. They also agree to submit themselves to the absolute judgment of the Transport Authority. That's us. You signed a document agreeing to what I've just laid out for you, and now you've been found to be in violation of Transport law. Do you understand what I'm saying to you?"

"I don't think so, sir. I don't understand what I've done that was wrong," Jed said.

"You engaged in a public conversation where blatant violations of law were discussed and planned. Specifically, traveler Jerry Rios, who is now in custody as well, discussed with you in detail his intention, upon his arrival in New Pennsylvania, to remove his TRID implant—which would be a felony—and then to escape and illegally join you in the AZ there. Do you deny these charges?"

"I don't deny that he said these things. I didn't say them, or agree with them though."

"Well, it doesn't matter anyway, even if you denied it. It doesn't matter if you said anything or agreed or disagreed. Failure to report insurrectionist activities immediately to Transport authorities is evidence of criminal conspiracy. We have the whole conversation recorded, and you have waived your right to trial. You've been declared guilty, and now it just remains for us to decide what to do with you." Conrad looked over at Rheems, then stared back at Jed with hostility in his eyes.

"Am I going to be sent to Oklahoma?" Jed asked. That was the worst thing he could think of, so he figured he'd get right to the point. He wanted to look the thing square in the face if that was what was going to happen to him. Nobody wanted to be sent into exile in Oklahoma... and exile was the punishment of choice for Transport crimes. The horror stories about Oklahoma were widely believed to be true. Exile was tantamount to the death penalty.

"Well, that's what we need to determine, Jed. Normally it would be an automatic thing. In fact, historically we would have taken you and Rios off of your airbus and put you directly on a prison airbus to Oklahoma."

Jed didn't know what to say to that. The fact that the normal response to his crime had not been followed gave him hope that he might still avoid permanent exile in the wastelands, where he would be helpless among the society's worst criminals. He just stared back at Rheems, not wanting to say anything that might make his case worse.

"But..." Conrad said, exhaling heavily, "there are some problems going on in the exile lands right now, and we can't get any Transport vehicles in or out. So we have to decide what to do with you and Rios short of just casting you into Oklahoma."

• • • •

Jed spent the next thirty minutes squirming in his chair. Rheems looked up from his work occasionally and scowled whenever Jed would inadvertently bang his knee against the desk or knock his elbow against the chair next to him. The area where the catheter had been placed itched and irritated him, and he kept imagining the ship leaving for New Pennsylvania without him. Conrad had, according to Rheems, "gone to see the magistrate," whatever that meant, and Jed was left to cool his heels, hanging perilously between the possibility of being exiled for life to Oklahoma, and some other fate he could not even imagine.

When Conrad returned to the security office, he didn't waste any time letting Jed know that his fate had been determined.

"Okay, get up. Get your shoes on. Looks like you got really lucky. You're going on your trip. The magistrate has decided to send you on to New Pennsylvania and remand your case over to the court there. We're not allowed to hold you here indefinitely, and we can't get any form of transport into the exile lands, so grab whatever belongs to you and let's get you on your ship."

Jed slipped on his shoes, and when he stood up, Hugh Conrad was standing only inches from him. The older man leaned in toward him in a way that seemed threatening. Jed wondered if the man had somehow seen the gold coin in his shoe. *No. There's no way he could have seen it.*

"Be glad you'll be asleep all the way to New PA, pal," Conrad said. "That way you can't get yourself into any more trouble."

The remainder of the boarding process passed in a flash compared to the torture of waiting in the security office to learn of his fate. As Jed walked into the ship, his heart pounded and his palms grew clammy and damp. An attendant, seeing that he was nervous, led him to his pod and helped him to settle in. The pods on this level were aligned not unlike the benches on the airbus that brought him to West Texas. Rather than rudimentary seats, however, the pods themselves were egg-shaped cocoons with heavy lids that could be closed once the passenger was lying inside and the takeoff process was about to begin. Each pod lid had a large glass window embedded in it so that the passengers who chose the active monitoring option could be checked regularly during the duration of the flight. Jed thought it strange that there were Transport employees who would make the flight in Earth time and, other than the regular kind of daily sleep, would remain awake for the entire voyage. This meant that they were giving up almost a decade of their lives to the one interstellar flight that they would ever make. *It's a good thing these flights are subsidized*, Jed thought. *No one could afford the trip otherwise.*

Jed's ticket had cost him five hundred thousand unis. He expected that he might have to spend another two hundred thousand in transit. Converted back into Amish money, a man couldn't even build a really good barn for that amount of money.

Before receiving the extra unis from Dawn, Jed had always figured he'd be broke upon arriving in New Pennsylvania, just like his ancestors had been when they first came to America. His land, if he qualified, would eventually be free. He was planning to live and work with his boyhood friend Matthias until he could build his own place. The Plain People took care of their own, so he knew if he could ever get to the AZ on his new planet, he'd be taken care of.

The nurse hooked up his life-support system, attached a tube to his catheter, and typed on some kind of computer screen that was built into the wall of the pod. Jed heard a beep, and then he felt a slight buzz of vibration emanating from the band on his wrist. He looked up at the nurse with a look of concern on his face, and she smiled back at him.

"That's just to indicate that your account has been charged the additional one hundred thousand unis to pay for active monitoring. You chose this option when you paid for your ticket, correct?"

"Yes, ma'am."

"Okay, good. We'll leave the lid open until we're just about ready to take off. Whenever you're set to go under, press the blue button near your right hand and you'll be out in less than a minute. A lot of people choose to go under immediately. I think it eliminates the short period of worry that people have at the beginning of any journey, and it makes the flight seem shorter to them. So, whenever you're ready, just hit the button, and when you open your eyes again, you'll be in New Pennsylvania!"

"Thank you, ma'am." He looked up at her, and he knew that the worry that he felt was not only his concern about being turned over to the courts when he got to his new home planet. Deep inside of him, perhaps unrecognized and unexamined until now, was a fear that the ship would never get to New Pennsylvania at all.

That's why he'd paid for active monitoring, even though the Amish colonization agent had advised him against it. He felt safer knowing that someone who was awake would check on him regularly to make sure nothing had gone wrong with his life-support system. Maybe doing it had showed a lack of faith, but it definitely made him feel better about the trip.

"Ma'am... have you or the pilots... well... have *any* of you done this before?"

The nurse laughed. "No. No one on this flight has ever done this before, sir. It's a one-way flight, remember?"

"Yes. I suppose."

"Don't worry now. It's as safe a trip as Transport, with all their technology and expertise, can make it. Everything is run by computers anyway. You'll open your eyes and it'll feel like you've just had a good night's rest, and we'll be there."

"Okay. And thank you."

"No problem. Get some sleep, and I'll see you on the other side."

The nurse walked away, and as she did, Jed tapped his toe and remembered that the gold coin was still in his shoe. He knew he was still going to be in trouble when... if... he ever made it to New Pennsylvania, and he didn't want to add to his crimes.

Without taking much time to think about it or debate with himself, he leaned forward and removed the coin from his shoe. He looked around to see if anyone was watching him, but everyone he could see was either already unconscious, or was busy preparing for the flight. He felt around under his chair with his right hand, and he found a tight joint between the chair pad and the frame.

He pressed the gold coin into the gap and felt around the joint with his finger to make sure the coin didn't stick out where it might be seen by a nurse checking on him during the long years of flight.

Moments later, he was glad he'd taken the coin out of his shoes. The same attendant came back through the level and asked everyone for their shoes. She took each pair and placed it in a spring-loaded box that was attached to the base of each pod. When she took Jed's shoes, she smiled at him and said, "There now, you look better already!"

He watched as she finished out the level and then disappeared through a curtain.

Lying there, he couldn't figure out a reason to stay awake any longer. He was already sick with worry, and he knew if he decided to lie there awhile, he'd fret about what was going to happen to him when the flight was over.

He took a deep breath, and images of his brother Amos and his mother and father flashed through his mind. As he reflected on them, he reached down with his right hand again and pressed the blue button. He almost immediately felt a cool sensation enter his veins, and the effect was startling, although strangely pleasant. As he lay back against the soft padding of the seat and turned his head to his right, he began to experience the strong narcotic effect of whatever medication was now coursing through him. He'd never experienced any drug—had never taken Quadrille. The sensation was bizarre.

Just before his eyes closed, he noticed a face in the pod next to him that was looking back at him with a smile. His eyes fluttered and he tried to concentrate, but the darkness was coming and he couldn't fight it off. He knew the face, but the name was slow in coming, and it occurred to him only just as the lights went out.

Dawn.

THE CITY

C oming out of suspended animation was as remarkable as going into it. Some level of consciousness returned quickly, but Jed remained in a state of torpor for a while as synapses, long unused, began to fire again. He didn't know where he was or what was going on, but he knew who he was, and this knowledge was the substantive thread he first grasped as he came out of his long sleep.

The cold in his veins was replaced by a slow, expanding feeling of warmth and well-being. To Jed, it seemed like he stayed in this middling state of consciousness for hours, but in reality it was only minutes. He heard the pod lid release, and then there was a sound of gas or air escaping as the lid rose automatically and light flooded in around him. That was when he noticed that a recording was playing in his ears, and he instantly knew that the recording was repeating. He'd heard it before, only now it was actually passing through his conscious mind.

...the ship. Everyone must stop at Medical for a release before entering the station. Do not be alarmed. The process of reanimation is proceeding normally. You will feel confused, lightheaded, and weak at first, but normal function will return quickly. Your muscles have been continuously stimulated during your voyage, and will function normally after a period of acclimation. After a short episode of reorientation, you will begin to be able to feel and move normally. Take your time exiting your pod. When you do exit, you will find Medical on your left as you disembark the ship. Everyone must stop at Medical for a release before entering the station. Do not be alarmed. The process...

· · · ·

Jed closed his eyes tightly and flexed his neck, turning his head from side to side. He was doing an inventory of his body, and as he did he felt his mind begin to warm and his consciousness grow. He remembered where he was and what he was doing. When he opened his eyes, he saw a face looking down on him, and he had to blink a few times for the face to come into some semblance of clarity. A name formed in his thoughts again, and he realized it was the last name he remembered before falling asleep... Dawn.

Dawn gazed down at him with a concerned look on her face before looking from left to right, as if she were in a hurry.

"Hurry up, Jed. We have to go," Dawn said.

"Uh... I..." he sputtered.

"Shut up. We don't have time for you to wake up and figure it out. We have to get out of here before everyone comes to." She reached into his pod and removed his waste tube from his catheter.

"We'll have to get that catheter out later," she said as she typed on the screen on the wall of his pod. When she finished, she started pulling him by his arm to get him moving.

"I..."

"Jed. Don't talk. You're in danger. We're *all* in danger. We have to get out of here. Just do what I say and don't ask questions, okay?"

He stared at her, not knowing what he should think or do.

Dawn put a finger in his face. "If we're still standing here in two minutes, you *will* be arrested and you will never, ever make it to the AZ. Do you understand me?"

Jed blinked.

"I am the only hope you have of getting out of here and getting home. So put on your shoes and let's go!"

He struggled to pull his shoes on his feet, and Dawn didn't give him enough time to lace them up. She pulled him by his arm and pushed him ahead of her until his feet started to cooperate with his brain. Pins and needles in his legs, arms, hands and feet gave him the first signs that life was returning to his extremities. Dawn continued to push and pull him, but after a few steps, he stopped and bent over at the waist. A deep, diaphragmatic cough shook him to his core, and a blackish-gray, gelatinous mass worked its way out of his lungs and mouth and was deposited on the floor.

"That's actually not uncommon," Dawn said, then reasserted herself by pulling him by both his arm and shoulder. He picked up the pace and soon his legs were carrying him along without Dawn having to do most of the work.

"Medical," he said through another cough.

"What?" Dawn replied.

"I'm supposed to stop in Medical." He pulled up as if to stop, but Dawn grabbed him again, shaking her head.

"If you stop at Medical, you'll never be a free man again. Do you understand me? We have to get out of here!"

They exited the long tunnel that led from the ship to the gates and concourse. As they hustled along, Jed noticed that the terminal looked identical to the one in Columbia, where he'd met Dawn before flying to West Texas. Identical. Only older. As they ran, he noticed that the gate area was unmanned, and the whole facility gave off the impression that it was nearly, but not quite, abandoned. It was as if a war were raging in and around the place, and only a few functions still remained. Some lights hung by wires overhead, and here and there the bench seats were pushed out of line or were turned over completely.

Jed looked over his shoulder as they ran, and he noticed the sign that hung at a crooked angle over the counter at the gate.

Gate 13.

They ran past where, back in Columbia—back on Earth—he'd purchased the soup and sandwich, but there was no vending machine in this terminal.

* * * *

He was beginning to breathe heavily from the exertion, and was still struggling with his equilibrium. Dawn kept a hand on his shoulder to steady him as they ran. They rounded another corner, and in the distance Jed could see the check-in area, and beyond that, the entry doors. He was shocked at how similar this terminal was to the one back on Earth. *Maybe they had the same people build it,* he thought.

Dawn pulled him into a small administrative alcove, and he bent over to put his hands on his knees and draw in deep breaths of the stale air. Alien air. *I'm on another planet,* he thought. *I guess I'm the alien, though.*

"I hope you guys aren't planning on blowing this popsicle stand without me," a voice said, and Dawn snapped to attention.

The man whose voice they heard was just rounding the corner to enter the alcove when Dawn stepped forward and drove her elbow surprisingly hard into the man's face.

The man was big. Very big. He dropped to one knee and his hand came up to his face. Dawn braced herself against the wall and kicked hard at his head, but this time he was ready and he caught her leg and tossed her easily to the ground.

"What is wrong with you, lady?" the man said. He was bleeding from his nose, and his eyes narrowed as he tried to focus through his blurry vision. When his hand dropped from his face, Jed recognized him. It was Jerry Rios.

Dawn was back on her feet and Jed could tell that she was ready to resume her attack, but he stepped in between her and Jerry and put his hands up, palms out, to convince her to stop.

"This is my friend," he said. "This is Jerry. He was arrested at the same time I was back in West Texas."

Dawn lowered her hands and rolled her eyes. She exhaled deeply, pursed her lips and shook her head before stepping past both Jed and Jerry to sneak a look back down the concourse to see if anyone was coming or had seen them.

"You guys were never in West Texas," she said. "Are you ready?"

* * * *

Dawn spoke matter-of-factly, with no hesitation or indication that she might have second thoughts. "Okay, from here on in we walk. Do not run. Walk quickly and act like you belong here." As she talked, Dawn examined the flat muscled area above her elbow that she'd used to hit Jerry in the face. Seeing that there were no lacerations, she rubbed it before looking back up. Jerry watched her do this and snarled as he checked his own nose to see if it was broken.

"Sorry about that," Dawn said.

"Sure," Jerry replied.

"Okay, pay attention," she continued. "If anyone says anything to you or asks you to stop, you keep walking.

Mutter something like you don't understand them, but keep walking. We're looking for a man named Donavan. Do not stop until we run into Donavan. Any other name on the tag, I don't care who it is, you do not stop! Got it?"

"Donavan," Jerry said. "Got it."

Before Jed could say "Got it," which he dearly wanted to say, Dawn had already turned the corner and was gone. Jerry and Jed had to walk hurriedly to catch up with her.

"We're going to turn left up here," she said, "then another quick left through a doorway. Someone will probably say something to us there, but keep walking."

"How do you know all of this?" Jed asked.

"I've been here before."

They turned to the left, and then Dawn headed immediately toward a door marked *Staff Only*. The door had a push bar release, and just as Dawn punched open the door, Jed heard a voice to his right say "Wait a minute!" Jed scampered through the door and saw that Dawn and Jerry had turned right after entering the hallway, and were walking at a fast clip toward another distant door.

Jed heard the door swing open behind him, then footsteps. Voices, one male and one female, shouted, "Sir! Sir! I need you to stop!" Jed didn't stop. He caught up with Jerry and Dawn and he could hear the footfalls behind him speeding up and they were catching him just as the trio of travelers reached the far door.

"Sir! All of you! All three of you! We're going to need you to stop and come back to the desk!"

A hand reached up and grabbed Jed by the shoulder

just as the door swung open and a uniformed man stepped through. *Donavan* was on the man's nametag.

Donavan recognized Dawn and looked past Jed toward the two staff members who had just reached him.

"Okay, you two. Back to work. I'll take care of this. Thank you for your diligence," Donavan said with authority.

"But sir!"

"Back to work. I'll take care of this."

Before Jed could fully process what was going on, the three had been shuffled past the second door and they were walking through a heavily fortified parking lot toward a waiting Transport Authority minivan.

• • • •

"You barely made it, Dawn," Donavan said. He guided the vehicle through a maze of heavy concrete barricades, and Jed could hear distant explosions. Fantastic beams of light sped by overhead like ethereal shots fired from nearby cannon, and when the explosions were close, the ground would shake, and night turned into day all around them. "And I was expecting two of you, not three. This'll cost you more."

"How much more?" Dawn asked.

"I don't know. Seven total."

"Seven hundred thousand unilets? Have you lost your mind?"

"I could take you back and you can work it out with Transport... if that's what you want."

Dawn was quiet for a few beats. "We'll make it

work... somehow," she replied.

An explosion off to the right, on the other side of the concrete barricade, shook the van violently. Jed looked at Jerry, and with their eyes they asked one another, *What have we gotten into?*

"How many unilets do you have left?" Dawn asked Jed under her breath.

"Let me see," he said. "Five hundred ninety-eight thousand... minus the one hundred thousand from the flight... Four hundred ninety eight thousand. And that will make me completely broke."

"We're all broke," Dawn whispered to him. Then she gestured toward Donavan. "He just doesn't know that unis will be worthless real soon."

"I have just a bit over one hundred thousand unis," Jerry added.

Dawn reached forward and tapped Donavan on the shoulder. "Six!" she said loudly. "We have six. You'll have to take that, Donavan. It's all we can get."

"Six? You're kidding me, right? The price was three for *one* person, and you want me to move three people for six? What do you think this is, some cut-rate BICE shop?"

"They'll only have to cut two of us, Donavan. The Plain kid doesn't have an implant."

"I only have a TRID, not a BICE," Jerry added. He looked at Jed and shrugged. He didn't know if it would help in the negotiations, but it couldn't hurt.

Donavan shook his head and pounded the console with his hand.

"Unbelievable. So now you have me doing discount

hack work! Okay. Okay. Listen, lady. I'm going to do it, but you owe me, do you hear me, Dawn? You owe me big!"

"Okay! Sheesh. Settle down, Donavan. You're making six for driving us a few blocks. Think of it that way."

This little response inflamed Donavan all the more. "Driving you a few blocks? Driving you a few blocks? Is that what you think this is? I just secured three *criminals* from a secure facility in the middle of a major enemy offensive... all at the risk of my own neck, don't you know!" He exhaled loudly and struck the console again with the flat of his hand. "Driving you a few blocks! Wow!" He turned to Dawn and pointed at her. "You owe me big, Dawn. *Big!*"

Dawn rolled her eyes and shook her head.

"Yes, Donavan. I owe you big. Are we there yet?"

NEW PENNSYLVANIA

I ndeed, Dawn did owe Donavan. She owed him even more after they arrived at the underground BICE chop shop, and Dawn discovered that Jed had hidden the gold coin in his pod. This little fact triggered another loud argument between Dawn and Donavan. In the end, after Dawn admitted that this time, she really, really, *really* owed him *big-time*, Donavan agreed to go back to the station for the coin. Jed told him precisely where it was, and Donavan wrote down the pod number on a piece of paper so he could remember it.

There was one last argument when Dawn told Donavan that she wasn't going to pay him the six hundred thousand unis until he returned with the coin, but this time the hostility storm blew in fast and didn't last long. Jed heard Donavan curse under his breath as he left.

Dawn went under the knife first. Removing a BICE was a complicated but minor operation, and they only used some form of local anesthetic. Jed and Jerry sat against a far wall, and the operation took place in the middle of an expansive room and not in any kind of specialty operating theater. A slice was made along the hairline at the rear of the neck, and the BICE unit was removed with practiced precision. *They've done this before,* Jed noted.

Jed and Jerry talked during Dawn's operation, but there wasn't too much they could say. All they had were questions, and there weren't many answers to those questions available to them. They were both just glad to be alive, and no matter how bad it was here, they both agreed that it had to be better than if they'd been sent to Oklahoma. At least now they had a lifeline, however tentative it might be.

Jerry went to the operating table next, but before he did, Dawn instructed him on how to transfer the unis from his TRID to Jed's wristband. Once the unis were on the band, Jerry headed to the table and Dawn filled Jed in on some of the things that were happening—or at least, what he could expect to happen next. TRID removal was a lot easier than removing a BICE, Dawn told him, and it wasn't nearly as dangerous. Being *caught* without a TRID was what was dangerous.

She told Jed that she hadn't expected to come on this trip, even right up to the moment when she'd given him the note and the coin. Coming along was a last-minute exigency that she'd have to explain in greater detail later.

They needed the gold to get into the Amish Zone.

Getting to the AZ meant that they would have to travel safely through the battle that currently raged all around them in this new world, and there was only one man Dawn knew who could accomplish such a thing. That man was her cousin. Pook Rayburn.

••••

A harrowing walk of a few blocks through a darkened city under siege brought them to Pook's place of business. From all appearances, Merrill's Grocery Supply was mostly a bombed-out shell of its former self. Broken crates of canned and packaged groceries and kitchen supplies were scattered helter-skelter around the place, and Jed was surprised when they found Pook Rayburn himself still working at his desk in his second-floor office.

"What in the world happened here?" Dawn asked, as she gave her cousin a hug.

"Which world?" Pook replied with a wink. "*We* happened here. We—that is, *the resistance*—happened. It's a major offensive. This is the closest they've ever come to the City. I barely learned about it in time to warn you. I'm glad you made the trip. There probably won't be any more after yours."

"It's that bad?"

"For now it is." Pook placed a file he'd been looking at back on his desk and sat down, indicating that the rest of them should sit down too.

Jed was surprised to notice that there were no computers, no electronic devices anywhere to be seen. Jerry must have noticed the same thing, because he leaned over to Jed and whispered to him. "Apparently the resistance is purely analog... like you folks in the Amish!"

Pook overheard the jest and smiled. "All of this," he pointed to the paperwork and files on his desk, "this all has to do with my legitimate business. Everything else, I keep up here," he said, pointing to his head. "Anything digital can be traced and tracked. A lot of things that are *not* digital can be traced and tracked. We try to avoid leaving a signature anywhere, but..." He hesitated a moment before speaking again. "...But as this war develops, it seems that there are no guarantees about anything. I suppose uncertainty is always the product of any war..." Pook looked up and appeared to decide against whatever it was he had been going to say.

"How did the trip go?" Pook asked.

"Not bad when you consider how bad it could have been," Dawn said with a sigh. "Things have obviously gone downhill since I was here last. The biggest road bump was when Jed here and his new friend Jerry got pinched by Transport for insurrectionist conversations during their holo-trip."

Pook looked at Jed and nodded his approval, as if he were impressed. Jed responded silently by pointing at Jerry.

"That's a story you'll have to tell me later." Pook looked at his cousin. "Do you have the gold to get yourself into the AZ?"

"Donavan had to go back and get it from the station."

"Donavan?" Pook snorted with obvious dissatisfaction.

"Jed thought he was busted, and he hid the gold in

the seat of his pod."

Pook nodded again. "Okay... well... Jed here is a thinker. I'll give him that, for sure. How do we know Donavan won't skedaddle with the gold?"

"I told him I wasn't paying for the exfil or the BICE removal until he shows up with the gold."

"Clever of you. Not so much of him. Doesn't he know that unis are basically worthless?"

"Apparently not."

"Well let's hope he gets here with the gold before he finds out," Pook said with a wink. He stood up and walked toward the door. "We'll have to go next door to the antique shop, that's where I keep the Transport forms for the AZ."

●●●●

Merrill's Antique Shoppe had been spared most of the damage from the recent battles that the grocery supply building had suffered. Pook unlocked the door with an old-fashioned metal key, and as they walked in, only a faint blue-grey light from the streetlamps filtered into the darkened building, casting a ghostly hue on the items in the shop.

Without even being able to see much of it, the old building gave Jed a brief feeling of comfort. He felt like he was in one of the ancient buildings on his family's farm back on Earth. Everything in the building was old—and for Jed, strangely, it was the first time he'd felt safe since he'd left the Amish Zone back home. Here he was on a planet in a completely different solar system, and everything around him looked vaguely familiar.

Pook pulled some heavy blanket curtains down over the glass windows in the storefront, leaving them in almost perfect darkness. Then he walked through the store, and as he did he paused occasionally to light some fuel-burning lanterns that hung from wrought-iron hooks throughout the building. Jed couldn't say what kind of fuel the lanterns burned, but in his melancholic reverie he could swear that it smelled just like kerosene. A golden glow flooded the store as Pook lit the last lantern.

"A lot of this stuff might look really familiar to you, Jed," Pook said, almost as if he sensed what Jed was feeling. "We buy a lot of old junk on our regular trips to the Amish Zone. People in the City like Amish stuff for some reason. They'll hang just about anything Amish on their walls. I sold a six-inch piece of rope the other day for a thousand unis." He shook his head and let out a little giggle. "Of course, now that unis are worthless, maybe *I* was the one who got the short end of that deal. Seemed good for me at the time, though."

"The paperwork?" Dawn asked. To Jed, Dawn now seemed like she was in a hurry. Like she had somewhere else to be.

"You have a date, cousin?" Pook asked.

"I... I just don't like hanging around in here," she replied. "It gives me the creeps. This is all great stuff, and it was super when it was in someone's home, but in here it seems almost sacrilegious. Being here in this city and separated from the people who loved it and who owned it. I don't know. Maybe I'm just weird."

"I don't think you're weird," Jed said. "I love this

place, but I don't think you're weird."

"I do," Pook said, laughing. "Okay, the paperwork. Follow me."

He made his way through the narrow walkways between mountains of antique furniture, carpets, tools, and household goods. When he got to the back of the store, he reached through the flickering shadows, and on the far wall his hands found an old, whitewashed frame that looked like it had once been a window. He placed the window down on a dusty tan sofa; attached to the back of the frame was an envelope stuffed with papers.

"Here they are," Pook said.

Pook, Jerry, and Dawn walked back toward the front of the store, but Jed couldn't move. He was staring at the window frame...

The bottom-right pane of glass was missing. In its place was a piece of metal, a section of an old coffee can. You could see that the can had once—long, long ago—been red with white print, the old-timey kind, stomped flat and cut to fit.

The window itself looked ancient, as it always had, but now the piece of metal coffee can looked ancient, too—maybe over a hundred years old. Jed stared at the old window and touched the replacement pane with his hand.

He could almost feel the years pulse through the cool of the metal as the coffee can stared at him, penetrating him with an ageless accusation.

KNOT 2:

NON-ELECTRIC
BOOGALOO

MERRILL'S ANTIQUE SHOPPE

Lantern light flickered throughout Merrill's Antique Shoppe. The yellow-gold radiance pierced the shadows and made them dance against the collections of old furniture, twisted wrought iron, tin signs, and mannequins posed like fashion models arrayed in ancient dresses. The waltz of light and darkness reminded Jedediah Troyer of dark winter nights sitting around the wood burner in the front room of the farmhouse, when the firelight would shine through the glass window of the stove and his father would tell the family stories of persecution, of Jakob Ammann, of the lives of the martyrs.

In *this* Pennsylvania, those stories were ancient history, mythology, anecdotes of another world altogether. In this Pennsylvania, a war raged just outside the front door of the Antique Shoppe—a war with lasers and flying ships and assassin drones floating in deathly silence, searching for rebels in the night.

Now and then frightening explosions sounded in the distance, and the buzzing zip of phosphorescent projectiles or the crackling beams of laser light would slice through the air over the antique shop, highlighting both the irony and the relentlessness of time as the group of rebels plotted amidst the relics of an era long past.

The City was under attack. Jed wasn't even sure what that meant or who might be fighting whom, but the fact that he was trapped in some acrimonious struggle between alien factions was clear to him. Englischers—and most other humans—were already aliens to him, so he had no trouble seeing the conflict as a foreign engagement, a war in which he had no interest.

Pook Rayburn had just finished forging the last of the transport papers he hoped would get Jed, Dawn, and Jerry Rios into the Amish Zone when they heard something heavy crash against the front door of the shop.

Jed snapped back to the present as the frightening and desperate alert coming from the front of the shop pried his eyes and thoughts from the window with the coffee-can replacement pane—a relic from another time and place. *His* time and place.

What in the world?

Before anyone could even ask what caused the noise, Pook was up and running towards the door. He drew an antique twelve-gauge shotgun from an old umbrella stand as he passed it, and pumped a shell into the receiver before cautiously unlocking the door with his left hand and pulling it open.

Slumped against the doorframe was a man in a dark, military-style trench coat, and when the door opened the man fell into the entryway. His black features were barely licked by the light of the kerosene lamps, but even from Jed's location fifteen feet away he could see that the man on the floor was Donavan, and that he was still alive.

Jerry Rios—a large man, but athletic and quick—was moving now, and so was Dawn. Together with Pook they dragged Donavan into the shop, Dawn unconsciously trying to avoid stepping in the blood that trailed onto the hardwood floor as they struggled to move the injured man. Once they'd cleared the doorway, Pook stuck his head outside and looked around, checking that Donavan had not been followed. Satisfied that there was no immediate threat, he closed the door.

Jed didn't know how to react and, peering over Jerry's shoulder, he could see that Donavan's eyes were open and blood was seeping out of the corner of his mouth. When the wounded man saw Dawn and Jed, he smiled and shook his head, before coughing out some of the blood that was beginning to build up in his throat, blocking his airway.

Dawn was searching Donavan to try to ascertain his injuries, probing with her hands, and Jerry was propping up the injured man's head when Pook returned from locking the door.

"What happened, Donavan?" Pook asked.

"They got me," Donavan said, and laughed again.

"Isn't that what they say in the old movies?"

"This isn't a movie, Donavan! Who got you? What happened?" Dawn asked.

"Transport."

"But you *work* for Transport!"

"I think I've been fired," Donavan replied wryly. "We mutually agreed that I had no future with the company."

"Are you going to tell us what happened?" Pook asked.

Donavan's head lolled to one side. "They showed up just as I was leaving the ship with the coin. They didn't have to say anything." He gasped and inhaled deeply before continuing. "I could tell by the way they were walking towards me with their hands reaching towards their guns that I was busted, so I ran."

Another laugh brought on a fit of coughing and more blood came up before Donavan spoke again. This time no one peppered him with questions. Their silence implored him to continue.

"I got out of the building, and I was almost back to the van when one of them got me. It was a good shot, man, I'm telling you. I was almost behind the van and one of them hit me in the lower back. Kidney shot. Game over."

Dawn gasped, and Jerry carefully rolled Donavan onto his side. Blackish blood was seeping from a hole in the trench coat and soaking into the ancient hardwood floor. Jerry gently eased Donavan onto his back again.

Donavan laughed again. "Sorry about your floor, Pook."

"Shut up, man. This is a serious wound. We can't get you to a doctor, and you know that."

"I know. I know it. I'm done. I'm just glad I made it back here." As he said this, his hand opened and in his bloody palm was Jed's gold coin.

"We can give you the unis we owe you, Donavan," Dawn said with obvious sadness in her voice, "but you'll never spend them."

"I know. You guys can keep them. They're almost worthless anyway." More coughing and wheezing as Donavan struggled to hang on to the thread of thought that was still pulling him onward. "I just waited too long to get out. I was planning to get my own BICE removed next week, but it's too late now."

"Ah, man," Pook exhaled and then looked around, "I didn't think about that." He slapped his hand against the door in anger. "Your BICE. They can track you here."

"No, they can't," Donavan said with a grunt. He brought his left hand up to the back of his head, and when he pulled his hand back it was covered in blood.

"I didn't even look at his head after he said he was shot in the back," Jerry said. He rolled Donavan's head to the side, and they could all see that Donavan's short, curly hair was matted with blackened blood.

"You cut it out yourself, you crazy fool?" Pook asked.

"Yeah. I ditched the van not far from the station and then I crawled down an alley. I cut the BICE out with a piece of sharp aluminum I found behind a recycling unit. You'd be surprised at what you're capable of doing when you still think you might survive." Donavan laughed again, which set him off on another coughing spell. He gagged a little on his own blood.

"Can't they track his TRID?" Jed asked. He had only the faintest idea what 'tracking' really was or how anyone could do it, but it seemed to him that if they could track a BICE they could track a TRID.

"No," Dawn said. "Most of the people, like me, who had the newest BICE units didn't require a Transport ID chip. They're all-in-one now. The Transport ID is in the BICE unit." She showed Jed the back of her hand and he could see an old, healed scar, barely visible in the dancing light from the lanterns. "I had my TRID removed when I got the new BICE unit a couple of years ago."

"Listen," Donavan sputtered. He was fading fast, and Jed could see that the man's life was coming to an end. "I don't have much time, so listen up." His voice was a low wheeze, and his eyes fluttered as he struggled to push out words. He coughed again, but this time it was weaker and he choked a little on the blood as he tried to raise his voice. "There are Transport units everywhere. They know there are TRACE resistance groups active in the City, so they're looking. They'll come here, and probably soon."

"Did you see them?" Dawn asked.

"They are... they... are... everywhere." Donavan breathed deeply, trying to access some last store of energy so that he could finish what he had to say. He blinked several times, and Jed could see the life draining from the man's eyes.

"They have Transport drones... TRACERs out there

too. Flying silent. Watch. Pook? Pook?"

"I'm right here, Donavan."

"Pook, if you don't have guns, you need to make some right now. I don't think you'll make it past the walls and to the AZ... Pook?"

"Here, Donavan."

"You'll have to fight your way out, most likely."

"I'll get us out, Donavan. Thanks to you. We'll make it, man."

"Make it," Donavan sighed.

"We'll make it!"

"Make... it."

"Thank you, Donavan," Dawn whispered. She was crying now, and Jed felt like he was going to cry too. He didn't even know Donavan, but he was moved by the man's sacrifice.

There was a final gasp, and then almost a "whoosh" sound as the last of the air escaped the dying man's lungs. As he died, his hand opened, and the gold coin rolled onto the wood floor, circling in a lazy arc before bouncing off of Jed's shoe and coming to a stop.

Pook looked down at the coin and said, "Heads," in almost a whisper. He looked at Jed and nodded his head slowly. "Pick it up, man. He died to get it to you."

●●●●

Working together with Jerry and Dawn, Pook wrapped Donavan's body in a tarp and secured it with several sections of hemp rope, tying it up tightly like a package.

Pook looked down on their work and shook his head. "We'll have to stow him in the back for now. I'll get some of my men to come and get the body and try to give him a proper burial."

Jerry bent down and lifted Donavan's body by the feet, and Pook grabbed the corpse by the shoulders. Together they shuffle-carried the dead man toward the rear of the store and into a darkened office near the back door.

As they hefted Donavan onto a dusty desk, a deep rumble shook the building, followed by a thunderous roar that caused Jed and Dawn to look at one another with unvoiced concern. A tear rolled unchecked down Dawn's face.

The rumble gradually died away into the distance, and Dawn looked upward, blinking through the moisture in her eyes, as if to check to see if the roof was going to cave in on them. When it didn't, she looked back at Jed.

Jed and Dawn stared deeply into one another's eyes, and for the first time he saw that she was not entirely the cool and dispassionate professional that she'd appeared to have been the entire time he'd known her. She wiped away the wetness from her cheek as she studied Jed's face for answers.

He had none.

Murder. Violence. War. These were things that were usually outside of his world, separate from his realm of experience. Death in the Amish world was structured, ordered, systematic. Even when an unexpected accident took the lives of the young—maybe a buggy overturned, or a boy fell under a plow—there was a system to things.

Everyone was on the same side, and all played their parts. Death was considered a stage of life, and it was integrated into the system in a way that left no room for confusion or doubt.

But this—people being gunned down in the streets— was a foreign concept to Jed. Implements of war loosed in the streets of cities, mindless tools of despotic governments seeking flesh to destroy. And for what? How could a young man like Jed understand the devilish and covetous motivations that could bring about such a way of living?

It didn't seem to Jed that Donavan had been a bad man. Donavan was just a Transport official who wanted *out*. Jed had to wonder... isn't *out* a primal desire? Isn't *out* a destination found in the heart of every man and woman?

When Pook and Jerry returned from stowing the body, the four of them stood wordlessly for a while, as if the moment transcended words and demanded silent recognition of the Transport man's sacrifice. As they stood in gauzy silence, Jed could hear a breeze bend its way around the building, on its journey from somewhere to eternity. The building creaked and whispered its age, and Jed identified the very faint *pop, pop, pop* of the lanterns sucking oxygen through their flames.

After an appropriately solemn period of respectful silence, Jerry turned to Pook and tapped him lightly on the arm.

"So what's this about making guns?" he asked.

"We'll have to go down to the basement."

"Lead the way."

Dawn and Jed stayed behind for a moment longer, and when the others were gone, Dawn's hand came up to her mouth.

Jed noticed a slight tremor in the hand, and that small involuntary expression communicated to him her fear and sorrow. He didn't know what to do, but he felt that he should do *something*, anything—so he did what he would have done for Amos, or even for his mother if they were upset. He put his arms around Dawn and drew her close to him in an embrace. He didn't second-guess his reasons for reaching out to Dawn, and she seemed to immediately submit to what the moment required.

As if the act of Jed embracing her gave her permission to release a pent-up torrent of emotion, Dawn collapsed into him, squeezing him tightly, and a loud sob escaped from her as the tears flowed freely.

"Thank you, Jed."

"No. Thank you for getting me out of that place, Dawn, and for watching over me on this trip."

"It was..." She paused a few beats. "It *is* my job."

Jed moved to pull away from her, his mind reeling at everything that had transpired since he'd left Old Pennsylvania on this journey.

"Your job?" he asked.

Dawn grabbed him as he pulled away, and pulled him back into her arms.

"Yes," she said. "Your safety is my job."

Jed continued to embrace her, and as his gaze drifted across the antiques, the light flickering among them, he saw them for what they were: moments that marked real lives that were lived.

"I have so many questions," Jed said as he pulled away from Dawn's embrace again.

"I know, Jed. I know you do. You have been very patient. But we don't have time to go through everything right now. Lives are at stake, and you know that. It would all blow your mind out of your ears... seriously."

"I know." Jed took a step backwards, then began to move towards the door that led down to the basement. When he did, Dawn's hand darted out and grabbed his hand.

"Jed, everything is not as it seems. I know you probably know that by now, but no matter what happens, you need to believe that you can trust me. I'm here to help you, and to keep you alive. I can't answer all of your questions, and I'm pretty sure you wouldn't believe me if I could. But I'll tell you whatever I can when the time is right. For right now, my job—*our* job—is to get you to the Amish Zone. That is my one and only mission in life."

Jed looked down at his boots, and then back up at Dawn. He was still holding her hand, so when he turned again he pulled her gently behind him.

"Let me show you something," Jed said softly over his shoulder.

"What? Here? In the shop?"

"Yes, it's back here where Pook kept his forgery papers."

"Okay" was all that Dawn could manage to say as she let herself be pulled down a dark aisle and then back up another row that was dimly lit by lantern light.

When they were back in the little nook where Pook had removed the old relic from the wall, Jed pointed to the antique window that now rested against an old, dusty couch. Jed went down to a knee and reached out to touch the flattened coffee can that served as a replacement to a long-ago broken pane.

"This window frame came from the old barn on my farm. Back in Old Pennsylvania."

Dawn stood quietly a while, and when Jed finally looked up at her, she was staring at him, as if she wasn't sure what she should say.

"I broke this window pane with my slingshot when I was fourteen years old. I replaced the pane myself with this coffee can. I looked up at this window in the gabled end of our barn only days ago, when I was leaving to board the airbus to start this trip."

"That wasn't days ago, Jed."

"I know. I know that. But at the most it was nine years ago, and that's if the window frame made the trip with us on the ship, and I don't believe that it did. It was here when we got here, and it was covered in a lot of dust. Something is wrong."

"Maybe it's another window and it just really looks like yours. Maybe you're homesick, and you remember a window a lot like this one?" Dawn didn't say these things as though she believed them. She said them as if she were offering them up as excuses... reasons to suspend disbelief for just a little while longer.

"No, Dawn." He touched the metal replacement pane again. "This is what I know. This is the only thing I know in the whole universe right now. This is my work. It was a point of humor between my dad and me. I looked at it all the time. I put this can here." His fingers traced the raised lettering on the flattened, ancient coffee can.

"There are a lot of things that I just can't tell you yet, Jedediah."

"Just tell me where I am, and what happened to my home."

"Where... well, *where* is an interesting question. And I don't mean to sound mysterious, or to put you off when you're obviously concerned and maybe worried too, but the real question—and it's another one that I can't yet answer for you—isn't *where* are you, but *when*."

Jed looked up at Dawn, but his hand didn't leave the metal can in the window frame.

"So answer it, then. *When am I*, Dawn?"

Dawn shook her head and tried to smile, though the smile came off more like a grimace than anything else.

"I can't tell you that, Jed. I just can't. Not yet. I would if I could, and you have to believe that. When you're safe, and when I have leave to tell you, I'll tell you everything I can. For now, we have to go join the others. We have work to do."

With that, Dawn turned and walked back through the piles of ancient goods toward the basement of Merrill's Antique Shoppe.

OKCILLIUM

The basement beneath the shop was lit by a dozen lanterns scattered around the place, and the flickering, golden light revealed a cavernous room that looked as old as anything Jed had ever seen in the Amish Zone back on Earth. Older even. The dark red bricks that made up the walls appeared to be of the handmade variety, imperfect and inconsistent, adhered together with ancient, sandy gray mortar that here and there had dripped down over the brick faces in haphazard fashion. The construction looked to Jed to be from the turn of the twentieth century, and widely scattered mold and mildew stains marked the faces of the walls. Bags and boxes of old clothing and antique bits and pieces of the flotsam of time were scattered in dusty piles around the basement and stacked high against the brick walls—all except for the north wall, which had been cleared of the residue of these once-loved, but now forgotten, material possessions. The detritus of former lives.

Along that north wall, standing like a line of mechanical soldiers—or the shiny, stainless steel milking machines that Jed had seen once in a more liberal Amish neighbor's barn—were ten complicated-looking machines. The cords from the machines ran along the base of the wall and were taped together where they terminated in an enormous plug the likes of which Jed had never seen.

Pook followed Jed's gaze. "We can't use grid power, even if the power were up right now. They track any anomalies in power usage very closely."

"Anomalies," Jed repeated, absentmindedly, as he stared at the machines.

"Freakin' anomalies," Jerry repeated with a smile on his face. He seemed to be enjoying the entire adventure immensely.

"We had a friend who was running a single one of these machines using grid power out in one of the suburbs of the City," Pook said as he worked. "This was years ago. Anyway, they toasted the whole subdivision with a micro-nuke just to make sure they got him. Killed hundreds of people."

"Who did that?" Jed asked. "Who would kill hundreds of people to get one person for using a machine?"

"Transport, that's who," Pook said through a barely disguised sneer.

"I don't understand what using a machine has to do with Transport," Jed said.

"*Everything* has to do with Transport," Pook said, holding his right hand out in a clenched fist. He squeezed the fist as if he were crushing anything that could have fit into it. "For all intents and purposes, Transport *is* the government here, just like where you're from. It all goes back to the founding of the United States and the misinterpretation and misuse of the Interstate Commerce Clause found in the Constitution of America. Through time, governments used that clause to rationalize that *everything*—especially in a global world with instantaneous communication and the blurring of state, national, and international lines, laws, and responsibilities—fell under Transport law. After the wars of the early twenty-first century and the globalization of the 'war on terror,' micromanaging Transport became the easiest way to control populations and govern human behavior."

"That's when private transport was outlawed," Jerry said, nodding his head toward Jed.

"That's right," Pook said. He was preaching now. It was a sermon he'd given before, and Jed got the feeling that Pook was very much a preacher at heart.

"They had to do it, considering their goals. The purpose of government had morphed from its original goal into the solitary objective of maintaining an environment in which business could take place without fear and panic. Government became nothing more than a mechanism of control, because the free flow of dollars and the success of markets were the only things keeping the whole thing afloat. If mitigating panic is the national goal and purpose, then you have to control the where, when, what, and how of transportation. It's a maxim. You have to take away the risk of someone attacking transportation and crippling the country. To make that process easier and less irritating for the public, you make public transport the only way to travel, and you streamline everything with implanted chips so everyone can flow through transport smoothly. You sell it as 'homeland security,' as an economic necessity, as 'greening' the planet. It's a cure-all for a broken and desperately sad world.

"After the wars, everyone went along with whatever Transport proposed. Everyone, that is, but the refuseniks: mainly the miners and the people who lived out in the countryside. Just like when everyone but the Amish went along with the implanted chips and the Transport IDs, the refuseniks refused to accept the outlawing of private transportation."

"We don't have time for a political discussion," Dawn cut in. "We're being hunted down, we have a dead friend lying on the back table in that office up there, and I doubt Jed cares about our problems. I suspect he just wants to get away from all of this craziness and into the safety of the Amish Zone."

"Yeah. Safety," Pook said drily.

"How are you going to run the printers?" Dawn asked. The last thing she needed was her cousin trying to radicalize an Amish dissenter. She was calmer now, and a few faint tracks on her face were the only reminder that she'd had an emotional episode over the death of Donavan.

Jerry Rios stood silently now, watching Pook with a curious look on his face. Jed could tell that Jerry couldn't wait to see what was going to happen next.

"I have an okcillium power generator," Pook said.

"That's how I can run ten of these machines at once without Transport detecting anything. "It'll run for a couple hundred hours on just a few grams of okcillium."

"Ok—freakin'—cillium!" Jerry said with a grin. "I knew it!"

"You did, did you?" Pook said.

"What is okcillium?" Jed asked before he could think better of it. His curiosity was piqued by the strangeness of the machines and what Pook might do with them.

"Okcillium?" Pook said. "Okcillium is the future, *and* it's the past. Okcillium is power and freedom, and it can also be control and tyranny. Okcillium is why there's a war going on out there, and I reckon it's why you're here too Jed, but we don't have time for that right now. Dawn is anxious and she wants us to get to work."

As if to emphasize the point, another explosion shook the building above their heads, and dust and dirt shook free from the rafters of the basement as the building creaked and moaned in protest.

Seemingly unconcerned, Pook went to work. He plugged the male end of the cord assembly into a female receptacle, and then walked over and pulled a bunch of flimsy cardboard boxes full of clothing from a pile. The cartons had lost most of their structural integrity and as he moved them they spilled some of their contents on the ground. After Pook had moved a few of the cartons, Jed could see a small machine that had been hidden among the antique treasures.

Pook cleared the area around the machine, and then pushed two buttons simultaneously on the face of the stainless metal cage that housed the okcillium generator. A slight hum and an almost imperceptible vibration indicated to Pook that the machine was running, and Jed noticed that the ten gray machines over near the north wall all came to life, beeping and humming in coordinated response.

"It runs almost totally silently and doesn't emit any fumes or off-gases," Pook said of the generator. "It doesn't produce a tremendous amount of heat either. That's one of the reasons okcillium is so valuable... and so illegal. It is quite nearly undetectable."

Jerry Rios pointed at the generator and winked at Jed. "Private power generation is like private transport, Jed. Forbidden."

Jed nodded his head. He wasn't sure what to think about that information, but it was scary—and, if he had to admit it, somewhat thrilling—to be standing there while Pook defiantly broke the law.

"Once upon a time," Pook said, "the powers that be just kept a lid on new inventions. They killed or financially ruined inventors, bought up patents, and spun conspiracy theories that kept people wondering whether cheap and clean home power was even possible. Mainstream electricity and grid power were kept so artificially inexpensive that most people didn't even really care if home power generation was a possibility. Thomas Edison once said something along the lines of, 'We intend to make electricity so inexpensive that only the rich will be able to afford candles.' And they did it, too. The problem with that is that it made everyone addicted to, and dependent upon, cheaply provided and ubiquitous grid power. Sure, the government didn't much care if you went solar, bought fossil-fuel generators, or put up wind generators, because those off-grid resources were finite, unsustainable, and would always require more input from the outside world. But when okcillium was discovered, all bets were off. It was outlawed pretty soon after it was discovered."

"What reason was given for outlawing it?" Jed asked.

"They just categorized it with other fissionable materials, even though okcillium is nothing like radioactive, nuclear substances."

"Okay," Dawn said firmly, making it obvious that she was exasperated with all of the talk. "It's not necessary that Jed get a complete briefing about all of the problems in this world. He isn't a part of this world. We need to get a move on, like immediately."

"Gotcha, cousin," Pook said with a smile.

Jerry, Dawn, and Jed could only watch as Pook went to work. The first thing he did was produce a black pistol from a drawer. He showed the pistol to everyone before placing it flat on a metal rolling cart that had a bright white tabletop. Jed had never seen a real gun, and had only heard of them through gossip and maybe in a few sermons back at home. Pook removed some sort of cartridge from the grip of the pistol and placed the cartridge on the table as well.

While Pook went and grabbed a few other boxes, Jerry picked up the weapon and examined it.

"Glock 21," he said. "Fires .45 ACP ammunition and is very deadly, especially at close range. This one is highly illegal. No tracking chip. No location-based disarming module. No serial numbers. No ID activation or remote jamming."

"You know your weapons," Pook said as he placed the boxes he'd retrieved near the machines. He walked back over to the gun and took it from Jerry's hand. "That's not very common back where you come from."

"Yeah," Jerry said, putting his hands into his pockets. "My dad was an enthusiast."

"You have some kind of military background?" Pook asked.

"Nah. I was way too young for the wars. I'm only twenty, but my father fought. He was in Kansas City before it was destroyed, and he was there when New Orleans fell. He used to take me out to the country to an old cabin where he'd hidden some weapons from the time before the banks collapsed and the wars broke out. I learned a lot about guns from my father."

"Interesting," Pook replied.

Pook placed the gun back down on the table, disassembled it into its several parts, and then propped up the pieces on tiny, clear blocks that elevated the gun from the table. He did the same with the black cartridge. "This will allow us to get a full 3D image of the items," he said as he worked.

"The units we're going to make will be one hundred percent polymer resin and ceramic, even the striker pin and spring, and they'll be undetectable by metal detector—even though almost no one really uses metal detectors anymore."

Pook opened up a cabinet and pulled out a large handheld device that, when plugged in, emitted a glowing red light. The luminous wand was connected to another device that Jed rightly identified as some kind of computer. He knew about computers from the studies he'd done to prepare himself for his trip, and he'd seen Dawn operate one back at check-in when he'd first arrived at Columbia.

"Back where you're from, guns were not only illegal, but they were manufactured so that they wouldn't fire unless they were in the hand of a certified Transport Officer. They were also disabled electronically whenever they were in or near any government facility." Pook began slowly moving the handheld device over and around the gun parts and the disassembled cartridge, and an image of the items began to appear on the computer screen.

"Guns are illegal here too, but the resistance has ways of arming themselves. Of course, that's always been true. The only people who are disarmed in this world are the Amish," he jerked his head toward Jed, "and all the other ignorant, urban civilians. We usually call them 'victims.'" Pook looked over to Jed and smiled. "Pardon my terminology, Jed. I'm sure you don't philosophically agree with the use of weapons."

Jed just shrugged and stared back at the pistol as its representation began to materialize on the computer screen. He certainly didn't intend to get into any religious or philosophical discussions while running for his life out among the English. He knew that back in his old life he'd be asleep in bed. In only a few hours, he'd be waking up to milk Zoe. None of this—this running around, hiding, fighting, making guns—none of it made food for people to eat or put clothing on their backs. He understood that perhaps these people felt like they needed to fight and struggle to be free, but the struggle was birthed from their departure from a simple worldview. The English had long since abandoned the idea that man needed only food, raiment, and perhaps shelter. Once man leaves the farm, he needs *more...* always *more.* The hunger for more inevitably leads to conflict, wars, tyranny, oppression. And always, always, always this *more* that man actually gets... comes in the form of more government.

Pook touched the screen a few times, moving the image about and checking it for any noticeable errors, and as he did this, he continued talking.

"This is all really old technology. This pistol and these printers and computers are all relics from the second decade of the twenty-first century. Being in the antique business has its benefits." Pook opened his hand as he touched the screen and the image grew larger. Jed could now see more detail in the animation.

"Once I get a complete scan of the gun, the clip, and all the parts," Pook said, "the computer will render a perfectly identical model—accurate within forty microns, or about half the breadth of a human hair. The printers will reproduce the item precisely, even down to the internal moving parts."

Pook then walked over and filled each of the machines in measured doses with resin powders from the different boxes he'd stacked in front of them. When he was ready and had double-checked all of the settings, he pressed some buttons on the computer, and the 3D printers jumped to life.

A gray arm on each of the machines began traveling back and forth within its case, laying down each micro-layer of polymer from the bottom up. After each pass, the panel that was holding these slowly forming weapons dropped down an almost infinitesimal distance, ready for the gray arm to make another pass. A white, drying powder also filled the case as the printing progressed, suspending the newly printed parts in three dimensions.

Pook turned and looked at Jed, who was staring, mouth agape, at the process, and smiled with amusement.

"Have you ever fired a gun, Jed?"

"No, sir. We don't hunt. Some of our people have small rifles for killing pigs or cattle, but we're all pacifists."

"Yes," Pook replied, smiling, "I suppose you are. It must be nice, having other people fight your battles for you."

Jerry seemed to bristle at this, and answered before Jed could think of what to say.

"He never asked anyone to fight for him, Pook," Jerry said. "I mean his people didn't. Jed doesn't owe you or me or anyone else anything at all. You can't force people to be thankful just because in your mind they seem to benefit from what you're doing... especially when what you're doing is something you would do anyway, even without them as an excuse."

"Well now!" Pook said, laughing all the while. "Irony always amuses me. It looks like now *you're* the one who's come to Jed's defense, but I don't suppose he owes you any thanks for that."

"No," Jerry replied, staring at Pook. "No, he doesn't."

"Well then," Pook smiled. "It looks like no one owes anyone anything!"

REPLICATIONS

Less than an hour later, there were ten finished polymer replicas of the Glock 21 sitting on the rolling table. Pook assembled the pistols, examining each one intently before handing it to Jerry, who inserted the clip and pulled back the slide, checking to see that the gun functioned properly.

"The ceramic and polymer resin produces a fine and lightweight weapon," Pook said. "Once you're used to it, you may like it even more than traditional, predominantly metal guns. I guess we won't know for sure that these are perfect until we're forced to fire one, but we've done this before and I've never had a problem."

"I'm anxious to try one out," Jerry said.

"I'm sure you'll be put to the test soon enough, Jerry," Pook said.

"I can't wait!"

"Good, then this one here is yours." Pook handed the last pistol to Jerry as if he were presenting a ceremonial sword to a newly christened knight.

"Really?" Jerry said, his face beaming.

"Really."

"What about ammo?" Jerry asked as he snapped one of the clips into place.

"We have our own underground version of that, too. The ammo we'll use is constructed of a synthesized material made up of polymer resin, ceramic, and okcillium. All of those materials—except the okcillium, of course—are easy to get on the black market and, luckily for us, here in the City I *am* the black market. Believe me, they didn't have anything like these where you came from."

"I'm sure they didn't," Jerry said.

"The good thing is that these guns and ammo are also undetectable by TRACER drones, which means we can go armed and shouldn't trigger any aerial attack."

"That *is* a good thing," Jerry said.

Pook opened an antique trunk, pulling out some old blankets and sheets and tossing them to the side before removing a false wooden bottom. He extracted six or seven small white boxes and then replaced the false bottom before closing the trunk. He tossed two of the boxes to Jerry, who began loading clips with the special ammunition from the boxes. The rest of the boxes Pook stuffed into a backpack.

"Load these in the same way as you're used to, Jerry. Thirteen per clip."

"You said something like that earlier," Jed interrupted. "You said 'TRACE resistance groups,' or something like that. Are TRACER drones in any way related to these groups?"

Pook laughed. "Yeah. Like a bird dog is related to a bird!"

"I don't get it," Jed said.

"Well, Jed, there's probably a ton of stuff you need to know, but we're on a short schedule here and we're going to have to get moving, so I'll need you to keep your questions to a minimum—but, since you asked... TRACE, well, that's us. There are a few hundred of us in the City. TRACE is the resistance. So when I say 'us,' I mean Dawn and me, the refuseniks, and the people like us who fight in an organized way against Transport and their schemes. TRACER drones, those are the aerial drones operated by Transport that hover in and around the city in order to find and kill people like us. That's why they call them TRACERs. TRACERs are designed to kill TRACE operatives. They track us. Most of the drones are probably grounded right now with this offensive going on. At least I hope like hell they are."

"You say they track and kill people like you? People in the resistance?"

"That's right."

"Are they ever successful?"

Pook shrugged and nodded. "Yeah. Yeah, sometimes they are."

●●●●

As Pook and Jerry were stowing the guns and ammunition in a large black canvas bag, Jed looked up and saw a face staring at him from the dark shadows of the stairs that led up into the antique store. Jed was startled at first, and his heart jumped in his chest. He was just about to shout when Pook, who must have noticed the face too, yelled "Billy!" in a good-natured way. The face smiled back and the man named Billy came down the stairs into the basement.

"Hey everyone, this is Billy, one of my minions." Pook smiled when he said this, and punched Billy playfully in the arm. "Not really. Actually, Billy is my best friend."

"Hey everyone," Billy said. He didn't look anyone directly in the eye except for Dawn, and Jed noticed that Billy seemed to be shy and unsure of himself compared to the confident and aggressive manner of both Pook and Jerry.

"Hey Billy," Jerry and Jed said in unison.

Dawn walked over and gave Billy a hug. "Hey Bill," she said, looking up into his face.

"Hey girl," Billy replied, smiling.

Jed noticed that Billy's hand hesitated for just a moment on Dawn's neck as the two separated. Billy nodded his head weakly at Jed, and then stepped over near Pook and began to brief his friend.

"The other guys are coming, but they were delayed. I left Will upstairs to wait for them and fill them in on what's happening."

Billy ran his hand through his hair and shook his head. No one said anything for a full minute, and Pook just stared at Billy, waiting to hear what his friend had to say.

"It's madness out there right now, Pook. Resistance

lasers and ordnance were hitting dangerously close to the safe house, and we were scared we'd be killed by friendly fire. So we got out of there and headed over here. Then a TRACER showed up out of nowhere and almost got us all. We were huddled in close together behind an apartment building when the TRACER found us, and if we hadn't seen it and reacted quickly it would have ended us all. After that we got separated, but I know the rest of them are heading this way."

"A TRACER? Damn. I thought they'd all be down," Pook said.

"I thought that too," Billy said. "The good news is that the TRACER that almost nailed us got hit not long after that. I saw it tumble and go down over by Locust and South 2nd. Took out a house over there, not far from the river."

"Hopefully Transport gets the message and keeps the rest of 'em grounded until this offensive winds down."

"You don't think the resistance will break into the City?"

"Nah. They never intended to. This offensive isn't the real thing, although I have to admit it's been impressive. TRACE couldn't get near this place with an army sizeable enough to take the City. At least not yet. Based on the mayhem that's being caused out there, this has to be Rover's unit, and the SOMA has to be hands on, calling the shots. But on the ground? Ten, maybe fifteen guys tops, causing this entire ruckus."

"You're kidding me," Jerry said, rolling his eyes in disbelief. And who's Rover? And who is the SOMA?"

Pook looked at Jerry and just shook his head slightly,

indicating that he had no intention of answering those questions. In reply, Jerry nodded his head to indicate that he understood.

"Wow. I'd have thought the whole resistance was bearing down on the City," Billy said.

"That's what we wanted it to seem like," Pook said with a smile. He reached into his jacket pocket and pulled out a cigar, loosed it from its cellophane wrapper, and bit off the tip before putting it into his mouth. "But even I didn't know it would be *this* devastating. Transport has to be in an uproar, messing their diapers over all this."

"Why the fuss, Pook?" Billy asked. "And why now?"

Pook produced a lighter from his pants pocket and held it up for everyone to admire. "Okcillium lighter. One of a kind," he said, grinning and speaking with the cigar between his teeth. He thumbed a button and a strange blue flame shot up an inch high and burned brightly. He placed the end of the cigar into the flame and rotated the stogie slowly between his thumb and forefinger, puffing large clouds of smoke into the air as he did. He held up the lighter again and smiled.

"There is enough okcillium in this lighter to blow up a city."

"That's reassuring," Jerry said, with a sideways glance at Jed.

"The fuss?" Pook took a long draw from the cigar and blew the smoke straight up into the air. He gestured at Jed with the thumb of the hand that clutched the cigar. "The fuss... apparently... is all about him."

Dawn shook her head and waved at the smoke in the air, trying to disperse it from in front of her face.

"Smoking is illegal. You know that, don't you cousin?"

"Everything is illegal, Dawn. Besides, what're they going to do, kill me with a TRACER for smoking?"

"That and a million other things."

"Then I guess the smoking doesn't matter much, does it?"

Pook then added, "I'll be surprised if any of us makes it through this day anyway." Only this time he said it so that everyone could hear him but Dawn.

Jed stared through the smoke at Pook. A hundred questions crossed his mind, but none of them seemed to want to form on his tongue, or break forth from his mouth. He was a long way from his home in the Amish Zone back on Earth.

* * * *

Jerry, Billy, and Pook stood talking in hushed tones, mostly about insurgency tactics and weapons. Dawn noticed that Jed seemed out of place and uncomfortable in the conversation, so she walked over to him and pulled him to the side.

"Thanks again for—well, you know... when I broke down a little up there," she said with a smile. "I really appreciate it, even if I know it made you uncomfortable."

"That's okay," Jed said.

"All of this is really overwhelming."

"Yeah."

"Probably more so for you."

"Probably," Jed said with a smile.

"Tell me about your farm back in Old PA, Jed. What was it like?"

Jed dipped his head and shuffled his feet, nervous to be talking to a girl face to face, despite everything that had already passed between them in such a short time.

"I don't know. What do you want to know?"

"Just tell me about your life there. You know, what it was like."

Jed narrowed his eyes a little and looked up at Dawn. He wasn't sure why she felt it was necessary to talk about his life. He understood that she was naturally curious, but his people were pretty private when it came right down to it. He was still suspicious of *Englischers*, and although he had nothing but good thoughts about Dawn personally, she was still an Englischer, and he still felt like he was reluctantly trapped in this uncontrollable chain of events.

Jerry was right, Jed thought. He'd not asked any of these people to help him or fight for him. Still, despite his discomfort, he couldn't help but feel glad that these strangers were willing to try to get him out of the City and to his people. It all mixed and mashed up together inside him into a confusing puzzle.

"Well, ours was an old-fashioned farm, even for the Amish," he finally said. "We didn't have milking machines or any of the other modern amenities that many of our wealthier, and maybe more worldly, neighbors had. My dad was... is... *was* a traditionalist. Real conservative. We had one milk cow and we milked her by hand. Her name was Zoe. Once I turned eighteen and I was approved by the elders to emigrate here, I started training my younger brother so he could take over the farm chores. We were a really small family compared to most of the Amish, and there were a lot of chores to do. But we were a subsistence farm and not a business. We produced what we consumed and not a whole lot more. For extra cash, my mother made baskets, and on sunny days we'd sell them on the side of the road, and during the growing season we had a little market garden."

"That sounds nice," Dawn said, smiling and nodding her head.

"It was nice. If there wasn't such a land crush, I mean, if there had been more land available, I would have gladly stayed. My father was a carpenter and made handmade furniture that we sold from the front lawn to the tourists for exorbitant prices. Englischers were glad to pay those prices, and who were we to argue if God wanted to reward us for living a simple life by having the English flock to buy our products? Still, we were an old-fashioned family. We didn't have a generator or even a propane stove or refrigerator. That's simple and plain, even for the Amish."

"That sounds so interesting, Jed."

"Maybe. I don't know. It was just the way we lived. I liked it. I still do. I can't wait to get back to it. After experiencing this world over the past... however long it's been... I think I'll be glad to be farming again."

"You haven't seen us at our best," Dawn said.

"Haven't I?"

Dawn blinked, but she didn't answer. They stood quietly for a few beats, neither one of them knowing exactly what to say. Dawn was the one who finally broke the silence.

"So you're eighteen? I would have thought you were younger if I didn't know better. You have a baby face."

Jed scowled. Not at all what he wanted to hear from a pretty girl.

"I'm sorry, Jed!" Dawn said, laughing. "I just mean that you have a youngish look about you. I'm not much older than you. I'm just barely twenty!"

"Oh" was all that Jed could think to say.

"Do you have a girlfriend back in Old Pennsylvania?" Dawn asked, smiling and giving Jed a teasing wink.

"No. That's not really allowed. At some point—*if* I'd stayed—I probably would have picked one out that I and my parents agreed would make a good wife, and if she picked me too, we'd have gotten married. But I wasn't really pursuing that kind of relationship back there. I knew I was coming here and I didn't need anything holding me back or tying me down. I want to build a good, productive farm here. If I meet someone down the road, later on, then I suppose all of that will take care of itself in time."

"Well now, aren't you a free spirit, then?" Dawn said, laughing.

"You tease me a lot, Dawn."

"I'm just making conversation, Mr. Serious."

"What about you?" Jed asked.

"What about me?"

"Do you have a... a... boyfriend?"

"Me? No. No. I mean, I've had a boyfriend before, but nothing now. I'm like you—too wrapped up in this colonization business and being part of the underground.

Haven't had much time for love."

"So, not Billy then?" Jed said, nodding his head toward where the three militants were chatting about guns and insurrection.

"Billy?"

"Billy."

"No!" Dawn looked over at Billy and then back at Jed. "No."

Jed tilted his head and raised his right eyebrow.

"No. Not Billy. No."

"Wow." That was all that Jed could say.

"No, listen. It's complicated," Dawn said, and unconsciously touched his arm to emphasize that he must be completely misunderstanding her.

"Take it easy. It was just a friendly question." Now Jed was teasing her.

"*You* take it easy!" Dawn said, pushing him back a step. She was smiling but not quite laughing, as if she didn't know if Jed really thought she was with Billy. "I said no, and if you think differently, then you're wrong."

"Just take it easy!" Jed said, eyes wide in mock outrage.

"*You* take it easy, Mister!" Dawn said, and smiled.

●●●●

"Tell me about your brother," Dawn said. "Were you two close?"

"Were?" Jed shook his head, still trying to get his mind around the ramifications of time and the confusions of interstellar travel. He'd left home nine years ago, and if all had gone according to plan, his brother should already be on his way to New Pennsylvania.

"I think almost all Amish families are close. We *are* close though." He smiled as he thought about his little brother. "Amos is the best. He's smart, wise, funny, and he is as earnest about our culture and lifestyle as any Amish man I ever met."

Dawn just nodded her head without saying anything.

"Amos didn't like the idea of me coming here. He was only fourteen then, but he always seemed to be older than his age to me. He thought it was a mistake, emigrating, but he decided that if I was going to come, then he was going to follow. I haven't had time to think about it yet, but I hope he was able to make it. I had so much trouble getting here that I hope he got through it all and is on his way."

Again, Dawn didn't say anything. Instead she stared deeply into his eyes with that faraway gaze—like she'd done when he'd first met her at the Columbia checkpoint. Only this time, he knew she wasn't on the Internet in her head. She'd had her BICE removed. And she wasn't on Quadrille either. In fact, he hadn't yet seen anyone that he thought was on Q, so Dawn's faraway look must have been rooted in something real, something deeper than drugs or the Internet. *Perhaps she's missing someone too,* Jed thought.

"How is your wound doing?" he asked.

"My wound?"

"Yeah," Jed said. "Where you had your BICE taken out."

Her hand went up to the bandage on the back of her

head. "Oh, it's fine."

"Do you miss it?"

"Maybe. A little. Maybe? I don't know. Having constant and seamless Internet access was like having a super-brain. It was distracting and sometimes frustrating, but it was still kind of handy. I feel a little dumber now, I guess."

Pook heard some activity upstairs and signaled to Dawn that they needed to be leaving. As the whole group filed up the dark stairs back into the Antique Shoppe, Jed noticed that Dawn left her hand very lightly on his elbow—almost, but not quite, taking his arm like his mother did his father's when they would walk toward the garden in the cool of the morning like lovers and friends.

WHO'S WHO?

More of Pook's team had arrived at Merrill's Antique Shoppe, and they were milling around upstairs, drinking coffee and chatting quietly when Pook, Jed, Jerry, Billy, and Dawn came back upstairs with the guns and ammunition. Pook handed out some of the pistols from his black bag, while one of his men—a short, powerful-looking man that Pook called "Ducky"—briefed him on the operation.

"We'll need to move quickly, boss," Ducky said in his gruff voice. "Transport is out in force, and there was at least one TRACER came down on us. Nasty bugger. Stumbled on us by accident I reckon, but with five of us bunched together and none of us emittin' a Transport ID signal, it didn't take them long to make us as TRACE. Clyde and Will took care of the TRACER, but there may be more of 'em out there. If you plan on takin' the package over the bridge, we can't all go in a large group like this—we'd be sittin' ducks. The rest of us—we'll just have to make our own way.

"Right," Pook said.

"And we cleaned up the door and the entryway here, and halfway up the block on the sidewalk and street out there. There was blood everywhere, man. You need to be more careful about cleanup, Pook. Someone might've called Transport if they'd seen it."

"That was my fault," Pook said. "We had a situation and we needed to move fast on getting these guns made."

"Do I even want to ask?" Ducky said.

"It was Donavan, one of our inside men in Transport. They got onto him and shot him. He made his way here to report before he died. Guy was a champion. We'll need to put up a statue for that man when we win this war."

"He marked?"

"He cut it out himself before he came here."

"Seriously?" Ducky said, screwing up his face.

"Seriously. I have it in my pack."

"Wouldn't that emit a signal that could be tracked here?" Jed asked.

"Nope. BICE units run on the electricity produced in the human brain," Pook pointed to his head and winked at Jed, "and the human brain produces a shocking amount of electricity!" He laughed at his own play on words, but Jed didn't really get it, so Pook continued. "Outside the brain, the BICE doesn't have a power source so it doesn't transmit. When they first came out with these, they installed them with built-in backup power supplies like in a LoJack or the older implanted ID chips that went in your hand or arm, but over time those things tended to leak—causing brain damage or worse—and when they failed that meant further surgeries. Before the BICE was rolled out for widespread use, Transport found a way to run them off of the electrical current that the brain naturally produces, so if you cut one out, it's a dead unit, unless you hook it up to an outside power source."

"Well, props to that dude, for sure—cutting out his own BICE! Where is he now?" Ducky asked. Jed noticed that the short soldier was all business.

"Back in the back room, wrapped in a tarp."

Ducky turned to a couple of his men and pointed with his thumb back towards the rear of the shop. "You two get rid of that body back there. Do it respectfully and properly because he was one of us. Don't leave any evidence. If we're gone when you get back, meet us on the other side of the river. Camp Echo. Now git!"

The two men nodded and walked toward the back of the building.

"What do we have outside?" Pook asked.

Ducky jerked his head toward the door while simultaneously indicating to Pook that he wanted a cigarette. "I've got two men watchin' this place, lookin' for eyes and tails, anyone gettin' too curious, you know? No one will ever see them. Invisible, they are. Like the wind."

Pook pulled out a pack, popped out a cigarette, and offered it to Ducky, who took it and nodded his thanks.

"I've got two more soldiers watchin' the bridge, makin' sure everstuff is copacetic, you know?" Ducky puffed on the cigarette and blew the smoke straight up into the air.

"What else?"

"It's a mess out there, Pook. Our own ordnance nearly took out a few of our safe houses. Whoever is callin' the shots on this offensive is makin' it look all too real, know what I'm sayin'?"

"That's what Billy said, and that was the plan," Pook said, "and the closer our offensive fire gets to our own safe houses, the less suspicious are those houses, right? I mean, who would fire on their own hideouts?"

"Only crazy people, I 'spect. Well, I hope we don't have any friendly-fire deaths before this thing is over."

"Everything that can be done to minimize our losses is being done, Ducky."

"You sound like one of *them*."

"The curse of management," Pook said and punched Ducky hard in the arm.

• • • •

As the two men continued their conversation, Jed noticed the knob on the front door twist and the door crack open slowly. What happened next occurred very quickly. Like a cool, rainy evening interrupted by a sudden strike of lightning, the familial atmosphere changed in an instant. Jed was one of the last to react. Everyone else had been intensively trained on how to deal with threats.

The door swung open and Jed instantly recognized the two men who pushed their way into the room. It was the two policemen who had arrested him during his trip:

Hugh Conrad of the Transport Authority and Officer Rheems of the Transport Police. The two men strained their eyes to see through the relative darkness and smiled when they saw Jed's face among those of the other rebels in the room.

Before the two men had even stepped fully inside, guns were snap-drawn throughout the shop, including the one wielded by Jerry Rios, who also recognized the two cops—who were now smiling at him too. Everyone moved into position wordlessly—even Dawn—as if they were practiced at dealing with just such an eventuality, and the tension in the room reached a new high as eyes peered down gun barrels and fingers tensed on triggers.

"Look, Rheems, it's Jerry Rios!" Hugh Conrad said with a laugh. Rheems nodded and smiled. There was a twinkle in his eye. "And there's the Amish kid!"

Most of the guns—the ones held by Pook's men—came down, but Jerry didn't lower his gun at all. He kept it pointed at Conrad's face.

"Drop the gun, Jerry," Pook said. "They're with us."

"They're with *you?*" Jerry said. There was incredulity in his voice. "How can they be with you? They arrested Jed and me during transport and almost kept us from making the trip! They wanted to send me to Oklahoma."

Ducky raised his pistol silently, but this time it was pointed at Jerry Rios.

"I told you, they're with us, Jerry," Pook said calmly. "So lower your weapon."

"Yeah," Conrad said. "We're with him."

Jerry moved the gun so that it was pointing at

Rheems. He wasn't talking now. The wheels were turning in his mind, but he didn't have an answer. He moved the gun back toward Conrad.

"Easy, tiger..." Pook said with a smile on his face.

"I don't understand," Jerry said. The tension in his voice was mirrored by a very slight tremor in his pistol hand. "If they're double agents working inside Transport, then why did they arrest us in West Texas? Why the charade? And why are they exposing themselves now?"

"You're new here, Jerry," Pook said calmly, "and I really don't have to answer your questions." Pook exhaled deeply, and Jed could see that the rebel leader was considering his options. "I'll tell you what I can. But in the future, if I—or any one of my men—tells you to drop your weapon, you will drop your weapon. There won't be a second request."

Everyone remained frozen as Jerry considered what Pook had said.

"So this is it, Jerry. Drop the weapon and I'll tell you what I can. Or don't drop it and we're going to smoke you and get on with our day."

Jerry slowly lowered the pistol and pointed it toward the floor.

"Good thinking," Pook said.

"So what's this all about?" Jerry said tersely.

"This is all about him," Pook said, pointing toward Jed. "We're doing whatever we have to do—putting everything and everyone at risk—to get him where he needs to be. Rheems and Conrad are here because we need their help if we're to get Jed out of the City and into the Amish Zone. That's our only mission right now."

"Got it," Jerry said.

"And going forward, I don't have time to brief every newbie and wannabe that hitches on to my mission, you understand?" Pook said.

"I said I got it," Jerry snapped.

Just then, one of Ducky's men burst through the door with a shout. "TRACER incoming!"

"MOVE!" Pook shouted, and just as he did, a thundering explosion rocked the front of the shop, blowing away the door and a portion of the building with it. The sentry who'd just warned everyone was killed instantly.

"Out the back!" Ducky yelled as smoke and dust and flying debris filled the air around the team.

Two more of the men on Ducky's squad were cut down immediately. Dawn grabbed Jed by the hand, and before he could really register everything that was happening she'd pulled him down so that they were low-crawling toward the rear of the building. Jerry was pushing Jed forward as they crawled, and seemed to be protecting him from fire from the rear. Phosphorescent projectiles sailed overhead and exploded when they came into contact with the structure, sending glowing plasma raining down like magma. Jed looked back over his shoulder, and over Jerry's head he could see a floating TRACER drone hovering just outside the massive new hole in the structure and firing rounds into the building. Red and green laser beams emitted by the drone crisscrossed through the smoke and dust, searching for targets to destroy.

Looking back where they were crawling, Jed saw the

rear door open, and he, Dawn, and Jerry bolted for it, falling in line with the rest of the team as they flowed out of the building like water escaping a crumbling dam.

In The Streets
Of the City

Jed and Dawn ran along an alleyway with Ducky's team, and gradually a protective formation of TRACE fighters took shape around Jed. The troops began barking to one another in staccato bursts of commands, signals, and responses that everyone else in the group understood, even if Jed found it hard to make heads or tails of any of it. Out in the open, TRACE worked like a well-oiled machine as they fled the scene of the destroyed antique shop.

Jed was impressed at the discipline displayed by the team as they moved deliberately and as clandestinely as possible through town. When the whole group reached a good chokepoint in a darkened alleyway, the unit that was surrounding Jed and Dawn pushed forward and took cover behind a series of large dumpsters while the rest of the squad scattered and took positions on both sides of the alley.

Two of the men scaled an ancient fire escape and Jed watched as Pook walked out into the middle of the alley. Pook pulled something out of his pocket, fiddled with it a moment, then dropped it on the ground and ran for cover.

From his position behind the dumpster, Jed finally made out what it was that Pook had dropped on the ground. It was the bloody **BICE** unit that Donavan had cut from his own head before he died. Pook must have attached some sort of battery to the device, which would have reactivated the signal. Dawn pushed Jed further in behind the dumpster and everyone went silent as they waited. Jerry, Dawn, and Billy had formed what seemed to Jed like a protective wall in front of him, and he could barely see what was happening over the backs and heads of his defenders. He also noticed that Billy took Dawn's hand for a second, but she turned her hand loose and thrust it into her pocket.

It seemed as though minutes passed, but it was probably only seconds before the **TRACER** unit that had attacked the antique shop came hovering around the corner from an adjacent street. A glowing missile fired from the drone destroyed the **BICE** unit as it lay on the ground, and tracking lasers began scanning the alley for signals or targets.

The men on the fire escape and those hidden in place in the alley opened fire on the **TRACER** unit before it could lock on to any other target, and a well-placed shot coming from one of the elevated positions struck the drone right above its laser-sighting lens. The machine hummed for a moment and shook with violence, spinning drunkenly as it attempted to maintain level flight, before it exploded and a thousand pieces of high-tech shrapnel scattered around the alley. The largest portion of the TRACER drone caromed down the alley like a beach ball until it bounced off of the dumpster that shielded Jed and his defenders from the battle.

Once again, the team wordlessly snapped into motion and Dawn was pushing Jed from behind out into the alley. Pook pulled on a heavy glove and he and Ducky began to remove smoking parts from the damaged portion of the drone, stuffing the parts into a backpack.

When Pook and Ducky were done stripping the drone, the team formed back up, and in moments they were all moving eastward again, leapfrogging forward in groups of two or three as they crossed the open and seemingly abandoned streets of the City on their way toward the river.

● ● ● ●

Ten minutes later, the squad gathered together outside a darkened tavern. The faintest hint of the coming morning was only then touching the eastern sky— or at least the bit of it that could be seen between city buildings. The tavern was still shrouded in darkness, and since most of the streetlights had been extinguished due to the rebel offensive, the squad was able to gather near the door of the tavern without worrying about alerting anyone who might be in the area, or peeping out the windows of nearby buildings.

Above the door where the team was gathered, the name of the tavern was written in Old English script, and Jed studied it with interest. If it weren't for the things he'd been through in the last few days, he might have laughed...

Ye Olde World English Tavern. Didn't that name just say it all?

Pook knocked on the door while sentries moved into position on both ends of the block. One of Ducky's men, with a long rifle slung over his shoulder, scaled the building across the street from the tavern with the skill and agility of a trained mountain climber, and in under a minute he was peering down at the rest of his team from the roof of the opposite building.

A dark figure came to the door, and after pleasantries were exchanged, Pook, Dawn, Ducky, Jed, and the remaining soldiers from Ducky's unit all filed into the tavern.

Two of Ducky's men helped a few of the bar employees as they darkened all the windows before lanterns were lit throughout the tavern. The man who'd opened the door to let them in stepped behind the bar for a moment and returned with a handheld electronic device that he held up in front of Pook.

"Sweep 'em all," Pook said.

As the man activated the device, Pook noticed that Jed and Jerry were looking at it curiously.

"BICE scanner," Pook explained. "Detects TRIDs, too. It's crazy expensive and highly illegal. We keep one here because most of our operational planning takes place here. There are only two other functional scanners in the whole resistance, as far as I know. We couldn't afford to lose one of these like we just lost my antique shop."

Wordlessly the man began to scan everyone in Pook's party with the device. He gestured to the two Transport officers, Conrad and Rheems. "What about those two?"

"They've turned their units off," Pook replied. "It's a workaround we came up with a few months ago. Sweep 'em anyway, though. Make sure they aren't broadcasting."

The man scanned Conrad and Rheems with the machine, and nodded affirmatively to indicate that they were clear.

Jed would later learn that the tavern owner—the man with the scanning machine—was a respected veteran resistance officer named Jeff Wainwright. Jeff and his people never asked any questions, and the bar was virtually silent as Jeff went from person to person, scanning them from head to toe.

The silence gave Jed his first chance to think, really think, since this whole thing began. Since arriving in the City, he'd witnessed three men murdered right in front of him. *Because* of him. Was it only three men? *Maybe it was four.* Or had there been more? Jed didn't even know. That realization filled him with shame. Was he losing his identity? His humanity? *How can human life*, he thought, *become so cheap?* The questions piled up like the firewood he would stack just outside the back door back home. Why were these people helping him? Why were they concerned at all about a young Amish immigrant? Strangers—the English—putting their lives and futures at risk so that a farmer could make it to the Amish

Zone? None of these questions had answers, or at least none of them had any answers that he could fathom. No one had asked him what he thought. No one had asked him his opinion or permission for anything at all. It was disconcerting to be swept along by events like a leaf floating down a stream. And were these deaths somehow being registered to his account? Perhaps that was the biggest question of them all.

"I should just go turn myself in," he said quietly.

Pook spun to face him. "Excuse me?"

"Too many people have died to protect me," Jed said. "This has to stop."

"This has to stop, does it?" Pook said. "What are you thinking? Do you think you're on a buggy ride in beautiful Amish Country, Jed?"

Jed stood silently, his eyes downcast.

Agitated now, Pook squared up with Jed and then poked him in the chest with his finger. "Listen, pal. You're right. We've already lost some good men and my whole antique shop for you. I'm outed, because they now know that I owned that shop. We're all fully invested in getting you out of town, so you can stop with all that crybaby nonsense right now. Don't you even *think* about surrendering yourself. You do what I say, when I say it. I'm not sure I understand all the ramifications of what just went down, but the whole resistance is at risk until we get you into the AZ, do you understand me?"

Jed nodded. "Yes, I understand. And I'll do what you say. But I didn't ask for any of this. I don't even know what's happening, or why all of this is going down. No one has told me anything." He looked Pook in the eye. "Just don't pretend you're doing this for me. You're not. You don't even know me. You're doing it for reasons of your own, and I can appreciate that, even if I don't agree with what you do. Once and for all though, I'd like you to get it through your head that I haven't asked for you to do *anything* for me. Our people believe that God is sovereign over everything that happens, and if He raises up a deliverer to help us, then that is His business. If you kill someone, or if someone working with you dies, it didn't happen because of me. Everyone makes their own choices and decisions and has their own motivations, and I haven't asked anyone to sacrifice themselves for me. I just want to get home, and I would rather not be the cause of anyone else getting killed."

"God, huh?" Pook said as he took a long draw from the cigarette. "Well, I'm not doing this for *him*, either."

"Your call." That was all Jed could say to that.

Pook shook his head, and spoke again with a softer tone. "We're going to get you home, Jed. I just pray that all of this is worth what it costs. I'm just a soldier. I take orders like everyone else here. So let's just all do what we have to do and get this mission finished."

* * * *

Half an hour later, the team had pulled several of the tables together to form one long conference table and Pook was addressing the assembled mass of rebels, briefing them all on the plan that was about to unfold.

"I can't tell you how difficult the next few hours are going to be. Our plan is workable, but flawed. It relies on precision timing, and to be frank with you, there are a whole lot of unknowns and things that can go wrong. I'm going to need you all to listen closely, and to know with certainty what you're expected to do and when.

"The first thing you need to know is that Hugh Conrad is going to put Jed on a secure airbus, alone. The airbus will exit the city over the river via the bridge air gate."

Ducky's hand went up almost immediately.

"They've already got an APB out on the kid, Pook."

"We know," Pook said. "That means that we need a window of time when the computer doesn't know that it's supposed to be searching for him. And if there's one thing we know about Transport, it's that Transport officials don't know anything the computer doesn't know."

"Will the bridge even be open, you know, with the offensive going on and all?" Dawn asked.

"The offensive is basically over. It was planned to culminate at first light, and first light is right about now. Still, the bridge will be open to Transport officials only. That's what we're expecting."

"How're you going to arrange for this blind window?" Ducky asked.

"We're going to hack Transport. Rheems is going to stay here and use Jeff's equipment. We know how to do it, and we know it'll be successful. We just don't know for how long."

"What's the probability that they don't make it over the bridge before Transport figures out they've been hacked?" Dawn said.

"Fifty-fifty," Pook said.

"That's encouraging," Conrad said with a nervous laugh.

"Listen," Pook said with his hands up in the air. "I'm going to need you all to pipe down for just a minute while I brief you. There'll be time for questions afterwards, okay?" Pook began walking now, circling the table, looking each man or woman in the eye as he walked. Heads nodded, so Pook continued.

"This thing is going to have to be timed perfectly. Rheems will hack in and try to blind the system for long enough to get Jed on an airbus headed for the AZ. Hugh, once you get him on the bus, you'll need to make your own way over the river. You're busted once they figure out that you put Jed on the bus. Don't get caught on this side of the river after you get the kid on the bus, got it?"

Hugh Conrad nodded his head, accepting the responsibility and the implied danger that came along with his mission.

"We don't figure he'll get many miles into the rural zone before Transport figures out what happened. They'll bring the bus down immediately," Pook said, "and lock it tight until a Transport team can go extricate Jed from the bus. We'll have maybe ten minutes to get there first."

"But—" Ducky started, before Pook's upraised hand silenced him.

"As you all know," Pook continued, "the rural zone between the river and the AZ is peopled mostly by gangs and independent salvagers. There's a strong possibility that they'll have that bus cracked open in less than two minutes."

Ducky was nodding his head vigorously. This was the reason he'd tried to interrupt.

"That's where the gold coin comes in," Pook said, looking at Jed now. "You all know that private ownership of gold is forbidden. That fact is precisely why gold is the preferred method of payment in the ungovernable rural zones. One gold coin should buy Jed here his safety—and if not safety, then at least some time. You still have the gold, Jed?"

Jed held up the gold coin, but didn't say a word. He felt like Donavan's blood was on the face of the precious metal, accusing him.

"Good deal. So Jed will have to do some acting. He should be the only person on the bus, and if he is, then that fact alone will indicate to the gangs that he's valuable. Nothing else has been moving during the offensive. If the gangs get to him first—and that's our preferred outcome— he's in good shape. They'll be glad to get the gold, and they'll probably protect and hide Jed until we can form up and get to him. If it's the salvagers that get to him—"

"—they'll want to sell him to the highest bidder," Ducky said.

"Yes. But they won't know we're on the way, or that he's with us. Salvagers are unpredictable and mercenary, but we're hoping that they think that Transport is their only problem, so maybe won't be in quite as much of a rush. If Jed can get them talking and delay them, maybe we can get to him before they're all through the hills and gone."

"But what if Transport gets to him first?" Jeff Wainwright asked. "This is a three-way race, after all."

"Then we'll have a fight on our hands," Pook answered soberly. "Jed, you'll have to really sell this thing," he added.

"What does that mean?" Jed said, as he pushed the coin deep into the pocket of his broadfall pants.

"That means you'll have to do a little bit of acting. You'll have to be confident and assertive, and the longer you can stall and delay whoever it is that's gotten to you first—especially if it's the salvagers—the better the chances are that we'll be able to get to you and secure your freedom."

Jed nodded his head. He still wasn't sure exactly what was expected from him, but he felt like he didn't have any other options other than to play it the way Pook had designed it.

"There'll be a race to get to you, Jed, once the airbus is electronically forced down in the rural zone. Worst case scenario, salvagers get you. If that happens, delay, delay, delay. Got it?"

"I think so. Why won't Transport just recall the airbus and fly it back over the bridge?" Jed asked. "Why force it down in what you call 'ungovernable' territory?"

"They used to do that," Pook said, but years ago the unaffiliated gangs and salvagers found ways to launch homemade sticky bombs that would adhere to the exterior of the buses. They'd rig the bombs with timing devices, and Transport would fly the buses right into the Transport station and then the bombs would go off. So they don't do that anymore. Now, if they know they have a high-value target on an airbus, they just bring the bus down and send a team to go and search the bus while it's still outside the City. It minimizes the terrorists' ability to attack Transport facilities.

"The problem now is that the salvagers and the gangs are so highly organized, they can often get to the buses and extract whatever's valuable before Transport can get to them. Transport hasn't come up with another protocol yet, so for now it's really just a race to any bus that's forced down.

"So you'll need to sell what it is you're doing, Jed. By that I mean that you need to be who you really are—a harmless young Amish boy trying to get home."

"Amish *man*," Dawn said. "He's not a *boy*, Pook, or a *kid*. Why don't we start treating him with the respect he deserves?"

Jerry nodded his head at Dawn approvingly.

"Whatever you say, cousin," Pook said dismissively. "Jed, you'll need to tell whoever gets to you first that you need them to take you to the Amish Zone, and take your time telling them about the gold coin. Depending on who captures you, you might find them to be tremendously helpful—"

"—or tremendously unhelpful," Dawn interjected.

"Yeah," Ducky said, "they might cut you up and cook you in their stew."

This made the rest of the team laugh, but Pook cut the joking short with a wave of his hand.

"We're all going to have to improvise and adapt. The rest of us are going to be crossing the river the old-fashioned way." Pook saw Jed's confused look and explained. "That means we'll be swimming over, Jed. That's the easiest way for anyone who is un-chipped to get into or out of the City on the western side. Transport believes they have the river sealed, but that has never been true. Now, just because I say it's the easiest way, don't take that to mean that it's easy. It isn't. We've got our points of ingress and egress, but we've got to be careful."

Pook turned to face Jerry. "Jerry, you've never done this river crossing before. Don't go improvising. You need to listen closely and do *exactly* what we tell you to do, or you'll mess this up for all of us."

Jerry narrowed his eyes coldly at Pook, but he nodded.

Pook went on. "We'll all form up once we're in the rural zone and try to locate the airbus before Transport can get there."

"How're we going to locate the bus?" Dawn asked.

"The same way that Transport will find it: by tracking the locating beacon on the bus. We're always stealing their technology, and we've developed a pretty good system of tracking Transport... almost as good as their system of tracking us."

"But he could be ten miles past the bridge when Transport brings him down."

"Right. We'll have to hustle."

The conversation went on like this for several more minutes, but Jed noticed that Dawn was growing increasingly agitated. He wasn't surprised, then, when she pushed out her chair and, interrupting the briefing, stood up and addressed Pook directly.

"I am not comfortable with this plan. I was given strict instructions from the SOMA that I was never to lose operational control of the subject. This plan requires me to relinquish control of Jed to Hugh Conrad. No offense, Hugh, but that isn't in my brief."

Hugh shrugged as if no offense was taken.

"I understand your concerns, Dawn, and they are duly noted, but there is no way we can get you on that bus," Pook replied. "You have no tracking chip, and we don't have time or, really, the ability to achieve that kind of hack in the time that we have. The forged transport papers may get you into the AZ once you arrive there, but we both know they're worthless as far as getting you on that airbus."

"I'm not saying we get me on the airbus. I'm saying that we get Jed into the rural zone the same way I'm getting into the rural zone... via the river."

"No way, Dawn," Ducky said. He slapped his hand down on the table, as if this was where he would definitely take a stand. "It's hard enough getting trained soldiers across that river safely, much less a farmer boy—er, farmer *man*. The current is so strong, and there are all kinds of sensors, even under the water. Getting Jerry across is going to be tough enough, and he seems to have had a little training. There is virtually a zero percent probability of Jed making it across that river without bringing all of Transport down on our heads."

"I'll take full responsibility for him," Dawn said.

"No you won't, Dawn," Pook said. "I understand that you have your orders, but your orders—even if they come from SOMA—are based on the overriding principle of operational security. If your orders guarantee failure, then they must be altered to allow for success."

"I formally protest this decision, Pook."

As Dawn sat down, her hand found Jed's under the table and she clasped it tightly and held on to it. Jed felt his face flush, and for some reason he looked over at Billy, but Billy couldn't see that Dawn was holding his hand. Jed felt Dawn exhale deeply, and he gave her hand a slight squeeze. Dawn squeezed back, and Jed saw her force a smile, as if she'd accepted the fact that her petition had failed. Jed didn't know how he felt about Dawn holding his hand, but he was convinced that she did have his best interests in mind.

"Protest noted," Pook said, "but overruled. Now, let's get to work."

CROSSING

The airbus lifted silently from the Transport bay until it reached twenty feet of altitude, and it was at this height that it crossed over the bridge that spanned the rushing green-blue waters of the river. The bridge itself was an ancient relic of a bygone time, and strictly speaking it hadn't been necessary ever since private transport had been abolished, but the stone and steel span marked the "safe portal" or air gate, by which the airbuses could officially enter or exit the city. If the Transport vehicle was too high, or if it tried to cross the river anywhere other than at the bridge, the City's air defenses would be engaged to bring down the wayward aircraft.

After crossing the bridge, the airbus climbed smoothly to one hundred feet of altitude as it automatically directed itself in its pre-programmed route toward the Amish Zone. The buses could fly lower when leaving the City than they could when approaching it. No one had ever bombed or rigged an airbus to blow as it was leaving the City.

Hugh Conrad, in his official position as a Transport Agent, had seen Jed onto the bus, and then had ordered his underlings in the terminal to see that Jed's airbus left promptly and without hindrance on its journey. Thankfully for Jed, and thanks to Officer Rheems and Jeff Wainwright, the computers just happened to be temporarily blinded to the fact that a wanted fugitive would be using Transport property to escape the City.

Looking out the rear window, Jed saw the bridge grow smaller behind him, and watched the ground slip farther away as the craft made its way into the fifty miles of rural zone that separated the Amish Zone from the City. All the while, the rest of the team, including Conrad and Rheems, had separated into units and were attempting to make their way out of the city using more traditional means of escape.

Jed didn't know with any certainty when, or if, Transport would learn of the security breach and bring the airbus to a halt on the ground, but he'd been assured by Pook that this was almost certain to happen at some point during the trip. He was nervous and a little frightened, just as he'd been when he'd first left Columbia in Old Pennsylvania back on Earth and headed to the Transport spaceport out in the desert of West Texas. That is, if he'd ever been to Texas at all...

"You guys were never in West Texas."

That's what Dawn had said to him and Jerry as the three of them were fleeing the Transport station.

Jed now felt like he needed to question every

experience he'd had since his journey first began. None of it made sense.

And then there was the coffee-can window—and that was the kicker of it all. That was the one piece of evidence that inexorably brought home the idea that he could not trust his senses, and that nothing was at all as it appeared. That window was the only thing *real* that Jed could identify. Everything else could be a trick.

Jed looked out the windows of the airbus, and watched as the early morning light illuminated the deep green of the countryside. Despite all of the weirdness he'd been through, these undulating hills and abundantly verdant swells of earth made him feel that he could easily be back in Pennsylvania—the old Pennsylvania, back on Earth. This place was different in many ways—it was wilder, and the old farms here were grown over with weeds, and trees, and brush—but the geography looked a lot like home.

The bus passed over a small town—or what used to be a small town, but now was just a bombed-out remnant of a town. Jed saw the piles of brick, and the burned-out businesses and homes, and he had to shake his head. Wherever this was, whether this was New Pennsylvania, or Mars, or the far side of the moon, it was clear that the wars the English insisted on fighting had followed them here from Earth.

"You guys were never in West Texas."

She might as well have said, "You can't trust anything."

For the first time in his journey, Jed was alone with his thoughts. All of the scenes from his long trek were now flashing before his eyes. He saw Conrad and Rheems arresting him, and the fear returned and he felt his heart race. He saw himself hiding the gold coin in his pod, and he saw himself waking up and racing with Dawn toward...

What?

Now, in his mind, he was back at the chop shop. Dawn and Jerry were going under the knife, and Donavan—smiling Donavan—was offering to run back to the Transport station to get the coin; to risk his own life for the lives of strangers. Or did he just do it for money? Then there was the ride to the grocery, to the antique shop. And then there was death. Omnipresent death. Surreal and immediate.

What should a man believe?

If West Texas wasn't real, was any of it real?

The window frame back in the antique store. *That* was real. Jed had no doubt at all in his mind that the window frame was reality. He could close his eyes right now and he was back on the farm, and he was fourteen again, and he was stomping and pounding that coffee can flat with his worn-out Amish boots and then cutting and shaping it so that it would fit perfectly in the space where the old broken pane had been carefully removed.

Yes. The window frame was real. That, at least, was something on which Jed could anchor his thoughts. Somewhere out there... or back there... somewhere in the universe, he still had family.

And that led him to think about Amos. Jed had told Dawn that Amos was wiser than his years. That was true. *If Amos were here*, Jed thought, *I think the two of us could sort this out.* He loved his younger brother so much, and he hoped with all of the hope that was within him that Amos was still on his way here. Wherever—or whenever—this *here* was. Amos *was* that window on the couch in the shop. He was real, and he was out there too. *Maybe somewhere between here and Earth.*

* * * *

Jed opened his eyes as he felt the airbus slow to a stop. The bus hovered in place for a full minute, and Jed felt his heart race again. Adrenaline flushed through his body, and he felt his stomach give way within him as if his heart had plunged into his gut. The silence was deafening.

Jed moved around the bus, looking toward the ground in every direction, and then his gaze darted along the horizon, trying to gauge where he might be so that he'd know once the bus was commanded to land. He couldn't see any groups—gangs or salvagers—out there. The bus hovered, shrouded in the miserable silence which permeated everything like a dense, malevolent fog.

Just as Jed moved back toward the rear of the bus in order to try to look eastward towards the City, a loud klaxon sounded, and the bus swerved and dropped radically, as if it was taking evasive maneuvers. For a fraction of a second, Jed saw a floating TRACER drone, but then it was gone.

A terrifying, deafening explosion rocked the airbus, and Jed felt his stomach rise again as the bus plummeted toward the ground.

A second explosion blew the windows out of the bus, and Jed was propelled backward, and only saved himself from falling out of the broken windows by catching a handrail with his flailing hand.

The bus hyper-rotated, as if to try anything to regain control and level flight, and for a moment the vehicle was able to arrest its own fall only ten feet or so from smashing into the earth. The airbus even managed to gain altitude briefly before another explosion violently pummeled the vehicle. This time, Jed saw what was happening. The drone that he'd seen was firing phosphorescent projectiles at the bus, and this last shot had found its mark. The bus cratered near the midsection, and fell the last twenty feet to the earth in a smoking, fiery heap.

●●●●

Jed blinked his eyes, trying to clear his vision. He'd been unconscious, but only for a few seconds. The impact of the crash had thrown him to the very back of the airbus. Fire was now racing through the crumpled seating area, and there was a solid wall of flames that blocked any attempt at exit through the front.

The smoke was beginning to choke him as he struggled to pull himself upright, and just as he felt as if he might be blacking out, a strong hand jerked him through the place where the windows had once been.

Jed found himself being dragged backward through heavy and unkempt underbrush, while struggling unsuccessfully to regain his feet.

"Wait... wait... wait..." he said.

"Not waiting for anything," the man who was dragging Jed replied.

Jed was finally able to turn his head, and he saw a brutish man with a heavy beard and a scowl on his face, dressed in animal skins and carrying an ancient-looking long rifle.

"Drone," Jed said. His voice sounded like the bark of a small dog.

"Drone being dead," the voice said.

"Who are you?" Jed asked.

The rugged man didn't reply. He just grunted and kept dragging Jed further into the overgrown thicket. Thorns and branches tore at Jed's clothes and scraped the bare skin on his arms and hands.

"Just... just... take me to the Amish Zone. I have money," Jed said.

"Ha!" the man said. "You having money! Right!"

The man spoke a very difficult-to-understand and guttural dialect of broken English. He'd obviously lived a long time separated from the comforts of city life and the society of men. He grunted again and pushed Jed to the ground. Jed jumped to his feet and tried to run, but the rough man was faster, and snagged Jed by the arm and tossed him back to the ground.

"I do have money. I have gold. I'll pay you to take me to the Amish Zone," Jed said.

"Don't wanting your gold, Amish boy. Gonna be paid many more much moneys than you *ever* paying me."

"Who?" Jed asked. "Who will pay you money for me?"

"Ha!" the man laughed again. "I will being a rich

one, because knowing that your brother will paying all the gold of Oklahoma getting you back from me!"

"My... brother?" Jed said.

"Yeah. Being your brother. Amos."

KNOT 3:

ALL QUIET IN THE AMISH ZONE

14

THE SOMA

The old man paced the command deck, hands behind him, eyes fixed on the floor before him as he walked out his frustrations. Despite his age and the weight of responsibility he carried on his back, he stood tall, exuding an air of noble authority.

His body reminded him that authority, like age, comes with sufferings that youth and ambition never consider. Tension in his neck caused his head to throb with dull, radiating pain. To say his headache was *splitting* would be accurate on multiple levels: his parents would have said he was of two minds; his brother would have told him that he was conflicted; the elders would have declared that his natural man was at war with his spirit man. But however his problems were characterized, they were inarguably rooted in conflict—both the internal and external kind.

Double-mindedness is frowned upon in Amish society. Still, he was torn. There had been a time when his brother would have told him to just grow up and do as he was told. A much simpler time. But that path was no longer available to him—not now, not here, in this world. He'd already grown old, and there was no one to tell him what he should do. Even the bishop would've said only for him to do nothing until he'd prayed and received an answer from God. He yearned for the early years when simple prayer would have been enough. But for a very long time now he'd been operating without even the pretense of being guided by Amish culture and community. A plain person wouldn't fight a physical war for freedom or survival. Perhaps in his heart he was still Amish, but to the Amish he was on his own. Not one of them at all.

And now, on top of all of his other responsibilities, he had his brother to deal with. A specter from his own past. A reminder of who he'd once been... of his Amish beginnings. So his mind was bifurcated, split in twain like that of many men who hold the reins of power.

For most of his adult life he'd been a part of the rebellion, a part of TRACE, and for all of that time TRACE had been at war... a war the resistance *must* win if freedom was ever again to raise its graying head in the universe. And now his brother had become the key pawn in the game.

He smoothed his hair. *This isn't a game. This is about liberty, life, death... blood... peace.*

One part of his mind wanted him to put his worries behind him, to concentrate on the war and the immediate concerns on his plate—problems over which he had some real tactical control. That part of his mind did not recognize ancient clan loyalties, familial bonds, and brotherly love. In fact, his carnal side didn't bow to any higher power at all. It was coldly rational and without natural affection. His carnal man was all about fighting and destroying Transport until the government decided it would allow men and women to live freely.

The other part of him—his spirit man—rebelled against his sterile, more mathematical inclinations. This second portion of his mind wanted to do whatever he must—damn the revolution—to save Jed at all costs. His older brother was out there, just a boy, young and afraid, with no understanding of the intricacies of this otherworldly conflict. Jed was pure. Maybe the only pure thing left in the universe.

The Tulsa—his flagship, and the largest ship in TRACE's fleet—hung still in space, five hundred miles southwest of the City and twenty-five miles above the battle-ravaged ground of New Pennsylvania. His mind reeled at the technology on display in the Tulsa. Its stillness alone was remarkable. The ship was virtually invisible to all existing technology: radar, laser, thermal, radiological tracking and scanning. If he ordered it, the Tulsa could sit directly over the City, and Transport wouldn't even know she was there. Her okcillium-powered weapons systems were unmatched—and some were even untested. The ship was that new.

If he didn't think about it, when his mind drifted, he could forget he was on a ship at all. The new okcillium drives didn't even hum, much less vibrate. And the Tulsa was twenty times larger than any other ship ever operated by anyone other than Transport. In fact, dozens of TRACE ships could fit inside the hold of the Tulsa. They not only *could*, they *did*. The Tulsa was going to put an end to the long war at last, and Transport didn't even know she existed. The tide had turned, and the end was very near. And it was all because he—the SOMA—controlled the mines where okcillium was extracted.

He glanced across the command deck. The Tulsa was a secret, even to most of the resistance military leaders who were currently in the field. He'd hand-picked the workers on this ship himself. Now he watched as the men and women of the Tulsa worked. TRACE officers and soldiers went about their shipboard duties unaware—so far—that their long-time commander was vacillating. Hindered from performing his own responsibilities while he waited to hear word about his brother. His hesitation, at this critical moment, was something completely out of character for him. His decisiveness was universally credited as the main reason that TRACE still existed, still fought, and still breathed in the air of liberty.

An assistant approached him and handed him a sheet of clear plastic. When his hands touched it, his

BICE activated the sheet and it became, to his eyes only, a document that could be read.

It was a report on the latest movements of Transport forces. This information had already been made available to his mind through his BICE—as it had been to every officer with the appropriate clearance. It was included here just for context and clarity. Nothing had changed in the last half hour.

There was a notation from the armorer that the weapons had been checked and readied. TRACE was poised to attack, but its leader waited.

It still amazed him to see so much firepower under his command. Things had surely changed in the past six decades. When he'd first arrived in Oklahoma, the rebels fought against Transport with sticks and rocks and ancient firearms that were as untrustworthy as they were rare. He remembered spending his eighteenth birthday making arrows from elm and hickory harvested from old, abandoned farms in the green country of northeastern Oklahoma. Now, in this one ship, he commanded enough power to take the City once and for all. Taking the City wouldn't end the war, not by a long shot, but it would signal the beginning of the end. His spies informed him that Transport—anticipating that a full-scale attack from TRACE could commence at any time—had already removed most executive functions and a good part of their military to the frontier cities behind the Great Shelf.

The old man sighed. They say the crown weighs

heavy on the head of a king. He was *the SOMA*—the title given to him forty years ago when he became the supreme commander and administrator of the Southern Oklahoma Militia. He was the king of the rebels, the absolute monarch of the revolutionary powers at war with Transport on New Pennsylvania. His authority was unquestioned, even by the members of the Council. He had the power to dissolve the Council with a wave of his hand—and every Councilor would happily obey him and be glad to be rid of the responsibility. He was the one who'd insisted on a governing council to begin with. There were no challengers to his power, no loyal opposition. He enjoyed complete support, which was something unheard of except in times of war. He wasn't foolish enough to believe that his universal approval would ever last past the war. But for now, the authority—and the responsibility—were fully his. That knowledge would have been crippling to a lesser man.

He had never asked for either the office or the power. Both had been thrust on him against his will, and he was not ignorant of the fact that in everything he did, he was watched—studied—on every side. And now, everyone was looking to see how he handled this business with his brother. They expected a miracle. Or they expected him to sacrifice his brother for the greater good—something horrific to imagine, but glorious and selfless just the same. Or they expected him to magically save his brother while using the opportunity to deal a crushing blow to the enemy. They all just expected these things, although no one offered him any comfort or solace—or advice as to how such miracles might come to pass.

He was an old man now, and tired. He'd tried to resign several times, but the council would never accept his resignation again while the war with Transport raged. Abdication? He'd tried that too, only to watch as the resistance faltered, headless and unable to maintain and extend the victories he'd given them over the many decades of battle. His retirement had lasted all of a month before he'd been re-drafted by universal mandate and forced back into power.

An ensign, a recruit, young and without any of the physical or mental scars of war, walked up to the SOMA and snapped to attention. "A moment, sir?"

"Go ahead."

"A report on Jedediah Troyer, sir."

"I said go ahead."

A slight nod. "According to intercepted signals coming from Transport, he is on the verge of being captured at any moment."

The SOMA flinched. "Captured?"

"The TRACE team has been unsuccessful in getting him to the Amish Zone, and they've been engaged by a superior force in the No Man's Land west of the City."

"Do we have any larger units nearby that can engage?"

Now it was the young soldier's turn to grimace.

"Yes... sir, we have."

The SOMA stared at the young recruit. "And why haven't they been activated?"

"Based on the situation on the ground, they wouldn't be able to guarantee the safety of your brother, sir."

No Man's Land

Jedediah Troyer screwed up his face in disgust. His sense of decency rebelled against the foulness of this man who'd captured him, this salvager who had dragged him from the wreckage of the airbus. The savage was chewing on some greenish vegetative concoction, and slobber ran down his beard and clumped in slobbery globules near the bottom of his lip.

"What the—"

The salvager cut Jed off before he could get the question out. "Being shut yourself, boy."

More thick, mucusy goo dripped from the man's beard as he earnestly chewed the wad of greenery.

Jed inhaled carefully, hissing, hoping not to catch a whiff of anything floating his way from the wild Englischer. "I just have to know what you're chewing and why."

"Shutting yourself."

"That's just not right," Jed said, "and you're making me sick having to watch you."

"Don't watching me then."

Jed tried to look away, but he couldn't for long. "Seriously, what are you chewing?"

The salvager glanced at Jed and exhaled in frustration. A large quantity of greenish viscous material flew out in various directions with his breath.

"Tobac."

Jed furrowed his brow. "Tobacco?"

"Yes. Tobac."

Again, Jed tried to look away, but it was like trying to not watch when his father had to pull a calf from a heifer giving birth for the first time. "Sir, you're doing it all wrong," Jed said.

"Shutting yourself. Being chew the tobac, and you shutting. That is all."

"Listen, you. Whatever your name is..."

"Goa Eeguls."

Jed hesitated. He stared at the salvager, expecting the man to explain, or at least repeat himself. The chewing had stopped for a moment. "Your... your name is Boll Weevils?"

"No. Not being boll weevils, stinking cronad. Name being Goa Eeguls. GOA. EEGULS." He paused for effect. "Goa. Eeguls." Pause. "Goa. Eeguls. Being understood?"

Jed narrowed his eyes and tried it. "Goa Eeguls."

The salvager nodded his head and pointed at himself. "Goa Eeguls."

"Is this name from your own language?" Jed asked. "Because you almost speak English, albeit poorly. Is *Goa Eeguls* a family name or something?"

The salvager shook his head and reached into his rough tunic—a filthy, handmade overcoat consisting of animal skins from indeterminate creatures mended here and there by reclaimed patchwork cloth. Withdrawing his hand, he produced an ancient green hand towel, and on it Jed could see a picture and some faded words. The picture he recognized. He'd seen it before, on the shirts and coats of some of the English tourists who would stop in front of the farm in airbuses and buy the Troyers' baskets, vegetables, and furniture. The image on the towel was of something called a "football helmet."

Football, like all major sports, was a game played at one time by the English in large stadiums all across the land. That was before the wars came and changed the world. After the wars, private travel was banned and large gatherings of people became magnets for terrorist bombs. Eventually—according to what Jed had learned from the elders and by rumor—the sporting events became available only via television, with the games and players manufactured artificially by computers. According to the English, the winners were supposedly determined secretly and fairly by private accounting firms using complicated data modeling. According to the elders, the whole thing was a sham, with the games being created and distributed by big entertainment corporations in order to keep the sheep occupied while they were being sheared. Bread and circuses.

Jed had seen a football once when he and his father took an airbus to Cruville to bid on some farmland. English children had been throwing the oblong ball back and forth in the park. One of the children would catch the ball and take off running, and all the other children would chase him and wrestle him to the ground and pounce up and down on him like wild beasts. To Jed, as a boy, it all looked like great fun.

The helmet on the towel was printed in white on faded green, and the cloth was marked with stains and a few rips here and there, but Jed could still see the stylized wings wrapping from the front of the helmet toward the rear. Under the helmet were the words *GO EAGLES!* Apparently the towel was a relic of some football competition.

"So you took the name 'Go Eagles' because it was written on that towel?"

The salvager nodded his head. "Name being Goa Eeguls. Being my name."

"Can I just call you Eagle?"

The salvager gave Jed a look of irritation, and spat a huge amount of greenish goo in a disgusting pile between himself and Jed. "Yes. Being Eeguls." The salvager emphasized the "s" at the end of the name. "Eegul*sss*. Now shutting yourself."

Jed pointed at Eagles's face. "You shouldn't chew that tobacco while it's green, Eagles. It's loaded with bad poisons that are only eliminated by aging and curing."

Eagles stood up and glared at Jed for a moment, then stomped off a couple of paces. "Boy need shutting himself!" Eagles spat and then, after a few seconds of preparation, began urinating on a bush.

Jed looked away and shook his head. His nerves were still on edge and his hands still shook when he rubbed his face. He'd been clean-shaven when he left the Amish Zone back home. They told him his hair wouldn't grow while he was in suspended animation, but apparently it had started again. Now, for the first time since he'd left on the trip, he noticed that he had the beginnings of a beard. He stretched his fingers out in front of his face and tried to will his hand to stop shaking. Only twenty minutes had passed since his airbus had been shot out of the sky—with him in it. He'd barely escaped death, and now here he was with this wild man named Eagles who chewed toxic green tobacco and hated to talk.

Where are Pook and his team? Is Dawn out looking for me?

In his post-crash confusion he'd momentarily forgotten that the team would be searching for him and that his job was to delay so that the TRACE unit could locate and rescue him. He reached down and unlaced his boot, and started to pull it off. Any minute now

Eagles would want to move on. Removing his shoes was the only thing Jed could think to do as a means of delaying.

Eagles turned around and held up his hand before pointing at Jed. "No! Doing not that!" The salvager grimaced. "Shoes on, boy!"

"I have a stone in there I need to remove."

"Shoes on, boy! Going."

Jed ignored Eagles and finished unlacing his boot. He pulled it off and slowly shook it, looked down into it, and then reached deep into the toe area as if searching for the non-existent pebble. After a few seconds, he began feeling on the ground, as if the pebble had come out and now he was trying to find it.

Eagles spat and chewed and then spat again, his jaw working furiously. "Hurry, boy."

Jed straightened his sock and then, as slowly as he could manage without enraging the salvager even more, he began putting his boot back on. He tried not to look up at the wild man for a full minute, but when he did, he saw that Eagles was lifting his rifle very slowly, and crouching down at the same time. The rifle came up and Jed could see all the way down the barrel. Thinking that Eagles was about to shoot him, he dove to the ground and put his hands over his head.

Eagles whispered. "Stopping that, boy. Friends being near. Making the noise too muches."

"Your friends?" Jed asked.

"Shhh... No. Being not mine. Being yours. Stupid

cronads." Eagles looked down at Jed and spat. The green saliva landed a foot from Jed's head. "Getting up, boy!"

Crawling to his knees, Jed felt the rifle barrel pressed against his temple.

Eagles shouted, and the sudden, scary holler drove Jed back to the ground.

"Getting out the open, Pook! Eeguls knowing you being out there!"

Jed turned his head, but couldn't see anything. He couldn't hear anything moving at all.

"Getting out the open, Pook! Or Eeguls shooting boy!"

Jed heard a snapping of twigs and a shuffling of feet before Pook—and about ten others, including Ducky, Jerry, Jeff, and Dawn—appeared from out of the heavy brush.

"Don't shoot him, you old nasty bastard," Pook said.

Ducky made a hand signal and the rest of Pook's team lowered their weapons.

"Give him to us, Eagles. You know who he is, and you know where he needs to go."

Eagles shook his head and spat. "Nope. Boy will bringing Eeguls many much moneys."

Pook reached into his pocket and pulled out a pack of cigarettes. He offered one to Eagles, who declined and pointed to the wad of green nastiness in his mouth. Pook screwed up his face and then popped one out of the pack for himself, lit it with the okcillium lighter, and smiled at Eagles. "We don't have time for this, old man."

"Boy being with me. Making Eeguls much rich."

Pook looked down at Jed, who began climbing back to his feet. "Didn't you offer him the gold like we said?"

"I did. He turned it down. Said my brother would pay more for me." Jed knelt down and finished lacing up his boot. "What did he mean by that, Pook?"

"He meant exactly what he said. Your brother would pay way more than one gold coin to get you back."

"My brother is either on his way here, in suspension, or he never left Old Pennsylvania. And he's four years younger than me."

"You're wrong, Jed. Way wrong. And on every count. But that's to be expected, since you don't have a clue what's going on."

"So why not tell me? It's not like I haven't asked."

Pook shrugged and pointed at Jed with the cigarette. "We have cross purposes, Jed. The first thing you should know is that I don't care about you. Don't care what you know, or who you are by accident of birth. You want to know things, and we've all been ordered to keep things secret." Pook took a long draw from the smoke and then closed his eyes as he exhaled. "But... but it looks like now the cat is out of the bag." Pook cocked his head and gave Jed a look that was half apology, and half "deal with it."

Dawn stepped up and grabbed Jed by the arm, pulling him closer to her. Eagles smiled, but he didn't lower his rifle. He kept it trained on Jed's head, and around his grin, spittle glistened in his facial hair.

Dawn reached over, and with a snarl she pushed Eagles's rifle barrel down, and Eagles let her. He looked amused. "Jed," Dawn said. "We've all known that you have a lot of questions, and I'm sorry we haven't answered them. It's frustrating, I know. But your brother had his reasons for keeping you in the dark. He wanted you to see things and understand them in their proper order and context."

"So my brother, Amos—he's here, in New Pennsylvania? Now?"

"Yes, Jed, he is." Dawn reached over with her other hand and pulled Jed even closer to her so that she could look him in the eye. "Everyone gets frustrated when there are more questions than answers. You're not the only one. We all do. And your brother understood that. He's the one who contacted me via my BICE when I met you at the Transport desk. He messaged me in my head—as you would say it—and ordered me to escort you here. He said that he wanted you to get to the City, and then to the Amish Zone, so you could see everything for yourself. You have to understand—"

"I *have* to understand? What do I *have* to understand, Dawn?"

Dawn's eyes narrowed, and he could tell that she

was irritated. "Do you think we've all *not* wanted to answer your questions? Do you think Ducky's men *wanted* to die last night to protect you and to try to get you where you want to go? Do you think Donavan wanted to bleed out onto the floor of an antique shop just so we could all keep secrets from you? Get some freaking perspective, will you Jed?"

Jed didn't respond. He didn't know what to say. The English were always trying to make the Amish feel guilty for decisions the strangers had made totally on their own. He was sorry about the deaths. Truly sorry. But he hadn't asked for anyone to die. He hadn't asked for any of this.

Dawn took a deep breath and softened her voice before continuing. "You have to understand that the story you need to know is bigger than you can possibly grasp all at once. You really need to see it *all*, so that you'll believe it and comprehend it. Your brother knew that. He's wiser than you can imagine, Jed. If we just dumped everything on you as soon as you got to the antique shop, you'd be even more overwhelmed than you already are. He believed that without the ability to see some things for yourself, you'd just be getting context-less information and you'd be liable to make bad decisions."

"That's what my brother said?"

"Yes."

"He's just a boy!"

"He's not a boy, Jed. Not at all. He's the leader of

the revolution against this present tyranny. And that isn't just what he *said*... that's what your brother *knows*," Dawn said.

"So where is he?"

Dawn hesitated. Jed tried to read her, but it was difficult. There were so many social and cultural differences. To him it seemed as if she was still trying to think of a way to continue on the mission as it had been designed.

"Our job is to keep you alive and get you to the Amish Zone," she said finally. "A lot of people have been hurt or killed to make sure that this is what happens. None of them asked a bunch of questions about what and why. They were all taking orders, and that's what we're doing too. We all trust your brother—*the SOMA*—with our lives. If we're going to have a future, we have to see the bigger picture, and we have to follow orders."

"The *SOMA*?" Jed shook his head. "Is that some kind of resistance joke? Because his name is Amos?"

"I can see why you'd think that."

There was a loud *harrumph*. Eagles had heard enough talk. He pushed Dawn aside and grabbed Jed by the coat, twisting him around until he was kneeling again. The old salvager pushed the rifle barrel up under Jed's chin and then turned to Pook. "Talking is enough now. Boy being with me."

Without needing a signal and in perfect synchronization, Ducky and the rest of the men fanned out so that there would be no crossfire. In unison, their pistols came up to the ready position, aimed directly at Eagles. Eagles just smiled and spat again. "Let's... partying!" he said, which made him laugh.

Pook raised his hands, trying to calm nerves and to interdict any itchy trigger fingers. "You monkeys calm down. Everybody get your booger-hooks off the bang buttons. Nobody's getting shot right now."

Eagles had fire in his eyes and a huge grin on his face. He was ready for some action. He looked at Pook and raised his eyebrows, then winked.

"Wanting boy? You paying me rich right now."

Jerry Rios, with his pistol aimed at the old man's head, whistled for Pook to look over to him. "Say the word, Pook," Jerry said. "Just say the word."

Pook didn't reply; he just held up his hand in a "stop" signal and turned back to Eagles. "Eagles, the only reason you're not dead and we're not already moving toward the AZ is because you're my friend. Keep that in mind. The Amish fellow offered you the gold and you turned him down. Now you want money?"

Eagles pointed at Pook and crooked his finger. "No gold. Gold being easy. Eeguls can always getting gold."

"Earlier you wanted gold from the SOMA, but now you don't? Well, how do you propose I pay you if you don't want gold?"

Eagle winked and crooked his finger again. "Giving Eeguls firing stick."

"Firing stick?"

"Putting in pocket. Firing stick. Give to Eeguls for boy."

Pook looked around the group from face to face. "Firing stick?"

"The okcillium lighter, Pook," Dawn said. "He wants the lighter."

Pook furrowed his brow. "Noooooo," he said slowly, shaking his head.

Dawn nodded her head and implored her cousin with her eyes.

"Not a chance," Pook said. He exhaled deeply and looked over at Ducky, who lowered his pistol and took a few steps toward Pook.

"Just give him the lighter, man! Let's get outta here. You know this is taking too long. We're exposed here, Pook."

Pook closed his eyes—then reached into his pocket and pulled out the lighter. He rubbed it longingly, then tossed it to Eagles, who caught it cleanly and almost immediately lowered his rifle.

Ducky was already in motion, "All right team, we're heading to the AZ taking Route Bravo. Everyone got it?"

Each member of the team said, "Roger that" in unison. Dawn took Jed by the hand and brought him over behind Ducky as the unit fanned out again, each member then dropping to a knee and checking weapons, waiting for an order from Pook or Ducky to move out.

Jed looked to the northwest, unconsciously gazing in the direction he believed the Amish Zone to be. That was where he wanted to go, and by their preparatory movements, it appeared to be the direction the team intended to go as well. As he stared off into the distance, it took him a moment to understand what he was seeing. In the distance, a half-dozen TRACERs—hovering white globes equipped with lenses and flashing lights—were approaching in formation, rapidly advancing toward the group. Jerry must have seen the drones at the same time, because Jed heard the big man's voice, thick with tension, "Here they come!" just as the fullness of what was happening flashed across Jed's mind.

Pook barked, "TRACERs! Everyone move!"

Eagles fired first; his shot caused one of the drones to shudder. The sound of the shot was like a starter's pistol and everyone sprang into motion just before a loud explosion rocked the ground and Jed felt dirt and debris raining down on him. It wasn't a miss. Some rebel had instantly ceased to be. Jed pulled Dawn to him and made for a low hill to the southwest just as a blast of laser light fried the ground where they'd been standing. The team opened fire at the drones, and orders echoed through the air like cracks of lightning as Jed now pulled Dawn into a low crawl. Another laser crackled past his head, and he could feel the heat and the electrical sensation of static as the shot went by.

The assault was overwhelming and brutal, and was met in earnest by Pook, Ducky, and the rest of the TRACE fighters. Billy—the man who had some kind of history with Dawn—raced through an electric mist of smoke and flying debris and slid in next to Dawn and Jed behind the low hill.

Billy grabbed Dawn's hand and pulled her closer so that he could be heard over the din of battle. "Take Jed now and get moving! Head northwest!"

Dawn shook her head. "We shouldn't leave the group!"

"They're looking for him!" Billy said with a jerk of his head toward Jed. "They'll kill everyone 'til they find him. If you don't want to die—with him dead beside you—then you need to get out of here, now!"

"We're staying with the team until Pook or Ducky order me to leave!" Dawn shouted over the noise.

Jed's attention was drawn to Ducky, who had moved out from behind cover and was systematically firing his pistol at one of the drones. Ducky had a good angle on the TRACER and was taking advantage of his position to try to bring the drone down with small-arms fire. As the soldier fired away, Jed saw another drone swinging into position to fire on Ducky. Before he could shout a warning, Eagles, who must have seen the same thing, sprinted the distance between himself and the rebel fighter and tackled him to the ground just as the second drone opened fire. The move saved Ducky's life, and Eagles rolled with the smaller man until they were both safely behind a low mound.

The drone Ducky had been firing at then took another direct hit from rebel fire, and it spun into the ground with a squeal and a piercing whistle. It crashed into the ground about fifty yards in front of Jed's hiding spot, and the explosion sent a shudder through the air that stunned everyone for a moment.

Ducky stared at Eagles for a moment, and then both warriors began laughing and Ducky slapped the salvager hard on his shoulder—his way of thanking the strange man for saving his life. Eagles just laughed and laughed, green slobber running down his face, before deciding to rejoin the fight.

The moment of victory was short-lived. Jed turned away from the remnants of the TRACER explosion just in time to see three of Ducky's men instantly vaporized in a shower of laser light and smoke, and a fourth cut cleanly in half by a phosphorescent round that hit him in the hip as he ran for cover. The suddenness and brutality of it all stunned Jed into closing his eyes for a moment, but the images of death and destruction seemed to be burned into his retinas. Closing his eyes changed nothing; the hellish assault on his senses continued. There was no escape. The land had become a killing field, and men were dying to his left and to his right.

Jed had almost despaired of *any* of their lives being spared when, as suddenly as the attack had commenced, the firing coming from the attacking

Transport craft stopped, and the remaining drones retreated and disappeared from view.

The smoky, mercurial haze sat low upon the ground. Small fires in the low brush crackled and hissed, and added more smoke that clouded the battlefield and stung the eyes. Jed found himself looking around dumbfounded—like everyone else in the rebel group—when a loud, amplified voice trembling with bass blasted over the battle scene.

"Attention rebel militia currently engaged in illegal combat with lawful Transport administration authorities! Pay strict attention to the following commands

"Give up Jedediah Troyer, alive or dead, and you will all be allowed to depart unhindered. I repeat: Give up Jedediah Troyer, alive or dead, and you will not face immediate death and/or capture.

"If our attack commences again, you will almost certainly be killed—and in the unlikely event that you are captured, you will be tried according to Transport law. If you do not face execution for your crimes against the people, you will face rehabilitation and resettlement to the frontier cities.

"This area is surrounded. There can be no escape. We have airships and ground units moving in on your location. Give up Jedediah Troyer and you will be allowed to depart unimpeded. You have sixty seconds to comply."

CAPTURED

Pook, Ducky, and the surviving resistance fighters were using the sixty seconds to reload and to prepare themselves for the renewal of the fight. It was obvious to Jed that Pook had no intention of surrendering. He and his team would battle to the death. There were no heroic speeches. The music did not build amid flashbacks to better times and shorter odds. No debate prevailed upon the stage. The men and women of TRACE simply went about their preparations as if living or dying were something completely outside of their control—and thus none of their concern.

Seeing the inevitability of defeat, and torn between competing duties and affections, Dawn finally succumbed to Billy's wishes and began pulling at Jed's hand, wordlessly making known her intention to sneak him off the battlefield toward the Amish Zone. Her orders came from the SOMA himself, and she had every intention of keeping Jed alive and getting him to his destination.

Jed watched all of this as the seconds ticked by, knowing that he alone had the power to save these brave men and women.

That was when he decided.

It wasn't a conscious thing. He didn't spend minutes pondering the different options that were available to him. He'd seen enough. Enough good people had died.

For what? For a poor farmer boy?

It was all too much to take in anyway, so he acted. Dawn had told him his brother was alive and leading the rebellion. How was that possible? And the Amish do not fight! He felt like he was in a bad dream, and that he couldn't wake up. At the same time, he hadn't slept or had anything to eat since... when? It was all too confusing. What he did next was more of an involuntary reflex than a decision.

Jed shook his hand loose of Dawn's grip, climbed to his feet, and walked out into the open field with his hands up.

"I am Jedediah Troyer! And I surrender!"

Pook sputtered and then shouted. "What? What the hell? Jed! Somebody grab—!"

Jed kept walking, and picked up his pace, making sure he was out in the open and easily identifiable. "I am Jedediah Troyer, and I accept the terms of surrender!"

A drone appeared and zipped toward him until it came to hover about fifty yards west of his position. A thin red beam lit the ground in front of Jed, scanning a few feet left to right before moving up and coming to rest squarely on Jed's chest. Ducky and his men raised their weapons again, ready to reengage on Pook's order, but everyone could see that it was too late. The drone could fire in a thousandth of a second and Jed would be dead before they could return fire. There was no way they could take the drone out fast enough to save him.

"Damn you, Jed!" Pook shouted, just as Transport foot soldiers appeared in the distance, moving their way inward from three different directions.

"Rebel forces! Follow these instructions and you will be permitted to depart safely. Leave Jedediah Troyer and exit the area to the south. If your forces move in any other direction, you will be engaged and terminated. Lower your weapons and move to the south immediately. *You have thirty seconds to comply."*

Pook's hand went up, and he commanded the rebel team to break contact and move out. Weapons were lowered and the team began slowly backing out of the area, heading south as instructed. It was obvious that Pook didn't trust Transport, but he had no other option. Retreat was the only way the team might live to fight another day. Transport wanted Jed, and it seemed like they wanted him alive. The government wanted him so badly that they were willing to let an armed resistance group escape when it could have been destroyed. Pook shouted to his men to stay alert, to be ready in case the Transport offer was a trap.

Billy tried to pull Dawn away, but she wasn't having it. She dropped his hand and shook her head. "I'm staying with Jed. No matter what."

Billy reached out to Dawn again, "But Dawn—"

"No matter what!"

She turned her back on Billy and walked out with her hands raised. Transport troops were moving in now, and Billy reluctantly turned and joined the retreating rebel force as Dawn joined Jed. He watched over his shoulder as Dawn and Jed were surrounded.

Dawn slowly put her hands behind her head, showing Jed by her actions what he should do to make sure that no Transport goon with an itchy trigger finger was going to shoot them.

As the soldiers arrived, those that were not involved in capturing the suspects moved outward to set up a defensive perimeter. Their training made them wary of a counterattack, but they seemed confident that the battle was over. Two soldiers grabbed Jed and pushed him roughly to the ground face first, then began zip-tying his hands behind him. The two troopers did not speak.

Dawn bristled. "Take it easy! He's surrendering!"

A gloved hand grabbed Dawn by the face and

shoved her roughly to the ground. Jed struggled, both against the men and against his conscience, but it was too late.

With Jed restrained, the troopers turned their attention to Dawn, and soon had her cuffed as well. The soldiers had just lifted both arrestees to their knees when a Transport officer walked up and lifted the visor on his helmet. He stared at Jed for several seconds without saying a word. After a few more intense moments of silence, he shifted his gaze to Dawn, and then back to Jed.

"So you're Jedediah Troyer, eh?"

Jed nodded his head. "Yes, sir."

The officer knelt down on one knee so that his face was only about eight inches from Jed's face. "Well Jed, it's nice to meet you. I'm Teddy Clarion, but you can just call me Clarion. Only my mom calls me Teddy."

Jed nodded his head again, but said nothing.

A small airship hovered in from the east and landed softly about seventy feet from where Jed and Dawn were being held. Clarion moved some of the soldiers out of the captives' field of view, and Jed and Dawn watched as two more arrestees were dragged from the ship. These men were also cuffed, but in addition they had black bags over their heads that had been tied loosely around their necks with white rope. They were thrown violently to the ground by Jed and Dawn, and struggled to rise to their knees in protest against their captors. Clarion walked over to the two new arrivals and, one at a time, loosened the ropes and removed the bags from the men's heads.

Jed recognized the men immediately. They were Hugh Conrad and Officer Rheems, formerly of Transport and currently rebels against the state.

Clarion pulled a pistol from his holster, and without any cinematic soliloquies or impassioned or sarcastic speeches, shot both men through the head. Their bodies flipped backward and shook on the ground, gyrating in their violent death throes.

Clarion watched the bodies as they twitched. "Disturbing, isn't it? Jed Troyer, I'm sure you haven't watched many movies, but the lady probably has. It's criminal they way they show people just falling over dead when they're shot in the head—flopping over like a sack of grain. In reality, the nerves and synapses continue to fire for some time. Muscles twitch, even if the whole brain is destroyed. It's quite gruesome and troubling, wouldn't you agree?"

Jed and Dawn just stared, neither of them able to respond.

Clarion walked back over to Jed with the pistol in his hand and pointed it at Jed's head. "So you surrender?"

Jed watched the bodies of Conrad and Rheems as the nerves that animated their spasms died, and their sickening jerks and twitches came to a halt. He just nodded his head.

Clarion stared at Jed with a fierce intensity—

attempting, it seemed, to peer into Jed's soul. After a long pause, he jerked his head a little to one side and smirked.

"Pity."

Just as the mystery of the word struck him, Jed was grabbed from behind; he flinched at the sharp stick of a needle going into the meat at the base of his neck. He tried to turn his head, but could only move it enough to see one of the soldiers jabbing Dawn as well before the darkness overwhelmed him and the lights went out.

●●●●

With the captives secured, Teddy Clarion surveyed the battlefield. Dead rebels were strewn here and there, and small fires burned among the ashes. As he took a step forward, he saw a small object near the toe of his boot. He picked it up and examined it. An odd item—a cigarette lighter, but strange in its manufacture. *Some kind of rebel technology*, he thought to himself. *I know someone who will want to take a look at this.*

●●●●

Lost in darkness, Jed felt like he was swimming toward a faint light, but he couldn't feel his body moving, and only sensed its motion by the cloudy shimmering of iridescence caused by his struggles. He could breathe easily enough, but the occlusion of his vision gave him the impression that he was underwater, and an unspecific panic reflex took hold of his mind.

Floating in the brown-gray darkness he saw images of things that he knew, visions floating in the water, or behind it and through it. He saw Zoe, his milk cow, struggling in the murk; he saw the window with the coffee can that had replaced the missing pane; and he saw the face of his brother leaning over to reach for him from the other side of a gulf that stretched between them. He reached up for his brother's hand, and as he did so he felt a sharp pain in the back of his head and his vision cleared instantaneously, as if someone had flipped a switch. And as instantly as his sight was made perfect, he now found that he was standing (if it can be called standing—he couldn't feel his body) on a hillside that was covered in the greenest grass he'd ever seen.

He realized that it may not have been his real self standing on that hillside. Maybe he was a boy; or maybe he was someone else entirely. He couldn't rightly tell. He looked up. The sky was so blue that it took his breath away, and as he looked around he could see the minutest details, as if his eyesight had improved a thousandfold in a moment.

He glanced back up at the blue sky—a blue like the blue he'd only seen on his mother's palette when she painted patterns on smoothed boards that she would sell to the tourists. His mother never painted natural things, like people, birds, or trees, because creating images of anything God had made was forbidden. It was against the *ordnung*: the rules of their community.

But she did like to paint patterns and hex signs in bright colors on pieces of plywood, cut round and sanded. The myth that Amish hex signs were always religious or superstitious, or that they were put up on barns to keep evil spirits away, was one that had been trumpeted by secular authorities and governments—and of course by the tourist industry, to add mystery to the Amish story, and thus attract tourist dollars. To the Troyer family, the hex signs were just a way for Jed's mother to express her artistic side, to display her ethnic identity, and experience the joy of painting. She always picked the most beautiful colors to use in her projects.

Jed was staring up into a sky that was *this* color of blue when he saw what looked to be meteors—or missiles?—falling from the sky and impacting the ground in brilliant oranges, reds, and browns. The display lasted for only seconds, but to Jed it felt like it went on much longer.

Then from the same blue sky—or, rather, in front of that sky, between him and the blueness—he looked on as numbers appeared, long rows of digits moving quickly from right to left, zeroes and ones and symbols that meant nothing to him. These numbers flashed and disappeared, and then he was in a darkened room and there was a screen of white suspended in the air in front of him. He looked down at his arms and legs and hands, and it was just as if they were his own, from his point of view, but the parts were somehow different, foreign to him. He lifted his hands and saw them rise up in front of his face. He examined them, but they looked artificial; he was moving them, but they didn't feel like *his*. It wasn't that they weren't right, it was that they were... *too* right. The tiny hairs on the backs of his hands moved as if molested by a gentle breeze that he could not feel. He could flutter his fingers and touch his nose, but the feelings were still just—not... quite... right.

On the white screen—which brought to mind what he'd heard of Englischers' televisions or movie screens—he could see his family's farm, as if from the road, and he found he could reach out and touch the screen and the image would react to his touch. He could zoom in any direction and look around the farm.

And they made an image of the beast, and did worship it...

The words of a sermon preached in his church by an elder came to him almost in spoken form, but then the thought was gone and he found he could interact with the picture on the screen simply by opening and closing his hand in front of him. He was just getting the hang of manipulating the image of the farm when everything in his view flashed white, and again he was submerged in the dirty waters, unable to feel anything, floating, reaching for the light. Feeling the urge to panic. Then blackness swarmed over him again, and he slept.

● ● ● ●

Jed awoke upon a firm and thin mattress in a

darkened room. The only light came in through a small square window on a door that was six or seven feet away from the bed. As his eyes slowly adapted to the darkness, he could make out that he was in some kind of cell. He was still wearing his Amish clothing—his broadfall pants, long-sleeved white shirt, suspenders, black boots—and his hat was near him on the bed. His hands and feet were no longer bound. He sat up on the bed, and as he did so a light came on in the room and some music started to play from somewhere. Soft piano music with no lyrics. He was trying to gather his mind and to get his thoughts in order when he heard a buzz, and the sound of air... like when an air compressor on one of his more liberal neighbors' farms was being voided of its compressed contents. He looked up, and from a crevice in the brick walls of his cell he saw a mist descending on him. It smelled like orange zest, and his mind zoomed back to the time when he was interrogated by Hugh Conrad in the Transport Security office and a canister had sprayed into the room, releasing that very same smell.

The scent relaxed him, and he leaned back on the bed and felt his vision go still and black. Once again the white screen appeared before him, and he felt like he was standing in front of it. The screen expanded until it wrapped all the way around him and over him, and on the screen a farm appeared. It was his farm, and he was standing in the paddock next to the milk barn, and Zoe walked up to him and reached toward him with her nose. She was hoping he had some sweet treat, some cow cubes perhaps, to give her. When he touched her nose she realized that he didn't have anything for her to eat, so she turned away, uninterested, and sauntered across the green grass of the paddock, her empty udder swinging with each step.

This time it was more real. Well... it *felt* real. There was still just the slightest hint of that sense of everything being *too* perfect, but for some reason Jed's mind was now taking over and fixing the "too-right" things that should have been "wrong." His brain roughed up the image until he agreed to be convinced that what he was experiencing was real. He looked up into the clouds and he could see the three dimensional wispiness that modern artists never seem to get right. (He'd seen art before, in school, or on trips to town with his father.) He looked toward the road, and his attention fell on a mud hollow the pigs had dug out while rooting. A recent rain had filled the little hollow with muddy water.

Jed turned and saw the barn. That beautiful, glorious structure that held so much meaning for him. His eyes tracked upward and he saw the place where the special window should have been in the gabled end of the uppermost peak of the barn. The window—frame and all—was missing. He looked back down, and at the base of the barn he saw a set of hay hooks he'd dropped there on the day he'd left for New Pennsylvania. He'd forgotten to put the hooks back in the barn—and there they were. Still there. The hay hooks were a detail, one of a thousand that convinced him the vision was real, not something concocted in order to trick him. Then he looked toward the house.

And he saw Dawn.

So beautiful. He heard the thought, and it embarrassed him.

She was standing only ten feet from him, and she was the most captivating thing he'd ever seen in his life. Everything about her was perfect, and she was smiling. Only, there was a sadness in her smile even though she looked authentically happy to see him. And she was dressed Amish, with cape and white apron and a white kapp with the ties hanging down.

He felt ashamed because a part of him knew that this *wasn't* real, it couldn't be, and that Dawn hadn't consented to be seen this way. His mind—just below his consciousness, but still invading it—noted the irony of a man feeling shame for imagining a woman in modest, plain, and unrevealing dress. But a fantasy is a fantasy, isn't it? It cannot be right. His face flushed red, and Dawn saw it.

She looked down at herself and smiled back at him. "Don't be surprised, Jed. I really like these clothes. I love being dressed like this. It's beautiful."

Jed shook his head. "Only it's not *you* saying that. It's all in my mind. It's what I would want you to say."

"You're wrong, Jed."

Jed looked around. "So is this heaven? Were we killed?"

Dawn shook her head, and the sadness in her eyes multiplied. "No."

Jed reached down and picked a piece of grass, then put it in his mouth. He chewed it and tasted its sweetness. He could feel the fibers on his tongue.

"Are you sure this isn't heaven?" he said.

"I'm sure, Jed. In fact, this is a whole lot more likely to be hell."

Q

Jed and Dawn walked toward the house, and as they walked Dawn took his hand in hers. At the house, they sat on the porch in wooden chairs that his father had made in his workshop using only hand tools. His parents were nowhere around. He didn't feel an urge to look around for them, because some part of him was still telling him that what he was seeing wasn't the real world. A gentle breeze touched his hair, and he felt it this time, like the wispy fingers of evening and history. He removed his hat, and he smiled when he heard the familiar creak of the porch as he pushed his legs out and crossed his boots.

Glancing again at Dawn, he almost couldn't stand to look upon her for fear that his heart would jump out of his chest, and because he thought that if she caught him looking she would read his thoughts. She was so stunning in her Amish dress that he had trouble controlling his breathing. He looked away rather than stare at her. "If this is hell," he said, "and I know it might be blasphemous... but..."

Dawn flinched and interrupted him with an upraised hand. "We can't stay here. It's not real, Jed." She pointed out across the farm. "This is all a lie."

"But you said you were real."

She grabbed his hand in hers and looked into his eyes. "*I'm* real, Jed, but this place is not. Transport Intelligence put a BICE unit in your head. In mine, too. I'm back online. And they have you on Quadrille—we call it *Q*—so that your mind will more easily accept the transplant... and believe the things you see and hear while they're trying to reprogram you."

Though he tried so hard not to, he found himself staring at Dawn's face. It was so *right* that he wanted to kiss her. He didn't want to talk at all. But then he knew it would be wrong to kiss her, so he tried to focus on what she was saying. "If this isn't real—" *But I know it isn't real.* "If this isn't real, then why are they letting you tell me this? Don't they control the computers? Aren't they listening to us right now?"

Dawn smiled. "Well, they don't know that TRACE has back doors, shells, and traps throughout their system. We've been infiltrating their programming for years, and there's been nothing they could do about it. It's a byproduct of a technological ecosystem: any system that relies on creative people to keep it running is going to be riddled with secrets and back doors. Most of the programmers who designed the BICE and integrated it with the Internet had hacker and rebel tendencies. Those people *always* do, God bless them. It's always been that way and it always *will* be that way. There was no way to keep us out. That's how the SOMA got in touch with me through my BICE when you were checking in at customs, back when I first met you."

Dawn was holding Jed's hand now, and she gave it a squeeze. He took it as a recognition of their shared adventure since that day, and how much they'd been through together.

She lifted his hand a little and looked at it closely before giving it another light squeeze. "Part of my job has been infiltrating Transport protocols and accessing TRACE backdoors to use the system against them. Right now they think we're both unconscious and recovering from the surgery and the drugs they gave us. They know that you're slowly adopting the BICE data into your cognitive stream. I have the data mirrored so they're seeing what I want them to see. Basically, I've hacked your brain, Jed. And I've also communicated to TRACE command everything that's happened."

Jed just stared, unsure what he should accept and what was still too fantastic to be believed.

"There's a war going on, Jed. And right now, one of the battlefields is your mind."

"I just want to be out of it all. I just want to be home."

"There is no out. There is no home. Unless we win."

Jed shook his head. "It's too much."

"Listen," Dawn said, "I don't expect you to get all of this at once. It's a lot to take in, and I understand that. We're just lucky they didn't shoot us back when they captured us just to be done with you."

"Blessed," Jed said.

"What?"

"Not lucky—blessed."

Dawn shrugged. "All right. Blessed, then."

"So what do we do next?"

Dawn stood up and turned to face him. She reached out with her hands and pulled him up out of his chair. When he stood, he was uncomfortably close to her, and she didn't step back to increase the space between them. She looked up at him as she spoke. "Next? You're going to go through all of their training and protocols." She reached up and fixed a wisp of hair that had escaped from her kapp. "The system does that automatically as you sleep, so you won't really notice it that much. Only fragments of notable instances here and there will occur to you. Without your even knowing about it, they'll train you to use the system, to access information unconsciously, and they'll program your BICE to send back information to Transport Intelligence. You're going to pretend to go along with everything they do."

She gave him a sideways smile, as if to say *sorry about this part.* "Actually, you won't have to pretend. My guess is that they're going to try to zap your memory of the last few days—going all the way back to when you first arrived at Transport Customs in Columbia, before you met me. I don't know exactly how they'll do it, but we'll soon see. Then they're going to deliver you to the Amish Zone—exactly as you'd originally intended before all hell broke loose. They'll expect that you won't know what's happening, and their plan is for you to serve as an unwitting spy, gathering data and transmitting it back to Transport."

Jed noticed that even though he was now standing, Dawn was still holding both of his hands. He wondered if that was part of the fantasy that his brain was concocting, or if she was really in control of what he saw in front of him.

"Why go to all of this trouble just to spy on the Amish? What harm can the plain people be to Transport?"

Dawn pushed the troublesome strand of hair back into her head covering and shrugged. "The plain people are never harmless."

"But they *are* harmless," Jed said. "They're pacifist. They don't take sides. They can't help or hurt anyone."

Dawn shook her head again. "Free people who produce everything they need to survive are never harmless, Jed. Because they're not dependent on government—and *that* makes them dangerous when governments are wicked. Add to that the fact that people on both sides of this conflict depend on Amish production for food... which means the plain people are strategically important. And don't forget that the resistance is led by a former Amish man."

"My brother."

"Yes."

Jed took a deep breath. "When am I going to find out about Amos?"

"Soon."

Jed reached over and touched Dawn's sleeve. The green fabric felt cool and very real to him. When he touched her, she turned to him and smiled.

"Your brother wanted you to see everything, to experience what's going on in the Amish Zone and in this world. He figured that maybe then you would understand his decisions."

"I don't understand them."

"This whole thing," Dawn said, "everything going on here... this is not some grand plan to torture you or keep you in the dark. You don't think every single one of us in the resistance isn't tired of saying 'Not yet, we can't tell you yet'? Of course we'd love to have just told you everything when you first arrived at customs. But then you'd never understand. You'd be like the elders here in New Pennsylvania—unable and unwilling to see what's really happening."

"The Amish will never change. They will never

fight."

Dawn smiled. "Your brother knows that. He doesn't want them to change or fight. They're too valuable to this world and the old world. He wants you to know the truth, so that at least you can communicate with them and let them know why he's made the decisions he's had to make. Why he's chosen to fight."

"I still don't understand."

"I know," Dawn said. "Hopefully someday you will."

Jed didn't reply. His hand moved up her sleeve, and then before he could stop himself he was touching her face. He couldn't help it. He wanted to know what she felt like, to get an understanding of what was real and what was not. Her skin was soft to the touch, and she leaned in to the contact and closed her eyes.

"If they zap my memory," Jed said, "then won't what they're trying to do to me... or with me... well, won't it work? Won't I forget everything and just go on without knowing what they've done to me?"

Dawn smiled again, and now she was the one to reach out and touch *his* face, as if she was checking to see if *he* was real. "They aren't going to zap *all* of your memory, because I'm going to keep them from doing it. They might accomplish it for a bit, but in the end you'll remember. I'm just going to teach you how to trick them so that they'll think they succeeded."

Jed didn't respond. He just looked into her eyes.

After a moment, her hand traveled upward until she

was pointing at the center of his forehead. "But never you worry, Jed." She smiled and his heart leapt. "All the while, I'll be right here."

His hand found hers and he pulled her finger down from his forehead until it was pointing at his heart. He held it that way for a moment, and then he released her hand.

"You're a very handsome man, Jed."

Her eyes closed and he could see that she was going to kiss him, or that she wanted him to kiss her. She hesitated, only centimeters away from his lips, expecting that he would meet her there.

He did not.

"I can't," he said. Her eyes opened and he blushed. "I don't know what's real."

Dawn dropped his hands, smiled again, then turned and stepped off the porch. She walked toward the water pump that was in the side yard under a large oak tree, and she turned and spoke over her shoulder as she walked. "Welcome to the world of the English, Jed. Almost no one knows what's real."

* * * *

Jed worked the pump handle while Dawn gathered water in her hands and splashed it on her face. He had so many questions, he wasn't completely sure where to start.

"What does the Q do? What part of what I'm

feeling is the drug?"

Dawn wiped her face with her sleeve, and Jed was fascinated to see the water spots on the sleeve of the green dress. Whatever kind of computer simulation this was, it was mind-blowing.

"Q gives you a feeling of euphoria," she said. "Of acceptance and acquiescence. It helps your brain meld the imagery that the computer is producing with the sensory perceptions that your brain adopts in order to help you believe the illusion. On Q, your brain 'fixes' things by adding in the imperfections and oddities that exist in real life. When computers try to do this alone, and your mind isn't on Q, the animation comes across as clunky and artificial. Animators and programmers call this 'the uncanny valley.' It's too real, so the mind rejects it as creepy and odd." Dawn pumped the handle a few times until some water spurted out. She caught the moisture in her hand and let it drip through her fingers in front of Jed's face. The sun glistened through the drops, and he was reminded of the drops on the grass on his last day in Old Pennsylvania, after he and Amos had milked Zoe.

Dawn continued. "The computer really only produces about fifteen percent of the image, and your mind produces the rest. Little-used parts of the brain are turned into supercomputers that render imagery based on the billions of microscopic memories stored throughout your brain. Your mind becomes the rendering chip. Q facilitates this pipeline. Back in the old world, television created these simulated realities—only slower and not as well. What the BICE can make is kinda cool and very technologically advanced, but even so, the brain always knows it isn't right. The Q helps your brain stop being so naturally cynical. It helps you suspend your disbelief. You become more accepting of the data you're receiving. That's why I wanted to be here for your first experience. When Transport showed that they would rather capture you than kill you, I figured they had a plan that involved implanting you and putting you on Q."

"Why didn't they kill *you*?" Jed asked.

"Good question," Dawn said. "I was hoping they wouldn't." She smiled at him, but he didn't seem to like her answer. "Because they don't know if they'll need me in the future to help control you. And they need *you* more than they need just about anything else."

"Why could they possibly need me?" Jed asked.

"Because every war has more than one facet. It's not all guns and bombs. There are things like public relations, propaganda, and public opinion. They need you—to use you as a tool against your brother and the resistance."

Jed was still worried about Dawn. "They already killed Conrad and Rheems as traitors. They'll kill you too if they don't think you can help them."

"Well, you're right. At some level, at least," she said. "Conrad and Rheems didn't have some of the capabilities that I have to disrupt and confuse their system if I need to." Dawn winked at him. "I might even be able to arrange for my own escape if I really have to."

"Then you should do that," Jed said. "Get out of here and don't look back."

Dawn laughed. It was almost an ironic laugh. "If you think I would abandon you here, Jed, or that I would neglect my duty to TRACE or the SOMA, then you don't know me as well as you should. As well as you will."

• • • •

Over the next few days, Jed's life settled into a pattern. He slept most of the time, and during this sleep—at first, anyway—he recognized that his mind was going through training. Often he would be standing in front of the white screen and he would find himself manipulating data, or filing information in folders that would appear before him. He learned how to categorize data, parse conversations, and add rankings to information before he filed it away.

When he awoke, sometimes he would forget the overall gist of what he'd been doing in his sleep, but he'd always remember that the training was moving forward.

On occasion—at random times when it was quite unexpected—Dawn would appear in his visions, and she would teach him things he needed to know: how to hide things, how to recall and change data even after the information had already been filed. She even taught him how to authentically alter his memories, so that the information that was filed was substantively different than what had actually happened.

And sometimes Dawn would take him to another place entirely. She showed him battles and wars. They stood on hilltops and on buildings and watched men and machines destroy and kill, and Dawn talked to him of history and the process that had brought this world to the edge of ruin. She showed him that the colonization of New Pennsylvania had been troubled from the very beginning. The same conflict and civil war that had marked the old world had carried over into the new.

A lot of what Jed learned from Dawn was data without context. He didn't gain true understanding because he didn't have all of the supporting information and experience that would help him truly make sense of it. He felt like a spectator, watching a show that had nothing to do with him, like he was being forced to see a movie about the world and everything that was wrong with it. He willed it to stop, but he had no power to control anything that was happening to him in the dream state.

One day (or maybe it was night? he had no way to know), Dawn took him on a journey to an area in the west called "the Great Shelf." There she showed him a massive line of limestone cliffs, hundreds and hundreds of feet high, bifurcating the whole continent from the north to the south. Atop the Shelf there were a dozen cities and towns, spread hundreds and hundreds of miles apart. Dawn explained that Transport had spent billions of tax unis to build cities that they'd hoped would eventually be filled with immigrants from the old world. But, she explained, things hadn't worked out as Transport had planned.

There were millions of people living beyond the Shelf, but the bulk of those colonists—along with their young, born on New Pennsylvania—avoided the planned cities as if they were filled with the plague. So the cities had only a token civilian presence, mostly colonists who relied on the government for sustenance and survival. Some of the cities had no more than a thousand to ten thousand souls living in them. The Shelf cities survived only thanks to the massive infusion of tax unis grafted from both the old and the new worlds. The old philosophy—where consumption, rather than production, provided for an unnatural and unsustainable system of urban living—wasn't workable in the new world. It didn't work in the old world either, but the old world system was slow in collapsing because it had thousands of years of production propping it up.

"Why do they even keep the cities if they can't support themselves?" Jed asked.

"No city of any meaningful size is ever self-sufficient," Dawn said. "Every city relies on production that happens in the countryside. Food, raw materials, goods, et cetera." Now she pointed out into the wilderness beyond the city. "In the old world, it took millennia to develop industrialized systems adequate to maintain large cities. Rome and Athens used slave labor, wars, and harsh taxation. Centuries later, machines did the job just as well, and even if the industrialized nations still relied on wars and taxation, they'd been around long enough to use sleight of hand to hide the reasons and purposes behind the wars." Dawn looked at him and saw that even in cyberspace she was losing him. There was still a huge culture gap. The Amish weren't dumb, she knew, they just had no point of reference when it came to human culture on such an urban scale.

"The point is that you can't just drop a city onto a new planet and expect it to work."

"I can see that," Jed said.

Dawn continued. "The government thought that the old world system could just be duplicated and transferred into the new world, but in this thinking they'd missed one very important fundamental truth: without several millennia of the compounded productive labors of individuals who'd systematically made goods and products by hard work, using raw materials gleaned from the real, tangible world... your cities aren't going to make it.

"The leaders of the world forgot where real wealth comes from. It's like thinking that you can take all of the flesh, sinews, ligaments, and tissues that make up a human, and just stick them all together in the right places and somehow you'll have life. You won't. You'll have a reconstituted corpse that's still dead.

"The nuts and the bolts of the issue," Dawn explained, "comes down to this: if the people of New Pennsylvania don't work with their hands to create the means of survival, production, and expansion, this world will collapse and regress. The only thing they'll be left with is the ancient Roman model of empire-building: endless war, slavery, and oppression. The people who have rejected the cities seem to grasp this. They're out there, beyond the Shelf, working, living, and surviving. Everyone else doesn't have a clue. This difference was the root of the war between TRACE and Transport," Dawn said. "In the countryside, TRACE is embraced and supported. In the cities, Transport is idol, king, and god."

Dawn was biased, and she admitted as much. According to her, TRACE wanted to free people from oppression so that they could work and produce and survive. According to her, Transport wanted to enslave generations of humans and force them to maintain a system that was already crumbling from its own internal corruptions and contradictions.

And whenever Jed was just beginning to get a modicum of understanding, the darkness and the sleep would overwhelm him again.

This became his pattern: sleep, training, long visits and conversations with Dawn. The information, relentless in its assault, pouring into his mind like water filling a cup. His thoughts alternated between murky confusion and stunning clarity. It became more and more difficult for him to keep track of what was real and what wasn't. Time passed, but he had no idea how long this pattern continued, until finally, something changed. He felt himself coming out of that deep and bottomless slumber, his consciousness returning to him only in fits and starts. He was disoriented, and awareness of his surroundings was slow to return to him. He struggled to focus his mind, to concentrate on anything at all that would help him gain some kind of center.

After a few long moments of nothingness, Dawn appeared in his mind. Not in his vision, but it was her essence, incorporeal. She didn't speak until his focus was entirely on her and not on his indistinct surroundings. When at last he'd cleared his mind enough to hear her, she spoke.

"Here we go."

● ● ● ●

Dawn was gone. But Jed knew that he was coming awake. He realized—almost as an afterthought—that he was very cold, but concurrent with that thought he began to feel warmth expand and spread throughout his body, tracing along his veins and arteries. The warmth brought his consciousness into greater clarity, and he heard an unlatching sound, and then the sound of air escaping. He opened his eyes and the lid of the pod rose slowly and light penetrated the darkness around him and he felt himself stirring into consciousness. There was a voice speaking...

"...Medical for a release before entering the station. Do not be alarmed. The process of reanimation is proceeding normally. You will feel confused, lightheaded, and weak at first, but normal function will return quickly. Your muscles have been continuously stimulated during your voyage, and will function normally after a period of acclimation. After a short episode of reorientation, you will begin to be able to feel and move normally. Take your time exiting your pod. When you do exit, you will find Medical on your left as you disembark the ship. Everyone must stop at Medical for a release before entering the station. Do not be alarmed. The process..."

He realized that he was in the Transport station: he'd arrived in New Pennsylvania. He reached down into the tight joint between his seat and the frame of the pod. For some reason he couldn't grasp, his hand searched there for something. Something that should have been there. But he found nothing.

What had he been looking for?

Mrs. Beachy

From his desk in his office aboard the Tulsa, Amos Troyer could glance up and see a dozen paper-thin screens that fed him information from everywhere that TRACE had a presence. Whether he chose to receive his intel from the screens, or from the BICE in his head, was a matter of multitasking and how deeply he needed to examine information. Sometimes the BICE was too cumbersome and resource-dependent for regular, everyday jobs. For a cursory idea of what was happening in the war, the wall screens were sufficient. But if something really needed his complete attention, then he would use the BICE.

It was interesting to note that the BICE, designed to be the single most efficient means of gathering and utilizing information, was often too unwieldy for the job when it came to the millions of bits of ordinary information humans gather casually every day. The BICE had become—for many people, including the head of the insurrection—something that was for entertainment, for escape, for personal or sensitive communications, or for deeper research. But the system proved to be less than ideal for the multitudes of daily transactions and computations that didn't require full concentration.

The human mind simply couldn't function well with ten programs running in the brain at one time. In the exterior world, men and women could perform quite well working with a wall full of monitors offering different flows of information. The brain's *latent inhibitions* sorted the information and threw most of it out as useless, focusing attention on what was most likely to be important. But the BICE system bypassed these latent inhibitions, and force-fed all of the information directly into the consciousness. Too much of that could cause insanity. The Q helped, but it couldn't help everyone.

Amos sighed. Ages ago, humanity foolishly believed that with the advent of the digital age their lives would soon be paper-free, but that dream had never been realized. Quite the opposite, actually. It took more paper than ever to support the paperless society. Likewise, many people once hoped that integrated computers—brain chips—would one day replace all stand-alone processing stations and displays. *Nope,* Amos thought. *We rely on them more now than we ever have.*

On one of the heads-up wall screens, a remote camera displayed what was happening in a sector a hundred miles south and west of the City. Amos watched as four TRACE units engaged and destroyed an armed Transport convoy—most likely transporting goods confiscated from the small towns and villages of the frontier.

The tide of the battle on every front had turned. TRACE was no longer just a gadfly and a nuisance. Everywhere, people were starting to realize that Transport was on the run, and the resistance was rising.

TRACE was winning the propaganda war, too. They'd successfully portrayed Transport as heartless and tyrannical, while showing the rebels as compassionate, measured, and just.

But even success and victory carried their share of challenges. With their increased capabilities came the necessity of restraint. Amos knew that he could end Transport's control of the capital city with the push of a button. Okcillium gave him that power. But then there would be no city left to claim. Scorched earth *is* a policy, it's just not usually the best one.

The rise of the resistance was directly attributable to the fact that Amos had increased TRACE's access to okcillium, an element that hadn't yet been found in the new world. Maybe there *wasn't* any okcillium on New Pennsylvania. The first decade here had seen an all-out search for the rare element.

And okcillium was thought to have been so completely depleted in the old world that for all intents and purposes it was considered an extinct element. However... okcillium did still exist in the old world; it had just taken the right man to know where to find it, and how to extract it. In fact, it was quite plentiful in one place on Earth: Oklahoma. But sometimes the hardest question isn't *where*; sometimes there are also questions of *when*.

Having access to okcillium made all the difference to the resistance. The element was the most valuable and useful material in the war, and TRACE alone was able to use it for advanced propulsion applications and for game-changing weapons systems. The enemy did not yet know where—or when—TRACE was getting its supply. But if ever they figured it out, there would be a war over Oklahoma like nothing the world had ever seen.

Amos watched the screens as his forces mopped up after the attack on Transport. Another victory. Even without it, his people were calling for decisive action. They were calling for the Hiroshima Option, something he was unwilling to do. Just having okcillium was not reason, in his mind, to destroy a city with all of its population still in it.

The full brunt of TRACE's newfound power could be unleashed on Transport's forces in and near the City at any time, but still he waited. He knew that Transport was in the process of abandoning the City and hightailing it out west, beyond the Shelf, where it would be easier for the government to regroup and rebuild. Getting control of the City was a chief war aim, but when TRACE *did* finally take control, Amos wanted there to be a city left. And he didn't want to kill hundreds of thousands of civilians in order to occupy a city that, in the long run, he didn't even want. So for now, it was a waiting game—and it seemed that Jed Troyer was the piece that was in play. What happened to him would determine the future of the City, and therefore the entire population of the east.

Amos knew that to the people, it might look like he was hesitating *only* because he wanted to spare Jed's life. That wasn't true, but the people didn't always know his mind. Of course Jed's life was critical to Amos as a man and as a brother, but TRACE—and eventual victory—was even more important. Amos knew that he didn't have critics now, but with the tide of war turning... As soon as it looked like his people might win, he'd have plenty of them. He knew all about Churchill, MacArthur, Patton, and other war heroes who had been cast to the winds once the threat they had fought no longer occupied the forefront of the people's minds, and ruling became all about the perks, with little risk. It was just the way of humanity, and he didn't expect anything to change.

He opened his desk drawer and grabbed one of the little white pills that lay among the pens, tweezers, and paperclips. He held the pill up before his face and examined it. Such a tiny thing. The tool of the devil, no doubt, and the legal drug of choice among the English. Q was both bane and boon to Amos. He wanted to be free of it in his old age, but he needed it to help him assimilate and sift through so much information. He popped the pill in his mouth and chewed it deliberately. It was bitter: wormwood and gall. *Consuming hell*—he thought—*one little white pill at a time.*

He closed his eyes, and in a few moments the familiar feelings of peace and acceptance swept over him. He thought about home, and Jed, and milking Zoe in the mornings and evenings without a care in the world. He activated his BICE, and the unit booted up in a tenth of a second.

Now, in his mind, he stood confidently. His avatar was him—young, as he'd once been. His powerful muscles pressed against the uniform that stretched over him like armor. He was a vibrant youth of thirty, and unquestionably the man for the job at hand.

He was in a darkened room, and he saw a cube floating in the center of the space. This was the way he'd personalized his filing system. There were a million other ways to do it: one could have a long wall of drawers or lockers, an endless filing cabinet, buttons that floated, or numbered kittens that mewed as they relaxed on sofas. But Amos liked the spinning box. Each side of the cube was divided into different-sized squares—drawers, actually—and the size of each drawer was correlated with how much information was in it and how often it was accessed. The entire parent box was a perfect cube, four feet to a side, and it hung in the room without any visible means of support. No wires were needed, because Amos was *in* the Internet. This room was his control room. The parent cube could be rotated, spun, inverted, or reversed, all with the flick of his wrist. He turned the box slowly with one hand until he saw a drawer marked DB.

Dawn Beachy.

He opened the drawer with a flick of a wrist, and a flat card came out and floated in front of him. The big square faded until it was just a ghosted image, and the two-dimensional card became brighter once it was floating in the open. It then expanded into the third dimension until it became a cube as well, three feet to a side and also covered on all six faces with different-sized drawers. Amos spun this cube end over end until what had been the top faced him, and he found a drawer with the letters DM.

Direct Message.

He opened the drawer with another flick, and in a split second, Dawn Beachy appeared before him. She was opaque, and her eyes were closed.

After a few seconds, her eyes flittered open and she became solid and real. Recognizing the younger Amos, she nodded. "Yes, sir. Awaiting your orders, sir."

Amos waved his hand and the two boxes faded until they were virtually invisible. "No orders. I just wanted to talk."

"Yes, sir," Dawn said. She cast her eyes downward, looking uncomfortable.

"Is something the matter?"

"Everything is fine, sir."

"Speak freely, Dawn. We're old friends. Is something wrong?"

"No, sir. It's just... I find it distracting to see you like this."

"Why's that?" Amos asked.

"Because you look like a slightly older version of your brother."

Amos nodded and laughed. He looked down, and in a blink he was his older self again. Still in uniform, but older and frailer.

Dawn nodded. "Thank you, sir. Better."

"How is everything progressing?" Amos asked.

Dawn put her arms behind her and came to an "at ease" position in front of the SOMA. "Things are going well enough, sir. He's made it to the AZ and he's going through their immigrant orientation. I'm giving him nudges now and then, to make sure his mind doesn't become completely submerged, but pretty soon we'll need to activate him."

"Let him go for a while," Amos said. "He needs to reconnect with his people, and then we'll let him see the world for what it is, and he'll have the context he needs."

Dawn nodded. "Yes, sir. But you should know that Transport is going to be using him to gather information. And immersion like this can be tricky to undo. Every day that he remains oblivious to what's going on inside his head, it will become increasingly difficult to pull him all the way out."

Amos waved his hand again and a white screen appeared. He glanced over at Dawn. "Work with him at night. Underneath his consciousness. Erase your tracks when you're done. But not *every* night. Randomly, and never more than a few times a week. Don't be predictable."

On the screen, the recording of Jed and Dawn talking near the water pump at the old farm appeared. Amos and Dawn both watched as Dawn almost kissed Jed before he pulled away at the last moment.

Dawn blushed and then nodded. "Yes, sir. I'll work with him as you direct."

"Have you convinced him you love him?" Amos said. He flicked his wrist and the screen disappeared.

"I think so, sir."

"Does he love you?"

"I don't know, sir."

"Does he?"

"Maybe."

Amos raised his hand and began to turn his wrist very slightly. The image of Dawn began to fade.

"You're going to break his heart, Mrs. Beachy. You know that, right?"

Amos emphasized the word *Mrs.*, and Dawn flinched. "I hope not, sir." She took a step back, taking her leave, but just before she blinked out, she looked Amos Troyer in the face. "And Ben is dead... sir."

Amos nodded, but Dawn was already gone.

ARRIVAL

The airbus came in low, descending until it landed smoothly up against the platform dock. The bus was about two-thirds full, and Jed waited until it was almost empty before he followed the crowd out onto the platform. There had been only a handful of Amish on board, and they filed into line under a sign that read "Amish Residents." The English flowed down a roped trail into a second line that terminated under a sign reading "Tourist Entry." No one waited in line at a third counter, where the sign read "Amish Immigrants—Please Check In."

Jed walked up to the Immigrants desk, and the woman behind the counter, who looked to be a Mennonite, was placing papers into a manila folder as he approached.

The woman smiled. "Welcome to York Amish Zone. For official purposes,"—the way she said this made it sound like "porpoises"—"I am speaking da English. Are y'uns having the papers?"

Jed remembered that when they'd removed his bio-identification band, he'd been handed an envelope with papers in it. He put his hand into his vest and found the envelope, then handed it to the heavyset Mennonite lady and smiled.

In the distance there was a rumbling sound, almost like thunder, and Jed turned his head, trying to identify the sound.

"Chust da Englischers, fighting," the woman said. "Always da fighting. It wonders me they all han't died."

"Does the fighting ever come here, ma'am?" Jed asked.

The woman smiled at Jed as if he'd said something cute or amusing. "No. Never. The fightings never comes here, because we are growing da foods for many of the Englischers!" She stamped some of his papers, then pulled out a few notes and handed them to Jed. "Here are da moneys, young man."

Jed saw that the customs official back at the Transport station must have exchanged his unis for Amish Barter Notes when his ID band was removed, because the small slips of paper she handed him were Amish notes.

"Do y'uns read, boy?" the woman asked.

"Yes, ma'am."

"Wunnerful gut." She handed him another printed sheet. "Here listing ist da *ordnung*. Normally *ordnung* never ist written, but during the immigration periods, rule ist setting aside. Read when y'uns can."

"I will, ma'am." Jed suddenly had one of those strange feelings of déjà vu. It wasn't *really* déjà vu, because it wasn't the feeling that he'd done all of this before, but the Mennonite woman's unique accent and dialect affected him strangely, as if he'd heard something similar to it recently. Similar, but not the same. Maybe a very rough and wild version of it.

Eagles.

Why did he think of the word *Eagles* just then? He shook his head and tried to push down the strange feeling. He'd been on a long journey. Perhaps he was just tired.

"Wunnerful gut. Okay," the woman said, "now, y'uns following line on da floor until are arriving at da airbus that take y'uns to da Greeting Center. Not costing moneys, young man. Y'uns stay at der Greeting Center until other housings are arranged, or y'uns are receiving allotment of da farming lands. Mr. Zook will take wunnerful gut care of thee."

"Okay, thanks," Jed said. And as he said it, he could hear another woman's voice—inside his head!— say, "This is real, Jed, but don't forget what's happening out there." He turned his head, but there was no one near him who could have spoken the words.

⬥ ⬥ ⬥ ⬥

The airbus floated over towering walls of indeterminate origin that circled the entirety of the York Amish Zone. Jed estimated that the walls must have been hundreds of feet high and at least as wide as a cornfield—stretching into the distance like the Great Wall of China he'd seen in a picture book, only far taller and wider. Taller than many of the great buildings he'd seen in photographic art books, and the outer portion that faced the world was a sheer wall that would only be scaled with much difficulty. Jed wondered who had built the walls and why. With airbuses and floating airships, the walls seemed kind of pointless and silly.

At the Immigrant Greeting Center, Jed was taken in by an Amish family who treated him like a king returning from a far country. He took a hot bath, and while he bathed his clothes were washed for him. He was given a loaner set of clothes while his dried on the line, and then he was measured for several more sets of Amish clothing. Jed was told that the women of the community would have his new clothes—made according to the local *ordnung*—ready for him in a week. In the meantime he'd have his own clothes and the ones he'd borrowed.

In this community, according to the *ordnung*, the button pattern was a little different on the front of the broadfall pants (there were two extra buttons that he felt were unnecessary, but those were the rules) and the hats had a slightly smaller brim and a narrower band. The work shirts—pullovers—could have pockets, and had three buttons instead of two. Other than that, Jed thought as he looked over the printed *ordnung*, not much was different than the *ordnung* he'd lived under his whole life. Buggies were the same color and styles, and the women's dress was almost identical to what he was used to seeing at home. It looked to Jed like as soon as he had his new clothes, he should fit right in here, and he was happy about that.

The waiting list for land distribution wasn't long, and he was thankful to learn that he'd be receiving his allotment of two hundred acres in a few weeks' time. Until then he was slated to stay with his old friend Matthias, another young, single farmer who was just getting started on his own farm. Matthias was supposed to come pick him up sometime the next day, and Jed was looking forward to seeing a friendly face from Old Pennsylvania.

Mr. Zook, the patriarch of the family that ran the Center, a strong man in his early thirties, talked to him and kept shaking his hand and patting him on the back like he was really excited to have him there in the community. Jed noticed that behind his back, or when people thought he wasn't looking, the local Amish stared at him and sometimes whispered.

The Greeting Center was more than a mile inside the AZ, and it was in a forested area dotted here and there with tobacco and cornfields fenced by split rails. Jed and Mr. Zook sat out on the porch of the Center, talking and watching the occasional buggy go by, and

Jed experienced that peculiarly Amish feeling of peace that overwhelmed him whenever he heard the clip-clop of hooves and the rattle of buggies as they passed. Mr. Zook spoke remarkably good English, with no trace of the Pennsylvania Dutch accent or dialect.

Jed would learn later that Mr. Zook had been a backsliding Amish who'd once left the fold to join the world back in Old Pennsylvania. He'd only agreed to rejoin the Church when he learned of the opportunity to emigrate to New Pennsylvania. As the operator of the Greeting Center, he still had some contact with both worlds, and that was the way he liked it. Jed's father had called men like Mr. Zook "political Amish" or "money Amish," since they weren't particularly religious men, and stayed in the Amish fold for reasons other than spiritual ones.

"Our community here is young, Jedediah. Our elders are mostly in their late twenties or early thirties. The few older folks we do have are converts who most likely came to New Pennsylvania as Englischers. Elders and bishops are still chosen by lots, so, as you can imagine, there are many more twenty-something-year-old Amishmen serving as elders than any other subset. That means we have a lot of energy but sometimes lack wisdom. I understand, though, and I know we'll grow into things after a few more decades."

An explosion, loud but distant, echoed through the air. Jed looked at Mr. Zook, who gave him a crooked half-grin.

"The war. It drags on and on. I follow the news more closely than many of the others. And I have the added opportunity to question a lot of travelers as they pass into the Amish Zone. It looks like the rebels have turned the tide. People are saying that the government is fleeing the city and moving their operations to the cities on the Shelf."

"What does that mean for the Amish?" Jed asked.

"We won't know for a while. There are some who say that the rebels are setting bombs in the roads and fields to harass Transport. Others say the rebels are honorable and would never do that. That they are careful not to kill civilians. But we have had some of our people die from the bombs. The rebels say it is because the government plants bombs so that they can blame it on the resistance. Both sides say they studiously avoid killing Amish.

"Most of our people just want the war to go away, but some whisper out of the other side of their mouths that they have to admit it: the Amish have grown wealthy selling food and supplies to both sides."

Jed whistled. "The Amish materially assist the rebels?"

"Not out in the open, but some do. Transport avoids searching Amish wagons and buggies when they leave the AZ out of fear of being seen as tyrants. I believe some of the Amish take advantage of this to deliver goods to the rebels. And many of our food shipments heading to the City are captured by TRACE units operating outside of town. Some say that's because our own people tip off the rebels as to when and where the shipments will be moving. Nobody cries or complains when shipments are taken. Nobody except the most mercenary among the Amish." Zook smiled at his own ironic claim.

"You talk freely of these things here?" Jed asked.

"I do," Zook said. "I find that it eliminates suspicion of all of the Amish if we are open about what is happening. And to be totally frank with you, most of the Amish don't think of these things at all. They just hear the bombs and want them to stop."

* * * *

Zook's wife had a full box of garden vegetables and other staples ready for Jed on the porch when Matthias pulled up in his buggy. Jed's friend bounded up the walk and shook Jed's hand vigorously with a huge smile on his face. "So good to see you, Jedediah Troyer!"

"I'm glad to finally be here, Matthias."

"How was your journey?"

"Just as the Englischers said it would be," Jed replied. "Scary, but safe and without any real incidents."

"Well, you'll fit right in here. It's very much like home. Today we will be helping my neighbors, the Schrocks, weed a cotton patch they've planted. I'm helping them with the crop from start to finish, and in the winter, the Schrocks will share some fabric with us."

Jed nodded. "That sounds great."

"It will be a short while before you get your allotment and can start on your own land, but take my word for it: without a family, it will be difficult. Many of the single men work together, and help out with the neighbors' farms. When we build, we'll have a lot of help too."

"I'm ready to get started, Matthias."

"Then off we go."

As they were loading the Zooks' vegetables into the buggy, Jed put his hand on Matthias's shoulder and smiled at his friend. "When Amos gets here in four years, we'll already be well on our way. In fact, Amos should be asleep right now in his pod, and when he opens his eyes, he'll be here."

Matthias didn't respond. He looked at Jed with sadness in his eyes. It looked to Jed like his friend's mouth wanted to form words, but could not. Then the moment passed, and Matthias smiled. "Let's go hoe weeds, Jedediah."

● ● ● ●

Jed's hoe worked expertly between the plants. Cotton here grew tall, and this crop, though still in its early stages, was already taller than most of the finished cotton Jed had seen back in the old world. But then again, most people didn't realize that cotton is a perennial bush, not an annual. In the old world, hybrid varieties were grown shorter so that machines and equipment could work the fields. Then chemicals were applied in the late fall to defoliate and kill the plant so that the stripping combines could get the cotton off cleanly. But true heritage cotton would grow as high as four or five feet, and once the bush became established, could produce crops year after year. This was the first year of this stand, and if things went well, Jed knew he'd be pulling cotton by October.

As he worked his blade between and around the plants, careful not to harm the roots, he thought of row crops he'd worked back in Old Pennsyvlania. Moving up and down the rows with Amos and his father, talking and laughing. Sometimes they would forget that they were working at all, and then they'd get to the end of a row and realize how much work they'd done while lost in conversation.

This is all real, Jed. But you need to remember what you've been through to get here. Don't forget the people who died in the City to get you out.

Jed heard the voice, but knew that there'd been no sound other than in his mind. It was a woman's voice, and it sounded very familiar. He looked around, and even checked around the adjacent rows to see if maybe one of the Amish girls was playing a joke on him.

Don't forget, Jed. I'm here for you, but they're *in*

here too.

He had a flash vision of a man holding a gun and pointing it at his face. He couldn't recall the place or the man, or anything else about the vision. It happened in the blink of an eye, but it felt like the beginnings of a memory. Then Matthias walked over with a canteen full of water. They both drank deeply, and as Jed watched Matthias drink, he tried to remember the vision, but could not.

"I'd like to go to that great wall, Matthias. The one that surrounds the AZ. I'd like to stand on it and look out over the world."

Matthias put the cap back on the canteen and wiped his mouth and his youthful beard with his sleeve. A drop of pure water glistened on the tip of his beard, and again Jed had that feeling that he should be remembering something.

"The Amish youth like to go up on the wall, but I've never seen the point in it," Matthias said. "We know what the English world is like, so I don't see any use in staring out at it."

"I'm new here, Matthias Miller. I'm like the English tourists, staring at our homes. I want to see it all."

Matthias chuckled. "All right, then. This evening, when work is done, we'll go stand on the wall and stare at the English world."

● ● ● ●

Jed smiled as he toured the tiny structure. Matthias's house was small and comfortable—more of a Dawdi Haus than a full-sized Amish home. In Amish culture, the *Dawdi Haus* is usually a smaller home, attached to or near the main house, which the farmer moves into when he retires and sells the farm and main house to one of his children. A large Amish family may sometimes have two or three Dawdi homes where the parents, grandparents, and even great-grandparents live and continue to participate as valuable members of the family.

It wasn't common for a new farmer to start with a Dawdi Haus, but these were interesting times on this new world, and Jed understood the necessity. At some point in the next few months, the community would show up at Jed's land and would build a similar house for him to live in. He heard his father's voice telling him to be thankful for all graces, and this made him smile the more.

"Why are you smiling like a cat, Jedediah?" Matthias asked. "Are you laughing at my tiny house?"

"I love it," Jed said. "I want one too."

Matthias nodded. "Well, you'll get one soon enough. In fact, the Church will be here to build my barn in a month's time. I've already been here awhile, and my turn for a barn is coming up quickly."

"A barn raising!" Jed said, and slapped Matthias on

the shoulder. "I haven't been to one since we put up the Stolzfuses' barn last summer."

"Not last summer, Jed," Matthias said. "A long time ago. You've been asleep for years."

Jed laughed. "Still. I'm looking forward to putting up a barn. You get out of practice, you know?"

Matthias showed him to his tiny room. It didn't take long. "On cold nights you'll want to do like me," Matthias said. "I sleep on fleeces in the kitchen near the wood stove. Not too many freezing nights this time of year, but sometimes." Matthias placed a full mason jar in Jed's hand. "Lard, for the lamp. Use it sparingly."

Once he'd shown Jed the room, Matthias left, and Jed checked out his new, temporary home. The small bed was of standard Amish make: instead of an Englischer mattress, ropes were stretched across the wooden frame to serve as springs, and these supported five boards, planed smooth, which in turn held piles of lamb's fleeces. The bed was pushed up against a wall, with little room to spare at the foot, and there was no dresser or other furniture, save for seven pegs that were set into the wall across from the bed at eye level. There was a single lamp that looked to be a fat lamp, and that was to suffice for his lighting.

Jed hung his spare set of clothing on one of the pegs, then sat on the bed and pulled off his boots. He placed the jar of lard under the bed, stretched out on the fleeces, and closed his eyes.

Matthias had told him that the Yoders would be

bringing by supper for a week or two, until Jed was settled in. "We'll have many meals out as well," Matthias had told him. "We work away a lot, so we eat very well."

Since he had an hour before supper, Jed decided to rest and try to calm himself of his excitement. He could hardly believe it: he was finally in New Pennsylvania! His dream was now within reach. He pressed his eyelids together and tried to imagine what his farm would be like.

But with his eyes closed tight, what he saw in his mind's eye was something else altogether. Jed saw the window from his barn back home. And strangely, it wasn't in the barn—it was sitting on a dirty old sofa in a dark room, lighted only by a lantern. Jed stared for a while at the old coffee can pane he'd used to fix the window, and then he fell asleep, and everything went black.

• • • •

Jed was standing in a darkened room, and the wall screen was there—a bright flat light that started out in two dimensions, and then grew until it surrounded him on every side like a cocoon. Then there were images on the screen, and they looked so real that he thought he was somewhere else entirely. His brother Amos was there, only he was an old man. And he seemed to be on trial. An Englischer read out crimes that Amos was supposed to have committed. Theft. Rebellion. Mass murder. The prosecutor offered evidence of these crimes, and Amos did not refute him. And images, like memories, flashed on the screen: of bombs, and war, and innocent people dead and dying. And then Amish men stood up, elders that Jed didn't recognize, and they offered testimony too. They said that Amos was guilty, and that he'd become as murderous as the Englischers, making war and killing.

Don't believe it, Jed. These are all lies.

Who are you? Jed thought.

It's Dawn. I'm your friend.

I love you.

I know.

＊＊＊＊

Later that evening, Jed and Matthias stood up on the great wall, facing east. It had taken them almost an hour to climb to the top, and Jed was exhausted. He'd been awakened from his nap by Matthias when the Yoders had shown up with the evening meal. After they'd supped, Matthias harnessed the horses and pulled the buggy out of the barn. It had taken forty-five minutes of driving to reach the wall.

"I don't come here much anymore," Matthias said. Darkness was falling, but from the top of the wall the two Amish men could see to the horizon. The blue of the gloaming was on the land, and lights were coming on in scattered country houses out in the English territory.

"Why not?" Jed asked.

"It's just the English. They come to stare at us. I don't spend much time staring back at them."

Gazing out over the landscape outside the wall, Jed examined the English homes, just their outlines as the light of day disappeared into the night. "The English are not unlike us in many ways," he said.

"That's a strange thing to say."

Jed looked over at his friend. "They just want to be happy, Matthias. They're just confused about what to do about it."

Matthias nodded. "I guess I never thought about it that way."

"I do," Jed said.

"I suppose they could start by ending all of their wars," Matthias said.

"That might be harder than we think."

Matthias thrust his hands down into the pockets of his broadfall pants. "What can be hard about choosing not to kill one another?"

"I don't think the English want to kill each other," Jed said. "At least most of them don't. They've been told what to want and what to think just like we have. They value different things."

"The elders say the English will always be at war. It's the way of their kind," Matthias said.

"I hope they're wrong," Jed said. And as he spoke the words, a blinding light—brighter than that of the sun—erupted in the distance. In a microsecond, the bright cloud broke over the horizon, turning night to day, and Jed instinctively pulled off his hat and covered his face. He turned to Matthias, who was doing the same thing.

Matthias tried to speak, but found that he could not. "What...?"

The bright light was somehow turning even brighter, and surrounded them in a glow that made it look like noon up on the wall.

"Don't look at it. We have to get down!" Jed shouted. He moved toward the stairs and pulled Matthias behind him. Once they were on the way down, they put their hats back on their heads and took the stairs two at a time. They were thirty feet down when the blast blew over the wall. It sounded exactly like they would have imagined the end of time would sound, and the hurricane winds blowing over their heads made a deafening roar.

"What could it be?" Matthias asked, out of breath from the running.

Jed steadied his friend as they continued their descent. "If it isn't the return of Christ, then something terrible bad has happened."

● ● ● ●

The City ceased to exist in a microsecond. Merrill's Antique Shoppe, Ye Olde World English Tavern, and thousands of other businesses, homes, and lives flashed into dust, and then blasted outward in a wind that reached hundreds of miles an hour in the blink of an eye.

On the command deck of the Tulsa, hundreds of miles away, an old man watched a wall screen, and what he saw took his breath and his words away. The mushroom cloud grew and grew. The old man's mouth flew open, but nothing came out.

From the telltale blues and purples, he could see that it had been an okcillium detonation. And because it was okcillium, the land would not be poisoned from radiation, and the sickness would not kill those who— thanks to distance or other geographical protection— weren't killed in the initial detonation of the bomb. The river would have boiled away nearest the City, and the land would be flat as a tabletop when and if intrepid explorers chose to investigate this spot. This vast, empty spot that had once been a large urban area, but was now, for all intents and purposes, a parking lot.

An officer appeared between Amos and the wall screen, and the man's eyes betrayed his fear and wonder. "Who—"

Amos didn't hesitate. "It was them." He ran his fingers through his graying hair. "They did it to themselves!"

Knot 4:

Thou Shalt Not

BREAKING GROUND

The plow dug into the soft loam, and the earth offered little resistance as the share turned the deep black soil up and out of the furrow. Jed clasped the reins in one hand, and used the other to pull off his hat and wipe his brow with his sleeve. This was going to be a new field for Matthias, beans for man and beast along with more nitrogen fixed in the soil. It was an important addition to Matthias's farm, as it meant independence from the feed store, and more product to share and trade in the community. Over the past year, the horses had grazed here, fertilizing the soil for the crop to come; now they'd been moved to the north field so that this one could go into production. As for Jedediah, he was being cut in on half of the prospective profits, to be used to pay for his barn when it came time to build it. Work like today's was money in the bank for a young Amishman.

The plow was fancy as far as Jedediah was

concerned—far more than he would need to get started. It was a two-bottom with step pedals in the forecart, so the farmer could plow in either direction without circling around each time like he had to with a single-bottom plow. Matthias had said he'd bought this plow from a young blacksmith who was fabricating them based on plans someone found in an old catalog from the City. Of course, that was back when there *was* a City. Back before the explosion.

Meeting tonight, Jed thought as he looked back across the field. The elders had called a voluntary meeting so that the Amish could talk about the destruction of the City, and what that portended for the community.

Ten days had passed since the big bomb had ended the plain people's love-hate relationship with the City. And with the closest urban center reduced to dust, ash, and soot, things had necessarily changed in the AZ. Things were tighter now. There was some trepidation and worry; some of the Amish had grown too dependent on city goods and services. Trade with the English had ground to a halt, traffic at the emigration point had virtually stopped, and memorial funerals for those Amish who'd been out of the AZ and doing business in or near the city were still taking place on Sundays. Ten at a time on most Sabbath days, and sometimes there was a single service for a whole family. The funerals would probably be going on for a month or more, Jed thought, as he pulled up at the end of the row. He tied the reins around the brake and stepped off the forecart to stretch his back and legs.

That's when the lights went off in his mind again—the

first time it had happened since the big bomb—and he found himself once again standing in the inky blackness, staring at the white screen. It always scared him when it happened, but somehow he knew, somewhere deep inside himself, that he wasn't going to be harmed.

He expected her. The woman he thought would soon appear before him. The woman that he knew he loved. He didn't know *how* he knew this, or who the woman might be, but still he knew that he loved her. Right now, standing in the darkness, he couldn't even picture her, but with only the bright glow of the screen illuminating his form, he waited for her. And then she was there.

"Jed," Dawn said.

"Yes."

"Do you remember me?"

"No."

"I'm Dawn, and I'm your friend."

"I know." Somehow he did. Now that she said it.

She took his hand, and when she did, a part of his mind engaged, and he remembered her more completely. The screen expanded and wrapped around them like he knew it would, and they were at his farm in Old Pennsylvania. It stopped being a screen, and it felt like they were really there. As they passed the barn, walking up to the old porch, he felt the pull, and he glanced up and saw that the window was still missing.

Dawn led him by the hand until they were seated on the porch. Jed felt the soft breeze and smelled foxglove and touch-me-nots in the air, and off in the distance he saw himself walking down the drive, away from his home, heading for the airbus stop up by the road. They were in his last day on Earth.

Just as Jed was becoming completely absorbed in the scene, Dawn threw up her hand, did a little tap with it, and everything around them froze. Then Dawn swiped her hand, and the scene shrank down to a tiny square that she moved to one side with her finger. As she did this, the word "minimized" appeared in Jed's view. The word followed the small picture, and once he'd noticed and absorbed its meaning, it faded away.

That's when Jed realized that some kind of program must be giving him the vocabulary for whatever was happening. It was a little alarming to him that he hadn't really registered this before, and yet all of this knowledge overflowed him like he was being baptized in it. He'd always been too wrapped up in the strangeness of it all to recognize the background reality. But now he understood that his mind was being rapidly trained to function in this new world, and he realized that Dawn—or someone else—had probably done this for him.

Once again, the two of them were standing together in the dark room.

"Do you know what year it is, Jed?" Dawn asked.

"This... this vision—when I left home—was nine years ago. When I emigrated. That was the day I met you. I was eighteen, and the year was 2068."

Dawn nodded again and smiled at him, "So what year is it now? Right now. While you're plowing that field in New Pennsylvania?"

"Nine years of travel," Jed said, "so it's 2077, right?"

Dawn smiled, but it was a nervous smile, as if she

wanted to soften a blow, but had something she really needed to say. "Wrong. It's 2121, Jed. You arrived here in the year 2121."

Jed's eyebrows lowered and he narrowed his eyes. "How can it be 2121? I'd be... I'd be... somewhere around seventy years old!"

"You slept for a very long time."

"I'm sleeping *now*," Jed said. "This is a dream."

"No, it isn't. It's real." Dawn reached over and took his hand in hers. "You have a BICE unit in your head, and I've hacked into it. Transport hasn't connected with you in a while. They've been busy ever since they destroyed their own city with an okcillium bomb."

"If I've been asleep for that long," Jed asked, "then why has the technology basically stayed the same?"

"Well, it's not exactly the same. This is a pretty advanced implanted reality system right here. Better than anything from the old world, but you wouldn't know anything about that."

"But there are airbuses, BICEs, Q, TRIDs. I just thought the future would be more... different."

"There are reasons for that," Dawn said. "Not the least of which is this war. But with access to okcillium now, TRACE is making advances greater than you can imagine."

Jed shrugged. "Well, I'm probably not the best judge of any of that." He looked at the minimized scene of his barn, and then he touched it and enlarged it just a bit. He flicked his finger, and the scene played forward. He watched himself boarding an airbus out on the lane, and then things started to occur to him. Forgotten memories began to surface, but they were random, and he wasn't sure how he knew things. He just knew them.

"But I'm not on Q now. I haven't smelled the orange zest smell," he said. He minimized the scene again and looked at Dawn.

She closed her eyes for a second and then opened them again. "The Yoders have been bringing you your meals, haven't they?"

"Yes, but—"

"Your food is laced with Q. You probably haven't noticed it because they kept you on it during your entire sleep cycle."

"The Yoders are working for Transport?"

"Yes, I'm afraid so. And they aren't the only government spies who've infiltrated the Amish community."

Jed was silent a while. Once again he enlarged the image of the farm and activated it—and watched as the airbus lifted off and departed. Then he flicked his finger and the scene disappeared. Dawn was still in front of him, still in her Amish dress. He shook his head, then looked down at her. "Do you know who they all are? The spies?"

"No, not all of them." Dawn said. "I'm doing the best I can with what I have to work with. Things are... tricky right now. With the bombing of the City, the war has moved into a new and more dangerous phase."

"And you're saying Transport bombed their own city? Why would they do that?" Jed asked.

Dawn responded with a question. "Who are the Amish saying did it?"

Jed took a deep breath. "According to Matthias, most

of them think the rebels did it."

"Exactly," Dawn said. "And are the Amish still trading with the rebels?"

"I don't know," Jed said. "Probably not as much as they were."

"Now you're answering your own questions. *That's* why Transport did it. They did it because they were going to lose the City anyway. The writing was on the wall. They didn't want to turn it over to TRACE, so they blew it up and blamed it on their enemy. It's called a 'false flag' attack. It's as old as war itself."

"So Transport just killed all those people? Even people that supported them? And all the Amish who were there?"

"They did."

Jed walked past Dawn, and with his hand he enlarged the white screen. He played with its size and then, without knowing just how he did it, he brought up his BICE control console. His was preset and organized in the form of a huge wall of drawers, like a filing cabinet. With his mind he changed the format so that the information bits appeared as envelopes, and then as glowing red dots, and then milk cows in stalls. All the while, as he played with his BICE control setup, Dawn just looked on patiently and did not interrupt.

After a few minutes, Jed changed the control icons back to drawers and then turned to Dawn. "It's a lot to take in," he said finally.

"I know it is," she said.

"The year 2121 you say?"

"Yes."

Jed reached out and opened a drawer with *BICE Control Programs* written on it. "How does this work? This information system in my head?"

"It integrates into your brain functions. Every brain deals with the information differently—so the question is hard to answer. Sometimes the brain takes the new reality and input and creates its own system of dealing with it."

Jed was nodding now. "Like when Carl Miller got kicked in the head by a horse?"

"I'm not sure what you mean," Dawn said.

"Well, due to the pressure and damage in his brain, doctors had to remove almost a quarter of it. They said he'd never talk again, and that the part of his brain that controlled walking was located in the portion that was removed, so... you know... he had to live in a wheelchair. Then... it's weird, but a few years later he started walking and talking again. The doctors said that his brain rewired itself. That it doesn't always happen, but it happens often enough."

"Yes," Dawn said. "It's like with Carl Miller, then. Every brain is different, and not every person processes information in the same way."

"Why are you so good at it?" Jed asked.

"I don't know," Dawn said, and as she spoke she brought up an animated schematic, which looked to Jed like an aerial view of a big city at night from high in an airbus. The lights moved somewhat chaotically, but at the same time they all seemed to follow paths and get where they needed to go. "I just *see* the information flow, like maybe when you're milking a cow or out plowing Matthias's field—how you just see what you should do, and all of your senses work together to show you what's happening and what you should do next."

"Can you show *me* how to do that?" Jed asked.

"I've been showing you—mostly while you've been sleeping. You'll recall more and more of what I've taught you when you need the information."

"I just wish you could stay here and teach me," Jed said.

Dawn was silent for a minute before she spoke again. "Jed?"

"Yes."

"Do you remember the stories your parents would teach you as a child about the early Anabaptists—the early Amish—and how they'd meet for worship out in the woods, or in a secluded barn?"

"Of course," Jed said. "We're all raised with stories of persecution. To remind us that it can come back at any time."

Dawn nodded. "Right. And do you remember anything about those stories of secret, underground meetings that applies to what we're learning now about your BICE?"

"I don't know," Jed said. "What... what do you want me to say?"

"Think about it."

Jed tried to imagine those meetings, when the Amish were being pursued by the Catholics or the Protestants, and how they'd always try to find a place where they could flee quickly if need be. "There was always a way out. Always a place to run."

Dawn smiled. "Exactly, Jed. In programming we call

those routes a 'back door.' And a back door goes both ways. It can be a secret way back into a program, or a secret way to get out."

Jed nodded, but he wasn't yet sure what she was trying to tell him.

"Always remember that just about every system, every program, has a back door. Almost invariably. All of this technology was designed by people, and many of those people had the same fears, and the same spirit of independence and freedom, that our—that *your*—ancestors had."

"But how does all this apply to what we're facing today?" Jed asked. "Tell me something I can use right now, Dawn."

"Well... how can I say it?"

"Just say it."

"New Pennsylvania was always a back door. And sometimes even back doors have back doors."

Dawn cleared the white screen and brought the farm back up, then maximized it until they were actually in the scene again, sitting on the Troyers' front porch.

Jed stood up and walked to the porch railing, looking out over the green yard toward a walnut tree he knew by heart. "And why did they leave me asleep so long? If it only takes nine years to get here?"

Dawn stood and placed a hand on Jed's back, and when he turned to her she looked up at him and smiled. "Jed. 'Here' is the issue. It's the one question you haven't known to ask, and it was the one we weren't authorized to answer."

"I'm still on Earth," Jed said. He looked into her

eyes. "You don't want to tell me anything because I'm still on Earth, aren't I?"

Dawn didn't answer him. She didn't say anything at all. And when the tension had risen to the point that Jed was going to speak, Dawn grabbed his face and kissed him, and this time he let her.

(21

TRACE AT THE BASE

Pook wrote down the numbers on the pad with the stub of a pencil he found lying on the old gray boards that Martinez was now calling his "desk." His unit had been in camp now for over a week, but in the confusion and disruption following the detonation of the okcillium bomb that had leveled the City, command was just now catching up and organizing after-action reports.

Ten days after that shocking event, TRACE Intelligence was reporting that most, if not all, of Transport's forces had abandoned the east and had retreated beyond the Great Shelf. Now, Pook was responsible for reporting on the state of his unit. With a pencil and a piece of paper. The numbers he'd written on the notepad were cold and sterile—digits without meaning, corpses without faces—but the figures stood in for the real men and women he'd lost in the failed operation to get the Amish boy to the AZ. Numbers rarely tell all of the truth, not even after an attack like the one on the City, with a body count that rose above the ability for humans to rightly comprehend it. But the TRACE fighters he'd lost were far more than numbers to Pook Rayburn. They were his friends. His comrades-in-arms. They were members of his family. And despite all the years he'd been a part of the resistance, he never got used to losing friends.

He told himself again that he was just a soldier, and that it wasn't his job to question the reason for losses, for the risks taken. He reminded himself that his duty was to follow orders, and that he had no cause at all—after all these years—to question the SOMA and his decisions. The old man had selflessly served, and brilliantly too, since before Pook was born. Still, the numbers glared back at him from the page. Their accusations goaded him, and he had to cover his face with his hand to hide from the things they prodded him to say and think.

Pook slipped the paper to Martinez without a word and walked out of the barn that served as their temporary base camp. He walked to where his crew stood outside, waiting to find out what would happen next. When he got to the men, he slapped Jeff Wainwright on the back, gripped the man's shoulder and turned to face him.

"You take Jerry Rios and see that he gets fully outfitted. Then walk him through all of our procedures and unit opsec, got it?"

Jeff nodded. "Yes, sir. What about weapons? He only has the pistol you printed back in the City."

There. That was it. A millisecond of shared recognition. Any mention of the City was a vivid reminder that they'd each barely escaped the flash death inflicted on the multitudes who'd remained there. That realization, unspoken, with its associated feelings of gratitude, grief, and unworthiness, settled on the squad.

Pook exhaled deeply. "Get with Martinez. Make sure everyone is back up to par, and that we're all ready to roll in five if we get the call."

"Yes, sir."

Jeff and Jerry headed for the barn, and Pook turned to the remainder of his unit. "We're on hold. Waiting again."

"Hurry up and wait, eh Pook?" Billy said.

"That's it," Pook said. "You all know the drill."

"Any word on Dawn?"

Pook shook his head. "The kid made it to the AZ—apparently after they chipped him and tried to reprogram his brain. Dawn got in there too, although we don't know where she is physically. She's out there somewhere, and Transport is holding her, but she's successfully hacked the system. So there's that." He pulled out a cigarette and put it between his lips. Then he smacked his pocket, looking for his okcillium lighter before realizing he didn't have it anymore.

"Damn."

Billy tossed him a book of matches—an old pack with the name and logo of a bar from the City on it. Pook looked at it and then back at Billy. He struck a match and lit the cigarette, then closed the matchbook and tossed it back. "That's a collector's item now."

Billy stuck the matchbook back in his pocket, then rolled his finger at Pook—a sign to get his leader talking again.

"I wish I could tell you more, but that's all there is to tell. No one on our side knows where she is," Pook said.

Billy looked down and kicked the stones with his boot. "I promised Ben I'd keep an eye on her."

Pook breathed deeply. "Your brother was a good man. He'd know you've done your best. We've *all* done our best. He'd also know that no one can really keep an eye on Dawn when she has her mind set on something. She's pigheaded; always has been. But he and Dawn fought side by side. They were more than husband and wife. They were teammates. He knew what we were facing, and he'd understand that she's working on a program totally outside of our area of operations. It's above our pay grade, too."

"It's hard to know what Ben would think," Billy said.

Ducky, the short, muscular man who was Pook's second in command, had stood silent throughout this exchange, like a tempest in the distance, barely stirring over the horizon. But now, as the topic turned to what was going on in the resistance, the storm blew in. "I can tell you one thing," Ducky said. He was visibly angry, and had to interrupt himself frequently to take a deep breath to calm himself. "Ben would probably have a *lot* to say about this crap going on with the Amish dude—Jed." Pause. Deep breath. "Good men and women getting killed to save the SOMA's kid brother!" Pause. Breath. "He'd definitely have something to say, I can tell ya that!"

"Careful, Duck," was all that Pook said. The two friends stared at one another before Duck broke the silence.

"I'm not being insubordinate, Pook. I'm here and I'm following orders no matter what. I'm just telling it how it is. We're out here dying, and for what?"

"We've always been out here dying, Duck," Pook said. "And always for the same reason. What's changed? We take orders, and we do what we're told. That's what we've always done. That's what we did when Ben Beachy was here, and that's what we're doing now."

"Except that then, we knew what we were doing was one-hundred-percent resistance business. We *knew* it, Pook. Not personal business."

Pook took a step toward Ducky. It wasn't in any way menacing, but the motion did carry with it the weight of authority. He spoke softly, evenly. "Every one of us would be dead, imprisoned, or worse if it weren't for the SOMA. I'm not the kind of guy who starts second-guessing a leader who has never—not once, *ever*, in my whole life—failed me or the resistance. If he'd made a bunch of mistakes, or if he'd brought us to the brink of defeat... you know, I'd still follow orders, but I'd feel more comfortable questioning his leadership. But what has the SOMA done for us? Has he ever failed us? Are we not on the very doorstep of wiping out Transport and winning the war? Do we not have the upper hand?" Pook pointed toward the sky and then swung his hand around, indicating the surrounding area. "Look at us. Standing under this blue sky and not hiding out in buildings or underground. When have we *ever* been comfortable doing this in the past five years? And why do we feel pretty safe right now? Because Transport has fled beyond the Shelf, Duck!"

Pook reached out his hand and put it on Ducky's

shoulder. It was a sign of understanding, and of peace, but it also was a symbol of steadfast obedience and loyalty to a superior. "So here's the deal, friend. All of you. I love you all. We've fought together and we've been through some tough things. We've bled, and some of our people have died for this..." Ducky nodded, as did everyone else in the unit.

After a short pause, Pook continued. "So for now... Ducky... all of you... just shut the hell up. Just—respectfully—*shut up.* If you have a problem, bottle it up and keep your mouth zipped about it. I don't want to hear one more word of negativity unless you have some grounds for it that'll stand up to scrutiny, and even then, it'd better be something that helps us all. Am I understood?"

Ducky looked up at Pook, who was a full six inches taller. "Yes, sir." There was still anger in his voice, but it was subdued, and he'd regained his composure.

"Yes, sir," everyone else said.

Goa Eagles—swarthy, unkempt, and now overloaded with partial bits of clothing and coats he'd somehow conned from the quartermaster—chose this moment to walk up to the group. As always, he was chewing vigorously on a greenish mass. He spat a huge globule and smiled.

"Good speeching, Pook." Eagles arched his neck and thrust out his arms in a cartoonish impersonation of Pook. He raised his voice an octave higher and began to pace back and forth, glowering at everyone. He spit out another big, nasty load of green slime and then wiped his mouth with his arm.

"Being shut! Words, wording, words! Shutting up!" Eagles looked over at Pook, who was trying hard not to laugh. "Looking at Eeguls! Eeguls being the Pook! Everyone shutting! Got it?" By this point, everyone in the unit was laughing, and Eagles took their laughter as further encouragement. He turned to Ducky. "You... you being shut!" He winked at Ducky, then looked the shorter fighter up and down. "Also being un-tall." With that, Eagles threw out his chest and walked away, to the raucous laughter of everyone who had heard him.

22

LIVING ON TULSA TIME

The Great Shelf was, for now, the new front in the war. This latest government attack—an air assault on TRACE reconnaissance forces patrolling on this side of the cliffs—was half-hearted, a token gesture. TRACE forces hadn't yet attempted to penetrate past the Great Shelf to pursue the Transport-controlled assets that had retreated from the City. When the resistance launched their offensive, that's when the real battle would begin.

The SOMA watched as two of his fighters took out a Transport attack craft, the defeated aircraft disintegrating and plummeting in parts and fire and smoke toward the earth. Thus far, it seemed like Transport was just doing their best to regroup and lick their wounds. For the most part they'd pulled in their horns. With the exception of the perfunctory action the SOMA was now observing, intelligence reported no evidence of a pending counterattack.

The view that the SOMA had on the big screens in his office constantly changed perspectives. Looking at the scenes on display, you'd think that dozens of camera ships or drones must be zipping around out there providing the coverage, but there were no actual cameras involved. Instead, the graphics were constructed very accurately based on data gathered by sensors on all of his ships—and by every other sensor within range of the battlefield. The new TRACE Optimal Battle System (TOBS) relied not only on TRACE-specific encrypted data, which provided real-time location and identification information, but also on other airborne information, including data that was never specifically intended for TRACE or battlefield use. In short, TOBS utilized *all* available wireless broadband data, because even if the data was from an email between two BICEs, or was part of a computer game, or the sharing of a salsa recipe, that bit of data still had to travel through the air from somewhere to somewhere else. And TOBS was able to use this data to more perfectly render the battlefield in real time, like an early twenty-first century Doppler radar could model a tornado based on wind direction, air pressure, the reflections from bits of sand and debris carried by the storm, temperature variations, and a variety of other sources.

Using TOBS in combination with the implanted TRACE *Corinth* chips, TRACE and enemy ships could be nearly perfectly rendered in 3-D space. As could lasers and other ordnance. Data was cross-referenced and processed, in real time, using information stored in multiple remote systems. This aggregated information then became the foundation of the rendering program.

And the beauty of TOBS was that the individual ships didn't need to carry and support the computing power required to produce the finished visual product, although a rough version of the information was available on each ship captain's BICE and support screens. The ships needed only to transmit the data for rendering off-vessel, and to have enough computing power to receive and display the final visual. And this off-vessel rendering wasn't dependent on the functioning of any one part. Flexibility and redundancy were the hallmarks of TOBS. In fact, the system was intentionally fluid, utilizing an AI management system that altered the system's architecture on the fly.

On each ship, one—or in some cases more than one—intelligence officer had been implanted with the *Corinth* chip. The Corinth was the heart and soul of the TOBS and was effectively the fourth-generation BICE chip, something beyond even what Transport could imagine in its utility and complexity. The *Corinth* was able to take the raw data stream and compress it, encrypt it, and hide it in regular or worthless bits of data always zipping around the planet in the air. The system had become so efficient and effective that it was now fully possible for battle commanders to do what gamers had been doing for a very long time: zoom around the battlefield and *virtually* see things that their forebears had only dreamed of seeing.

The TRACE rebel ships weren't entirely dependent on this advanced TOBS technology, though. The ships could just as easily fly and fight without the lightning-fast rendering or the off-vessel intelligence support. If they had to. And they could fly and fight old-school if need be: dog-fighting, just as air forces had been doing for over two hundred years. But experience showed that when TRACE ships had access to TOBS, their forces were nearly impossible to defeat.

TRACE's technological advantage—itself a fairly recent reality—was a product of the fact that tech-loving geeks and programmers almost invariably end up siding against any system that is anti-freedom. A fact that governments throughout time have had a tendency to forget... to their own detriment. And the slow brain drain of programmers and technicians from Transport to TRACE had turned into a tidal wave once it began to look very much like TRACE could actually win the war. Geniuses who'd been raised on Q had held off on giving the government their newest and best ideas and improvements, because foundationally they'd never really supported Transport's imperial aims. Most of these technical personnel had applied for, or been recruited into, Transport jobs only because they were the only game in town, if you wanted to work with the best resources on the most advanced projects.

And now that TRACE had not only the brain power, but ready access to okcillium—enough that they could use it for something other than "clean" bombs, a few neat gadgets, and impressive parlor tricks—the technological leap forward in the last few years had been remarkable.

Amos Troyer leaned back in his chair. For an instant his mind flashed back to the Battle of Lawton, when Transport had surrounded the entire Southern Oklahoma Militia and defeat had been nigh; and he—just a young Amish teenager holding a World-War-II-era rifle with no ammunition left in it—had taken a battle knife from a dead Transport soldier, thinking it would be the last tool he'd ever use before dying. Terrified and clutching that knife, he'd closed his eyes and imagined his older brother Jed, sleeping peacefully in a spaceship bound for a virginal planet lush with verdant life. That thought had given him comfort when he thought his own days were numbered.

Amos felt like closing his eyes now. Here on this ship, an old man, and a tired one at that, he could imagine the end of the war, and his own inevitable exodus from power. Whoever and whatever government formed in the vacuum left by the destruction of Transport—whenever that occurred—would have access to technology the likes of which no people anywhere had ever mastered. That fact meant that when this war was over, freedom would face an even greater peril than it had ever faced before. Irony, like sin, never rests. The technology to control and destroy people always has in it the seeds of tyranny, and is forever subject to the lowest angels of human nature. And now he, Amos Troyer, controlled that power; and it frightened him more than he'd ever admit to his subordinates.

The SOMA opened his desk to grab a Q tablet, and as he reached for the pill, he saw the old battle knife—the same blade he'd relied on those many years ago outside Lawton, Oklahoma, when he knew for sure that he was going to die. The knife he'd used to kill countless men in his determination to set other people free.

Thou Shalt Not Kill.

The phrase rang in his mind again whenever he looked at the weapon. He unsheathed the blade, held it up before his face, and studied it. Though he knew every ding and every scratch on its surface, it always caused his heart to skip whenever he held it. Slowly, he slid the knife back into the sheath and then exhaled. He threw the pill into his mouth and chewed it up quickly, then leaned back in his chair and closed his eyes. Almost immediately his young avatar appeared in his BICE control room. Through the fog, he heard someone enter his office and say, "Sir, your report—", but he held up his hand to silence and dismiss the ensign, and his surroundings became quiet again. The almond bitterness on his tongue always accompanied the peace that flooded him when he was on Q.

For a moment, he felt his consciousness existing in three places. The feeling of being in his office, reclining in his chair, faded first. He was also in his BICE room, watching as his filing cube floated in the center of the space. His third self was, for a moment, back in Old Pennsylvania, with the young boys playing corner ball after a wedding, but that memory faded quickly too. In short order his consciousness was one again, and he was fully present in the darkness of his BICE control room.

He reached out and turned the floating cube with his hand, and when the far face of the cube came to the front, he saw that one of the drawers glowed, indicating he had an important message.

DB

Amos looked down at himself—at his avatar—and saw that he was his youthful, muscular, and vibrant self, so he immediately changed his avatar to match his sixty-seven-year-old reality. Then he flicked open the file, and when that cube instantly appeared and enlarged, he flicked his wrist to open the *Direct Message* square. In a flash, Dawn was standing in front of him. For the first time, he saw her in the new form and dress she'd adopted for her avatar. She was translucent, but appeared clad in Amish garb: a dark blue dress with white cape and apron. Her avatar appeared to sleep, but her right hand glowed, indicating that there was no stored message. Dawn, wherever she was, was waiting for him to appear so that she could talk to the SOMA directly.

Dawn's avatar awoke and became solid. She nodded her head at her commanding officer and said, "Sir." The resistance had long given up formal ranks, addresses, and salutes—other than the simple terms of address "sir" and "ma'am," which were usually reserved for officers.

Dawn and Amos had once been very close friends, especially after the commander of the Southern Oklahoma Militia had presided over her wedding to Ben Beachy. Ben, another young former Amishman, had been exiled to Oklahoma after being arrested for bartering with individuals wanted by the government for aiding the resistance—and he had lived a life that, until its violent end, had closely modeled Amos's own. Since those early days, Amos's and Dawn's fates had taken them down very different paths, but the SOMA still had a fondness and a paternal affection for Dawn—even if the nature of their working relationship added a certain stress and awkwardness to their friendship.

"You have a report for me?" Amos said.

Dawn nodded and assumed an "at ease" stance that looked strange and ironic in the dress she'd chosen for her avatar. "As you know, sir, civilian Internet communications have been spotty since the bomb went off. It's fortunate that we were able to mirror so many of Transport's data hubs before it happened. And thanks to our recent technological advances, we've been able to re-route our own data quicker than we'd originally thought. Between TOBS and the Corinth, we're now nearly one hundred percent independent of terrestrial systems and hubs."

"Good." Amos waved for Dawn to continue.

"I'm in contact with Jedediah. We're making progress through his BICE, but I still don't know what he remembers when he's awake in the real world. Transport is trying hard to reconnect with him, but thus far I've been able to block and confuse their attempts, and I've given them clues to suggest that the fault lies with the bomb's substantial damage to the Internet infrastructure. But that little trick won't work much longer. Their data flow looks like they've called out all the dogs, and their spiders are searching hard for whatever's causing the disruption. If they have one programmer who's half as good as I am, they'll have it figured out soon enough."

Dawn called up an image that expanded until it took up half of the control room and the screen filled with lighted lines, glowing cables, through which data bits were flowing. The flow didn't look like water in a pipeline, but like little glowing bullets, all of different colors—some larger and some smaller—streaming down each of the cables. Data trackers, taking the form of small mechanized spiders with glowing eyes, were scouring each line. Each spider would skitter a few steps, then stop and analyze the information bullets as they passed. The animation was a real-time representation of Transport's search for the interruption in their communications with Jedediah Troyer. "This is only one hub. Imagine this on a global scale," Dawn said.

Amos nodded. "Have you left any clues that will lead them to you?"

"I hope not, sir." She shifted her weight, a sign of nervousness. "I can't know how good their techs are. If they suck, like they usually do, we have a little time, but not much."

"Here's hoping they suck," Amos said with a smile.

"I've told Jed what I think I'm allowed to tell him. But now..."

"But now... what?" Amos asked.

"But now I'm asking your permission to tell him everything. Where we are. What's happening."

"No." Amos shook his head. "Not yet."

"But, sir—"

"No." Now Amos paced back and forth, his hands behind his back. "Let's not forget that capturing Jed is intended to be a public relations coup for Transport. They're back on their heels now. Reeling. They foolishly think they still have an opportunity to win the hearts and minds of the people; and perhaps they believe they'll convince the elders of the Amish to stop their people from feeding us or providing material aid to the resistance. The retreat to the Shelf has them on life support. Their goal has been to embed Jed with the Amish, and then use him to get to me. We can't risk them finding out that we're using Jed too."

"They've blamed the bombing of the City on you, sir," Dawn said.

"I know, but that lie will never stand for long. And when people find out that they destroyed their own city and killed thousands of people, the whole move will backfire."

Dawn looked the SOMA in the eye. "He's hanging by a thread, sir. He needs to know."

Amos paused, and met Dawn's stare. "Give him what you have to, but remember, if they crack him, they'll turn anything you've said to him around. They'll twist it, and it will all be worse for him in the long run."

Dawn shrugged. "I understand."

Amos exhaled, an indication that he intended to change the subject. "I'm putting Pook and his unit on standby. In case they need to go in and get you."

"They should be focused on Jedediah, sir. If anyone is going to need exfil when the time comes, it'll be Jed."

"You let me handle giving orders, Dawn," Amos said. His tone was stern, but not too harsh. "That's my job." He glanced back up at the screen, where the spiders were still scanning the data streams looking for clues. "You've done well, Dawn. And you have your hands full. Get Jed fully ready, because they'll have him back soon enough."

Dawn looked at Amos. "All of this for a PR victory."

Amos put his hands behind his back and fixed the stare of his avatar on Dawn. "A PR victory? That's what Transport wants out of him. But Jed means so much more than that to me. He's not only my brother, whom I love dearly. He's a Trojan horse."

Dawn nodded, and for a moment she had a faraway look on her face. "Is that why you've had me implant so many rapid learning programs into his BICE?"

Amos's nod was almost imperceptible. "I remember when I was him... a young Amish man with a pure heart. Mostly uncorrupted except for what I did in the war." He winced and bit his lip when he thought about it. His eyes closed for a moment before he continued. "And I hacked into the TRIDs on just my second time in the system! Nobody could believe it. But I did it because I didn't know I couldn't."

"I've read about that," Dawn said.

"People don't realize that the Amish think differently than everyone else," Amos touched his avatar face, which was smooth and shaved, and inhaled deeply. "It's not just that we—they—don't use a lot of the technology the world uses. It's that their brains are actually wired differently. All of this wiring starts for all of us when we're just babies, you know?"

Dawn nodded, but she didn't want to interrupt, so she remained silent.

"And Jed was always so clever," Amos said. "Smarter than even the elders. It's like that piece of coffee can he formed to take the place of the windowpane in our barn. His mind worked like that. He was a puzzle solver. He already thought differently than everyone else."

Just then, Dawn's avatar pitched forward. She was still standing, but something had happened. Her head twitched and then her eyes closed and she went translucent. Transport had figured out what she was up to, and they'd finally gotten to her.

To Amos, it wasn't entirely unexpected. He'd known they'd sniff her out eventually. It was all part of his larger plan. Still, it was startling to see her shut down right in front of his eyes.

Almost at the same moment—just a few beats after the data stream with Dawn had been compromised—the Tulsa lurched under Amos's feet, and his own stream blanked out. Sitting at his desk, he was thrown violently out of his chair and he sprawled across the floor. A sharp pain stabbed through his chest and immediately registered, even through the Q—

A broken rib.

The Tulsa was shaking and groaning, something he'd never before experienced with the ultra-silent ship. He grimaced and tried to pull himself to his feet.

The door slid open and an ensign ran in with two officers, McKay and Warren.

"Sir!" McKay shouted.

They helped him to his feet and then sat his chair upright so that he could sit in it.

"Are you all right, sir?" McKay asked.

"Don't worry about me," Amos barked. "What's happening?"

McKay straightened up and reactivated the screens in Amos's office; they'd gone into hibernation mode while he was on his BICE.

"We're under attack, sir," McKay said matter-of-factly. "Three warships, Berlin class. Apparently they've located the Tulsa and they've engaged."

"We didn't see them coming?"

"No, sir."

"How did they breach our defenses?"

Warren winced noticeably. "Somehow they hacked us, sir."

The ensign was trying to unbutton the SOMA's shirt to inspect the injury, but Amos was ignoring him and pushed the young man away. "Someone... *somewhere...* has tracked and penetrated our data stream?" Amos said, pointing to McKay. "An impossibility! Shut down Corinth communications... *NOW!*"

(23

HACKER

Jed floated in the inky blackness, wondering how long he'd been in that state. Ages? Lifetimes? Then slowly, his consciousness returned to him, and he was in his black room with the glowing screen. He remembered now: he'd been talking to the woman named Dawn, and he'd asked her if he was on Earth. He remembered kissing her. He could recall it now that the darkness was rolled back a bit, with the white screen shining garishly in the darkness and illuminating his body.

And then he remembered something else. Matthias shaking him; he'd opened his eyes and found himself standing next to the horses and the plow, and Dawn had disappeared, never able to answer the question about where he was. That was all a memory, too.

Matthias had been worried, and despite Jed's insistence, had made Jed go lie down for a nap. Jed remembered that now, Matthias pushing him toward the little house. And he remembered that he didn't argue too much, because he wanted to be with Dawn. *Was that her name?* Yes. Dawn. He'd thought then that if he could go to sleep, Dawn would come back for him. So he'd gone to his room and climbed on the fleeces he used for a mattress, and before long he was in a deep sleep.

Sometime during his slumber he'd entered this present blackness. And now the screen was here, and he could remember Dawn, and was hoping that she'd be back to get him. To take him somewhere to talk. But she didn't appear this time; another woman did.

It was his mother. Only it wasn't his mother. He knew that. The word "avatar" floated over her head and then disappeared. It wasn't her, but it *looked* like her. And she was talking to him, and pulling up data as she talked. Reorganizing files. Telling him that someone evil—someone named Dawn—had hacked into his mind, but that now he was safe again.

Jed watched as files opened, and the thing that looked like his mother was erasing and changing the information in them. And then he had other memories—memories that didn't seem right. He remembered watching battles with Dawn, but this time the Transport forces were performing heroically, and as the battles progressed, martial music played. He saw an image of a city being destroyed, and there was death, destruction, and horror, and words appeared in the smoke and clouds...

TRACE DID THIS.

While the woman worked in front of a long wall of file drawers, Jed searched in his memory for Dawn. He found her, and he remembered that she had once taught him how to hide data. She'd taught him so many things that he was only now recalling. So he gathered all of the information and conversations he'd had with her. He did it in his mind so that his avatar didn't move, and he tagged all the data just like Dawn had told him to. The woman worked away in the drawers and mostly ignored him.

Jed found that his ability to manipulate the data happened faster and cleaner the more he worked with it. He was even able to retrieve files directly from the woman without her knowing he'd done it. Once he stole a file right out of her hand, and the avatar of his mother kept moving as if she still had it. She continued to file a piece of information that she could see, but which was no longer really there. She began humming as she worked, in the same way Jed's mother used to hum, and he knew then that they were mining his memories in order to trick him.

While the woman hummed and worked, Jed worked too. He flicked his wrist, and a keypad appeared before him, and it had the letters of the alphabet on it, and numbers, and symbols too. The words for everything he needed appeared before him and were logged into his memory. Jed typed in the words COFFEE CAN out of pure instinct, and a drawer slid open next to him. He quickly dropped all the tagged files into the drawer and pushed it closed, just as the woman who looked like his mother turned to face him. She saw nothing.

"There," she said, and smiled at him. "Everything back as it should be." Then she reached up to him and waved her hand in front of his face, and the darkness swallowed him again.

• • • •

Only, this time *he* controlled the switch. She thought she'd powered him down, but he willed himself to stand—and then he brought the screen back up.

And he worked.

He didn't know for how long, but it seemed like he explored the BICE system for hours. For him, it all was just beginning to make sense, like when he'd first learned to work the horses. And just like Dawn had said, he could now *see* how the BICE interacted with his brain and his nervous system. He practiced controlling the electrical flow of impulses, changing the way that synapses fired.

Often he ran into roadblocks. The words *Access Denied* would appear whenever he tried something his BICE wasn't cleared for. So he'd experiment around the edges of the information, looking for things he *could* see and know.

Then he began manipulating the screen in his room. He brought up a scene from his childhood—a Thanksgiving with his family—and he zoomed his consciousness around the room while his family ate their meal. He could smell the turkey, and his mouth watered at the wonderful aroma.

Then he zoomed out through the front door like a bird, and his mind took flight. He shot straight upward and hovered over the farm; then traveled like a rocket or an airbus until he was floating over the City. The City, long before it had been destroyed by a bomb. He tried to zoom in on the Transport station, but when he did, the image froze and *Access Denied* flashed before his eyes.

He blinked his eyes, and the City was gone, but he was still hovering over the planet, so he began to look for other things. For storms and squalls and flocks of birds moving en masse. When he saw these things, he looked deeper, and found that he could see the very pixels that made up the wind, and the invisible streams of data that flowed constantly around the planet, wirelessly, through the air.

And he understood it all. It made *sense* to him.

He blinked again and he called up Dawn.

Her avatar appeared before him in her beautiful navy dress and her white cape and apron. Her likeness seemed to be asleep, and her whole appearance was not quite solid. He stood in front of her and touched her face, but she didn't stir.

"Dawn," he said.

He flicked his hand, trying to activate her avatar, but nothing happened. He tried a dozen other tricks and motions to wake her up, but none of them worked.

Jed paced the room, rubbing his head with his hands to try to stimulate thoughts and answers. His frustration grew, and when he knew that he had no solution to the problem he screamed at the top of his lungs: "DAWN!"

Dawn's avatar flickered. Her head raised and she sucked in air. As the flickering stopped and her form became solid, she opened her eyes. And then it was as if a bolt of electricity hit her, and Jed reached for her hand, and when he touched her the two of them rocketed up and through the ceiling, and wordlessly they soared over the Amish Zone, and Dawn took him until they were hovering over a farmhouse at the end of a lane. Then she blinked out and disappeared, and Jed awoke in his bed.

•••

"There's a farmhouse not two miles from here," Jed told Matthias as they ate. He knew the food was laced with Q but for now he didn't mind. He wanted to be sure he had access to the full capabilities of his BICE, in case he needed it. "There are three lightning rods on the roof of a banked barn that has green trim, and there's a young orchard to the east of the barn with a white picket fence around the orchard."

Matthias laughed as he took a bite of home-baked bread. "You just described most of the farms in the Amish Zone."

"This one was different," Jed said. He took a drink of lemonade. "It's at the end of a lane, and there's a creek that runs right through the property."

"That sounds familiar," Matthias said. "Marcus Yoder's place, I think. He's cousin to the man whose family is bringing us the meals." Matthias ripped off another chunk of fresh bread and then used his pocketknife to spread a chunk of homemade butter on it. "Speaking of which, the Yoders' food... it's the best I've ever had. I feel so peaceful after I eat it. Maybe it has something to do with this alien planet, but I don't look forward to the day when the Yoders stop delivering my meals."

Jed just nodded and kept eating. He knew that Matthias was reacting to the Q in the food, but he didn't say anything about it. All of this would have to be part of a long conversation he'd have with Matthias once he knew more about what was going on.

"Why are you asking about the Marcus Yoder farm?" Matthias asked.

And that was one more thing he couldn't tell Matthias about. As if Jed could even explain how he suspected that a woman named Dawn was being held on Marcus Yoder's farm somewhere.

And what did Jed plan to do about it, anyway? He was Amish. He couldn't just take a gun and run over there to try to rescue her. She obviously wanted him to know where she was being held, but he felt like if she was in some kind of imminent danger she would have said something to him. Still, he wanted to find a reason to go search for her.

Jed shrugged. "I'm just thinking about going to look at some of the unique farms in the zone, to get ideas for my own place when I get my allotment."

"How do you know about that place?" Matthias asked. He motioned for Jed to pass the peach preserves.

"Oh, I think Mr. Zook at the immigration center might have mentioned it. I'd just like to go take a look at it."

Mathias laughed. "You sound like the English, or some young Amish girl wanting to get married."

Jed smiled, "I like to get ideas."

"An Amish farm is an Amish farm." Matthias stuck his knife into the jar of preserves and pulled out a dollop of jam, then winked at Jed as he stuck the sugary mass in his mouth. He sat the knife down and twisted the lid back on the jar. "Well, this Sabbath is Visitation Sabbath. We could always go over there and ask to look around."

"That's two days from now," Jed said. "Any way we could do it sooner?"

Matthias wiped his knife on his broadfall pants, then closed the blade and tucked it back into his pants' inner pocket. "I suppose we could go tomorrow, but it'll look odd. Nobody visits on Saturday."

"Who cares if it looks odd?" Jed said. "Let's do it."

Matthias stood up and pushed in his chair. "All right, I'll talk to Marcus at the meeting tonight. But for now... you've been napping while I finished the plowing. So you get dishes duty while I go do the evening milking. If we can get all of our chores done before the meeting, maybe we can make a few more fat lamps after we get home so we can get more light in this dreary place."

"Now who sounds like a woman?" Jed said as he slapped Matthias on the shoulder. "No, I'm thinking of turning in early."

"After the meeting?"

"After the meeting."

"And after you napped the day away?" Matthias laughed.

"I'm starting to appreciate the value of a lot of rest," Jed said as he began to clear away the dishes.

• • • •

When the chores were finished and Matthias had filtered the milk, Jed helped his friend pour the finished product into sterilized five-gallon canisters. The canisters were then loaded into the buckboard wagon, and the two young men harnessed the horses and drove the milk over to the neighbor's farm. The clip-clop of the horses' hooves on the road was soothing, and Jed remembered riding in the buggy with his parents as a little boy, how he'd sing or make up rhymes that went with the beat of horse travel. He recalled traveling in the winter as a child—burrowing into the lap blanket and wishing that nothing would ever change in his perfect life, that his parents would always be there with him. These thoughts brought on a feeling of nostalgia and melancholy like a fog, which only lifted when they'd pulled the wagon up to the neighbor's barn.

Tom Hochstetler helped the two carry the canisters into his stone springhouse, and the milk containers were lowered into the icy water that flowed around the stone trough built into the wall of the springhouse. The pure, cool water came from a spring, flowed through the troughs, then down into a large cistern that served for the Hochstetlers' animal-watering needs. An overflow in the cistern routed the water back into a small creek that flowed down to a stock pond.

The milk would be bartered for lumber and supplies, to be stored up for Matthias' barn-raising, which was coming up soon. Altogether, Matthias was hopeful that when the time came for the barn-raising, he'd already be free of any debt related to the construction. Jedediah was hopeful too. He was looking forward to the fellowship time, because barn-raisings provided some of the fondest memories from his childhood.

• • • •

Later that evening, Matthias sat by lantern light at the oaken kitchen table in his tiny house, and Jedediah excused himself for the evening. He was anxious to go to bed, not because he was sleepy—he wasn't tired at all—but because there were things he needed to know, and the only place he felt comfortable accessing his BICE was in his own room, lying on the fleeces.

The meeting earlier that evening had taken place at the house of Arthur Lapp. Standing outside with the other Amish men beforehand, Jed had felt the intense stares coming at him; Matthias had warned him that people were suspicious because Jed's brother was head of the resistance. No one was openly rude, although speakers did tend to point in his direction whenever they spoke about TRACE and whether or not the rebels had set off the bomb that destroyed the City.

Jed had been surprised to see so many young faces there, even though he'd been told by Mr. Zook at the immigration center to expect it. The average age of the men who attended the meeting was probably around twenty-five. And when the meeting was brought to order, Jed noticed that the elders, all seated along one wall, were perhaps only a year or two older than the rest of the group, on average.

The meeting was conducted in English, and since most everyone was young, the English that was used was fairly modern and would have been considered "worldly" back in his home district. It made it easier for Jed to follow along; he didn't like it when meetings were held in either Pennsylvania Dutch or the weird hybridized slang that was often used by his elders in the AZ back home.

Ultimately, nothing concrete was decided. The meeting served more as a forum for airing out pent-up stress and pressure than it did as a call to action. There was a lot of complaining and accusing going on, but the group, and even the elders, were evenly split in their opinions about who was to blame for the bombing, and whether or not the community should continue to trade with the rebels. Tensions eased once the topic changed to giving aid and comfort to those who'd lost loved ones in the bombing, and the meeting took on a more temperate feel.

The last major topic for discussion was Matthias's barn-raising. It was a bittersweet thing for Matthias to learn that, since another family who'd planned a barn-raising for the next week had been killed in the destruction of the City, Matthias's barn-raising was now moved up. It would be held in eight days, the following Saturday. Moving the barn-raising up a month would create some tactical difficulties, but Matthias was excited about the prospect just the same.

Jed noticed that the Yoders were not present or represented at the meeting by anyone else from their family. He found that curious, especially if they were truly working for Transport, but he still didn't know what to do with that piece of information. He hoped to learn more on his next excursion into the cyber-world.

Toward the end of the evening, the floor was opened up to anyone who had anything to say, so Jed decided that it would be as good a time as any to introduce himself, and to perhaps assuage some fears and concerns about his presence among the people in the community.

"I haven't been here long," he said. "And I'm still trying to learn everything that's happened here in New Pennsylvania, and even about my brother's role in it. As you can imagine, I'm very lost right now, and I don't really know what to think. Still, I am Amish. I was born Amish, and I intend to die that way. Understanding all of this is something I struggle with, and I know that peace and comfort may be long in coming. I do appreciate all the love and care I've received since I first arrived, and I hope to be a productive member of the community here. I thank you all for your patience and kindness."

When he finished, one of the elders rose to speak. "You do know that your brother has violated both our *ordnung*, and every other rule we have as a people, by choosing to fight and to make war against the government?"

"I know that," Jed responded.

"And you know that we have chosen to remove him from our number, as we must do, and that he has been shunned from the fellowship of the beloved?"

"I do."

"All right, then. This meeting is adjourned. May God's grace be upon all of us."

24

ATLOS

Lying on his bunk among the fleeces, Jed prayed to God to watch over him before focusing his thoughts in order to enter his BICE control room. Before retiring to his bed, he'd downed a full glass of lemonade brought over by the Yoders, knowing that the drink would likely be laced with more Q. It was.

Almost immediately, instead of playing with the capabilities of the system like he'd done before, he dove into the Internet's data on the history of New Pennsylvania and the old world. According to the official government version, the first rebel wars had begun in the year 2018 and ended in the year 2040 with an overwhelming victory by "the forces of the people." The twenty-two years of almost constant battles—warfare that had eventually spread around the globe—resulted in the loss of almost fifty percent of the world's population. Transport, whose power and authority had grown throughout the period of this first global rebellion, became the sole governing body after the wars.

The Amish had been encouraged to spread out and to farm more land, and by 2042 the first officially protected Amish Zone—the first of the five that would eventually be developed—was established. During this time, in contrast to what was going on in the rest of the world, the Amish experienced unparalleled freedom and autonomy. As had been the pattern in old Europe, wars and starvation had a tendency, if only a temporary one, to convince nations that agrarianism was a good philosophy.

In the years during and just after the wars, technological advances had almost stopped, and worldwide economies either slowed or completely collapsed. This was often called "The Dying Time." Starvation was rampant, and disorder and violence plagued much of the world. Due to ongoing terrorist attacks by groups allied with the rebels, private transport was outlawed. Roads, some of them over a hundred years old, were ripped up in order to "disincentivize ground travel" and to hinder terrorist activities. The Transport authority implemented the first TRID system, using Unis as the form of currency, in 2050.

According to official government sites (or sites using government information), colonization of New Pennsylvania began just as the TRID system was being implemented—first with the establishment of the City, and almost immediately after that with the transplanting of a new colony of Amish into the Amish Zone far to the west of the urban area.

What the sites did not explain—at least, not to Jed's

satisfaction—is why the buildings he'd seen and entered in New Pennsylvania had looked so old. If, as the government was saying, he'd arrived on the planet in 2077, then the oldest buildings in the City should have been no older than twenty-seven years old. Yet he'd been in the basement of Pook's antique shop, and the cellar had looked as if it could be a hundred years old. And where did the salvagers like Eagles come from? And what were they salvaging? Where did Eagles get his Go Eagles towel?

And then there was the matter of the wall. Other than explaining that the massive wall around the AZ in New Pennsylvania was originally built to keep wild animals and other creatures out of the Amish Zone, the information sites that Jed visited did not explain its incredible scale—it was higher, wider, and longer than any wall he'd ever heard of before. From Jed's understanding, walls such as this were built by primitive peoples to keep out invaders and marauders, not by modern folk to hinder foxes and wildcats.

Information about the new planet was even more scant. According to the historical documents, scientists had identified New Pennsylvania as one of millions of Earth-like planets in Earth-like orbital distance from suns the same size as the one that heated the Earth. Probes from the early twenty-first century had then determined that the planet supported life, but had no intelligent alien species at all. This was the story painted by official government data sites. After traveling light years in suspended animation, the first human astronauts to land on New Pennsylvania found it to be a planet much like the Earth in every respect, except without intelligent life. If there ever had been intelligent life on the planet, it had either died away or departed the place long ago: no archeological anomalies or structures had been located on New Pennsylvania.

Jed shook his head as he studied all of the information. The most remarkable thing about it all was that people seemed to believe it, both here and back on Earth. That is, if indeed this place and Earth were two different planets, something about which he was no longer certain.

Tired of reading propaganda, he decided to try to contact Dawn again. Despite numerous attempts, he found that he was unable to locate her, or even to call up her avatar at all. Not knowing what else to do, he went back into the master file that he'd hidden from the avatar that had looked so much like his own mother.

He studied everything he could find in the files. Most of the information consisted of video files of Dawn's first training sessions with him—when he'd still been unconscious and not aware what was happening to him. He pulled up a file that was labeled "The Shelf," and this one he could *almost*—barely—remember. He played the video and watched as Dawn flew him in the direction of the west, and they ended up looking out from a great height over the cities on the plain beyond the Great Shelf. He watched and listened as Dawn taught him about the cities, and how the government had hoped to relocate millions of Earth residents into these large urban centers, and she explained how the whole plan had been a failure. This time, though, Jed noticed something that he hadn't seen the first time he'd experienced this vision. As he watched it now in "third person," separated from his other avatar self and floating in the distance, he noticed that up in the sky some letters and numbers would occasionally appear very faintly throughout the lesson. Then after several minutes, they'd disappear, only to reappear some time later.

He pulled up other training sessions, and when he searched through the videos, he noticed again that the same set of letters and numbers would often appear for a few minutes, barely visible, and then disappear. This time when it happened, he raised his hand, tapped, and froze the scene. He enlarged the area near the figures until he could read them...

AT10S

...the letters AT, then the number 10, and then the letter S.

What can that be? A training file code? Advanced Training? No. He shook his head. If it was a training code, he thought, then it should change with every lesson. He racked his brain, but he couldn't figure it out. He watched a few other videos, but he found himself growing very sleepy, so eventually he had to shut down the system and actually go to sleep.

He awoke with the first light of a beautiful Saturday morning, but he didn't feel rested. Out of instinct, or fear, or some other impulse he couldn't define, he looked around himself quickly, up into every corner of the room.

Perhaps he expected to see the AT10S floating up there somewhere, indicating that he was still in some kind of training mode. But the code wasn't there. He was actually in a tiny bedroom in a tiny Amish house in New Pennsylvania, and no matter what he thought about that, some very real cows waited to be milked.

THE END OF THE ROAD

The assault on the Tulsa didn't last long. Once the SOMA was aware that his Corinth system had been breached, he was able to secure the ship and harden it before launching a full counterattack that scattered the enemy warships, which then retreated under the withering fire of the Tulsa's support craft.

It was just a probing action, Amos thought, *but now they know we're here.*

And now my people have another reason to doubt me.

"We were caught with our pants down," he told his officers. "We got arrogant. Relied on our technological superiority. Underestimated our enemy. Basically, we did what Transport has done for the last twenty years. But it won't happen again. From now on this ship is on full battle footing at all times."

His next step was to get his systems officers actively

looking for the data breach. Just as Transport had been scouring the digital world looking for Dawn, TRACE's spiders now went on the hunt for the leak in their own system. Amos knew all about back doors and the damage they could cause. In fact, he'd been the first one to find the back door in the original TRID system. Since that time, he and his programmers—including Dawn Beachy—had regularly infiltrated Transport's system and used it to gain tactical superiority (or at least parity) in their fight with the government. Then when the BICE system was first introduced, it was intended to be a completely sterile environment—free from any flaws or bugs that could be exploited by the resistance. But that, like every such plan, was a fantasy. Amos, Dawn, and other techs sympathetic to the resistance had riddled the system with back doors and hacks—so much so that, in most cases, Transport didn't even know that a good portion of the data sent through the BICE system at any one time flowed directly through portals and hubs run by TRACE.

The whole thing reminded Amos of a story he'd read about as a young man. An actual event that had really happened in the history of espionage. In 1969, the United States government rather unwisely entered a contract with their Cold War enemy, the Soviets, to build a new American embassy in Moscow. In order to speed the job along, and in the spirit of détente that existed at the time, in 1972 the Americans agreed to allow the Russians to build the embassy. The result was not just the most sophisticated bugging of a building in all of history (before the BICE enterprise, anyway). It wasn't just that there were listening and recording devices throughout the building; that might have even been expected. And it wasn't just that there were other, more difficult-to-discover bugs actually *built* into the building. The result was that, taken altogether, the *entire structure* became a huge radio device that could broadcast every single spoken and written communication taking place in the building to Soviet intelligence. The building itself could not be salvaged or fixed. Sophisticated new spying technologies, some that had never been known to exist before, were actually built *into* concrete structures, in supporting walls, and through the concrete floors. The new U.S. embassy did not *have* bugs. The embassy itself *was* a bug.

American intelligence knew that a bugging operation was going on, but their arrogance convinced them that once they had full access to the building, they'd be able to find and remove or neutralize all of the devices. As is often the case when institutional hubris is involved, they completely misjudged the enormity of their problem.

This situation roughly equated with what **TRACE** had been able to do with the **TRID** and **BICE** systems. But now it seemed the tables might be turned. **TRACE** had always used technology as an ancillary or support element in their war against Transport. Advanced technology was just another tool. Sometimes it even became a second front. But things were different now. With **TRACE** producing their own ships and increasingly relying on cyberwar as an element of their war plans, the **SOMA** had to be worried about his own systems being hacked and used against him. Maybe, like when the Americans had eventually learned about their embassy, it was already too late.

Well, he thought to himself, *the geeks should be on our side, so at least we can rely on them—*

As soon as he thought it, he knew it was wrong. *When we're on top, some of them will defect back to Transport. If they haven't done so already.* Among programmers and geeks there are always rebels—even rebels that rebel against the rebellion. Counter-revolution is revolution's fickle twin. His shadow. Instability is the geek's favorite environment, and anarchy is their oxygen. Now Amos made a mental note of what he'd learned. For decades his mantra had been that within every technological advancement lie the seeds of tyranny and slavery. Now, in his heart, he codified its natural consequent: any society or government that relies too heavily on technology will find itself perched perilously on a crumbling precipice over the valley of death and destruction. In the new world, the geeks had become gods—or devils, depending on how you looked at it. Perspective is everything after all.

The bombing of the City, the weak and transparent probing action near the shelf, and the half-hearted attack on the Tulsa... all of these things were pointing to the fact that somehow, he was missing something. Something rather large. All of this added to the pressure of trying to win the war while still maintaining his identity and humanity.

Sometimes he felt like he'd give anything to go back and just *be* Amish. If only there were a button he could push that would erase all of the technology and put everyone back on the farm for a few thousand years. Make them fight with rocks and sticks again, if they must fight.

I have such a button, he thought, and then shook his head. Okcillium gave him this power. He inhaled deeply and then exhaled.

Despotism and genocide are born in moments like this.

●●●●

Amos examined the thin sheet of plastic handed to him by an ensign. The latest field reports. Most of the units engaging in surface operations did not have implanted BICE chips, and had to communicate through officers staged in base camps. He dropped the plastic sheet in a trash receptacle. The sheet display wouldn't work for anyone but him, because it was *EYES ONLY* and was activated by his own BICE.

Most of the ground units east of the Shelf—between there and the AZ—were now functionally out of the fight. Transport wasn't operating in the east anymore. Of course, that didn't mean that their field agents and insurgency units weren't still operating. Just as TRACE had once had resistance fighters and spies in place throughout the City, they also now had agents embedded in all the cities on the Shelf. East of the shelf though, everyone was just waiting. And there was no doubt in anyone's mind that Transport was now the insurgency in the east.

Amos looked at the ensign and nodded. "Activate Rayburn's people and get him to a communication deck. I want to talk to him myself."

The ensign nodded. "Yes, sir."

"That'll be all."

"Yes, sir."

When the ensign was gone, Amos popped another Q tablet and sat back in his chair. He didn't really want to do any BICE work, and Dawn Beachy was offline for the time being, so he didn't have anyone to talk to. But he took the pill because he liked the feeling, and it tended to smooth the edges. Made him feel calmer and more confident. Somehow, on the first wave of a hit of Q, his doubts and insecurities paled and faded. Not completely. They didn't disappear altogether—that would be too much to ask of a drug that didn't kill you in just a few years from insanity and addiction. For Amos, taking Q was like drinking a beer was to some other people. It leveled him out, helped him find some satisfaction in his otherwise stressful existence.

Just in case Dawn had reconnected and was trying to reach him, he pulled up and entered his control room, and when the floating cube materialized, he spun it slowly with his hand. He didn't expect Dawn to be there. In fact, he'd arranged for her *not* to be available. All part of his plot to get his brother to dig deeper into the operation of his BICE. A pure Amish mind, flexible and resilient, systemically agnostic, and clear of technological biases... that was just what was needed at this moment. It was exactly what his own mind had been like when he'd first cracked the TRIDs and the early BICE units in 2075. Jed was now a *tabula rasa*, a clean slate—and also a very clever young man who wanted only the truth. *Like I was once*, Amos thought. For now, Jed was the perfect weapon.

Transport wanted Jed because the government needed an unwitting spy *and* a propaganda victory. Amos wanted Jed because he needed victory.

Amos knew that Dawn wouldn't be able to retrieve any DM until the Yoders had fulfilled their purpose, but he wanted to drop her a message anyway. He was just about to send her a DM when he remembered again to change his avatar so that he would appear as his real self. An old man. And that's when he decided to get rid of his youthful avatar altogether. It was a vanity, a joke he was playing only on himself. He accepted fully, maybe for the first time, that he was past middle age, and to the rest of this young world he was just plain old. He flicked his wrist and brought up the box that asked him if he wanted to make his old man avatar his permanent one. He ticked "Yes" and then closed the profile cube.

He'd just reached out to touch his master cube, when the last person he would ever have expected to see at that moment appeared before him. His brother, Jed. With the exception of a new and scrawny beard, the boy looked exactly as Amos remembered him—the last time he'd seen him in the flesh.

The two brothers looked at one another, and did not speak for a moment as they each caught their breath.

It was Jed who spoke first.

"Amos," he said with a nod.

Amos put his hands behind his back, then nodded in return. "Jedediah." Then, "You got here faster than I'd expected."

There was another extended period of silence before Jed spoke again. "Listen... Amos... I don't know much about what's going on, but I'm learning. I learned how to get here to talk to you. And I've also learned something else."

"What have you learned, big brother?" Amos asked.

Jed scowled when he heard the emphasis Amos placed on the phrase *big brother*, but he shook off the urge to launch into a scathing attack on Amos.

"I figured out how they're doing it," he said.

Amos flinched. He wasn't sure what Jed was talking about, and for a split second he had a flash of doubt. Perhaps this person standing before him wasn't Jedediah at all? After all, his system had just recently been hacked. But then the doubt passed, at least for a moment. He'd expected Jed to get into the system and start figuring things out. In fact, he'd counted on it. Just not this soon. Maybe Jed was even more clever than his younger brother gave him credit for.

"Let's not drag this out, Jed. What is it that you've discovered?"

Jed took a deep breath. He knew that he was out of his depth, but what he'd seen needed to be known. "First, I figured out that Transport is gathering tons of okcillium, and then I figured out how they're doing it."

Amos blinked. "What?"

"They're ripping up the roads. Starting back in 2050 on Earth. That's the real reason behind the laws to ban private transport. The okcillium is in the road base. It always has been."

26

THE INFORMATION SUPERHIGHWAY

The avatar that represented his younger brother disconcerted Jed. He wasn't sure what he expected to see, but here before him was Amos as an old man, gray-headed and marked by years and the pressures of governing. It was tough to accept. But he knew it was Amos, or at least an accurate computer rendering of what his brother must surely look like.

"How did you work it out?" his brother asked. The old man looked at his wrist where a watch would be, even though he didn't wear one. "It's late Saturday morning, and you haven't had much time. We'll get to the okcillium and the roads in a minute. But I'm curious how you found me so fast. Here. In the system."

Jed shrugged. "It started with the code AT10S. It showed up whenever you were looking over Dawn's shoulder while she was training me. It was something in the picture that shouldn't have been there. I didn't see it when I was experiencing the training in real time, but later, when I went in as an observer using the COFFEE CAN password... I saw your code in the rendering."

"I was watching and keeping tabs to make sure that Dawn didn't disclose anything too soon," Amos said, nodding. "But that code shouldn't have been visible in the rendering. I know the code. You saw it because of who you are."

"Too soon—" Jed said. He was about to pounce on this, but Amos continued.

"You've picked up the terminology and the engineering lingo pretty fast, brother," Amos said. "Let me ask you a question: when you were milking Zoe, which one of her teats often had a mastitis problem?"

Jed stared at his brother for a long while. Then he realized that Amos still wasn't sure about him. There was fear there. Almost latent and mostly hidden, but it was still there. The head of the resistance didn't know if this avatar of his brother standing before him was perhaps being operated by some Transport hacker.

"That's not a good question, Amos. After all, I could guess. I'd have a one in four possibility of getting it right."

"Well, at least you know a cow has four quarters to her udder and four teats," Amos said. "Not many Transport hackers would know that."

"The answer is *none of them*, Amos. Zoe never had mastitis that I ever knew about. We only kept one milk cow and we cleaned her teats thoroughly every time we milked her. We never had the problems so many other farmers faced."

"Okay then," Amos said, "so tell me about this expansive technology vocabulary you have all of a sudden. How'd you come upon it?"

Jed nodded. "Dawn helped with that. She programmed a computing lexicon into my BICE. Every time I'm looking for a word or experiencing anything new when I'm in the system, the word appears almost before I realize I need it." He fixed his brother with an accusatory glare. "And I suppose if she did that, it was because you told her to do it. She anticipated that I'd be mucking around in the system."

"And from that you conclude... what?"

"That you knew I'd be doing this. That you planned it." He pointed his finger at his younger brother. "This whole thing... all along. Your plan, ever since I first came here, wherever *here* is, was to get me into the system to help you. And you knew I'd never do it unless I decided to do so on my own. Everyone kept telling me, 'We can't tell you anything' and 'Your brother wants you to see it for yourself.' And Dawn would say, 'If you get sterile information without the context you'll make wrong decisions.' What that really meant was that you wanted me to be your puppet. You wanted me to hack into Transport's system, for some reason I don't know yet. And I did exactly as you planned."

Amos waved his hand dismissively, as if to say *none of that matters now.* "So you saw the code. How did you figure out that it was me?"

Jed let out a derisive chuckle. "Changing the subject, huh? Your code was AT10S? Amos Troyer, tenth seat.

You don't think I remember school, Amos? It wasn't that long ago for me. We Amish may only go through the eighth grade, but I was only eighteen when I left home. In fact, as crazy as it sounds to me now, I'm still only eighteen."

Amos smiled, but there was pain in that smile. "And I'm sixty-seven, brother. Sixty-seven *real* years old."

Now it was Jed's turn to wave off Amos. He wasn't in the mood to either embrace or sorrow over his brother's troubles just yet. He put up his hand and continued his explanation. "Mrs. Holtzclaw numbered the desks in that one-room schoolhouse, and we had to file in and out of class by number. Our personal number—in your case 10S—was on anything and everything that had to do with school. Mine was 15S. That little bit of information came in handy just a short while ago when I needed to get into your files about me."

"You've read your files, then?" Amos asked. His face was a mask. Jed couldn't really read what was going on in his brother's mind, except that none of this seemed to surprise him. It was almost as if Jed had completed some farming task, and now his brother was just pressing him to find out everything he'd done and in what order.

"None of this is that difficult, Amos," Jed said. "You planted the code so I could see it. The rest of it follows easily."

Amos shook his head. "Easily for *you*, Jed. Because of who you are and what you are. It's like when we used to line up dominoes in patterns and we'd have so much fun watching them fall. The first one has to go, brother. If the first one doesn't go, the rest don't fall. You found and knocked over the first domino. It only seemed easy to you, well... because you're you."

Jed crossed his arms and just stared at his brother. There were so many things he wanted to say, but he didn't want his emotions to take over.

"Sorry to interrupt you," Amos said. "You were saying about the files?"

Jed uncrossed his arms and began to pace back and forth. "Yes. First I had to hack into your files," Jed said.

"I see." Amos had the air of a teacher interrogating a student. "And how did you manage that?"

"I used what I knew of you. I tried AT10S for your password, but that didn't work. So I tried 'Zoe' and that didn't work either. Then I tried ZOE10S. Still no luck. So then I took a wild shot at it. When you were twelve father bought you a cat. You called him Mr. Claws. So I typed in MRCLAWS and I was in."

"Not very clever of me," Amos said. "I should have set a better password."

"Unless you *wanted* me following this trail," Jed said. "Unless you *wanted* me rummaging around in your files. Many of the things I find seem to be placed there purposely for me. Like maybe the window from our barn I found in Pook's antique store. Maybe that was the first domino."

Just the hint of a smile touched Amos's lips. "So what happened next?"

"I was in the door, but I couldn't get anything to work. Your password had to be matched with data from your BICE, so next I had to look for a back door."

"And how did you locate it?"

"From your interface, and using your AT10S code, I went to our old farm." Jed noticed the smile start to spread across his brother's face. "And then I went to our bedroom. You kept a coffee can—identical to the one I'd smashed flat to make the windowpane. You always stashed it under the bed, as if you didn't think anyone would ever think to look there. And you kept all your secrets in it."

"I was a simpler person back then," Amos said, looking down. "And what did you find there, brother?"

"When I opened the coffee can, your whole system just opened up to me. I had free access."

Amos was still smiling, and it irritated Jed to watch his brother gloat. It was as if he was proud of Jed or something.

"You're still my little brother, Amos," Jed said. "Don't gloat."

"I'm just very pleased with you," Amos said. "You're every bit as smart as I remember. It's like I'm back in our room, listening to you explain how you solved a particularly perplexing puzzle." Amos reached up and dried a tear that had slipped from his eye. "You were my hero, Jed. You still are."

Jed didn't reply. He just studied his brother. He still wasn't sure what to think about everything that was happening, so for a minute he just stared... until his brother broke the silence.

"So then, you read my files?"

"Not a lot of them. I perused them. That was when I had the idea that Transport might have someone looking for Dawn. I went back to your files and started with every document that began with a 'D', and went through until I found your personal file on her. Her last name is Beachy. She was married. You presided at her wedding."

Amos was silent now. His eyes scanned his older brother's face. Jed wondered if the system was properly rendering his own real reactions—showing his brother something of what he was feeling.

Jed removed his hat and rubbed his head. "Once I found Dawn's personal code, I changed it just a bit to make it look suspicious—though I'd stripped it of any real data—and then I took it back out of your BICE and I planted it in some innocuous history files I'd found on Transport's open servers. Then I sat back and waited to see who would show up. When their spiders appeared and gathered the new data, I followed them back to their source. Something Dawn told me struck me then. She said, 'Every system or program has a back door.' I'd found one into your BICE, and I figured that if there was a back door into the TRACE Commander's head, then there must be back doors everywhere."

"So you went searching for a way into their system?"

"Yes. It actually wasn't that hard to figure out," Jed said.

Amos began to pace back and forth with his hands clasped behind his back. Jed noticed that the old man's jaw worked as he thought, something he remembered young Amos doing when they were boys back on the farm. "We've obviously been in and out of their system for decades," Amos said, "but I'm a little surprised to see you got in so easily. But maybe I shouldn't be surprised at all. How did you do it?"

"First, I stripped myself of all identifying information. Then I started by going to TRACE's hubs and looking at what information they were getting when they interrogated their own spiders. I rightly guessed that Transport's spiders were probably programmed by the same people, so I knew what type of information the portal would be looking for. Then I disguised myself as one of their spiders and I walked right in."

"The back door was the front door," Amos said.

"Yes, but I found out later that Dawn had done some hacking work on their system. She's fundamentally rewired their security infrastructure so that if her own scanners detect a break-in, the standard data circles back around and obscures the breach. Basically she created a cloaking device for anyone at all who wants to hack into Transport's system."

Amos shrugged. "Who else would want to do such a thing? I mean... other than us?"

Jed put his hat back on and stuck his hands deep into the pockets of his broadfall pants. "I don't know. I'm not an expert on any of this. I'm just pointing out that if *I* could get in there, then just about anyone else could too."

"Are you suggesting that there could be a third party involved in our little war?" Amos asked.

Jed cocked his head to one side and then nodded. "I'd be surprised if there wasn't."

● ● ● ●

Amos pulled up a white screen and then turned to face Jed. "Tell me about the okcillium in the roads."

Jed pulled up a document, and an embedded video began to play. It showed Transport machines ripping up the highways after the law was passed outlawing private transport. He muted the audio and spoke over the video as it played.

"Okcillium—the very existence of it—had always been a very closely held secret," Jed said. "How you and your people in TRACE are getting your okcillium, I haven't discovered yet. But when I started really digging into Transport's *real* files—not just the ones they've sanitized and altered for public consumption, but their internal files—I saw some things that made me believe that recently—*very* recently—they've come upon a new source of okcillium."

"A new source?" Amos asked.

"Actually, a very old one. It turns out that America's earliest highways, including the interstate highway system, used a very specific mineral aggregate in their road base. A substantial portion of that mineral aggregate was mined in Oklahoma."

"The only place in the old world where okcillium has been found," Amos added.

"Right," Jed said. "Okcillium was first identified in 2005, but it was in such trace amounts that it was almost disregarded, except as a scientific oddity. The U.S. government classified as Top Secret everything to do with okcillium, and since there were no large deposits discovered, very few people even cared about the discovery. Non-governmental scientists weren't even let in on the find."

Amos rolled his hand to indicate that he knew all of

this. "Get to the part about the roads."

"There isn't much to figure out. Most of the okcillium in Oklahoma was dug out prior to anyone knowing what it was or that it even existed. It was in the mineral aggregate that went into the interstate highways. And now Transport knows about it, and they've gone back to rip up the roads and dig it out," Jed said.

Amos nodded, but he didn't speak.

"I guess I don't see the point in sucking me into all of this, Amos," Jed said. "Dawn could have done everything I've done, and probably faster."

Amos smiled. "That's where you're wrong, brother. Dawn would never have found out about the roads."

"Why do you say that?"

"Because she would never have thought to look back in 2050," Amos said.

There was silence again for the space of a few minutes, and during that time a very rudimentary avatar appeared in the room. Amos turned to the avatar and greeted it. The avatar had no identifying characteristics— just a plain face and no expression.

"Ah... Mr. Rayburn," Amos said.

"It's Pook," the avatar said, "or just Rayburn. I'm not an officer, sir."

Amos put his hands behind his back and approached Pook. "Well, that is an oversight I intend to remedy, Mr. Rayburn."

"Why does his avatar look that crude?" Jed asked.

"Mr. Rayburn?" Amos said. "I take it that you've met my brother, Jed?"

"We've met," Pook said without any emotion. Pook

was all business.

Amos turned back to Jed and explained. "Mr. Rayburn does not have a BICE implant. The rendering you see here is done by a special helmet. He is also wearing—temporarily, of course—an electronic bracelet I invented that reads the movements of the ligaments in his hand. He can use his hand to interact with the system."

"Interesting," Jed said. He nodded at Pook. "Well... *Mr. Rayburn...*"

"Pook."

"Okay, then. Pook. If you'll just give me a moment with my brother, I want to finish up and then I have to get back."

"Yes," Amos said. "Jed here has *farming* to do."

It was a jab, but Jed ignored it. He actually wanted to hurry and go look for Dawn, but he wasn't going to let anyone know that. Pook's avatar nodded, and then went dormant. Once it was clear that Pook was no longer there, Jed turned to his brother.

"TRACE," Jed said.

Amos looked at Jed, but didn't speak.

"The name of the resistance is 'TRACE,'" Jed said. "I find that fascinating. All the documents I read said that only *trace* amounts of okcillium were found in 2005."

"A coincidence."

"Or maybe not. Maybe it's like that window in the basement of Pook's shop."

Amos shrugged. "And what else, brother?"

Jed fixed his gaze on his brother once again. "I also find it interesting that Transport has suddenly come upon a source of okcillium, at the same time that you seem to be flush with it."

"The coincidences are unrelated," Amos said. "Correlation does not necessarily imply causation, and all that."

"I have to go harrow Matthias's new field," Jed said.

"Send him my best."

27

LOST AND FOUND

Matthias rubbed his head and sat back in his chair. "This is a pretty fantastic story, Jed."

"I know it is," Jed said.

"And by 'fantastic,' I mean unbelievable."

"I know."

Matthias stood up and went to one of his kitchen cabinets. He pulled out a bottle of some clear liquid and a glass, then sat back down at the table.

"What's that?" Jed asked.

"Rheumatism medicine," Matthias said. "Gerald Miller makes it."

"It's booze?"

"Well, that is kind of a crude and English way to put it, but yes. I need something right now after hearing that story." Matthias poured a small amount into the glass, then hesitated before taking a long pull directly from the bottle instead. "I'm sorry," he said, wiping his mouth. "Do you want some?"

Jed shook his head. "No. I want to go find Dawn."

"Right," Matthias said, then he downed the liquor that was in the glass.

"So you say it's unbelievable, Matthias. Does that mean you don't believe me?"

Matthias laughed. "No. It doesn't mean that. That's why I needed the drink. I *do* believe you, and that is now my problem."

Jed had told his friend the whole story. From the beginning all the way through to his conversation with his sixty-seven-year-old brother. Throughout the telling of it, his friend hadn't said much at all. He'd asked a few questions now and then, especially when it came to the parts about the window with the coffee can pane, and the wild savage named Eagles with the green towel.

"So what are you going to do?" Jed asked.

Matthias pushed the cork into the bottle, walked to the cabinet, and put the bottle away. "I suppose I'm going to help you find your girlfriend."

"She's not my... well... she's..."

"She's your girlfriend and you love her, so we need to go find her," Matthias said.

"Okay."

●●●●

Their conversation during the buggy ride was a little more animated than Jed had expected. Matthias was full of questions, particularly about the animated BICE visions and how Jed had hacked into his brother's head. The questions didn't stop until the two young men were standing on the Yoders' porch and knocking on the door.

Marcus Yoder answered the knock, and when he opened it Jed could see that two of Marcus's cousins—a husband and wife from the family that had been bringing food to Jed and Matthias—were seated in the great room. Matthias had arranged with Marcus to give Jed a tour of the farm, so Jed was a little curious as to why the other Yoders would be there.

Introductions were made, and Jed and Matthias were invited to sit.

"It is a strange thing, Jedediah Troyer," Marcus said, "for visitation to be taking place on a Saturday. As you know—and I suppose it is still the way things are done back in the old world—every other Sabbath day is set aside for such things."

"I understand," Jed said, "and I'm very thankful that you were willing to receive us today." He didn't offer an explanation, though it was obvious Marcus and the rest of the Yoders were expecting one.

"Well, then," Marcus said. "Shall we take a look around?"

· · · ·

Marcus Yoder gave them a fairly comprehensive tour. He started by showing the two friends his house, which was an unremarkable and very typical Amish dwelling. The cooking and lighting in the house was provided by either propane or natural gas, but Jed didn't bother to ask which it was. There was a large area rug in the great room—something that was definitely not typical for an Amish house. Jed wondered to himself if the *ordnung* allowed for the rug, and he made a mental note to ask Matthias about it later.

There were five bedrooms in the large home, and the windows had green shades on them as the *ordnung* required. There were no closets—clothes were hung on pegs—so Jed didn't have to go around peering behind closed doors looking to see where Dawn might be hidden.

After the tour of the dwelling, Marcus took them on a walk around the property. Jed was curious why Marcus didn't take them directly to the large banked barn, and he wondered if maybe Dawn might be in there.

Yoder spent a long time showing his guests his plowing and farming implements, particularly (and maybe a little too pridefully) his new threshing machine—one that was operated using a large belt that, when it was in use, stretched to the barn where Jed assumed there would be either a tractor or a large generator.

"May we look in the barn?" Jed asked. He was getting anxious and a little impatient with the length and detail of the tour.

Yoder hesitated, but only for a moment. "Yes. Jedediah Troyer, if you'd like to see the barn, we can go take a look at it."

Matthias looked at Jed and showed by the slightest furrowing of his brow that he wasn't too pleased with Jed rushing the search.

"I have always loved barns," Jed said, smiling, "and with Matthias having his barn-raising in a week, I'd really just like to take a look at yours, Marcus."

The men walked to the barn in silence and the

tension between the three was palpable. The things that were unsaid seemed to multiply as they walked, and Jed began to wonder what he would do even if he were to find Dawn in the barn.

When Marcus slid open the huge door, the darkness inside was a little disappointing to Jed. Part of him wished that the light would flood in and he'd see Dawn there, waiting for him to save her. Another part of him hoped that he'd been mistaken all along, and that Dawn wouldn't be there at all. He did wonder why, if Dawn was being held in the barn, Marcus Yoder would freely allow Jed and Matthias to look there. *Maybe he plans to capture us, too?* Jed thought.

The three men walked tentatively into the barn because of the darkness.

"Let me go slide open the far door," Marcus said. "Then we'll have more light."

When he walked away, Matthias leaned in and spoke into Jed's ear. "What will you do if you find her here?"

Jed shrugged. "I don't know."

As the far door slid open and the light began to flood the large structure, Jed and Matthias held their breath. But Dawn was nowhere in sight. From all appearances, it was just an Amish barn.

"Do you mind if I look around?" Jed asked.

Marcus just nodded his head. While Jed poked around, Marcus and Matthias chatted. From what Jed could hear of their conversation, Marcus was asking Matthias about the details of his new barn that was scheduled to be built in just a week.

After a full inspection of the place, even the upper

portions that included the hayloft and the cubbies for tack storage, Jed was unable to locate Dawn... or any place where she might be hidden.

"Satisfied?" Marcus asked.

It seemed to Jed that there was more to the question than an inquiry about a barn tour.

"I suppose I've seen everything I came to see," Jed replied, and smiled.

● ● ● ●

They were back in the Yoders' great room, which included the kitchen, and as Elizabeth Yoder was pouring lemonade for the four men Jed noticed the area rug again. It was out of place. It didn't fit. It was like the AT10S floating in the sky in its incongruity. He spoke before he really had time to think about it, or gauge how his words might be received.

"I'd like to look under that rug," Jed said, pointing at the floor

Yoder actually flinched. Jed saw it on his face and in his manner as the question rang through the silence in the kitchen. "Excuse me?"

"I'd like to look at the flooring under that rug," Jed repeated. "Our district *ordnung* in the old world didn't allow for such things, so I am interested in why it's there."

Yoder stared at Jed for a moment with a look that bordered on hostility. "The floor is damaged. That's why the rug is there."

"I'd like to look at it," Jed insisted.

"This is not possible," Elizabeth Yoder interrupted.

She was tense, and somewhere in her look Jed could see that she was afraid, too. That's when he became certain that Dawn was down there—somewhere.

He moved without premeditation. His body took over even while his mind was reeling. He was all emotion and intensity. He leapt forward and reached for the rug. Marcus Yoder moved forward too, as if to stop him, but Jed pointed a finger directly at Yoder's face, stopping the man in his tracks. "Stand back," Jed said firmly.

He pulled the rug and then flipped it back on itself, exposing the cellar door that was built into the floor.

"Stop!" Elizabeth yelled. "It's not what you are thinking!"

Jed reached for the cellar door and pulled it open. "What am I thinking?" Jed said. There was fire in his eyes.

"I see that you are violent, like your brother," Marcus said, but he didn't move to stop Jed from going down the steps.

"I'm nothing like my brother," Jed snapped.

The space under the kitchen was dark, and when Jed reached the bottom of the stairs he could only see faintly into the room. What he could see, however, made him catch his breath.

His heart pounded in his chest. Dawn was there. Tied to a chair. Her eyes met his and he could see by the expressive movement around the eyes that she was excited to see him. He pulled out his knife, and in seconds he had the ropes cut. Dawn fell into his arms, and he pulled the gag off. She spit out another rag that had been stuffed into her mouth, and her hand came up to massage her jaw.

"Jed!" she said, as soon as she could speak.

Jed steadied her and lifted her to her feet. "I have you."

"I knew you'd come."

"Let's get you out of here." He looked up, and Yoder was standing at the top of the steps.

"Jedediah," Yoder said. "Don't jump to conclusions. We work for the SOMA. For your brother."

"That's impossible," Jed said.

Yoder leaned into the darkness, and only then could Jed see the Amish man's face. "It's true," Yoder said.

Just then, Jed heard a commotion above him. Shots rang out, and he heard loud thumps, as if bodies were landing hard on the floor over his head.

"What—" he started, but Dawn grabbed him and pulled him away from the stairs and into the shadows just as something struck Yoder from behind and he tumbled down the stairs. Blood poured from wounds to his neck and the back of his head.

The figure of a man appeared where Marcus had stood, the light from behind him causing him to appear as just a menacing silhouette. Dawn and Jed tried to push themselves farther back into the shadows.

"Just come on up here, Jed Troyer and Dawn Beachy," the man said. "Let's get this over with."

Jed knew the voice, but he couldn't quite place it. *Who could it be?*

"Get up here," the voice said, "now!"

Dawn leaned forward even though Jed tried to pull her back. "I know that voice," she said.

"Then get moving," the voice said.

Dawn stepped out and, avoiding the body of Marcus Yoder, held tightly to Jed's hand and pulled him forward too. "Teddy Clarion," she said.

"Only my mother calls me Teddy," the man said. And that's when Jed knew. It was the Transport official who'd captured them in the No Man's Land west of the City. The man who had killed Conrad and Rheems.

"I'll give you five more seconds, and if you aren't up here, I'll come down and kill you there," Clarion said.

● ● ● ●

When Jed emerged from the cellar, he felt as though he were entering some kind of nightmarish alternate universe. The same serene Amish great room in which he'd sat politely just moments earlier had now been stained by violence and death. The bodies of Elizabeth Yoder, her husband, and Matthias lay lifelessly on the floor, blood pooling around them. Jed could only stare in shock at his friend Matthias, a good and peaceful man who now lay facedown in his own blood. Four Transport officers in full battle gear stood around the room, eyeing Jed and Dawn warily.

"Your time is up," Clarion said. "We'd hoped to use you two for... morale purposes... among the plain people here, but you just couldn't leave things alone, could you, Mrs. Beachy?"

Dawn didn't reply.

"You should have known we'd find out you were trying to help the boy."

Dawn sneered. "You brought me here. What did you think I'd do?"

"We hoped that we could just hold you and produce you if ever Jed here needed convincing," Clarion said. "Of course, we didn't know at the time that our insiders here, the Yoders, were working with the rebels too."

"There seems to be a lot you didn't know," Dawn said.

"I know what happens next," Clarion said, smiling.

"I'm a soldier," Dawn said.

"Soldiers die."

"Then we all know where we stand," Dawn replied.

Clarion didn't speak again. He turned and gave some orders to his men, and as he did, Jed noticed a slight motion on the floor. He glanced down at Matthias and saw his friend's hand move. Matthias was still alive!

"Hold it!" Jed shouted, and when Clarion looked at him, Jed acted like he'd been speaking to the Transport men, rather than to his friend.

"We'll hold nothing," Clarion replied with a smirk and raised his weapon. "Like I said. Time's up."

● ● ● ●

The noise was deafening as the windows of the Yoder house exploded inward and the green blinds were ripped from their moorings. Jed sensed the impact coming before it came, or perhaps he'd seen a shadow move through the blinds, but in any event he grabbed Dawn firmly by the arm and, as the impact happened, pulled her to the ground.

Clarion and his men reacted slowly. Too slowly. And most of them were dead before they'd even realized what happened. The windows of the Yoder house imploded as men smashed through them simultaneously. Jed recognized Pook Rayburn as he pulled the trigger on his pistol and fired the shot that hit Teddy Clarion in the head, killing him. The wild man named Eagles appeared like a specter behind one of the Transport soldiers and, lightning-fast, produced a knife from somewhere in his mass of odd and mismatched clothing and cut the soldier's throat, throwing him to the ground.

Flying head first through the far window, Jerry Rios hit the floor and rolled, and came up shooting, taking down the last two soldiers. In the blink of an eye all of the Transport fighters were dead or dying.

Eagles, the unkempt savage, was standing in front of Dawn and Jed with a bloody knife clutched in his mammoth hand, and when the two looked up at him he smiled. There was a huge wad of tobac in his mouth, and saliva—mixed liberally with greenish particles and pieces of glass—was in his beard. He was the most beautiful thing that Jed had ever seen, other than Dawn.

Spittle flew from Eagles's mouth as he shouted triumphantly. "Goa Eeguls saving the Amish boy and girl!" He lifted his hands into the air dramatically. "Ta-daa!"

KNOT 5:

THE PEACEFUL KIND

A LONG HAUL

NOW

Jed rocked back and forth beneath the wide blue sky. He was lying on his back, a green soldier's blanket laid over his chest, as he was carried on a stretcher held aloft by four men. He saw the beautiful wispy clouds, some connected by gossamer threads of vapor and others seemingly more solid, like great billowy ships adrift in a heavenly sea, and he felt the rhythm of the swaying as the men walked. He had a headache, there was no denying that, and he could hear the people who traveled with him talking as the group moved.

"The only portal left is up on the Shelf, and now with the AZ gone, it's our only hope." It was Pook Rayburn talking, and Jed smiled when he recognized the voice. He'd grown to like Pook while working with him on the farm over this past week. He closed his eyes and focused his attention on the voices, hoping that by doing so maybe the headache would fade.

"It's a long haul, but we'll make it." This time it was Dawn Beachy speaking. "We don't really have any other choice."

"I hope he's going to be able to walk at least part of the way," a third voice said.

There was a loud, derisive sound as one of the men snorted aloud and then spat. "Boy being hurting," that deep and easily identifiable voice scolded. "Eeguls and boys carrying he all everywhere if needing be."

"I understand, Eagles," the third voice said. *Ducky*, Jed thought. *I know his voice and his tendency to worry.* "And I'm not complaining," Ducky added. "Besides, as short as I am I'm not really carrying any of Jed's weight at all. I'm just saying it would be nice if he improves and he can walk part of the way."

"He's had a major head injury," Dawn said. "Angelo and I had to do four hours of surgery just to get all the shrapnel from his shattered BICE out of him... all so no little piece would get into his bloodstream or work its way around so that it cut something important."

"He's lucky to be alive after that fall," Pook added.

"Okay!" Ducky said with a sigh. "Just so everyone knows: I'm not complaining about us having to carry Jed. Not at all."

"We all want him to improve and get better, Ducky," Dawn said.

"That's all I was saying," Ducky said.

Jed opened his eyes again and stared into the sky. So beautiful. The headache blurred a little around the edges, and he concentrated on breathing deeply, tried to focus his attention on where he was and what might be happening. So: his BICE was gone. Shattered in a fall. That was one thing. He tried to access it, as if he believed that what he'd just heard wasn't true. He concentrated and imagined his BICE control panel coming up, but however much he focused, nothing happened.

He watched the clouds again as they moved, and then closed his eyes and took several very deep breaths. He tried to let all of the tension go out of his body, noting that as he did so, the headache seemed to lessen just a bit. Then he opened his eyes again. He imagined the sky and the clouds as being made of tiny pixels, and he tried to soar up there so he could get a closer look. Nothing happened, so he settled himself again. To be without the BICE interface now... it seemed like trying to think or operate without part of his own mind. Surely all of his new powers hadn't been stripped from him?

He tried to remember everything he'd been told about how the brain worked. He evened out his breathing again, and this time he *really* concentrated. He imagined the new synapses that had been formed when the BICE was first installed, and he tried to think of them as little switches that could be flipped on and off at will. He once again pictured himself bringing up his BICE control interface. And this time, something spectacular happened.

Darkness permeated his mind, and in moments the white screen appeared before him. He immediately reacted by dividing the screen into nine windows, just as he'd done the last time he'd used his BICE.

Next, he imagined himself dividing his mind—his

own consciousness—so that a whole new Jed was operating each screen, and simultaneously all nine of the windows came to life, each monitor showing him different data.

Now he was faced with a whole new reality. What was happening to him? He could feel the sway of the stretcher, and the cool breeze on his face. He could still faintly hear the voices of his friends as they carried him along. But in his mind, he was looking up at nine view screens, like nine panes of glass in a window. He looked closely at the bottom right-hand pane, and on that ninth video screen the image of the coffee can appeared.

Either he was suffering from brain damage and he was now hallucinating that his BICE was still functioning, or... *could it be?* Could his brain have been permanently altered by the presence of his BICE? He remembered back to the early days, when he was just studying about the BICE and how it worked. He remembered someone... maybe it was Dawn... telling him about experiments that had been done on the brain in the past. In one such experiment, soldiers were given goggles that inverted their vision, and therefore the world that they saw. Since the lenses naturally inverted every bit of light that enters the eyes, the brain had the job of flipping the upside-down images into a right-side-up picture. With the inversion goggles on, everything looked upside-down. The soldiers' feet touched the ground above their eyes, and the sky hovered below. A tool lying on the ground would appear to be "up," but if they tilted their head up to look at it, their view would pan in the opposite direction—toward the sky. Which was "down."

In short, the goggles were very disorienting, and at first, the soldiers often got very sick. Doing the simplest tasks became extremely difficult. But then a strange thing happened. After several days of wearing the goggles non-stop, their brains eventually began to *re*-invert the images. The brain was able to *correct* for the inversion goggles, by turning the images back over so that the men began to see things right-side-up again. Their brains had re-trained themselves.

Then the goggles were removed—and the brain, having grown accustomed to inverting upside-down visual inputs, continued to invert the images. As a result, the men once again had the feeling that everything was upside down, even though they weren't wearing the goggles. Fortunately, within a few days their brains had *re*-re-trained themselves, and everyone's vision had returned to normal.

Overall, it was a fascinating lesson in how the brain can learn to function and adapt to alterations to its normal input.

Jed's brain (it seemed) had learned to work as if the BICE was still there, providing him visual input so that the newer, higher-functioning areas of his mind could interpret data. On one screen, an image was displayed. It showed a large empty area, devoid of hills or valleys, where the Amish Zone should have been. It was as if the whole community had just disappeared. He didn't know how he knew that this had once been where the Amish Zone was, but he did. Even the immense walls were completely gone. On another screen he was seeing the process of okcillium being extracted from reclaimed road base, back in the old world. On still another screen, he examined maps and data that appeared to show a location up on the Great Shelf. All of these things—except for the image of the empty space where the Amish Zone had been—were things his brain already knew. His mind was simply using a new process for interpreting and organizing data, having learned this method from working with the BICE.

The other screens showed things like force readiness reports, and files about the history of the AZ and the building of the wall. All things he'd read before. He thought of Dawn Beachy, and a file containing her picture appeared on one of the screens. He scrolled to an overall summary of the information Transport had about her. He had the feeling that, if he'd ever looked at or studied a piece of information before in all of his life, he now had access to it in real time.

This was all impossible, of course. If he had no BICE interface, he couldn't be accessing the Internet. Maybe he was just having hallucinations. Maybe his brain was somehow responding to the injury, and as a result he was flashing back to an earlier episode in his bizarre experience.

He felt a drowsiness coming over him then, and he breathed deeply again. He heard voices: those of his friends as they carried him along on the stretcher. And there were other voices, too. The voices of strangers he'd never met.

He squeezed his eyes tightly, and he saw the screens in his mind, and they'd gone dark.

Ask questions.

He thought for a moment. *What is the next step? Where do we go from here?*

And the screens answered him.

About Time

ONE WEEK EARLIER: SUNDAY

In his sleep, Jed soared high above the Amish Zone and looked down on it from the air. Down below, his body was ostensibly sleeping, cramped but not too uncomfortable, on the floor of Matthias's kitchen, along with Pook, Billy, and Ducky.

At altitude, he took it all in. He could see the entire extent of the Amish Zone, and the incredibly high and thick walls that surrounded it. Looking closer, he discovered that the walls appeared to have been constructed of rubble, pushed into the form of perimeter walls. But the top of the wall and the inside—facing the Amish countryside—had been finished and smoothed with concrete. Stairs and railings had been added here and there, so that anyone from inside the Zone could scale to the top if they felt like it.

Jed still didn't have answers about who had first built the walls... or why. The barrier had not been built to keep the community safe from animal predators, this much he knew. He studied the walls a while longer, then shifted his perspective so that he could see the whole community in one scene—and found himself deeply moved by the awesomeness of it all. This plain community, connected by blood and heritage to the old world of before, and even to the still-older world of medieval Europe, had survived and thrived—while the largest empires ever built by humans had all come and gone.

Although it was night, Jed could still see every detail, and he adjusted the light until it was perfect for his purposes. He could see the rich soil, the tree-lined lanes, the perfect intersecting lines of plowed fields and fences. He could see the immaculate houses and yards and barns set in stark relief against the verdant nature the community revered and managed. He saw a people who'd determined that they would define *themselves* rather than have their reality and culture defined by the times. That thought satisfied Jed, and soothed his soul.

He came to a stop and hovered in space, just studying it all awhile, reveling in the same beauty that had made Amish communities the target of tourism for hundreds of years. After a bit of reflection, Jed took a few deep breaths and then brought up his BICE control interface. He examined the file drawers for a moment.

He tried unsuccessfully to bring up Dawn's avatar, but wasn't surprised by that; he was starting to suspect that her BICE had somehow been removed or turned off while she was being held by the Yoders. He regretted now that he hadn't cleared up that little mystery with Dawn before setting her up in his bedroom for the night. When he'd told her goodnight, she'd given him the bottle of Quadrille, so he knew she expected him to get online. But if she'd planned on joining him in cyberspace... well, he had no way of knowing.

Regardless, Jed certainly wasn't going to waste the whole night sleeping. He wanted to know more about what was going on, and how he was being used by both his brother and Transport. It was like he was being pulled in a single direction, but by two diametrically opposed forces—if such a thing could be possible. He wanted to be online, because he wanted to know more about this place, and what was happening to him, and, at the same time, he wanted to find out why he was being used... why his being online was so important to his brother.

He started reading through the files again, repeating his process of hacking into Transport's system. He accessed the information on how Transport had determined that they could mine okcillium from the road base back on Earth. It was all right there in a memo sent to Transport command:

"We already ripped up the roads the first time around, only for a different purpose. This time, we'll just put the road base material through a few more steps, and we can extract the okcillium at the rate of ten grams per one hundred metric tons."

This information perplexed Jed. If Transport hadn't harvested the okcillium from the road base the "first time around" (whatever that meant), and had only subsequently learned that the okcillium was in the road base, then what did that mean? That they went back to Earth to get it? *So they went back in time?*

He'd always liked puzzles, but this one seemed to be unsolvable. So he switched gears. Rather than study events in time, why not study time itself? He searched for anything he could find about the basis and science of time... and time travel. He studied documents and reports from throughout written history. For the most part, these papers were written in a style and manner that was completely over his head. He couldn't make head nor tail out of them. So he closed his eyes, looked out into the universe above the Amish Zone, and tried to imagine what time must *look* like. He tried visualizing many different concepts, but every time he would encounter some flaw in his analogy. That is, until he struck on the idea of thinking of time as a long string—or, rather, an immense fabric made up of a large number of strings. This analogy wasn't perfect, but it held up better than any other he'd come up with.

He remembered that as a boy his father had once told him that space was like an enormous blanket, or carpet, which God had stretched into place starting from a single point. Not like a blanket that swaddled the Earth like a baby, but more like an unimaginably large fabric that stretched through nothingness and the void. And the planet Earth was just one little element embedded in the fabric.

He'd seen Amish women making fabric on looms, so he understood that process. And, he thought, his own life had been like a journey along one of these threads. It started at one point and had progressed "normally" in one direction. Even if someone had tied a knot in the string (a concept he could understand), he'd still only traveled forward, and never any other way.

Two ants traveling on a string in this manner could have different journeys. An ant walking along the top of a taut, straight string would never loop back to where he'd already been. But another ant, perhaps walking along the bottom of the same string, could detour around a loose, hanging knot or loop, circling back to where he'd been before, while the ant on top of the thread kept right on walking.

Now Jed thought of an almost (but not quite) infinite number of threads—enough threads to form a fabric containing everything that is. Any single thread in that fabric could be crossed or looped at any point along any of the threads. This thought process helped him get his bearings, even if it didn't help him solve any of his immediate problems.

As an Amish man, Jed had never progressed beyond the eighth grade in his education. Amish education existed mainly to prepare the plain people to deal with real-life issues and challenges. Things like communication, simple work, fellowship, humility, and submission were emphasized. For Amish men and women, education and job training would go on for life, but the primary, community level of education finished when one was about fourteen years old. Logic was learned by solving real-life problems in real time.

Well, he thought. *Apparently, time travel has just become a real-life issue.*

But Jed also recognized that if an education beyond the eighth grade automatically helped in solving time-travel problems, then probably a whole lot of the English would already be bopping around time by now, and it didn't seem like they were. So maybe he didn't need a public education. Maybe what he needed was just the ability to think things through.

He wondered: maybe some force had been applied to loop the thread of time back on itself. If time is an immense fabric, then like fabric, it can be wrinkled, looped, or folded. Jed remembered playing a game with Matthias where they would put a heavy leather ball (a toy they called a "corner ball") in a small baby's blanket, and then each of them would take two corners of the blanket. They'd pull tight and rocket the corner ball into the air. Then, when the ball descended, they would catch it in the blanket. As it came down with great force, they would lessen the tension on the blanket, and the ball would push the blanket down and curl the fabric back around on itself. From this loose analogy, it seemed to Jed that bending time might be possible if only the one wishing to do the bending could apply enough power, force, speed, or some such expression of energy.

Bending the fabric of time? That would take a lot of energy, he thought.

It seemed logical that the energy behind this time-bending force must be okcillium. He didn't even know what okcillium was or what it did, but he knew that it was a unique and very efficient power source, and that both sides in the current war were keen to have a lot of it. Perhaps some enterprising scientist working for the government had been the first to use okcillium power to bend time?

Jed immediately pulled up a file that discussed the attributes of okcillium. He had dozens of documents to choose from, so he just pulled one randomly from the cabinet and began to read. It was a paper done for a university back on Earth. From what Jed could gather, okcillium was a completely new and different kind of power source. And it was incredibly efficient; this fact was repeated over and over again. Power generated by okcillium produced very little resistance as it traveled through just about any material at all. That means it didn't produce a tremendous amount of heat, or a lot of noise either. A common piece of copper electrical wire was sufficient to send enough power to light a small town.

Here, he thought, *is enough energy to produce a bend or loop in the fabric of time.* So somehow, during his travels, he'd been tossed forward in time. His mind reeled at the thought of it.

He reflected on his journey to New Pennsylvania. How Dawn had told him that he'd never really ever gone to Texas. That apparently that part of the journey had been a show—a sham—perhaps some government method used to track down rebels trying to pass through time using Transport resources.

But then he'd been released by the Transport Authority, put inside his pod, and prepped by the woman whose job it was to monitor him on his trip. He remembered now that the woman hooked a tube up to his catheter. That was supposed to be his waste-processing system. Before now, he'd never considered that the catheter might have been for some other purpose. He pressed his eyes closed and tried to amplify his recollection of events. He remembered pushing the blue button, and he recalled the almost immediate cool sensation of some liquid pulsing through his veins. He remembered thinking that the cooling of his veins was odd, but not unpleasant, and then he remembered being surprised to see Dawn in the pod next to him, right before the lights went out for him.

Was it possible that he'd been drugged just so that, while he took some strange loop along the thread of time, he wouldn't know what was happening? Could it be that he'd never really left Columbia, Pennsylvania at all? That somehow he'd been kept in suspended animation for some requisite time while he and the ship he was in merely passed forward into another era?

Dawn. She said she'd been back and forth several times.

She knew Billy and Pook and Ducky like they'd been friends forever. Yet she also knew Amos from when they were both back on Earth, and Amos had contacted her and asked her to travel with Jed to New Pennsylvania.

Then there was the window with the coffee-can pane. That was easy enough to explain if the window had come through the same portal. Maybe not at the same time, but who knew? Pook had stored his forged papers in the back of the window frame. *No way was that a coincidence.* Jed knew that his brother had intended for him to see the window. When he'd mentioned as much to Amos, his brother had smiled.

Jed's thoughts raced now.

Here's what he knew. He was either completely insane, or... well, he felt like he could safely assume four things: 1. The Columbia Transport Station was (or contained) some kind of okcillium time-bending device. 2. Transport, at some point, had figured out how to perform this time bending, and was using it to colonize... what? Some future Earth? Was he in the future? Was he still on Earth? 3. The limited amount of okcillium available on Earth at the time meant that TRACE was forced to use Transport's travel portal. 4. The City was gone.

Also this: Transport now had access to a large supply of okcillium back on Earth. Conclusion? *Everything has changed.*

30

THE COUNCIL

This Council meeting was unlike any the SOMA had experienced in all his years of leading TRACE. For the first time, *his* leadership and decisions were being questioned—openly. His natural fighting instinct inclined him to threaten to retire again. In the past, that ploy had usually worked to get the council to back off—but with so many pieces of the endgame finally in place, he was just a little afraid they might actually accept his resignation this time, and move on without him. That was a fear he'd never really experienced before in all his time as the supreme commander of TRACE forces. And now, at long last, he had his brother in play, and things were going so well in that regard.

Councilman Bennings stood and placed both hands on the table. Bennings was a traditionally contrarian voice on the council. Slow to move and difficult to convince. Amos was also convinced that the man wanted power, and the sooner the better.

"Now that Transport has retreated beyond the Shelf, why have they not moved against the Amish? Either to take the Amish with them, or to destroy their community so that it cannot exist to support and feed the resistance?" Bennings asked. "We're all sure that the government didn't bring the Amish here in order to abandon them to us. So why not destroy them?"

Bennings didn't direct his questions to anyone in particular, but all eyes turned to Amos anyway. He was always expected to have all the answers.

"The only reason the Amish haven't been destroyed in the new world," Amos replied, "is because they produce raw materials from nothing—from the ground—and most of the new world would starve without them." He put his hands behind his back and began to pace slowly back and forth before the giant screen that showed a map of the Amish Zone.

"Colonization of the Great Shelf has largely failed," he continued. "Despite all of Transport's schemes and machinations, the big cities are still only lightly populated, and the immigrants who have chosen to live there work for slave wages, earning unbacked and inflated unis in the factories and service industries, to support Transport's imperial plans. The cities are not cities in any real sense of the word. They are basically large factory prisons. Just because the prisoners choose to remain there as some quirk of their makeup doesn't make the prison any less real."

Bennings nodded. "These are all things we know, Commander. But they don't explain why Transport hasn't yet attacked the AZ."

"It is the foundation of my answer, Councilman," Amos said. "If you'll allow me to continue?"

Bennings nodded and waved his hand, almost dismissively.

Amos resumed his speech. "Transport's hope has been that the population of the cities would explode—through immigration *and* through natural population growth. The government's erroneous belief has been that where there's a growing population, eventually productivity will follow suit. The theory, as backward as we know it to be, is that the more consumers there are, the more consumables can be produced in the factories, and the better everyone will do. Of course, we know that population growth does not just magically spawn productivity. Building factories and stocking them full of people does not mystically produce either raw materials *or* good ideas. But understanding Transport's thinking helps us to predict how they might act. For example, since they believe that population equals production, and that city folk are more compliant and more easily governed, we can expect that they are incentivizing births in the cities. We were able to predict this even before we learned from our spies that the city folk up on the shelf are encouraged to reproduce offspring wildly, while country folk—if they are caught—are *punished* for having children, unless they commit to having their children schooled by the government and trained for city work.

"Understanding Transport helps us know what we need to do to defeat them," Amos said.

"And what if they're successful?" It was

Councilwoman Reynosa. She sat back and fixed her eyes on Amos. She spoke respectfully, but with firm intent. "What if they're able to begin making these factories more productive than they are currently?"

Amos nodded at the Councilwoman. "Those who are creative or who can *produce* have mostly escaped the cities and are now living in the countryside—off-grid—much like the Amish in the east. The brain drain is almost absolute."

"If you are correct," Reynosa said, "then we should be able to sit back and wait. Eventually the cities will collapse, and Transport will have failed to rebuild."

"Unfortunately, that is not true," Amos said. "They have access to a portal. And with it, they can bring through raw materials, even okcillium, all taken from the old world. History shows us that many tyrannical governments have been able to build up large and powerful armies using coercive industrialism. Nazi Germany is one example." Amos paused for a moment to let the visual sink in. "If Transport hadn't found a way to access okcillium from the old world, I would completely agree with you, Councilwoman. We could contain them, and just wait for their system to collapse. But as we have seen... okcillium changes everything."

Bennings scowled. He was growing frustrated. "That still doesn't explain why the Amish have not been destroyed." The Councilman stood and walked closer to where Amos stood. The approach wasn't threatening, but it carried with it a message; and that message was understood by everyone in the room. "If the Amish aren't in a position to supply goods and services to Transport up on the Shelf, why does the government allow them to survive—when they know all the Amish will be doing is producing for us?"

Amos looked down at the floor and sighed. "I don't know." He looked up again. "I only know that food production up on the Shelf is not sufficient to provide for the cities for very long. We know it, and they know it."

"And what, then, are we to conclude from these facts?" Bennings asked.

"They must attack at some point," Amos said. "As soon as they feel they are strong enough, or that they have an advantage."

"If we know this, and we expect an attack on the AZ, what are we going to do to protect the Amish there?"

"Everything that can be done."

"Can we guarantee that they will not be harmed?"

"No."

This answer caused a general buzz to run through the room. The voices carried with them every form of human emotion. Anger. Concern. Fear. Amos knew that fear, when properly curated, could be a great ally. *It is good that they fear,* he thought. *If they are not afraid, then they are stupid. And if they are afraid, then they should listen to me.*

Amos spoke loudly to be heard over the general din. "On this side of the cliffs, Transport forces are only performing occasional probing actions. But we should not get cavalier and forget the dangers. We've seen what they did to their own city."

"What you *say* they did to their own city!" It was Councilman Graham, a politician who represented rebels who lived in the countryside beyond the Shelf.

Amos Troyer smiled, but it was a smile dripping with irony. "If you have information about the bombing that contradicts the facts we know, Councilman Graham, I'd love to receive them." He knew that Graham was a great supporter of his. The man was just making a joke to lighten the mood and to emphasize that some members of the Council didn't trust Amos Troyer with power. Not now that TRACE was winning the war.

Bennings waved off the small performance between the two allies. "What about our soldiers who stopped the attack on your brother in the AZ?"

Amos noted—and not for the first time—that whenever his military actions were successful, Bennings would refer to the soldiers as *our* soldiers. *Our* forces. *Our* actions. But if something failed, as it did in the recent limited attack on the Tulsa, Bennings had emphasized that "*Your* people were not ready." "*Your* people were caught by surprise," he'd said. Amos decided, wisely, not to point out this anomaly, but he intended to mention it to some of the other Council members in private conversations later.

"*Our* people," Amos said, "have been permitted by the elders in the AZ to stay for one week, to tend to their wounded or to make other arrangements. But after that, they'll have to go. This is in accord with the agreement the Amish have with Transport, going back to the foundation of the colony."

"But Transport has no authority there now!" Councilman Bennings shouted. "They're gone from the east. Why are the Amish still obeying Transport?"

Amos stared at Bennings for a moment before answering. "The Amish have their own reasons for everything they do, and you know that," he said. "They don't have to answer to me or to you. However, they've graciously given us some insight into their decisions. The elders realize that their colonization agreement may be voided now that Transport has fled beyond the Shelf, but they don't want to be harboring violent rebels beyond the time limit that they believe allows them to satisfy the Biblical requirement for charity and mercy. This is the best that we can expect."

"And what about your brother?" Bennings asked.

"Yes?" Amos said. "What about him?"

"Are the Amish going to ask him to leave, too?"

"No."

Bennings nodded. "And how does this affect the war?"

"Although they cannot yet ask Jedediah to leave, the elders also voiced the opinion that he should pray about whether or not he is becoming a detriment to the future happiness of the colony. Jed was not found to have engaged in any violence, or to have encouraged it in any way, but they ask that he consider whether or not his presence among the plain people is likely to encourage more violence to happen in the Amish Zone."

"And how does Jedediah figure in your plans?"

Amos smiled. "I'm not free to divulge that yet, other than to say that my brother is of primary importance to our war effort."

At this point, Bennings stood and threw his hands into the air. "So you don't even feel the need to inform this council of your plans?"

Amos shook his head. "I do not."

Councilman Graham interrupted. He had his hands spread apart like he was separating two prizefighters in the ring. "Can you at least tell us why you don't just mount a full attack on Transport? Those of us who live on the Shelf would greatly appreciate the relief. We've given you the Tulsa, as you asked. We've achieved air superiority. We have them on the run beyond the Shelf—"

Amos raised his hand, palm out, to silence his friend. "If we defeat them here... if we destroy them, and any means or method they have to travel back to the old world—which is no easy task... we still have the fundamental problem."

"And what problem is that, sir?" Bennings asked.

"They still have control of the old world. According to my brother, they have now discovered a means to gather and utilize an enormous amount of okcillium. If we win the war here, the fight only shifts back to the old world. From there, if they are not stopped, they can build a *thousand* portals—and flood this world again in a way that we'll never stop."

Bennings looked around at the other faces and frowned. "But if we don't win the war here first, then they *still* control both worlds, and can shut the portal any time they please..."

"Something they've already done by destroying the City, haven't they?" Reynosa asked.

Amos Troyer put up his hands again, indicating a request for silence. After a moment, the talking and bickering quieted down, and Amos waited a few more beats before speaking.

"By destroying the City, Transport succeeded in destroying the only... *official...* travel portal between the old world and New Pennsylvania. This is true. But we should all be prepared to accept the reality that they would not have done this if they didn't already have another portal ready and operating. We suspect that this new portal is somewhere beyond the Shelf."

Bennings sat down in frustration. He sighed deeply and rubbed his face with his hands. "I guess I hadn't really thought about that with everything going on here. The Transport station in the City was our main means of maintaining the war in both worlds... and now it's gone."

Silence reigned for a few moments, and all eyes were on Amos.

"The good news is that *we* have another portal, too," he said. He began pacing again, but looked at each Council member in turn as he spoke. "The existence and location of that portal is currently a military secret. I will not divulge it to this council or to any other person at this time."

Silence.

Bennings stood again. "Either we must win *here*, or we must win *there*—in order to guarantee ourselves a future."

"That is incorrect," Amos said. "We must win here *and* there, or we are all finished."

"Which war is more winnable?" Graham asked.

"This one."

"Then we must win this one first, and win that one eventually," Bennings said.

"I agree," Amos said, nodding. "And I have every intention of making certain our eventual victory."

When it appeared that no one had anything else to add, Amos fixed his eyes on Bennings and approached the man, who turned in his chair to face the SOMA.

"If we are done here," Amos said, "I am going to ask *you* to get out of *my* office—and off *my* ship." He paused for a moment and then smiled. He directed his next statement to the rest of the Council. "If the rest of you want this little man running your war, just let me know, and I'll turn over the keys to him. If not, then I don't want to see him on my ship again until this war is over and I'm retired."

31

LIGHTER

saiah King's family took Matthias into their home—to care for him and tend to his bullet wound. Of course, this was after he'd received first aid from Pook's unit medic (a tall man named Angelo), and after he'd been seen by Elder Bontrager at the Amish clinic. The Kings were an Amish family who'd come to New Pennsylvania from the smaller Missouri Amish Zone in one of the earliest migrations from the old world.

The Amish of the New Pennsylvania colony were an amalgamated people. The community was made up of converts from among the English back in the old world, Amish-raised transplants from the four different AZ's of Earth, and even some other plain people who didn't self-identify as Amish. But one thing the community in New Pennsylvania had that has always been common to communities of plain people the world over, was a sense of obligation to care for one another. They all possessed an intense desire to feed the hungry and clothe the naked, and to take care of the aged and infirm no matter the cost.

Matthias's life had been spared because the bullet fired at him from the pistol of a Transport soldier had missed an artery in his shoulder by an eighth of an inch. Despite the close call, and the fact that Matthias was still not out of the woods, everyone was hopeful that he'd make a full recovery. They were hopeful, but not deceived. They wanted him to live and thrive, but no one could really know for sure that he would—not yet. There were no hospitals in the Amish Zone (though there was a clinic) and with the destruction of the City, critical medical care had become something that, once again, they couldn't depend on. Though they weren't at all hesitant to make use of advanced medical care when it was available, and when it fit with their overall worldview, the Amish generally relied on common sense, intensive personal attention to the sick or injured, and prayer, more than they ever relied on some system devised by the English.

After he'd made assurances that Matthias was being well cared for, Jed, Dawn, and Pook's soldiers had all made their way back to Matthias's farm where, by agreement with the elders, they would stay until after the barn-raising, which was scheduled for the coming Saturday. Even with Matthias injured, the barn-raising would go forward. However dour and serious the Amish might seem to outsiders, they are an overwhelmingly optimistic people. Their faith, and the evidence of a thousand years, convinced them that plowing forward despite the obstacles was always the best policy.

But while it is true that they are an optimistic people, they are not particularly *inclusive*. They have their own culture and rules, and they expect to be left alone to live according to them. So once the barn was raised, the rebel soldiers being housed at Matthias's house would be expected to leave the Amish Zone—and the elders were not-so-privately hoping that Jedediah would go with them.

Back at Matthias's small farmhouse, the tiny structure became the temporary home of Jed, Dawn, Billy, Pook, and Ducky—which was all the people the little cottage could comfortably hold. The rest of the rebel squad bedded down in Matthias's temporary "barn." He called it a barn because it was where he stored his buggy, wagon, and tack, but for all intents and purposes it was a small shed that was barely weatherproof. Built of old, re-purposed barn wood, the shed had taken four days of lonely labor for Matthias to construct, and the young Amish man had been clear in pointing out that he looked forward to tearing the shed down so that he could reuse the wood yet again.

The shed was no motel, but it was plenty fine according to the standards of the TRACE soldiers. It was certainly better than they could expect most anywhere they'd be billeted outside the Amish Zone. Many times in the past, through their battles and travels, the team had slept in caves, or dens of rocks. They'd often stretched themselves out on the frozen ground of New Pennsylvania for a shivery night of very little sleep. No, for them, Matthias's shed would do just fine for the week, and they were glad to have it.

Being dead, the Yoders could no longer be relied upon to bring meals, so a committee of the Amish had created a rotating meal-assignment list that would spread the responsibility of feeding the inhabitants of Matthias's farm until it came time for them all to leave. These arrangements were a matter of course for the Amish, and were never seen as a burden. Jed remembered that his family back in the old world was constantly preparing food to be delivered somewhere, for some charitable reason or another. Among the Amish, a person's sense of self-worth and personal value was intricately tied to the communal idea of helping others. Independence and individuality were never considered positive things to be sought after. Dependence on one another, and losing oneself in the body of the brethren, were the foundations of the community. To *not* have that extra work to do would have been quite troubling for the plain people.

Jed gave his little bedroom over to Dawn, and the four other men bedded down on fleeces and blankets in the tiny kitchen. They all slept well after the ordeal of the previous day. Just before bed, Dawn had pressed a small bottle of white pills into Jed's hand. "Q," she'd said. "In case you need it."

• • • •

On Sunday morning, Jed awoke early and cleaned up his area, stowing his fleece and blanket out of the way so that the kitchen could be used. He wanted to be up early enough to show the soldiers who'd slept out in the barn how to perform many of the daily farm tasks. Since they'd be there for a week, and since Matthias wouldn't be able to work, the soldiers were expected to pitch in. It was the Amish way.

Jed stepped out into the cool morning air and inhaled deeply. The scents of manured fields and fresh hay, and the pungent aroma of damp grass made him feel almost like he was at home. Almost. There were lingering doubts in him that threw everything just a little off kilter. It isn't natural for a human to *not* be grounded in "place" and "time." To be cast adrift unsettles the soul, and until a new place becomes home, it remains foreign. Jed felt unmoored from the foundations of his life, and even his Amishness wasn't quite the anchor that it had always been for him.

He wasn't excited about waking the soldiers in the milking shed at 4:30 a.m. either, but it needed to be done, and the cows certainly wouldn't milk themselves. They were used to being milked at this hour, which meant that their udders would be full and giving the animals a feeling of urgency. The cows knew when it was almost time to let down their milk, and Jed had seen Zoe so eager to be milked at milking time that her teats were literally leaking the fluid when he'd gone in to start the process.

He pulled open the shed door, expecting to be an irritant to the soldiers, only to be pleasantly surprised by what he saw. Several lanterns were already burning in the small shed, and their yellow-orange light flickered and cast long shadows against the walls. It seems Jed wouldn't have to wake the men after all. Apparently, Eagles had already—to his own evident joy and amusement—rudely woken the other men, and he was now showing the sleepy team how to milk the cows. The soldiers were all crowded around a stall while the burly wild man tried to explain the process of milking in his broken English.

"Eeguls juicing cow!" he said to Jed as soon as he noticed him watching from the doorway. He had a huge smile on his face. It was evident that the salvager was very pleased with himself for recognizing the need, and for taking on the task.

Jed had never seen Eagles without a big chunk of uncured *tobac* in his mouth, so he was a little surprised that greenish goo didn't fly from the man's lips as he spoke. In fact, the man wasn't chewing the green tobacco at all.

"Squeezing teat down. Topping to bottom. Ziiiip! Juicing!" Eagles repeated the feat again and again, and then added his other hand. "Ziiip! Ziip! Bothing hands now playing musics!"

"I'll never figure that out," Ducky said with a sleepy scowl.

"Little man figuring out!" Eagles shouted angrily. "Little man eating not if not juicing cow!" The big man pointed around the barn randomly and said, "Farm!" Then he pointed at the cow and said, "Cow!" Then he pointed at the teats and said, "Juice!" Then he pointed at his mouth and said, "And eating only then!" To conclude his filibuster, he pointed at Ducky. "Juicing cow no? Eating no!"

"Somebody give this man some tobacco," Pook said, shaking his head. "He's a little cranky in the morning."

"Not cranking, dummy! Shutting the Pook!" Eagles snapped. His right hand continued the milking, but his free hand began to strike out, flailing at the soldiers wildly, and he succeeded in knocking Billy off the neighboring stool. Eagles stopped milking then and stood up, glaring at

Pook. "You!" He narrowed his eyes in a threatening way, pointing at the rebel leader.

Pook looked around. "Me?"

"You!"

"Me what?"

"Juicing cow."

"Wait. *I'm* juicing the cow?"

Eagles nodded. "Now!"

Pook grinned. "You're kidding me, right?"

Eagles glared at Pook, but didn't say a word.

Pook shook his head. "I'm an officer now. I'm not milking any cow."

The wild man snarled and then nodded again. He shrugged, and then hauled back and punched Ducky right in the face. The little man flew backward and landed on his rump, skidding up against the wall of the shed.

"Whoa!" Pook yelled, and pulled his weapon, pointing it at Eagles. "What did you do that for?"

Ducky, now propped up against the far wall, shook his head and rubbed his jaw. He tried to clear his vision, and a few of the other soldiers ran to help him up.

"Pook juicing cow!" Eagles demanded.

Pook was pointing the weapon at Eagles and trying to figure out what had just happened. He backed up slowly and then reached over to steady Ducky. "Why did you punch *him* and not *me?*"

Eagles made another fist, and then reached behind him with his other hand and snatched Billy up from the stool. "Being Pook is boss!"

Ducky looked up at Pook while still rubbing his jaw. "I think he's saying that if you don't get milking, he's going to kick all of our butts."

"What the—?" Pook said.

Eagles tightened his fist and looked at Billy.

"Okay! Okay!" Pook said. "Sheesh! Unbelievable."

"Juicing, now!" Eagles said.

"Juicing now," Pook said. He exhaled deeply and sat down on the stool and took the teats in his hands.

Eagles looked around and smiled. He smacked his hand together like he was done with his work, and winked at Jed. "Timing for tobac!" he said as he walked out of the shed.

Jed watched as the wild salvager skipped across the dirt drive on his way to the small house. As Eagles walked, he tossed up a piece of metal that glinted in the moonlight, commanding Jed's attention. Eagles caught the piece of metal deftly and then tossed it up again. Just then, Ducky walked up next to Jed, still working his jaw back and forth and stretching his neck.

"Hmmm..." Ducky said to Jed. "I wonder if Eagles got that okcillium lighter back somehow. I thought he'd lost it in the firefight with Transport in No Man's Land, when you and Dawn were first captured."

32

THE PEACEFUL KIND

MONDAY

A dozen Amish men arrived at Matthias's farm just as the pink-orange glow of sunrise began to paint the eastern sky. They brought two large wagons, filled with tons of lumber and building supplies for the new barn. Heavy beams cut from ancient trees, rough-cut studs, and one inch-thick siding boards were strapped on with heavy hand-made ropes.

Pook's team worked alongside the Amish men, unloading all of the materials. Then two of the Amish craftsmen began leveling and laying out the foundation and base of the banked barn, while another team began cutting and notching the heavy beams like puzzle pieces, according to plans they stored only in their heads. By noon, the Amish artisans were teaching Pook and his team how to lay concrete block. Although the barn would be built on Saturday, this prep team was sent to make sure that things went smoothly on barn-raising day.

Jed and Dawn took the opportunity to spend some time together, so in minutes they were walking along the tree-lined roads of the Amish Zone, stopping every once in a while to study neighboring farms and structures. As they walked, Dawn briefed Jed on what had happened to her after she'd been captured by the Yoders.

"They had been working for Transport, but Amos turned them," Dawn said. "Or the other way around—I'm not sure. Anyway, they were double agents. And maybe we'll never really learn where their real allegiances lay."

Jed reached up and touched the back of Dawn's kapp. "They removed your BICE? Is it healing up all right? Do you have any pain?"

"I've had a BICE removed before, remember?" Dawn said. "I'll be all right. It *is* kind of hard to get used to not having Internet access, but I think I kind of like it."

Jed just nodded. He wasn't sure he wanted to be without the chip just yet. Certainly in the long run he wanted to be done with it all, but having the chip gave him a strange and even eerie sense of comfort. It was a very non-Amish feeling, but however paradoxical it was, the feeling was there nonetheless.

"Being here," Dawn said, "walking these lanes and being with you... Well, it shows me that I'd like to live here when this is all over," Dawn said.

Jed blushed and put his hands into the pockets of his broadfall pants. "I'd like for you to live here, too."

Dawn took his elbow and pulled him to a stop, turning toward him. "So, do you think we could get married? You and I? And live with the Amish here in this community?"

Jed blushed. He didn't know what to say. He studied Dawn's face to see if she was serious about what she was saying. It was different to actually be talking to her face to face, without the subconscious knowledge that what he was looking at was actually just her avatar. "I don't know," he said. He turned and began walking again, so Dawn followed him. "The elders have made it pretty clear that they don't want me here."

"Once this is all over," Dawn said, "they'll know you didn't participate in any violence. They'll know you were just trying to survive in a peaceful way, Jed."

"*I* don't even know if that's true," Jed said. "I don't know myself well enough to know if I'm the peaceful kind."

Dawn put her hand on his back. "You are, Jed."

"I don't know," Jed repeated. "Maybe I'm more like my brother."

"I know you both," Dawn said. "And I love your brother. He's been like a father to me. But you and he are nothing alike, Jed."

"He brought me here. He planned all of this so that I'd join in the fight with him," Jed said.

Dawn pursed her lips. "I don't think so. He brought you here, for sure. And there's no doubt that he's been using you to help the resistance. That part is also true. But he hasn't asked you to fight."

Jed didn't say anything for a while after that. They walked on, and after a short spell he took her hand and squeezed it. "I would very much like to marry you, Dawn.

Wherever we end up." He smiled at her. "I'll be Amish wherever I am, I know that. And I hope you know that too."

They walked up to a large clearing that looked very familiar to Jed. There were a few low rises that seemed out of place, but if he didn't know better, he'd have said that this land could have been the location of his family's farm.

"I brought you here on purpose," Dawn said. "I thought you would recognize it." She put her hands behind her back as they walked. "I thought you might be ready to see it."

Jed didn't speak as he looked around. He wasn't sure what he thought about seeing the place.

"I was raised Amish," Dawn said.

Jed's attention was on the land—he was trying to compare it with his memories of his old farm—but when he realized that Dawn was being serious, he turned to her. "You were raised Amish?" Jed asked. "What happened?"

"My father left the Amish when I was ten years old. After my mother died." Dawn looked down at the ground and shuffled her feet. "He wasn't excommunicated or anything. He just said he couldn't stand to see the Amish life continue without her. Like it sullied his memory of her or something. It never did make sense to me."

Jed didn't know what to say to that.

"You don't have to say anything," Dawn said, as if she'd read his mind. "It's just something that happened. I guess that's why I married so young, and married a former Amish boy."

"Ben Beachy?" Jed said.

"Yeah. Ben."

"He died?"

"Yes. In this war." Dawn walked up the long, weed-strewn drive that led onto the empty property. "He was Pook's best friend. Billy is Ben's younger brother. The three of them were inseparable."

Jed just nodded. He still didn't know what to say, and it didn't seem like Dawn expected him to say anything. It was like she was unburdening her soul. Like she was clearing the decks so that her relationship with him could go forward unhindered. So he just let her talk.

"Billy was in love with me too," Dawn said. "Still is, I think. There could never be anything between us, though. But we both loved Ben very much. I think of Billy as if he were my brother." She nodded very faintly, as if giving herself permission to admit something. "In that way, he *is* my brother."

"Having a brother can be tough," Jed said.

"Yes. And pretty great."

"Yes."

As they walked up the lane, Jed was getting the strong feeling that he'd been on this property before. The bend of the road, even though it was unkempt and covered over with weeds, was very familiar to him.

"I was ordered to make you fall in love with me, Jed," Dawn said. "Might as well get it all out in the open at once."

Jed stopped and looked at her. It was all so overwhelming, so he just blinked and nodded his head. Somehow he knew that what she was saying was the truth.

Dawn pulled him by his hands until he took a

reluctant step toward her. "But that doesn't mean I didn't *really* fall in love with *you.*"

"So how does it stand with us now?" Jed asked.

"I love you," Dawn said.

"I love you, too."

●●●●

"This is my old farm," Jed said, and pointed out at the land. "It just feels like it. It has to be. I halfway recognize some of the trees, though they're a lot larger than I remember."

Dawn didn't say anything for a few moments. They walked up onto a low hill that seemed to have been made artificially.

"This would be where the barn was," Jed said.

Dawn just nodded.

"What happened to it all?" Jed asked.

"Fire," Dawn said.

"Everything?" Jed asked. "Everything burned?"

"Twenty percent of the homes and other structures burned down when the community first got here."

"The community?"

"The whole thing. The entire Amish Zone," Dawn said.

"I don't get it," Jed said. "If this is my old farm, then it has always been here."

Dawn shook her head. "You'll need to talk to Amos to get all the details."

"Are you saying the whole community, land and all, was somehow transported here from the old world?"

Dawn nodded. "Talk to your brother, Jed."

(33

ANOTHER EARTH

TUESDAY

The next morning, the Amish women from the community showed up to clean and work on Matthias's little house. This was a common practice in plain communities, a unifying tradition that, renewed generation by generation, tied the people together and made everyone's life easier. Even weekly worship meetings are held house to house, every other weekend, so that a different family hosts the meeting each time. Every two weeks, on the weekend when a meeting was scheduled to be held, a group of community members would show up at the host's house—usually on Friday afternoon—and the home would be readied for the meeting. Needful repairs would be made, no questions asked. Sprucing up, sometimes even including major projects, would be completed so that the house would be ready for the Sunday meeting.

On the Saturday afternoon before a typical Sunday meeting, a wagon appears at the host's home. In the wagon are all of the portable pews for the Sunday fellowship. The pews are unloaded, and the wagon is carefully re-loaded with furniture from the parts of the house that are to be used for the meeting. Then the pews are arranged in the vacated rooms. In this way, the plain people believe that they are carrying on the practices of the Apostles and the early Church in holding their fellowship meetings house to house.

The cleaning going on in Matthias's house, however, was not for a scheduled Sabbath meeting. This was instead for the barn-raising scheduled for Saturday. On this Tuesday morning in Matthias's cottage, screens were fixed, blinds were dusted, and the whole house was given a thorough cleaning from top to bottom. Dawn joined in, and spent most of the day chatting and making friends with the young Amish women from the community, many of whom were close to her age. Though she'd been raised Amish, she'd been gone for many years, and was surprised to find out that the Amish girls were so goofy and full of joy. They joked around a lot, and teased one another incessantly. And even though Dawn was dressed in Amish garb, the girls all called her "The Englischer," but they did so with a wink and a smile. Overall, she felt very comfortable with the girls of the community. That is, until two of the girls asked her about Jed.

For the most part, this was a forbidden thing in an Amish society, this talking about an unmarried young man. Girls did not talk about boys, except maybe to their closest sisters. Dawn was a little surprised that in this young colony, the girls seemed to be more forward about male/female relationships than she remembered from her own district back in the old world. In most traditionalist districts, there was no talk at all about relationships between men and women. Most people (even parents and siblings) found out that a young couple was in love at the moment they announced their marital intentions to the family. But that had been a long time ago.

Dawn couldn't really tell if these girls were actually interested in Jed, or if they were just curious and looking for gossip, but both girls specifically asked if Jed might be looking for a wife, and if Dawn had any intentions toward him. Although she was embarrassed to be asked, and she blushed when she answered, she admitted that she did care very much for Jed, and that she was hopeful that he cared for her too. Both girls smiled and seemed to be authentically happy for her. Their curiosities sated, they all got back to work.

How exciting to be thinking about love, Dawn thought. *Even if things don't work out for us, it has been a pleasant interlude in my life of war: to be dressed for peace, and in love with a man like Jed.*

Out in the barn, Pook's team took the opportunity to clean their weapons. This was another thing that was frowned upon in Amish society, but the squad felt that it was necessary that they keep up their battle readiness even during this peaceful respite. Eagles also gave knife-throwing lessons to any of the squad who were interested. He just called it "knifing," but nobody could get him to change his word for the activity. Eagles was good at "knifing." *Very* good. He always tried to throw a knife in such a way that the blade would stick into the gouge left in the beam from the last throw. He called his perfect throws "bullsings." He wasn't always successful, but he was always close. And when he did hit the mark perfectly, he would yell "Bullsing!" at the top of his lungs, and then crush anyone within reach with an almost paralyzing bear hug. It got to the point that when the soldiers of TRACE heard the cry "Bullsing!" they would all jump out of the way and run to the corners of the shed.

After the knifing lesson, Jed showed the squad how to hook up the milk wagon to the horses, and to prepare the milk to be hauled away. Prepping the horses and the wagon was something all the members of the TRACE team grew to love. Already, this early in the week, they would race one another to get to work with the horses and attach the wagon.

As for Jed, he wanted to find a place where he could spend some time alone... so he could get on the Internet and learn more about his situation. A man's mind can float around untethered in the sea for only so long before it seeks a lighthouse, or at least a bird with leaves in its beak. So, after delivering the milk to the neighbor's springhouse, Jed received Tom Hochstetler's permission to crawl up into the man's hayloft so he could "rest" while the women worked on Matthias's house. Eagles and Ducky drove the wagon back to Matthias's place (Eagles loved driving the horses) while Jed stayed behind.

After he'd found a good resting spot in the loft, Jed took a Quadrille tablet and lay down. He calmed his mind and tried his best to relax himself. Closing his eyes, he felt the calm feeling grow in him, and when he felt he was ready, he brought up his BICE interface.

This time he didn't soar up into the sky, something he dearly liked to do. He didn't zip through immersive Transport maps of the cities on the Shelf, and he didn't study the geography of New Pennsylvania from on high, trying to figure out the "where" of his life. This time he immediately went to his messaging interface and sent an alert to his brother. Only moments later, he saw Amos's avatar, transparent and seemingly sleeping, appear in the control room. As he watched, the avatar became opaque, then the eyes opened, and Jed's brother Amos was standing before him.

When Jed saw his brother, he felt a chill go up his spine. For the first time, he really got a sense of the years having gone by in Amos's life. Jed felt that the man he was looking at wasn't just an avatar displaying for him what his brother would look like as he approached seventy. No, this really *was* his brother—though not in the flesh—and those decades that showed so plainly on his skin and weighed so heavily on his shoulders had really happened to the man.

"Jed," Amos said with a nod, by way of greeting.

"Amos," Jed said, nodding in return.

"How is life in the Amish Zone, brother?"

Jed scowled a little at his brother's familiarity. "A little confusing, Amos."

"Confusing? How so?"

"Dawn took me to the location of our old farm. I could see the foundations of the house and the barn. It was very troubling."

"Fifty-three years have come and gone since you left that place. A lot can happen in over five decades." Amos paused for a moment, choking back a sob. "A lot *has* happened..."

"She said that the whole Amish Zone traveled to this new world."

Amos looked at his brother. A whole range of emotions flooded over the older man. He longed to bring his brother into his arms—to hug him in a long embrace. And to tell the boy everything... everything he could possibly want to know. *It won't work*, he thought. *You've known it from the beginning. He can't take it all at once. No one could.* "She did, did she?" he said.

"She did."

"And what else did she say?"

Jed put one hand in his pocket, but with the other he pointed at Amos. "She said I needed to talk to *you* about it."

Amos nodded. He exhaled, and his eyes scanned his brother's face as he considered how best to explain things in a way that wouldn't confuse Jed even more than he already was. "I understand that this is all still perplexing to you, Jedediah," he finally said. "With everything you've discovered, there is still so much about what's going on that you don't know."

"So why don't you tell me about this part," Jed said.

The brothers stared at one another for a long moment. Jed could see that even the idea of explaining it all was taxing on Amos. The leader of the resistance was, after all, an old man—regardless of the fact that he'd been born four years after Jed.

"There was a war that broke out," Amos began. "Shortly after you left for New Pennsylvania. We all call it the Second Transport War. In fact, it was breaking out in Oklahoma even as you were boarding your ship." Amos put both hands in his pockets and rocked back on his heels. "The war was confusing at first. There were a lot of factions. Eventually foreign governments got involved. It got ugly fast."

"A World War?" Jed asked.

"In a way," Amos said. "And in that war, several major cities not far from the Amish Zone on Earth were destroyed. Most of Columbia, Pennsylvania was destroyed as well. That's the city from which you embarked on your journey, and the same city where you landed when you arrived in New Pennsylvania. Now," Amos raised up an old, wrinkled hand, "not all of Columbia was destroyed. Luckily for you—and for all of us—the Transport Station in Columbia survived. But most of the city became a huge pile of rubble. And with all these cities reduced to nothing but bricks and rocks and ashes, someone decided that all of the rubble—the shattered structures, the concrete; the bricks, rebar, and wiring that make up a modern metropolis—should be hauled off."

Jed could see it all happening in his mind's eye. But just in case he couldn't, Amos brought up a white screen, and a video began to play on it. It showed enormous pieces of construction equipment clearing away the remains of a city.

Amos pointed with his finger. "All of that debris went to build—"

"—the Great Wall," Jed interrupted.

Amos sighed deeply and began to pace as he talked. "Yes. At some point, the decision was made by Transport to construct a wall around the Amish Zone."

The video screen began to show images of the wall being constructed. "Many reasons were given for the construction of the wall. Some said it was to protect the Amish from the war, and from the refugees who flooded the AZ after the destruction of the cities. Those were very real problems that needed to be addressed. Some said that the wall was designed to keep the Amish from openly trading with the rebels." Amos had a sad look of chagrin on his face. "This was also a very real issue, I must admit." He flipped his hand as if indicating some imaginary other group. "Still others—the more conspiracy-minded among us—believed that the plan all along had been to intentionally... How should I say this?" He made a flipping motion with his fingers, like he was turning on a light. "Transport... the AZ to New Pennsylvania."

Jed was confused. "But there was already an AZ in New Pennsylvania before I even went through the emigration process," Jed said. "I saw pictures."

"That's right," Amos said.

"Which was before the war started."

"That's right. Think back on those pictures, Jed," Amos said. "Did they look anything like the Amish Zone you found when you arrived here?"

Jed closed his eyes and tried to access that part of his memory. "Well, now that you mention it," Jed said, "the brochures mentioned that the AZ in New Pennsylvania was still a tiny village. It never mentioned a wall at all."

"Over thirty-five thousand *miles* of copper cable and

wiring—debris from destroyed cities—was laid out in the construction of the wall. All the power lines, wire, and cable that existed in several major metropolises near the AZ. Not to mention all the steel rebar, re-mesh, and reinforcing materials that existed in the piles of rubble."

"What does that have to do with anything?" Jed asked.

"It has everything to do with *everything*," Amos said. "Basically, the designers of the wall created the world's largest portal—a huge Faraday cage that could take an unprecedented burst of pure energy and cycle it through the walls."

Jed narrowed his eyes and chewed on his lip. He took a step closer and stared at the video screen. "You say 'energy.' By that do you mean *electricity?*"

"Everyone still uses the term 'electricity' to explain the energy that is produced by okcillium, but strictly speaking, it's not electricity at all. It is a whole new thing altogether. It's like the English using the term 'horsepower' to describe the locomotive force produced by their automobiles. It is something people understand because when the term was coined it hearkened back to what they used to know. But it is not strictly accurate."

Jed nodded. "So okcillium produces an enormous amount of energy, right? Enough to fundamentally affect the physics around us?"

"It does," Amos said.

"To bend time?" Jed asked.

"Yes," Amos said. "To bend time." He brought up the image of a large coil of cables suspended in the center of what looked to be a laboratory. "The first okcillium portals were very simple and small-scale. How the scientists figured out that there was a *where*—a real location, even if they didn't know where the *where* was— where all of the stuff that disappeared through this portal was going, is a story in itself. Books could be written on the experiments that happened in a very short window of time."

"'Window of time,'" Jed said and smiled. "Very clever.'"

"Unintentionally so," Amos said with a dismissive wave. "Through trial and error, and a whole lot of math, the people running the experiments were able to—in a general way—control the process, and even came up with a way to send a human through the portal and bring them back. They didn't really go anywhere. It was time that moved, not them... but that's a lecture for another day. Anyway, within a few years the phenomenon had been perfected, and Transport had the okcillium portal built into the Transport Station at Columbia. The emigration system—the whole process—was really an elaborate ruse designed to colonize New Pennsylvania while leaving the rebellion and all elements of TRACE behind."

"Wow," Jed said.

"Yes. Wow. They hoped to steal away with millions of potential slaves, and leave the rebellion behind on a planet they'd ruined."

"So they... they... took the *whole* AZ?"

Amos nodded. "Of course, at the beginning they were just taking people, like you and hundreds of others. They'd built in the nine-year delay to explain away the distance traveled and so forth. But as the war heated up, they changed their plan. They took the whole AZ, and all at one time."

"Unbelievable!" Jed said.

"All it required was a low-yield okcillium explosion, perfectly placed and timed, to send the whole Zone away... into the future. Or, if you prefer, into another dimension."

"That sounds impossible," Jed said.

"With all prior technologies, it was," Amos said. "And frankly, they didn't know it would work. A lot of good Amish folk died in the translation. Including..." He trailed off.

"Our parents."

Amos couldn't answer. He just nodded. Both men were silent, and the old man wiped away a tear. After a long period of quiet reflection, Amos continued. "There were a lot of fires... I... can't even think about it without..."

Jed nodded. "I understand."

Amos gathered himself and cleared his throat. "But okcillium changed everything. It allowed for a shocking amount of power to be transmitted down wires and through metals without it creating much heat or resistance. You know that when electricity flows through a coil of wires it produces electromagnetism, right?"

Jed shrugged. "I guess. But I never really thought about it."

"In effect," Amos said, "Transport did the same thing. Only with the astronomical amount of energy produced by okcillium, the process created enough gravitational disruption to transport the entire Amish Zone."

"So... *where* did it go?" Jed asked.

"The Amish Zone? Well, in a way it went here, to New Pennsylvania. It became part of the reality of this new place."

"In a way?"

"My scientist friends tell me it never went anywhere. Einstein, they say, talked of time as if it were a long, lazy, meandering river, and said that everything along that river of time always existed at that place. We *perceive* time as passing because we are traveling along with the river. But if we could go back up the river, we would find that everything that has ever happened is *still happening* back where we'd been. So, in this sense, the Amish Zone never went anywhere. The Zone stayed in place. The time around it changed. In essence, you could say that the zone just changed epochs or dimensions, but in reality it never moved."

Jed's mind spun. "And New Pennsylvania is the Earth in the future?"

Amos laughed. "Well, that's the joke of the thing, brother. We don't know for sure." Amos threw his hands up as if his guess was as good as anyone's. "No one does. We think so. Much of the old world was still present in the new one. Basements in Columbia were still intact when New Pennsylvania first began to be explored. You just recently saw the foundations and 'tells' of our old farm. In some ways it was as if the community was just transported forward in time. New Pennsylvania was very much like the Earth... but in the future."

Jed had a pensive look on his face, and he narrowed his eyes at his brother. "Very much like?" He said. "But in some ways it was different?"

"In some ways it was remarkably different," Amos said. "The Great Shelf, for example. The geography of the planet is fundamentally changed in a lot of ways. So it's like I said... very much alike, but also changed. The Great Shelf looks as though the New Madrid fault, running through the Midwest, suffered a massive, world-changing earthquake that elevated the land to the west of it, and created the massive cliffs we call the Shelf. That event would have changed the makeup of the continent forever." Amos looked at Jed, scanning him to see if the young man believed what he was being told. "The Mississippi River, for another example, isn't there anymore."

"But we *are* on Earth, right?" Jed said.

"That's the thing," Amos replied. "Everything *mostly* lines up with that theory. But it still... it still seems to be another Earth altogether. Like maybe we came to a parallel Earth, where subtle things are different."

"Subtle things?" Jed said. His mind was racing back through the facts he knew, trying to make sense of this new information.

"Like the weather, for example," Amos said. "The weather here is more stable and predictable, with fewer devastating storms. In the years the Amish have been here, the dates of the first and last freeze have been so consistent that they don't even speak of those events in relation to 'dates' anymore. They predict the first and last freeze of the season to the closest hour!"

Jed just shook his head. He thought of all the times a late freeze had done damage to the fruit trees or to the gardens on the old farm.

"And there were very few humans on the planet when it was discovered... or re-discovered."

Jed was taken aback. He shook his head, "Very *few* humans? So there were some?"

"Yes," Amos said.

"Because I was told that the planet was devoid of intelligent life when the first explorers arrived here."

"That's not true," Amos said. "There were the wild people. Your friend Eagles is one of them. These were indigenous people, or maybe humans who had reverted back to a more wild and natural kind of life. They didn't come here through the portal. They lived through the time in between."

"How many years was that?" Jed asked. "Because Dawn told me it's now the year 2121. So it was like... I don't know, fifty years?"

Amos grimaced.

"You said fifty-three years, Amos," Jed said.

"I *did* say that, but it's not... It's just what we say. You don't know, and nobody else does either," Amos said. "The current year has been reckoned based on the differences in the ages of people who came through the portal at different times, and on estimations of the age of ruins and rubble found here when we got here."

"Couldn't we determine the year by looking at the stars and the locations of the planets?"

"That's one of the problematic things," Amos said. "Remember? I said that some subtle things were different? Well, that's one of them."

"The stars?"

"The stars. The planets. All the heavenly bodies," Amos said. "Things just don't add up."

Jed was speechless. He stared at his brother, not sure exactly what he should be thinking or believing.

"Anyway," Amos continued, "the indigenous people mostly lived in the wilderness, like the tribes in early America: warlike and highly intelligent. They'd developed their own very peculiar language that seemed to have its roots in our own English."

Jed nodded his head. "The 'salvagers,' right?"

"There are a lot of names applied to them. The salvagers are just a subset. Others have established trading clans. Some of them live in the remote areas of the wastes and are very peaceful and pastoral—almost like they're Amish. Our people get along very well with most of them."

"And they speak a form of English?" Jed asked.

"It's a strange thing, brother," Amos said. "It's a form of English, but if you listen very closely, you can almost hear an Amish foundation to it. In Old Pennsylvania, many of our people spoke a broken English that was a combination of Pennsylvania Deutsch and English, with a lot of made-up words thrown in here and there. The wild people have some hints of this in their own dialect."

"So maybe they're made up of people who left, or were kicked out of, the Amish communities."

"This too," Amos said, "lends credence to the theory that we're in the future. But we can't be certain. There are other theories that could also be true. We could be all the way across the universe, on another Earth that developed in parallel to our own. That one is tough for me to swallow, because I don't know what intelligence had us land here instead of on any of the billions of planets that could never support human life... or in the middle of the vacuum of space where we would all have died instantly.

"So yes, we could be on the same planet on which we were born. That's my prevailing theory. Or we could be on a different plane of existence altogether, as if this planet is right on top of the other one, only with each inhabiting different dimensions of space-time. We just don't know. And for most of the Amish, this isn't a question they spend too much time thinking about. They don't reckon it's profitable. To them, they left one place and ended up in another."

Jed inhaled deeply, then exhaled. Amos was right: this was too much to take in all at once. "I want to learn all of this," he said finally, "but maybe in a way that's a little more spread out."

"Now you see what I've been saying," Amos said. "It's a lot to take in."

Jed paused, then broached a new subject. "Tell me about your plans against Transport."

"I thought you were a man of peace."

"I am," Jed said.

"Then you have no need to know of my plans," Amos said. "You have your BICE, and you can do your own research. I would appreciate one thing, though: if you do learn anything that will be of assistance in protecting and serving the people of New Pennsylvania, will you inform me?"

"I don't know what I'm going to do, Amos."

For a long moment, there were no words. Then,

when the silence became too heavy for either of them to lift, Amos spoke.

"I'm not asking you to fight, brother. I know you wouldn't, and you've helped us enough already. I respect who you are and what you are, and I always will. I hope you know that. I'm just asking you to go be what the rest of us are fighting for. Maybe that's something we can both get behind."

34

DIGGING IN

WEDNESDAY

On Wednesday, after the chores were done, two of the Amish elders showed up at Matthias's farm to help with the next step of preparing for the barn-raising. These were the two men who had the most experience with these events, so they were put in charge of the construction of Matthias's barn.

As part of the overall project, Matthias would also, eventually, be getting a springhouse. Just like Tom Hochstetler's, the partially buried building would serve as a place for him to store his fresh milk until it could be delivered or processed into another product. The springhouse wouldn't be built on Saturday, but the hole for the project was going to be dug now. It was really the dirt from the hole that they needed immediately, in order to bank the barn—the hole for the future springhouse was just an additional benefit.

A banked barn is a handy thing, because it means that the barn (usually) is built into a hillside. Having the barn built into the side of a hill means that the upper level of the barn is reachable directly by vehicle. So rather than lift heavy hay bales or other weighty items using a block and tackle, the farmer can haul these items into the barn directly from a wagon or other conveyance, which can be pulled up to—even backed into—the barn from the upper level. Hay or other crops can be easily stored upstairs, and then, as needed, dropped through a great opening in the middle of the barn to the animals—who, in the wintertime, are housed in the lower level.

The land Matthias's farm sat on had a few slight elevation changes, but no slopes dramatic enough to support a banked barn. So instead, a suitable hill was going to be *made*. In effect, a banked hill of dirt would form a large, very gradual ramp up to the second floor of the barn. Such a project would require even more dirt than they'd get from digging the hole for the springhouse, so there would need to be a second excavation later in the week. But today they would just tackle the springhouse excavation.

The TRACE soldiers were all given shovels and other digging implements, and the Amish men marked out the area where the springhouse would go. The new structure wouldn't have to be built directly on a spring. The cold water from the nearby spring, when developed, could flow into the springhouse through a piece of pipe, or a channel or tunnel formed by the careful laying of smooth rocks.

The Amish elders wanted a hole that was four meters square and two meters deep. And they made sure that the Englischer soldiers took turns with the hard digging. The dirt was scooped into wheelbarrows and carted the seventy meters to the location of the banked barn. The dirt wouldn't be pushed up against the barn's concrete and cinderblock foundation until Friday afternoon, to make sure the foundation had enough time to dry and cure before adding any lateral pressure to the new walls.

For the first time since he'd arrived in New Pennsylvania, Jed felt like he was able to immerse himself in farm work to the point that he was able to forget everything else that was going on outside the walls of the AZ. If only for a moment, his mind was completely absorbed in thoughts about the soil. He could breathe in the pure air, and dream of the process of building his own farm—maybe someday with a wife of his own. And for just that beautiful sliver of time, Jed was more than willing to let the Englischers have their own war, and hoped they could just leave him out of it.

* * * *

Amos Troyer busied himself making sure the Tulsa was fully battle-ready. He and his officers personally toured the Tulsa's massive platforms and decks, observing as the attack craft and support vehicles were made ready for the coming battle. Amos watched as the ships were being loaded with armaments, supplies, and equipment, and he sat in as the pilots were briefed on their missions. He visited the engineering and maintenance decks and personally interviewed the officers there to make certain that everyone was on the same page.

Just as he'd always been, Amos was a hands-on commander. He was briefed by the team that was implementing the now redesigned *Corinth* battlefield intelligence system, and he even observed as a few of the remaining intelligence officers had their Corinth chips flash-updated in the medical bays. Transport had hacked the Corinth chips once before, and he hoped now that the vulnerability issues had been fixed.

Amos didn't know what event or proximate cause would act as the trigger for the next phase of the war. But while the council and the people waited and watched, he was preparing his force to invade the area beyond the Great Shelf—to find Transport's forces and ships, and destroy them.

•••

That night, Jed didn't even get online. He was so exhausted from the digging, and so pleased with the day's work, that he never even logged on to see if he had any messages from his brother. Had he gotten online—and had he, perhaps, hacked into Transport's communications from out beyond the Shelf—he might have noticed some anomalies. There was some interesting chatter that might have indicated to him that something interesting was taking place out west. All of TRACE's analysts missed it, but maybe Jed wouldn't have. It could have been that with Jed's unique perspective, and his willingness to question everything, he would have noticed something: some track, or trail, or telltale clue that an amassing armada must, inevitably, leave behind.

Because out beyond the Shelf, Transport's forces were gathering. Hundreds of attack airships were being prepared, and a thousand unmarked white orbs—unmanned Transport drones, manufactured in the old world and relayed to New Pennsylvania through a makeshift portal hidden in a large factory in a mostly unpopulated city—were receiving their final memory updates from Transport command.

It's possible that Jed would have missed all the signs. But it's also possible that had he taken a look, he might have seen something that no one else did. And maybe he would have given his brother—and the whole world—another twenty-four hours to act. But such surmisings aren't usually profitable. Who can say what *might have* happened in any situation?

What matters is what *did* happen.

And what did happen is, Jed didn't get online. He was still an Amish man after all, and averse to getting involved in conflict. So Jed didn't notice the signs of a pending Transport counteroffensive for another full day. And in that full day, while Jed slept and woke and worked and loved, the forces in the world around him rushed headlong toward an inevitable, and violent, climax.

THE WASP

THURSDAY

On Thursday, after the milking and a large breakfast, the TRACE squad joined a dozen Amish men who showed up to move even more dirt. The concrete and cinderblock foundation walls they'd constructed a few days earlier were now sturdy enough to hold up against the strain. so half of the men were assigned to start forming the long, gradual ramp that would lead to the second floor of the barn. The soldiers, and the other half of the Amish men, would be digging a hole for a small stock pond.

First, the sod was cut from the whole area of the future pond, and the grassy turf was carefully laid aside. This grass would eventually be placed on the embankment they'd be building that day. After the sod was cut, a half dozen wheelbarrows trucked dirt back and forth from the site of the new pond to the barn. The barn needed the dirt, and the farm needed the pond, in order to trap and hold more surface moisture for the watering of animals. Digging, then, was on tap for the second straight day.

On this Thursday, Dawn and Jed worked together. The women didn't usually join the men in their building chores, but Dawn insisted that she wanted to help, and no one was willing to tell her no. And if the truth be told, she wanted to spend some time with Jed as well. So she put her muscles to work and dug out big shovelfuls of deep, black soil, dumping them into the wheelbarrow; and when it was so full that she was afraid it might tip over, Jed would push the load up the low hill to the foundation of the new barn, where men were placing the soil, spreading it, and tamping it down to make the bank.

This process gave the two of them a lot of time to talk, because between runs, Jed would flop down on the grass while Dawn was digging (she got to rest while he was hauling).

"Do you want to swap jobs?" Jed asked.

"Nah, I'm all right," Dawn said. "Besides, I have the easy job."

"Digging's not easy!" Jed said. "And I have the blisters from yesterday to prove it!"

"That's why you should wear gloves," Dawn said with a smile, and held up a gloved hand. "You may be the strongest one in this relationship, but I think I'm the smartest." She winked at Jed.

"Oh, I don't doubt that one single bit," Jed said, nodding his head.

Dawn went back to digging, and Jed reached up and

smoothed out a pile in the wheelbarrow that was looking like it might make the thing lean too much to one side. "Relationship, huh?" he said.

Dawn stopped digging and leaned on the shovel. "What?"

"You said 'this relationship,' and I wondered what you meant by that."

"Uh... I don't know," Dawn said. "I thought we both said we might want to get married or something. Was I dreaming that part? Or..."

"No," Jed said, "you weren't dreaming at all. I just... It was just weird hearing it all official like."

"Weird, huh?"

"No... no." Jed held up his hands in mock surrender. "Wait a minute. I don't mean weird. I meant it was... nice. It was nice to hear you say it. That's all I meant to say."

Dawn scowled at him. "Yes, I'm sure that is what you meant to say, Jed."

"It was. I liked hearing it."

"Yeah, well, maybe I'd like hearing it too."

Jed looked down at his boots, and shuffled them for a moment before he spoke again. "Dawn... listen... we have ways we do things. You know that. We don't have girlfriends and stuff. We don't 'date.'"

"I know," Dawn said. "But your parents aren't around, and mine aren't either. I mean, who are we going to ask for permission, or tell, so we can make things official?"

"When we're ready, we'll talk to the elders," Jed said.

"I've been married before, and I'm not Amish." Dawn didn't say it like she was apologizing, because she wasn't. She spoke in a very matter-of-fact tone, as if to say, "Okay, how do we deal with these facts?"

"You're a widow, and you can be Amish again whenever you want to be," Jed said.

"It's just..." Dawn threw down the shovel and climbed up out of the low hole. She stood very close to him, and looked deeply into his eyes. "All I've wanted to do since Ben died was fight his enemies. It's all I *have* done. But now..."

"But now?" Jed asked.

"But now, all I want to do is be with you. Wherever you are. I just want to build a life with you, Jed."

Jed looked at Dawn and inhaled deeply. This was what he'd hoped for—maybe not openly, but he'd felt very strongly for Dawn almost from the moment he'd met her. From the instant his eyes had opened up in that pod in the Transport Station and he'd seen her looking down at him.

"Billy talked to me yesterday," Dawn said.

"Oh... Oh, he did? What..." He put his hands into his pockets. "Well, I guess it's not my business to ask."

"Of course it's your business, Jed. That's why I'm telling you."

"Okay, so..." He threw up his hands, showing that he was flustered.

"He asked me if there was any hope for the two of us," Dawn said. "He wanted to know if he could take care of me. Like Ben did."

"And what did you say?"

"I told him that I loved *you*, Jed. That's what I told him."

Jed smiled. "I love you, too."

"I just want to be with you."

"Okay, so you'll give up TRACE? You'll leave the resistance?"

"I... I... I don't know. I don't know what to say. I haven't thought it all out yet. I don't know what to do."

Jed smiled at her. "I understand." He pushed a loose strand of hair out of her face, and smiled wider when he saw a grin break across her face. "We'll wait until we know exactly what we should do, okay?"

Dawn looked up at him for a moment and then nodded.

"Okay."

● ● ● ●

That night, worn out and dirty from a day's work, and while they were delivering the evening milk to the neighbor, Jed asked Tom Hochstetler if he could sleep in his barn again. He didn't mind sleeping on the floor of Matthias's little house, but Jed thought back to how comfortable he'd been in the Hochstetlers' hayloft, and he wanted to get online to see if there were any messages from his brother.

Once the milk was unloaded, and after Eagles and Ducky had turned the wagon around to head back to Matthias's place, Jed took a sponge bath in some of the frigid water he drew from the springhouse. Not long after, shivering while he drip-dried in the evening air, he climbed into the hayloft for the night.

The sun was just dipping down below the horizon

out to the west as Jed sat down in the hayloft door and took in the beauty of the evening. It was the gloaming; dark blues and shadows were becoming one, and fading pink-orange fingers of light touched the few puffy clouds still visible in the sky. Jed watched as the last sliver of the golden orb disappeared below the high walls of the Amish Zone—the tops of which barely poked up over the hills in the distance. The first stars—he couldn't name them, and after what his brother had told him, he wasn't sure if anyone could—were blinking on in the deepening sky, and a soft breeze made him shiver again, but not really from the cold. The weather was perfect, and taken altogether it was a scene out of a picture book, and Jed reveled in it, so exactly did it bring back to his memory the halcyon days of his youth.

From down below he heard a mild disturbance coming from the chicken coop as the Hochstetlers' hens established their own sleeping roosts for the night. Even the simplest of God's animals argue and fret over position and authority... asserting, sometimes with force, just who deserves what. The difference is, of course, that the wars of the chickens won't ever break the world.

After he'd taken in his fill of the beautiful evening, Jed opened the small package—a meal wrapped in rough brown paper—which Dawn had given him when he told her he was going to stay in the neighbors' barn for the night. He spread the paper with his hands and examined his supper. There was a piece of cornbread, with home-churned butter already spread on it, and three thick slices of bacon too. There was a pint-sized mason jar, with lemonade sweetened with the very smoky caramel-tinged sugar that was made by another one of Matthias's neighbors.

Jed prayed over his meal and then chewed in silence as he watched the world get bathed in darkness. He lit one of the small lanterns and hung it on a hook from an overhead beam, making sure to be extra careful with it. Barn fires were still quite common in Amish country, so he was always very aware of how he worked with fire in any structure such as this one. In his mind's eye, just for a moment, he was back in the old barn... back in the old world. He could see himself hanging a lantern on a hook up in the hayloft, and when he turned, he could just make out the window in the gabled end, and the coffee-can pane winking at him from the lower right-hand corner.

But he wasn't in Old Pennsylvania. Wherever he was now, it was a different world altogether. He popped a Q pill in his mouth and chewed it up, and while the drug began to take effect, he prepared himself a little pallet and made it into a bed for the night.

● ● ● ●

There weren't any messages from Amos, so Jed decided to take a look around in Transport's files to see if he could get any news about what might be happening in the world of the English.

He searched through some file areas he was familiar with, and started to ask himself questions. This is how he sometimes made breakthroughs. Because even if he didn't know what he was looking for, if he asked himself enough questions, usually he'd get onto an interesting trail at some point in the journey.

Is Transport's Internet system still up and running at full capacity?

It seemed to Jed like it was. He did some cursory checks around many of the major hubs he knew about, and he didn't see any serious problems with the flow of data.

What is Transport doing now that they've fled beyond the Shelf?

Jed found the data routes with the most traffic passing between points to the west, and tagged along—disguising himself as an innocuous email—until he found a portal where the messages were being distributed. Once there, he used some of his previous methods (along with Dawn's pre-placed camouflage tactics) to hack in and begin scanning some of the raw data.

He brought up his viewscreen and had the data projected onto it, but even then the sheer amount of information was overwhelming, so he decided to improvise. He hacked a nearby hub and borrowed some of the processing power to implement some word searches. Every "war" word he could think of he then programmed into the search, and he fed "hits" to the main screen. This worked a lot better, and slowed down the mammoth amount of data by vetting most of it out, but it still didn't give him a clear enough picture of what he wanted to see.

Now he had to really think. He wasn't hamstrung by artificial or self-imposed limitations—that was the main reason why his brother had recruited him. His gift was that he didn't know what he could do until he did it. He solved problems more like a farmer than like a technician, who can often be limited by artificial protocols or learned patterns. A farmer had a tendency to just try things until something worked, and the task was the main thing, not the method.

As Jed pondered on problems or obstructions, the words he needed (along with their definitions) and instructions would appear to him floating in the darkness. This was part of the program Dawn had placed into his BICE from the beginning.

The term *multi-task* appeared in the ether, and the definition explained to him that he could use the computing power to do several things at once. Without even a second of doubt as to whether his ideas could even be accomplished, he thought about it, and instantly the screen expanded and then divided into nine smaller screens laid out like panes of glass in a window. Now he could watch data stream by, and his eyes just naturally followed it all. Then he focused again and assigned a certain amount of his BICE chip's computing power to each of the nine screens. Soon enough, he was flying through the data as it flowed by, and he was understanding everything he was seeing.

Drones.

The word caught his attention, so he focused his whole mind on it. He re-established all of the search parameters on all of the screens until they were all focused on finding anything and everything being said about drones.

He wanted to get comfortable in a way he couldn't really explain if someone asked him, so he made up a grassy hillside in his mind, and he sat down to study the data as it arrived.

Drones, manufactured in the old world, and brought here using a secret portal somewhere beyond the shelf, were being prepared for an attack...

An attack on what?

Hard to say. Overall, there was a gist... a *leaning*... in the chatter that seemed to make Jed think that perhaps an attack on the east by Transport might be imminent. He paused his searches and pulled up his communications interface. He sent a message to Amos, and then went back to his work.

Amos.

He wondered if his brother was watching him work, so he looked around in the corners of his vision to see if he could see the AT10S code anywhere. He didn't, so he just shook his head and laughed.

Well, if Amos is watching me, he probably wouldn't let me know at this point. He only did that before because he was using the information to drag me into this world. It was only bait, and I was the fish. Now look at me, swimming in this ocean of the Englischers' data. My brother is the high prophet of the worldlings, and I'm his little prize.

He wondered then if he could catch his brother spying on him. In those previous iterations, Amos had made the code visible in order to ensnare him; but what if the code was still there—only invisible—when Amos *didn't* want to get caught? Was Amos a good enough hacker to hide from his younger/older brother?

The next thing Jed did was to disguise himself. He

left an avatar of himself sitting on the hill, and made himself invisible to his own rendering system. He hid himself in the numbers and code, until even *he* couldn't see where he ended and the data began.

Jed looked up into the corners again, but now he looked even deeper. Of course, the "corners" were not really there. All of this—everything he could see—was just part of the interface that the BICE and his brain had concocted to help him understand the bits of data that were flooding through his mind. So he looked still deeper. He made himself an invisible part of the code and began processing it all, looking for anything that was out of place. Combing through bits and elements, scanning for something that stood out.

And that's when he found it: another entity. Another code looking down on his avatar, spying, taking it all in. But this time it wasn't his brother. Even his brother was not this clever. This entity was watching Jed's avatar watch the data he'd hacked, and up until now, the entity had been totally invisible.

Jed studied the entity's data with intensity and caution. He parsed all of the code that made up the entity, and examined it until he knew what data was part of that code, and what data the entity was using outside of itself. Then Jed wrote a quick program, using his imagination with some help from Dawn's helper program, and created an avatar for the entity. An avatar that only he would see. He didn't know what made him think of it—of the figure he'd bestow upon this being. He didn't know if this entity was good or evil. He didn't know if it was friend or foe. But Jed created an avatar based on one of the most hated antagonists of his youth: the mahogany wasp. The rendering was done so quickly, and so perfectly from his memory, that Jed actually shivered and shrank away when he saw it.

Now, he could pull back and watch the wasp watch the avatar he'd made of himself.

I have to find out who is controlling this thing, Jed thought.

So he caused his **BICE** to stop rendering the drone data. Then he walked his own avatar back through the process that he'd used to break into the hubs in the first place. And as he pulled back, the wasp followed. The wasp appeared to be heedless of the drone information. It didn't care about preparations for war. It was following Jed.

THE FARM BUREAU

FRIDAY

A red light in the corner of his vision and a chiming sound woke Jed from his sleep. It was around three a.m., and it took him a moment to figure out what was happening. But then he remembered that he'd made sure to set up an alert in case Amos tried to contact him during the night.

Jed shook the cobwebs from his head, and then, when he was fully awake, he pulled up his **BICE** control interface. He hadn't taken a **Q** since early in the previous evening, but the system still seemed to work pretty well for him.

Once he'd logged in and entered his control room, he found Amos there waiting for him.

"I got your messages, brother," Amos said.

"Then you know?"

"I know. But I'd like you to brief me."

"I hacked into Transport's—"

"Just... please," Amos said, "get to the part about the drones."

Jed paused, and then nodded. "I put it all into the files I sent to you, but here's the gist of it: Transport has an armada of aerial attack drones, white spheres much like the ones I saw when I was in the City. They have other support and attack craft readied as well. They're preparing an offensive as we speak."

"Any ideas about their targets?" Amos asked.

"Your ship, for one," Jed replied.

"Of course. Any other targets?"

"I saw general plans for searching out and destroying your attack aircraft using something called a *Corinth* hack? I didn't have time to figure out what that meant. All of this is in the file I sent you."

Amos nodded his head. "The Corinth chip was hardened after we discovered their hack. That must have been old information. Any terrestrial targets you could identify?"

"Not that I know of. Why?"

"Although these drone orbs can be used in air-to-air combat, that is not their primary purpose," Amos said. "They're designed for police work and population control. They were made to engage terrestrial based targets: cities, ground units, convoys... that sort of thing."

Amos put his hands in his pockets and rocked back and forth in place. It was obvious he was nervous, and maybe a little scared. "As you can imagine, we're on a war footing here now. I don't know how our enemy got this far without us discovering his plans. But I thank you, Jed, for this information. Hopefully we can use it to save lives. Our people are going through the files you sent as we speak, and we're preparing to meet their attack..." His voice trailed off. He knew that Jed didn't care to hear about the specifics of the war that raged around them all. "Is there anything else you need to tell me, Jed? Anything at all that isn't in your file?"

Jed looked down for a moment, thinking. A few seconds later, he looked up at Amos and nodded his head. "I found... Do you... Do you remember when I said there might be a third party involved in all of this?"

Amos nodded his head. "Yes, brother, I do."

"Well, I think I've learned something about that."

"Which is?"

Jed pointed with his thumb over his shoulder, as if to say *back there*, but then he dropped his hand again and eventually worked it back into his pocket. "I tracked another hacker that was spying on me as I did my work. At first I thought it was you, so I set a trap for it, to try to figure out who it could be."

"And what did you discover?" Amos asked.

"I tracked it back here," Jed answered.

"Back here? To this side of the Shelf?"

"No. Back *here*. Back to the Amish Zone," Jed said. "Apparently the Yoders—that family that you recruited as double agents, the ones you ordered to kidnap Dawn— well, apparently that family is bigger than I first thought. I traced the hacker back to the Yoders' farm. It seems that they're running some kind of operation out of that basement where they were holding Dawn."

"What kind of operation?" Amos asked.

"From what I could learn in only a few hours of digging, it seems they're playing both sides against the middle."

"I'm not sure I understand," Amos said.

Jed looked up at his brother and grinned sheepishly as he shook his head. "Apparently they're... I don't know what you'd call them... *techno-Amish terrorists* is a descriptive enough title. Anyway, they're doing their best to see that both TRACE and Transport lose the war for New Pennsylvania."

Amos just stared at Jed without blinking. "Get me Pook Rayburn please, and find a way to get him in touch with me as soon as possible."

●●●●

When Eagles and Pook showed up at the Hochstetlers' with the morning milk, Jed brought Pook up into the hayloft and contacted Amos again through his BICE. When Amos appeared, Jed communicated between the two military men as a sort of translator. Even while he was doing it, he wondered if he was crossing some kind of line in supporting the resistance in the war. He was certain that Transport would see it that way. If, somehow, they were hacking Jed's BICE, the last two days' activities could definitely be interpreted as acts of warfare perpetrated against the government, with those acts stemming from an Amish man in the Amish Zone. That fact alone would be enough for Transport to order an attack on the AZ.

So, what to do? Jed wasn't sure what was the right

thing, but he knew he needed to see this through. He didn't know what else he *could* do. When in doubt, his father would tell him, plow forward.

Before he signed off, Jed remembered one more thing he needed to tell his brother.

"The Yoders took Dawn's BICE chip," Jed said.

"I know this," Amos replied. "That was part of the plan from the beginning. To force you to use your chip and expand your participation with the system."

"But you don't know what the Yoders did with it. I mean... Dawn had a *Corinth* chip. Knowing what we know now about the Yoders, don't you think it's possible that this third-party group of Amish people... that they've hacked the chip? Or that they might have given it to the government?"

"It wouldn't help them to just have the chip," Amos said. "Although Transport having it is certainly not a good thing. They'll definitely reverse-engineer it and probably copy the hardware. But they can't hack it; once we had that hacking issue with Corinth before, we totally rewrote the software, and Dawn's chip was never flashed with the new updates. No one outside of my inner circle or the Council has access to any of the data."

Jed just stared at his brother, unflinching. "Could *I* hack the chip, Amos?"

"What?"

"Do you think I could hack into the Corinth chip?"

Amos shook his head. "I don't know."

"Then don't be so sure these techno-Amish haven't done it."

• • • •

Back at the farm, a few of the Amish craftsmen were preparing work stations for the different teams that would be working on the following morning. Working with the TRACE soldiers, Amish men in suspenders and straw hats prepared an area for the timber framers. Weatherproofed boxes of tools—containing flarens, adzes, axes, shovel gouges, mallets, and other hardened tools used for moving and shaping heavy beams—were put in position. Then the men hauled all of the siding materials to the area where the siders would be stationed. They made certain that the blacksmith had provided enough nails for the siding and roofing. The rest of the structure would be fitted together using timber-framing notches, mortises, and tenons, and a dozen other advanced joints that would tighten and strengthen the structure so that, if God willed it, the barn could stand for centuries.

Once the structure started going up, the process would move very quickly. Even for Amishmen like Jed it was hard to imagine that the barn would be up and dried-in in a single day, but the plain people had become very adept at these complicated projects. Most of the workers, both men and women, would have an assigned task they'd done dozens and dozens of times before, and the day would fly by for them. To the Amish, a barn-raising is more a time of great fellowship than a time of work. To the outsiders, it can be almost a spiritual experience. The TRACE squad members were talking about the barn-raising in hushed and reverent tones, like they would be building a cathedral on the Temple Mount or some such thing.

The barn-raising is one of the most fundamental and necessary of the traditions that hold the plain people together. Working together on a project that is both necessary and important links families, and even generations, of the Amish together. When an Amish person looks at a neighbor's farm and sees a barn that he or she helped build, it is reinforced that they are all together in this life. The Amish, therefore, are invested in one another. They are not strangers; they are family. Whether the English recognize this or not, they still know it, and their hearts burn when they see such a loving tribute to community played out in a land they call "Amish Country." This is why the Amish barn-raising is held in esteem by every culture everywhere. It is a holy thing, even to the world 'round about.

• • • •

"It's a tunnel," Ducky said. He held a lantern out in front of him and strained his eyes to see past the very edges of the orange-yellow light thrown by the lamp. Ducky, Pook, Eagles, and Billy were down in the basement of the Yoder house, and after moving old boxes and some broken furniture away from the walls, Ducky had spied a door that was *almost* hidden. It was a panel that was just not *quite* flush against the rest of the wall.

"Yep," Ducky said. "It's a tunnel, and it's pretty long."

"Well, we might as well find out where it leads," Pook said. He turned to Eagles and smirked.

"Yippee," Eagles said flatly.

The tunnel led downward and then broke hard to the left after about fifteen meters. The downward angle of the slope increased after that, and for a while they had to hold on to the sides of the walls so that they didn't slide down the slick, damp floor. Another twenty meters and they came upon a part of the tunnel that had been heavily reinforced. Water dripped down from the ceiling and gathered in a low area off to the side of the walking path.

"We must be under the creek," Pook said.

"Creeking must being up there," Eagles repeated from behind Pook.

As they stepped carefully past the wet portion, the tunnel leveled out and started to angle upward again, only at a shallower slope than the section they'd just walked down. The tunnel continued straight and slightly upward for another fifty meters, then took a right turn and began to decline again.

The four men were wondering aloud how far the tunnel ran, when up ahead of them on the right, a door opened and a young Amish man stepped out. He was a tall man, about twenty years of age, and he wasn't wearing his Amish hat. He didn't run or try to scramble back through the doorway from whence he'd come. When he saw the TRACE men coming toward him, he just thrust his hands deeply into the pockets of his broadfall pants and cast his gaze downward at his boots.

Ducky had drawn his weapon and was hustling forward, but the rest of the men kept their pistols hidden, not wanting to have an accident or to fire the weapons indiscriminately in such a cramped tunnel. Ducky trained his pistol on the Amish man, and when he reached him, he asked the young man to put his hands up in the air. The man obeyed, and then Ducky gently pushed the man into the room he'd come from.

Inside the room were four other Amish men, all seated at desks. The room was filled with computer equipment, and it was obvious to Pook that they'd found the *other* Yoders—the rest of the extended family that had been wreaking havoc against both sides in the Transport war.

The men surrendered immediately and were submissive, and answered all of Pook's questions without equivocation.

"So you're the Techno-Amish Terrorists?" Pook asked.

The leader of the Amish group smiled. "We prefer to call ourselves the Farm Bureau."

The Amish men admitted that they were operating on their own, and that they had learned to use the computer equipment from Amos Troyer's spies and agents in the City back before it was blown to pieces. They'd procured pirated BICE chips, laptop computers, and other equipment, and they'd made contact with Transport too, promising to spy for the government in the Amish Zone. In this way, they'd triangulated themselves, putting themselves in a position to throw both military groups into disarray, and spreading both information and disinformation as needed to keep either side from winning the war. The men insisted that they'd never been involved in any violence, although when Ducky challenged them on that and said that their actions had almost certainly led to violence and death, the men just nodded, without saying anything more on the topic.

"What did you hope to accomplish?" Pook asked the leader of the group.

"Confusion," the Amish man said. "And we hoped to exhaust both sides, hoping they would both give up and go home... or just quit."

"What did you have to fear from the rebels?" Pook asked. "All we want is for everyone to be free."

"Inherent in the power to make men free by force is the power to enslave them again," the Amish leader said.

"You do realize that Transport is planning to attack and destroy this place—this Amish Zone—don't you?" Billy asked.

The Amish leader's head dropped again, and he looked at his boots for a moment before looking up again at Billy. "We have only just realized this."

"And what do you plan to do about it?" Pook asked.

The Amish man stared into Pook's eyes. "We will not fight them. But if it comes down to it, we will thwart their plans."

"How?"

"Come," the man said. "I'll show you."

37

BARN RAISING

SATURDAY

The day dawned fresh and cool, and it wasn't long after the sun was up that buggies began appearing at Matthias's farm from every direction.

A long table was set up with hot coffee, tea, and every form and fashion of muffin, donut, and pastry, along with biscuits and pots of gravy and plates of thick-cut bacon.

From the buggies, ladies in pristine white kapps and long, somewhat formal Amish dresses of almost every color (although all of their capes and aprons were black) began to unload pans of roasted chickens and bowls of salads and fruit.

Most of the men, all wearing black broadfalls and roughspun shirts with suspenders crossing in the back, neatly folded their jackets and handed them to their wives, mothers, or sisters. They then grabbed hot coffee and a light breakfast, and ate it as they headed to their work stations.

Before long, the sounds of construction filled the air in the Amish Zone of New Pennsylvania. Boards were being sawn and then handed up to men who were standing on the already-completed concrete and cinderblock foundation. Within a half hour, the rough-sawn timbers were being fitted together, and the sounds of heavy mallets could be heard as the timbers were assembled and then raised into position using pikes and ropes.

The whole event was a symphony of cooperation and friendship. Young girls and boys carried pitchers of lemonade and filled glasses to the rim anywhere they could find someone willing to have another glass. To the Amish, a work time is simply a fellowship time where work happens to take place too. Although the job continued at a comparatively rapid pace, at any one time—if one were to take a snapshot (which would be frowned upon)—one might have seen groups of two or four or six Amish men leaning on their tools as they talked in an animated way. Breaks were common, but unspoken. Everyone just seemed to be where they were supposed to be when the time came for them to be useful. If a board was needed, the dimensions were shouted down from up top, and someone grabbed a hand saw and cut the board perfectly to fit. The board would then be handed up, and on its journey it might pass through the hands of a dozen men, crawling upon the structure like ants, before it reached its predestined location.

Jedediah Troyer had participated in many barn

raisings, and he always loved the experience. Like the coffee-can window pane—still perfect in his mind—the barn raising kept him in touch with his roots. It reminded him of who he was, and what he stood for. It was an anchor... but only a temporary one.

Dawn Beachy couldn't remember ever seeing a barn raising. She surely must have watched several as a young girl, but if she had, she couldn't now remember them. For her, this was a very special day. A perfect day. And for a time, she was able to put the other world, and the war that had killed her husband Ben, out of her mind.

She looked up at Jed, up at the very top of the barn, sitting astride the center beam like he was riding a horse. Men were handing up roof rafters and Jed was hammering them into place, one after another.

Dawn smiled. This was the life she wanted to live, and this was the man she wanted to live it with.

Before noon, the frame of the barn was already in place, and when the midday meal was called, the siding was already beginning to go up.

● ● ● ●

A light and perfect breeze accented the day, moving just lightly enough to keep everyone cool in the bright sunlight, and the smell of mown grass, cut lumber, and roasted chicken mixed in the air.

The women were laughing and clearing the long wooden tables of empty platters and bowls when the first sounds of war were heard.

Dawn was doing what many of the young ladies had

done just after the dinner was over. She was the last of the ladies who'd climbed up a very tall ladder to the peak of the new barn so that she could look out over New Pennsylvania from the very top. Jed was seated on the center beam, straddling it and nailing in a rafter, when he turned and saw Dawn looking at him with a big smile on her face.

"Get ye down before ye hurt ye by fallin'!" Jed said with a laugh.

"I just wanted to see what all the fuss was about," Dawn said with a playful smile on her face.

"It's just a barn," Jed said.

Dawn laughed. "Oh, so you think all those single Amish beauties just climbed this rickety ladder one after another to look at a barn?"

"What else is there to look at?" Jed asked.

"*Jedediah Troyer*, that's what!" Dawn said.

"Oh, get ye down!"

A low rumble shook the ground just then, and both Jed and Dawn looked up as a formation of maybe a dozen or more white drones, spherical and without markings, appeared over the high perimeter wall that ringed the Amish Zone.

"Dawn, get down!" Jed shouted. But Dawn, like everyone else who saw the sight, was frozen in place.

Just then, an attack craft—from Jed's point of view it had to be a TRACE fighter—sped from his left and engaged the drones, shooting two of them down in a shower of laser light and sparks. The two drones exploded and spun toward the ground, crashing in balls of fire and smoke.

One of the drones dropped precipitously, then shot back upward and fired a long volley of phosphorescent projectiles that struck the TRACE fighter and blew it out of the sky.

Now chaos reigned. Explosions rocked the ground, and more drones appeared on the horizon. An endless number, seeming to stretch from one end of the heavens to the other.

"Dawn!" Jed yelled, and she looked up and caught his glance. "Please get down!" he hollered, as four TRACE fighters zoomed overhead and then banked toward the approaching drones.

"You too!" Dawn shouted, but not before a flash of laser light split the air near her, sending crackling electricity like lightning through the air. She was halfway down the ladder when another explosion hit Matthias's little house, and almost at the same instant several of the buggies were struck and exploded, cartwheeling through the air before crashing down to the earth in splinters.

Another drone crashed nearby, and Dawn looked up in time to see three more TRACE fighters zip overhead at an extremely high speed. By now, Amish families were gathering together, and the parents were leading their children to run and hide—rushing to anywhere that might offer them safety. Dawn saw a family running across a field of low, green tobacco, and could only watch as a large TRACE ship crash-landed right in front of them. The family stared for a moment, and then turned and ran the other way.

The ship was huge, and Dawn was thankful that it hadn't exploded on impact. As it was, the crash landing had gouged up several acres of cropland. She shook her head and stared out at the confusion and destruction. War had erupted in the Amish Zone, and death and destruction now rained down from the sky. This certainly wasn't the first time a devilish government had unleashed its military to try destroy the Amish—but for those who were experiencing it, the scene was like none they'd ever imagined.

The Amish are raised on stories of persecution and violence. They know the tales by heart from the time they are children in the crib. They've always known that such things have happened often enough in the past. But the human mind is alike in every race and sect of people: when the danger isn't close enough, or when enough generations have passed so that the reality of hardship and persecution ceases to be real, the threats fade. They take on the quality of interesting fiction. But now, on this Saturday, as the blood of saints and tyrants began to mingle in the soil of New Pennsylvania, the ghosts and pains of the past took on new life for the residents of the Amish Zone.

From the wreckage of the downed TRACE aircraft, Dawn saw a figure appear. Old, and bowed down a bit from age and circumstance, the figure crawled out of the fighter and began to walk stoically toward the new barn.

Amos.

Dawn began to run toward her friend, but she'd only taken a few steps when she remembered that Jed was still atop the barn. She skidded to a stop and swung around just in time to see a phosphorescent projectile split the center beam of the barn—which gave way under Jed's weight.

Dawn's eyes met Jed's for just a moment as he began to fall, but in an instant he had flipped over backward and plummeted to the ground, landing beyond her view. Her breath caught in her throat and her hands came up to her mouth and she had to look away. As she did, she saw that Amos was running toward her with a hand outstretched. He got to her just as she pushed away and ran inside the barn.

As the two friends stepped over a portion of the shattered beam, they saw Jed lying in the rubble. He was bloody, and he looked for all the world like he was dead.

• • • •

A buggy pulled by two galloping black horses sped up the lane and then turned into the drive at Matthias's farm. Black buggies were everywhere: some scattered as horses bolted in fear, some shattered from explosions, and others being used by Amish farmers to get their families to safety.

Eagles was driving the horses hard, and Pook and Ducky were crammed into the buggy, holding on for dear life. Another buggy backed out into the drive as an Amish man tried to get control of his horses, and to avoid a collision Eagles turned the horses through a hedge. Their buggy nearly launched into the air as it crashed through the bushes and slid across the lawn, and the weight of the three militia soldiers, all thrown against one side of the buggy, flipped the vehicle over, separating it from the horses, who broke and ran across the field in terror.

Just as another buggy pulled up next to the destroyed one, Pook Rayburn kicked open the side door of the crashed vehicle—the side door which was now pointed straight upward toward the sky—and he and Ducky crawled stiffly out of the wrecked pile of wood and metal. Once they'd made their way to the ground, they checked one another for injuries and, finding none, looked around to see what might have happened to Eagles. But the salvager was nowhere in sight. Two of the Yoder boys climbed out of the newly arrived buggy and joined Ducky and Pook next to the wreckage.

They all looked at one another and started to walk around the wrecked buggy when they saw the whole shattered vehicle shift and move. From the midst of the debris, Eagles stood slowly to his feet. He had splinters and pieces of shrapnel in his beard, and there was blood running down one side of his face. The wild man spat his wad of green tobac on the busted-up buggy and then looked up at Pook, Ducky, and the Yoder boys.

"Taadaa?" he said.

• • • •

Pook found the rest of his squad, along with Dawn, his supreme commander Amos Troyer, and an injured and unconscious Jedediah Troyer, huddled next to the damaged and smoking skeleton that used to be Matthias's house.

Pook rushed to his team and did a quick numbers check to make sure everyone was accounted for.

"Where's Billy?" Dawn asked

"He had to stay behind to finish a critical task," Pook answered. "But we don't have time to talk about that. We have to get all of us, especially Amos, outside of the Amish Zone, and we only have about twenty minutes left before it'll be too late."

"I don't understand," Dawn said. "Is Transport going to destroy the AZ and kill everyone? Because if they are, we need to fight!"

"I'll explain it all when we're on the move," Pook said. He began to shout orders to his squad, then he pointed at Eagles and Ducky and told them to locate a working buggy.

"Load Jed into it and get him outside the walls as quickly as you can," he said. "The rest of us will find our way out and meet you due east of the AZ in the next thirty minutes. Got it?"

Eagles and Ducky nodded and rushed off to complete their orders.

"Okay, the rest of you, we're going to hoof it out of here. The Amish are going to need as many of these buggies as possible to use as ambulances, so we're going to have to double-time it out of the Zone on foot." He turned to Amos. "Except you, sir. We need you out for certain. You'll ride with Jed."

"No," Amos said, and closed his eyes.

"What do you mean?" Pook asked. "We need to get you out of here."

"I'm staying."

"Sir, you can't." Pook put his hands on his hips, ready to dig in if Amos wanted to argue.

"You don't *tell* me what I *can't do*, officer," Amos

snapped. "I know what you have planned, and it may work; but if it does, someone needs to stay on this side who knows what's going on."

"But..." Pook said. "But... who will command if you're gone?"

Amos put his hand on Pook's shoulder. "*You* will, son."

"Wait," Dawn interrupted. "I don't understand what's happening! Where is Amos going? Why are we fleeing the Zone?"

Pook turned to Dawn and reached out to hold her by the shoulders, steadying her. "Because in twenty minutes—less than that now—there's going to be an explosion and a blinding white light in the sky over the Zone. That'll be an okcillium explosion, and it will cause something very much like an electromagnetic pulse. It will destroy anything in the air in a fifty-mile radius, including every warship or drone on both sides of this battle. They'll all crash to the ground."

Just as he said "crash," a drone that had been shot down by a TRACE fighter crashed in the neighbors' field, sending forth a shower of sparks, fire, and smoke. Pook waited until the sound died down before he spoke again.

"And then, immediately after that, there'll be a smaller explosion, but you won't see or hear that one. You'll only see the results."

"What... what will happen? What will we see?" Dawn asked.

"This whole place," Pook answered, pointing all around them. "The whole Amish Zone, and everything in it, is going to disappear."

"Disappear?" Dawn said. "But where will it go?"

Pook shook his head, shrugged, and began to walk away, shouting orders to his men. Then he stopped and took a step back toward Dawn before reaching out and taking her by the hand.

"We don't know for sure," he said. "Maybe a hundred years in the future. Maybe the past? Can't be sure. But it'll go someplace."

Dawn held Pook's hand tightly, not about to let him leave again.

"Why don't we just go with it?" she asked. "Go with the Zone to wherever it ends up?"

Pook pulled on her hand and the two began to walk. "Because if we want to have any opportunity, any opportunity at all, to finish this for final and for good... then we have to stay here, in *this* time, and figure it out."

WINDOW PANE

NOW

Jed rocked back and forth beneath the wide blue sky. He was lying on his back, a green soldier's blanket laid over his chest, as he was carried on a stretcher held aloft by four men. He saw the beautiful wispy clouds, some connected by gossamer threads of vapor and others seemingly more solid, like great billowy ships adrift in a heavenly sea, and he felt the rhythm of the swaying as the men walked. He had a headache, there was no denying that, and he could hear the people who traveled with him talking as the group moved.

"The only portal left is up on the Shelf, and now with the AZ gone, it's our only hope." It was Pook Rayburn talking, and Jed smiled when he recognized the voice. He'd grown to like Pook while working with him on the farm over this past week. He closed his eyes and focused his attention on the voices, hoping that by doing so maybe the headache would fade.

"It's a long haul, but we'll make it." This time it was Dawn Beachy speaking. "We don't really have any other choice."

"I hope he's going to be able to walk at least part of the way," a third voice said.

* * * *

Jed's brain had learned to work as if the BICE was still there, providing him visual input so that the newer, higher-functioning areas of his mind could interpret data. On one screen, an image was displayed. It showed a large empty area, devoid of hills or valleys, where the Amish Zone should have been. It was as if the whole community had just disappeared. He didn't know how he knew that this had once been where the Amish Zone was, but he did. Even the immense walls were completely gone. On another screen he was seeing the process of okcillium being extracted from reclaimed road base, back in the old world. On still another screen, he examined maps and data that appeared to show a location up on the Great Shelf. All of these things—except for the image of the empty space where the Amish Zone had been—were things his brain already knew. His mind was simply using a new process for interpreting and organizing data, having learned this method from working with the BICE.

The other screens showed things like force readiness reports, and files about the history of the AZ and the building of the wall. All things he'd read before. He thought of Dawn Beachy, and a file containing her picture appeared on one of the screens. He scrolled to an overall summary of the information Transport had about her. He had the feeling that, if he'd ever looked at or studied a piece of information before in all of his life, he now had access to it in real time.

He squeezed his eyes tightly, and he saw the screens in his mind, and they'd all gone dark. All of them except one. The one there on the bottom right, with the picture of the faded and embossed coffee can, stomped flat and cut to fit. That screen didn't change. In his mind it was permanent—like an anchor, grounding him to...

...to what?

And then that screen faded to black as well.

And now he had another anchor. He felt his hand being clasped by someone, and when he concentrated, and really *felt* the other hand, he knew it to be Dawn's. As the team walked and carried him along on the stretcher, Dawn was holding his hand, letting him know that she was there, that she was a part of him, and a part of his life. Something that was real, tangible. Solid. Something on which he could depend. Someone he could love. She was his window...

Ask questions.

He thought for a moment. *What is the next step?
Where do we go from here?*

And the black screens answered him. A single word
in all caps. Italicized in white print. Stark against the
darkness of the screens...

OKLAHOMA

www.MichaelBunker.com

Sign up to Michael's Email Newsletter:

http://eepurl.com/enJeQ